The Advernox Project

To order additional copies, please contact us.
BookSurge, LLC
www.booksurge.com
1-866-308-6235
orders@booksurge.com

RICK NAYLOR

THE ADVERNOX PROJECT

Book One of
The BMX Conspiracy

2006

The Advernox Project

CONTENT

CHARACTERS

- Richard E. Naylor—Lead Scientist
- Candis Lockhart—Scientist
- William Winters—BMX CEO
- J.T. Barrows—BMX CFO
- Leon Kenton—Judge
- Steven Blair—English Scientist
- Evan Batiste—French Scientist
- Kathy Levens—WPP Chemist
- Charley Johnson—Fisherman
- Cliff Miller -BMX Security
- Jackson Legitt—BMX Attorney
- Clause Vonhart—WPP Attorney
- Mercedes Joyner—Rick's Admin Asst.
- Franklin Davis—Intel
- Marvin Edwards—WPP CEO
- Darius Pollard—FDA

SYNOPSIS

A well known Pharmaceutical company that has been a leader in its field for more than seventy years has hit on hard times. The past three years have been especially rough. Pensions and job security are now in jeopardy.

The company's only option for avoiding bankruptcy is a new wonder drug call Advernox. The only problem is this drug has a major side effect, which is well known by the company's board of directors. The decision of the board director is to find another option and hope things turn around in the next quarter.

However, there is a secret meeting held with a couple of members that refuse to leave their future in the hands of fate. They decide to move forward with this drug hoping to reformulate it at a later date.

Advernox surprisingly receives fast approval from the FDA and for the first four months the money is rolling in at an unprecedented rate until...

A small company called Warrenton Pharmaceutical claims the drug was stolen from them. If what they say is true not only is BMX Pharmaceutical guilty of thief but they might also be guilty of murder. In the shadows a trial is about to commence to get to the bottom of these allegations.

BMX Pharmaceutical is aware of their plight and knows that there is only one man that can help them. A former employee named Richard Naylor. Mr. Naylor is thought by some to be the smartest scientist alive. The only problem is he hates BMX Pharmaceutical and refuses to help them. History had shown him that dealing with BMX can only lead to heartache and pain.

BMX must have his services so they approach him with a very generous offer. When he refuses threats are made on his kid's life and the woman that he loves. This starts a whirl wind of events that lead to murder, suspense, intrigue and love. Enjoy!!

My Daughters: Brittany And Kimberly
My Sons: Derrick And Brandon

Special Thanks
To
Nora and Edi

For letting me know how good but also how confusing my early works could be...

Enjoy book one
Of
"The BMX Conspiracy"

PREFACE

The decision to publish this book in its unedited version was a stroke of genius by the author. Initially this unedited version was produced only for friends and family of the author who had read parts of this book when it was still in manuscript form and couldn't wait to get their hands on the finished version. However, the demand for this unedited version has been so great that it is now available for all to enjoy.

***

Everyday somewhere in this world a pharmaceutical company introduces a new drug to the public. The majority of these new drugs have a known side effect but some are not known until it's too late. Some of these side effects are harmless, while others are not. In most cases the good of the drug out way the negatives. However....

***

This story is fiction. Neither of these pharmaceutical companies existed when this book was written.

The author was inspired to write this book because he felt that it's important for people to understand some of the hardships that the families and loved ones of these scientists and chemists have to deal with in their everyday lives.

Rick has worked in the Pharmaceutical Industry for over twelve years and nothing in this book is a reflection on the great companies that he worked for, "any similarities are simply that."

Anyone that has worked in this industry will recognize some of the situations that he has written about and although this book is indeed fiction, the things that you will read about can and do happen.

Some of you may not understand the terminology but all of you will understand the plot and for the rest of your life before you take any medication you will think about this book and the characters in it. You will wonder just what it took to get that pill or that cold tablet to you.

"You will never view a Pharmaceutical company the same again."

INTRODUCTION

Gentlemen I asked you to meet me here tonight because we have a huge decision to make. I don't have to tell you how disappointed I was with that meeting in Washington yesterday.

Now I don't know about you but I have not spent the past twenty-five years of my life at this company working my ass off just to let my retirement slip through my fingers because the damn stock is doing badly.

The past three or four years we have barely been hanging on. If we don't do something quick, someone is going to buy this company right from under our asses and we all know what happens to management when a company is acquired.

What can we do William? Our pipeline of future products are so weak.

I have an idea J.T. It may save our pension as well as this company.

Remember that joint venture that we had a few years ago with that small generic company on Long Island. It shouldn't be that hard to remember, it was the one with the possible blockbuster drug for pregnant women.

Hold on a minute William! "That product wasn't cleared to go into production," said Randolph. I don't even know if Warrenton is still working on it.

He's right said J.T., remember we got out of it because of all the money it was costing us to try and reformulate it.

If I remember correctly gentlemen the reason we got involved in the first place was because it was going to be a huge money maker, said William. I suggest that we try to get our hands on it and get it on the market as soon as possible. If we can pull this off we can save our pension as well as our company from a hostile take over.

How are we going to get our hand on the formula said Randolph? If I remember correctly, Warrenton Pharmaceutical owns the rights.

Then we'll just have to find a way to steal it from them, said William.

"That's crazy and so is this damn meeting," shouted Randolph! I'm going home. Don't call me again unless you have both come to your senses. Good night...

***

He's right William but I'm curious as to what's cooking in that big head of yours.

It's simple John. We are in a lot of trouble if we don't turn this company around soon. We can't wait another quarter and hope things turn around on its own because things are only going to get worst. That product that Warrenton has could save us.

What makes you think they will sell it to us?

Who said anything about buying it?

I thought you were joking about stealing it but you are serious aren't you? Yes John, I'm serious...more serious than I have ever been in my life.

William please come back to earth. What you're suggesting is impossible! Warrenton Pharmaceutical probably has the formulation locked up. It would probably take an army to get in there and get it. Besides they haven't figured out the side effect issues or the product would have been released to the market already and they would be one rich company right now.

You worry too much my friend. First of all our scientists and chemists are smarter than theirs. I'm sure once we get the formula we can reformulate it quickly. Secondly, we don't need an Army to get into that place.

I still think it's impossible William.

It's not impossible J.T., I have a plan...

CHAPTER 1

Good morning sweetheart.
Good morning my love. How are you and the baby this morning? He woke me up early kicking again. I can tell he's going to have his father's big feet. This has been the hardest pregnancy yet. I'm ready for him to be born already. The other five kids didn't give me any trouble at all. That's probably because they were all girls.

Sweetheart please be patient just a few months more and our little bundle of joy will be here before you know it.

Marvin...you didn't sleep well last night.

Did I keep you awake?

Well..."you seemed to be having another nightmare."

I'm sorry..."I don't know why I keep having that same stupid dream." Do you want to talk about it? Maybe we can talk about it when I get home tonight but I have to get to work.

Okay Marvin, I love you. "I love you more pumpkin."

***

Marvin and his wife were very average looking people from the island of Hawaii. They had decided to move to New Jersey fifteen years ago after a hurricane had wiped out their village there. Although New Jersey offered assurance that they would never have to endure the heartaches of a hurricane, they both longed to return to their home someday.

***

Good morning everyone, said Marvin. I pray that all of you slept well last night and I hope that we are finally ready to vote on this extremely important issue, however, before we proceed, I would like for us to have one last discussion on this topic. Edwin, "I would like to hear from you first."

Thank you Marvin. "I will be brief."

For the past four years we have spent countless hours working on this project. We are so close to discovering the unlimited potential of this great drug. I know many of you if not all will agree with me when I say that it would be advantageous for us to continue to research and develop this drug.

Additionally, "I might add that this is going to be a blockbuster drug that is greatly needed." It is our responsibility to make sure that all of our hard efforts don't go unrewarded. Anything else would be completely ludicrous.

Thank you Edwin. Is there anyone else that would like to speak?

Marvin, "I would like to say something."

The floor is yours Kathy.

Thank you Marvin, "I promise to be brief".

As most of you are aware, I was one of the first members of this team.

In the four years that we have worked on this project I have seen some very good scientists come through this company. The majority of them have agreed that there is a very high possibility that a terrible side effect is associated with this drug. This was a fact on day one of this project and it remains a fact today.

We have done countless studies and all have returned with the same result. The environmental monitoring has shown us that the incubation period is far too long.

"We can not over look what this could potentially mean!"

If I believed that this drug was safe I would be the first one on the band wagon because women really need a product like this but only, "if it's safe". We have to forget about the great potential of this drug or how much money it will make this company, "until we are one hundred and ten percent sure that it is safe".

Please don't forget that we have tried countless reformulations on this drug and none of them have worked. This is an unsafe drug and this fact alone should be the deciding factor on how we vote.

For the one millionth time, "I disagree with her Marvin!"

Keep your voice down Edwin! "No one interrupted you when you were speaking", said Marvin.

"It seems that the only time anyone around here listens to me is when I raise my voice."

Edwin, just because you raise your voice doesn't mean anyone is listening to you. It only means that they hear you. "Of course you know the difference, right." Now I'm telling you to lower your voice and I strongly suggest that you do it now!

Ok Marvin, I'm sorry but I know we can reformulate Advernox, "all we need is a little more time." Once we have done so, we will be the envy of the entire Pharmaceutical Industry.

Kathy I apologize for Edwin's outburst. Is there anything else that you would like to say?

No Marvin…"I pray that I have said enough".

***

Would anyone else like to speak, said Marvin?

"I hate to admit it but I agree with Edwin," said Brandon.

"How on earth can you agree with him," said Victoria?

It's easy when you consider that we are not dealing with an Aseptic environment here.

So Brandon…"what is your point?"

Let me give you an example: take "nicotine gum", which is supposed to help the consumer quit smoking. Only God knows what's really in that stuff. I've known companies to know that there was ground up metal and oil residual in their gum but the Department Manager, Quality Assurance and Quality Control still allowed it to be put out on the market for consumption.

It's no wonder that some of the people that buy this product have health issues that are not related to smoking.

I am so disappointed with you Brandon and that is such a crazy statement. The fact that you would even compare nicotine gum to a product like Advernox makes me wonder about your commitment to this project.

I'm sure these companies have chemists in their labs that do stability tests and check for all the things that you just mentioned.

Vicky the point that I'm trying to make is," there are a lot of pharmaceutical companies that take short cuts in their process." The sad part is it normally comes down to schedule attainment and making money and that my dear is the bottom line. "The customer is only an after thought with some of them!"

Maybe you're right Brandon but I'd only go as far as to say some pharmaceutical companies but definitely not all.

"Victoria you of all people should understand what I'm saying." Now, it might not seem that important to you or anyone else in this room but I have seen first hand what happens to a person when they bite down on a piece of "nicotine gum," that's full of metal.

Brandon may I interrupt?

"Sure Marvin"

We all realize that you have an issue with the companies that produce, nicotine gum. We are also aware of one particular company and I will not mention their name, however we are here today to discuss the future of Advernox, a product that might be produced by our company.

"You are an excellent scientist Brandon and your opinion is very valuable to us." So please give us a break from the nicotine gum horror stories today and tell us your opinion on Advernox?

"Marvin I apologize." I suggest that we continue on our current course with Advernox but we should periodically monitor any contamination concerns with a microbial air sampler until the incubation period is over.

Brandon, "thank you for your support," said Edwin.

You don't have to thank me Ed. We are all well aware that most clinical manufacturing carries a certain level of risk but in this particular case maybe we can try to offset these concerns by simply consolidating the data from our environmental control investigation reports. We have already spent four years on the development of Advernox. A few more months can't hurt.

"Brandon thank you for your input," said Marvin. Now, I'd like to hear what Stacey thinks.

"Marvin I think it's unsafe," said Stacey. How much more time are we going to waste on it?

Mildred what do you think, said Marvin?

Marvin my decision is the same today as it was a year ago when, "I said we should dump it!" The possibility of this negative side effect simply out weighs the benefit of this drug. "I hope I'm not sitting here a year from today voting on this same issue!"

Thank you Mildred.

Several of you have not commented, said Marvin. This will be your last opportunity to speak before we vote.

What about you Leo?

Robert, Paul and I have worked on this project for over two years, said Leo and we all feel the same way. We will express how we feel when it's time to vote.

Very well...said Marvin, "if everyone has said their piece," I'm going to step outside of this room for about ten minutes. While I'm away I want each of you to ask yourself this one simple question.

Would you give this drug to a loved one? When I return, "we will vote."

***

Sandi can you make me a quick cup of coffee?

Of course I can...by the way have you finished your Christmas shopping yet Marvin?

No Sandi, "I'm ashamed to admit that I haven't."

Well you better get on it mister. Remember what almost happened last year Marvin. Don't expect me to perform a miracle like I did last year and the year before that and the...

I get the point Sandi but shopping isn't any fun for me unless I do it at the last moment, besides Christmas is still two weeks away.

"It's less than two weeks Marvin."

***

As Marvin listened to Sandi scold him once again about his Christmas shopping short comings, he wonder why his beautiful Norwegian assistance hadn't found a man to settle down with. She was like a sister to him and he knew many men that would love to run their fingers through the beautiful dark skinned lady's long auburn hair. She worked out rigorously three days a week and didn't seem to have an ounce of fat anywhere on her 6 foot frame. She was in her early thirties so there was still time for someone...

Marvin can I ask you a question?

Sure you can Sandi, "as long as it doesn't upset my ulcer".

Marvin please tell me that you're not going to allow them to put that product on the market.

"It's not entirely up to me Sandi."

"Are you sure about that Marvin?"

"Those walls are paper thin today Marvin". I've worked for you over ten years now and I have never felt the kind of tension that I felt when I went into that conference room this morning.

Those people act as if they have the weight of the world on their shoulders.

Unfortunately Sandi, "they are not acting."

"That was a very good cup of coffee, thank you". I have to go back in now but before I do I want you to know that your opinion means a lot to me. You are more than a secretary to me, "you are family." I just want you to know that I have always tried to do what is right and I think you know that. What is happening in that conference room today is more difficult than anything that I've had to deal with in my twenty-eight years in this industry.

I can only pray that the people in that room vote with their mind as well as with their heart, however, "I can tell you that the two are seldom in agreement with each other."

"Do you understand Sandi?"

Yes, "Marvin I do."

Good…now get a pen and paper and follow me.

***

As Marvin walked back into the old conference room, he didn't notice the chipped paint on the walls or the sun faded drapes that should have been replaced two years ago.

Sandi was right he thought, "there is a heavy presence in this room."

Marvin took his seat at the head of the table and for the first time didn't notice the dull shine on the once magnificent oval table that he had complained about a million times.

What he did notice was the look on each member of his team's face as he looked deeply into each of their eyes and searched their souls before he spoke.

The first person that he looked at was Leo. He was from the republic of Russia. He was a slender man with a wealth of knowledge. He had been a member of this team for three years and he was a no nonsense kind of guy. He played strictly by the rules.

Then there was Mildred. She was the mother of three and weighed a hundred pounds soak and wet. Her hair was forever braided and she was a beast when it came to following procedure. The African American woman always felt pressure to excel amongst her peers and most times did.

Robert was the prankster of the bunch but he was an excellent scientist and was the lead on many assignments. He was the shortest member of the team by far and was obviously annoyed when his team members addressed his height.

He looked at Kathy was the voice of the group. She was over fifty and had a body that would rival most teen age girls. Strangely she had never been married. She didn't flinch as Marvin looked into her soul.

Edwin was the Dr. Jekyll of the group. Just when you thought you knew where he was coming from he'd do an about face. Except when it came to Advernox. On this one subject he stood firm. The six foot 7inch giant could intimidate most.

Stacey was the most normal member of the team. She did her job and headed home, along the way she would stop at Jenny Craig and purchase her meals for the week. She didn't make any waves and was often the outsider during many group arguments.

Brandon was from the island of Haiti. Most of his days were spent with a cell phone to his ear as he tried to decide which lady he would wine and dine on the weekend. He was an excellent scientist.

Victoria stared at the wall not allowing Marvin to look into her soul. She was unofficially the boss of the group when Marvin wasn't around. She was an attractive Latino woman who was barely 5 feet 2 inches tall, yet she still towered over Robert. She had been in the industry longer than Marvin and often times rubbed shoulders with him over issues. She believed if she were a man. Marvin's job would be hers. Despite her obvious annoyance at this issue, she was a valued member of this team.

And then there was Paul. The rich kid that was smart enough to make it through college and onto this team but not smart enough to act like he cared. He was a necessary evil per say. He was also dating Sandi and they thought no one knew. Marvin tolerated Paul because of Sandi but his tolerance was wearing thin.

Marvin finally took a deep breath and calmly said, "After four long years we have finally reached the moment of truth."

***

Mildred are you ready to vote? "Yes I am Marvin."
Leo are you ready to vote? Leo is ready to vote.
Victoria are you ready to vote? "Yes Marvin."
Edwin are you ready to vote? I am ready Marvin
Robert are you ready to vote? Marvin…"I'm ready."
Paul are you ready to vote? Sure Marvin lets vote.
Stacey are you ready to vote. Yes sir, Marvin.
Brandon are you ready to vote? "I'm ready."
"Are there any questions," said Marvin?
I have a question Marvin.

What is your question Mildred? Are you ready to vote Marvin?

Marvin paused for about five seconds but it seemed like an eternity to his team. When he finally replied it was with confidence and authority.

Yes Mildred…I'm ready.

"Sandi please record each members vote," said Marvin. All those in favor of continuing this project raise your hand: all those in favor of ending the project raise your hand.

"Well there you have it."

By a vote of eight to one this project is officially over. All records will be officially sealed and all test and development is to cease effective today, December 15th' 2003.

"Good day and may God bless each of you," said Marvin.

"You idiots," yelled Edwin! "Do you have any idea what you've done?"

"Yes Edwin," said Victoria, "we know exactly what we have done". "We have stopped a madman!"

(One week later)

We are so sorry for your lost Mrs. Edwards. "If your family needs anything don't hesitate to ask," we are here for you.

"Suzanne your husband was a great man." He was loved by all that knew him. Life for us at Warrenton Pharmaceutical will not be the same without him. If you need help with anything please don't hesitate to call us.

"If you people really want to help my family you will find out who killed my husband," cried Mrs. Edwards!

I know it's hard for you to understand right now Suzanne but "he committed suicide," said Douglas. The police are investigating but it clearly looks like your husband took his life.

"He would not (sob) do that to us," yelled Suzanne!

My husband loved life, "he loved me and our kids." He was a great husband and father. He had so much to live for… "We had so many plans."

The only thing that might have been a concern to him was that damn drug that was such a hot topic at his job.

Do you mean Advernox?

Yes, "that's it"…that's the name he was yelling out in the middle of the night as we slept. I believe, "that drug is the reason that he is no longer with us."

For Christ's sake Suzy, "do you realize what you are implying," said Douglas?

Yes Douglas but I'm not implying it, "I'm stating a fact."

"If you weren't such a terrible boss Doug," it would be clear to you also. All you do is look down on others from your house on the hill.

My husband came to you for support. From day one you shunned him. He wanted to meet with you and see what your plans were for the department. He didn't take it personal though because you didn't meet with any of the African American supervision when you first took over the department.

Most managers meet with their team and discuss plans for the department's future. You only meet with a few people and Marvin wasn't one of them.

Furthermore...when he wanted his old job back you and all your friends ignored him.

Please calm down Suzanne, I do admit in the beginning, "I might have ignored him a little but it wasn't on purpose." I was in a new job and I was trying to learn as much about the department as I could.

Ha..."what a joke Douglas."

Anyone would tell you that my husband was the department. Did it feel good to stab him in the back, time after time? You don't have an answer for that Doug do you?

"He's gone now," so it doesn't really matter but I want you to know that despite it all, "he liked you and he also respected you."

I'm sorry Suzanne; I don't know what to say but I do realize a lot of people feel the same way that you do about me. Marvin was a good man and if he were alive today, "I would shake his hand and apologize to him."

"Too little...too late Douglas!"

Suzanne everyone loved your husband but if you are implying that he is dead because of Advernox, "I sincerely believe that you are wrong."

"I am not wrong and if anyone in this room needs me to spell it out," I will. "My husband was killed because someone didn't like the fact that he helped keep a dangerous drug off the street!"

***

"Suzanne please calm down," said Sandi. We know that you are in pain (sob) but please try to calm down for the kids sake. Maybe you should go upstairs and lay down for a little while, "I'll (sob) keep an eye on the kids for you."

Thank you Sandi, "you have been such a good friend." Marvin thought a lot of you. He told me more than once that you were like family. I'm sure you understand my pain better than anyone else.

Yes...I understand your pain and I know it's going to take both of us a while to stop hurting so much. "I loved him to Suzanne."

Yes Sandi, "I know you did." He loved you also.

Everyone may I have your attention please. I want to (sob) thank all of you for coming but I (sob) think it's time for you to leave. Tomorrow is Christmas and my kids and I need some time alone together.

"Merry (sob) Christmas everyone and thank you for coming," said Suzanne. Please (sob) see yourself out.

CHAPTER 2

J udge Leon Kenton stood before the mirror in his chamber and adjusted his tie. He couldn't help but chuckle as he looked at the figure staring back at him in the mirror.

"When did all these changes take place," he thought? The mirror hadn't changed but the figure staring back at him certainly had.

At the age of forty-seven his hair line was starting to recede and his stomach muscles were starting to lose a battle that his robe couldn't hide much longer.

Leon wasn't a big man but he was well aware that he could no longer eat what he wanted, when he wanted. Fifty was right around the corner and he knew it wasn't going to wait for him to get there. "It was obvious that he had to do something about his weight before it was too late."

"How does Roxanne do it," he wondered? His wife was just as beautiful as the day he met her and she hadn't gained and ounce. Lord only knows how she manages to do it, even after three kids and home cooked meals everyday.

One last glance as he turned away from mirror assured him that he still wasn't a bad looking man, "despite what father time was doing to him."

He took a seat in his large rich Italian leather chair and stared at his huge eighteenth century mahogany desk that he had hand picked five months ago. He was sure no other judge in the greater New York area had one like it.

He leaned back in his chair and surveyed the ceiling. "The brown spot was still there." It seemed to change a little every time there was a heavy rained. When is the county going to take care of that water stain?

He knew all he really had to do was pick up the phone and make a call but he also knew he would miss staring at the silly spot. He had made many important decisions, while staring at that damn spot. Even as a lawyer twelve years ago, "some of his best ideas came while staring at that spot."

***

It had been odd practicing out of a court house office as an attorney years ago but in this small town just outside of New York City a lot of odd things happened every day. Despite it all, "he loved his small crummy office and this is why he wouldn't leave it when he became Judge."

He didn't know which surprised everyone more; him making Judge at such a young age or the fact that he stayed in this small crummy office when he could have move into the Grand Chamber just up the hallway.

The fact that he graduated from law school early combined with the fact that he never lost a case in his short but glorious career as an attorney could help explain his quick ascension to the bench but staying in this small crummy office was only understood by himself.

As he looked around in his study, his mind was flooded with memories.

Had he really been in this same office for twenty years now? Where did the time go?

His eyes finally came to rest on a picture of his family. The picture was enough to confirm it. It was over fifteen years old.

He glanced at the walls of his office. They were tastefully decorated with his awards, certificates and a lone picture on Thurgood Marshall.

The first robe that he had ever worn was hanging in the corner. It was too snug on him now and the zipper didn't work but he wouldn't part with it for the world.

"Twenty years in the court room," he thought, maybe that's long enough? "This will probably be my last hearing," he thought. If there is enough evidence to go to trial, "it will be my last trial." Some how there was comfort in his decision. He knew twenty years wasn't long to be hanging around a court room but he wanted more.

He hadn't discussed his decision with Roxanne yet but she would be happy about his decision, "he was sure of that". She had devoted the last twenty-five years to him and the kids. It was time for her to reap the rewards of being such a dedicated mother and wife.

The kids are all away at college. "It would be like starting over again for them." He knew that the house would have a certain degree of emptiness without the kids running through it and shouting at each other.

***

One of the most important things that he had learned while being a lawyer and a Judge, "is that the truth is always on the verge of being exposed." You just have to be willing to allow it time." He hated a liar and those who lied in his court room paid a stiff penalty.

Some cases are so simple it's ridiculous; others are so complex that the truth looks as if it may never be known.

It's the ones where the defense appears guilty right from the start that intrigued the Judge the most. When this happened, he always reminded himself of a case when he was growing up in a small southern town in Alabama.

The case involved a man named Charley Johnson.

"Mr. Johnson was an honest man."

He was so skinny that you could actually hear his heart beat if you stood close enough. He was over six feet tall but he walked slumped over and this made him appear much shorter.

His only real friends were a bottle of Jim Beam and a pint of Seagram's Gin and he kept these friends close to him at all times. Surprisingly, "he never drank enough to get drunk."

Except for that one time...

***

Charley's summers were consumed with fishing and tending his rather large garden at the family's homestead. In the winter he would hunt deer and chop firewood. The firewood he would sell to the people in the next town but the deer he kept for himself.

Charley was the only boy in a family of six kids. The old house that was constantly in need of repair was given to him after his parents went on to glory.

The poor guy had never been in trouble a day in his life but on this warm September morning that was all about to change.

Charlie's only defense on this particular day was simply being in the wrong place at the wrong time; however, "no one was buying it." When three of the towns' most respected gentlemen find you kneeling over the body of a dead woman, "they pretty much figure they have you dead too right."

So in this small town where everyone knew everyone the news spread like wild fire. Charley Johnson was sentenced by the town folk practically before the case went to court and the trial, well..."that was just a formality."

Everyone was so sure that Charlie was guilty. They believed that he had gotten tired of his fat wife Edi and wanted the beautiful Daria.

Most of the men in town wanted the beautiful gold skinned housemaid but they knew they couldn't be caught alone with the beautiful Negro woman.

Yes, what had happened on that muggy September morning was crystal clear to everyone...or so they thought.

Fortunately for Mr. Johnson, a young boy barely nine years old was able to put aside his own fears of what he witnessed that day and come to his rescue.

"Leon Kenton was that boy."

He told his father what he had seen. His father told the Judge and the sheriff. They reluctantly accepted the story and Charlie was released.

What the Judge saw on that day kept him awake on many nights, "even into his adult hood." The nightmares are not as bad as they used to be but every now and then something will trigger the memory.

That was almost forty years ago but the memory is as clear as if it were yesterday.

**

Today Judge Kenton will be proceeding over a case involving two pharmaceutical companies. Although he hid it well, "he hated most of them."

"His experience had shown him, that all were simply after a buck and that was the bottom line." The companies put profit ahead of everything and everyone.

"Sure their ads made them seem sincere but it was only an act."

The judge was convinced that no matter how sincere their ads made them appear, the bottom line was how much of your money can we take out of your pockets today...and tomorrow?

He did realize however, "that they were a necessary evil."

His one dream was helping to create a system that made branded products affordable to everyone.

"Why should only the rich afford to be healthy?"

He knew that this was just a dream because the people that could do something about it are getting filthy rich as the big boys in the pharmaceutical industry stuffed their wallets.

***

Judge...it's time.

Thanks Nora, "I'll be there in a couple of minutes."

"Leon took a deep breath."

After all these years he was still a little nervous before a hearing. He bowed his head and asked the Lord to guide him once again. He made a slight adjustment to his robe and headed to the court room

***

"All rise."

Please be seated.

Judge today's hearing is Warrenton Pharmaceutical vs BMX Pharmaceutical.

Very well..."thank you Robin."

Is the attorney for the plaintiff here? Yes, Your Honor, "Warrenton Pharmaceutical Products, will be represented by Clause Vonhart."

Is the attorney for the defense here? Yes Your Honor, "BMX Pharmaceutical will be represented by Jackson Legitt and Associates."

Before we begin Mr. Legitt what does BMX stand for?

Your Honor the Initials BMX stands for Bernstein Medicines and Xenobiotics. Ok, Mr. Legitt, thank you for clarifying that for me. Let me remind both of you that this is a hearing not a trial. Only the rules that apply to a hearing are to be applied here. Does everyone understand?

"Yes Your Honor."

Good, "I'll hear from the plaintiff first."

Good morning Your Honor. Good morning Mr. Vonhart

Presently the generic business represents almost two thirds of my client's business; however, they are trying to expand their branded division market.

One of the ways that they had hoped to do this was by introducing a new product.

From May 2000 to April 2004 my client had been developing a new prescription drug designed specifically to treat the occasional dizziness, fatigue and stomach cramps that pregnant women have to endure.

Numerous tests on this new drug had been very positive. However, there was one test that this drug failed over and over again.

My client made countless attempts to correct this flaw or side effect but they couldn't. The decision of the board was to stop all development and testing of this drug. At this point, my client strongly believed that this drug was unsafe and should never be released to the public.

However, after months of debate, a special team of mostly chemists were allowed to continue to work on the drug. Their results and finding were the same as the previous groups and once again the project was ceased.

A week after the project had been stopped for the second time, "there was a fire at the research lab." Unfortunately, all records were lost when the lab burned to the ground on the 17th of August 2004.

However in October of 2004, BMX Pharmaceutical released a new drug to the market called Advernox. My client strongly believes that Advernox it is the same drug that they had been developing for the past four years.

We even have a hunch about how BMX came to obtain the formulation for Advernox.

If given a chance we will prove it in open court. After we have proven this, we will ask for a twenty billion dollar settlement. This is the projected amount that my client's drug would have generated while on patent.

However, if the defense is willing to settle today, we will accept ten billion dollars and take no further action.

Thank you, Your Honor.

***

Did I hear you say twenty billion dollars Mr. Vonhart?

Yes…"that is correct," Your Honor.

That seems a little high don't you think, said Judge Kenton?

With all due respect Your Honor, my client feels it's a bargain.

Mr. Vonhart, what is the name of your client's drug?

My client had not decided on a name yet Your Honor

"Isn't that kind of odd Mr. Vonhart?"

"Odd...maybe...Your Honor but not unheard of." My client knew that this would be a blockbuster drug and they had hoped that by not giving it a name, it would help protect its identity and discourage thief.

"Unfortunately their plan didn't work."

Very well Mr. Vonhart...

I would like to hear from the defense now.

Good morning Your Honor. Good morning Mr. Legitt.

What the plaintiff has just said before this court is a ball face lie!

"Please lower your voice Mr. Legitt."

"Yes of course," I apologize Your Honor."

My client is a well respected company that's been in the pharmaceutical business over a hundred years. "Never and I repeat never in their proud history has there been such a ludicrous claim against them!"

"My client does not need to stoop to the level of a common criminal to survive." This is nothing more than an old fashion witch hunt by the plaintiff.

Furthermore, it is not unusual for pharmaceutical companies to be working on similar products at the same time. We all know this happens everyday. In this particular case my client simply beat Warrenton Pharmaceutical to market with Advernox.

Thank you Your Honor.

Very well.... now Mr. Vonhart, the defense does make a very strong argument. "It is indeed true what they say about companies working on similar products at the very same time."

Are you aware of this fact?

Yes, "I am aware of that fact," Your Honor and my client is also aware of that fact. However, "that is not the case this time."

Mr. Vonhart, you stated in your opening that you have a hunch that Advernox is your client's drug but unless you have more to add, I'm afraid that I will have to deny your claim that appears to be based simply on "just a hunch."

Your Honor, we do have more to add. May I proceed?

"Yes, by all means."

On the day that the lab burned to the ground five innocent people perished. We strongly believed that the fire was not an accident as first believed but a deliberate attempt to steal the formulation for my client's drug.

Objection! Your Honor, Objection!

Please continue Mr. Vonhart.

Thank you Your Honor. We have done our home work on this case and we have found that BMX Pharmaceutical did not have any products similar too Advernox in their research pipeline until one month before it was released to the market.

"It's as though it just appeared over night."

Also, if our hunch is correct not only is BMX guilty of theft but also cold-blooded murder!

Objection Your Honor, Objection! This is a hearing Legitt, not a trial, therefore you cannot object. You should know that, said Judge Kenton.

I'm sorry Your Honor but these allegations have just gone to far. "First they accuse my client of theft and now murder."

They are liars, Your Honor!

BMX records show that Advernox was in research for three years, before being sent to the FDA for approval in October of 2004.

"We truly sympathize with them over their terrible tragedy Your Honor", "we truly do," but we, "strongly deny their allegations!"

Sit down Mr. Legitt you are out of order!

"I will have order in my court room!"

I think it might benefit us all if the defense takes a few minutes to calm down, said Judge Kenton.

Now Mr. Vonhart, "these allegations are huge!"

"Are you sure about this?"

Yes, "I'm sure," Your Honor, we have a hunch that...

Stop right there Mr. Vonhart!

"I'm not talking about some hunch." "No one has ever been convicted because the attorney said, "Judge we have a hunch that they did it."

Now Mr. Vonhart, "if you are going to come into my court room with these types of allegations," "you had better be ready to provide some proof."

"Do you understand what I'm saying?

"Of course I do Your Honor."

So do you have proof or not?

"I'm afraid not," everything is simply based on our hunch.

Well I'm afraid for your sake and the sake of your client that might not be enough, said Judge Kenton.

Your Honor please a horrific crime has taken place here. I'm sure that BMX has covered their tracks very well but they are guilty and if we go to trial I can prove it.

Mr. Vonhart there is no mistaking that you are very passionate about this matter; however, "that same passion should have been used to gather evidence against the defense."

"I realize that Your Honor but it's not always easy to catch a thief or a murderer for that matter."

Please have a seat Mr. Vonhart.

Mr. Legitt is there anything else that you would like to add? Yes, "I most certainly would". First of all, my client's reputation speaks for its self Your Honor.

BMX has been in business over a hundred years and in that time they have earned the respect and admiration of billions of people that have taken their products.

These charges by Warrenton Pharmaceutical are ludicrous and I ask that they be dismissed immediately before we waste any more of the good tax payer's hard earned money.

That's all I have Your Honor.

Very well gentlemen, if no one has anything further to add this hearing is adjourned until 1:00p.m. "I'll render my decision at that time."

"All rise."

***

Nora this might be a tough one.

What do you know about BMX Pharmaceutical?

Leon my parents and my grandparent's cabinets were always stuffed with their products. When I was a little girl, I thought all medicine was made by them. They always had good products back then but until that new product came along a few months ago things had been rough for them for several years.

Yes Nora, I've heard that also. I've taken everything from aspirin to God knows what, that they make. I just find it very hard to believe that they could be involved in something like this.

"It would be very disappointing if they are Judge."

Yes Nora, "it would be sad but let's not forget we are talking about a pharmaceutical company."

I know that look Leon.

What are you thinking about?

Old Charley Johnson just crossed my mind.

Now that's a name I haven't heard in a long time.

Can you get him on the line for me?

Is his number the same?

Yes, "I think so."

Judge, he's on line two.

Charley this is Judge Kenton. How are you?

"I'm doing fine judge."

I went fishing today and caught me a nice mess of fish. So I'm doing just fine.

"I'm glad to hear that Charley."

Charley, do you remember a year ago when you showed up at my door steps at one o'clock in the morning, "with that crazy story about what you saw at the lab?"

How could I forget that Judge? I was drunk as a skunk.

"It's no surprise that you didn't believe me."

Well…old friend, "I'm afraid that you might have been right after all."

"Why after all this time do you believe me?"

Let's just say it's a hunch and leave it at that for now. Charley is there anything else that you'd like to add to your story?

Oh yes Judge, there is a lot more to that story but I can't talk about it over the phone. I understand Charley. Can you meet me today, so we can discuss this?

I can't show my face around that court house, said Charley. I wouldn't dream of asking you to come here Charley but I could come out to your house.

When would you like to come?

I can be there in less than an hour. You make it seem awful urgent Judge. It's already taken a year Charley; I wouldn't call that too urgent.

Very well Judge but you'll have to meet me at the lake just before you get to my house.

"I don't want to upset my wife."

I understand Charley, "I'll call you back in about five minutes."

***

Nora ask the gentlemen if they can come back tomorrow morning around nine o'clock. "Let me know their answer right away."

Gentlemen the judge has requested more time before making his decision. How much time does he need, said Mr. Legitt?

He would like for you to return tomorrow morning at 9:00am. Is that alright with you Mr. Vonhart? Sure…"I don't have a problem with that."

Well…that's not a good time for me!

Are you sure Mr. Legitt?

Yes, "I'm sure."

Unlike Mr. Vonhart, I have other clients you know.

Well…I'll tell the Judge, Mr. Legitt if you insist but I don't think it was a request.

***

Judge Mr. Legitt has a scheduling conflict with tomorrow. I get the feeling that he really doesn't want to wait.

Well…he's going to have to wait.

"I have to go meet Charley for a few minutes." "Tell them to be back here at four o'clock this afternoon and that's final."

Charley this is Judge Kenton again. I'll meet you at the lake in about forty minutes.

"Should I bring my fishing poles," said Charley?

"That sounds great Charley," you bring the poles and I'll bring the worms.

***

As Leon drove toward the lake he thought about the night that he was awaken out of a comfortable sleep at two o'clock in the morning.

Someone was beating on the door so hard that it had set off the security alarm.

He glanced out the second story window of his brownstone and strained his eyes to see through the horrific down pour of rain. He was shocked when he noticed the unmistakable form of his friend Charley standing under the maple tree near the edge of the steps that led to the front door.

The Maple tree was over a hundred years old and wasn't doing a good job of sheltering his life long friend from the down pour.

Leon remembered almost falling down at the top of the stairs as he rushed to rescue his friend from the typhoon like weather. When he swung open the door it was ever so apparent that Charley was sloppy drunk. He had never seen him like that before.

Suddenly, Leon was just as paralyzed as the Statue of Liberty. He could only stand there in awe as his bewildered friend told him a story that was so unbelievable he knew it had to be the alcohol talking.

After what seemed an eternity Charley calmed down enough to realize it would be better for everyone if he came inside.

Leon gave his friend some dry clothes and escorted him to the guest room to sleep off his apparent drunkenness.

As Leon slowly ascended the staircase to his bedroom, there were two things troubling his mind; the first was what would have happened to him if he had indeed fallen down these stairs; the other and maybe even more important was the look of fear that was in Charley's eyes.

"Could the story he just told me be true?" Maybe I should call the Police. No way..."it had to be the alcohol," he thought. I'm going to sleep.

The following morning when Roxanne went to wake Charley for breakfast, he was gone. There had been very little contact with him since that night.

***

The drive out to the country was a very pleasant one.

"The air seemed so fresh up here in the hills."

It was nice to get away from the big city even for a short period of time. Before Leon knew it, he was approaching the lake. There weren't many people out today.

He slowed down and made the turn into the entrance of the lake area. It only took a second to find Charley. He put the car in park and raced to meet his friend.

Hi Judge, I see you're right on time like always. Hello Charley, "you look good for an old fart".

"How old are you now?"

"I'm sixty-nine and counting thanks to you."

Where are the worms, said Charley? They are in the car. Well go get them son, "even a fisherman as good as myself needs his worms."

"Sit tight old fellow," I'll get them.

Here you go Charley. Hey...just look at them wiggle.

These are some good ones, said Charley. "Yeah, they cost me a pretty penny but they're worth it."

So tell me young man, what's going on?

As always Charley any thing that I tell you is strictly confidential.

"My lips are sealed."

In a matter of weeks there might be a trial involving two pharmaceutical companies, I have a hunch that what you saw at the lab last year is going to be very important.

"I need you to tell me again, exactly what you saw."

It's a pretty crazy story Judge. I doubt if you will believe a word of it.

Come on Charley, other than my wife there is no one I trust more than you. That means an awful lot to me judge... thank you.

Hey, I think I got one, said Charley.

"You just put the bait in the water a few seconds ago."

"It doesn't matter how long it's in the water son." What matters is what you do with it while it's in there.

Ha, ha, we are talking about fishing aren't we Charley? Of course we are. Wow look at it Judge, a blue striped bass, must weigh at least ten pounds. "It will make for some good eating."

"That's a nice one Charley".

"It's definitely a keeper."

Now Charley, you said there was something else that you wanted to add to what you had already told me. What is it?

Oh heck Judge no good story is told in bits and pieces. I have to start at the beginning. Hey I think I've got another one.

Looks like you do, "you are the king of the lake aren't you." It's another bass and it's bigger than the last one. "I think you're right," said Charley, "it is a little bigger but there is one out there bigger than both of these put together." Come on Charley, "bigger than these two put together?"

"He's a sneaky one though," I keep telling my wife about him but she just laughs at me.

Can we get back to the story Charley?

Like I've told you before there is this nice little creek about half a mile from that lab. The creek runs into the lake that's just behind the lab. I hope those chemicals aren't hurting my fish.

Any way, since they put up that darn fence several years ago, "I have to go almost a mile out of my way just to get to the creek," said Charley but once in a blue moon, someone will forget to lock the gate and I can walk right up to where the creek empties into the lake.

"That's where most of the good fishing is."

They have no trespassing signs posted everywhere. I don't pay them any mind though because I was fishing at that lake long before that lab was there and even though I know the gate is always locked I push against it anyway.

As luck would have it on this particular day when I pushed on the gate it was open. I couldn't believe my good fortune. It didn't last long though because when I pushed it closed it snapped shut. I pulled on it but it was locked. I stood there for a few seconds trying to figure out how I had locked it, when out of no where this small truck came barreling up the road.

"I thought I was caught but I was able to duck behind a big tree." I lay on the ground not ten feet from the truck afraid to move. "I still can't believe they didn't see me."

Two men got out of the truck and walked up to the fence. One guy looked to be in his late fifties and was very short. His partner was much younger and well over six feet tall.

The small man pushed against the fence and when it didn't open, he started yelling at the big guy. He called him everything but a child of God. The big guy didn't say a word; he just turned and went to the back of the truck. When he came back he had a set of bolt cutters, which he threw at the feet of the little man. He said, "use this little stupid man".

This made the little man very angry.

He said to the big guy, if you ever call me stupid again, "I kill you".

The big guy laughed and went back to the truck and watched the little guy wrestle with the lock unsuccessfully. He finally got out of the truck and took the bolt cutters from the little man and cut off the lock like it was a stick of butter.

"The little guy didn't say a word."

They got in the truck and drove through the gate, not bothering to close it behind them.

By now I had forgot all about those fish, all I was waiting for was a chance to run out that gate before they saw me.

"I watched them closely as they parked the truck."

"To my horror," when they got out of the truck they were wearing ski masks.

They went to the back of the truck and got a shotgun and headed into the lab at the rear entrance. I know you think I should have got out of there and called the police but my curiosity had gotten the better of me.

"I was also starting to come to my senses." These two fellows were not guards.

That's right Charley but you should have figured that out when they had to use the bolt cutters.

I waited for about fifteen minutes and then the big guy came out and went to the back of the truck and got a large grey bag. He must have thought he heard something because he stopped dead in his tracks and looked in my direction.

When he did my heart stopped and it didn't start again until he had gone back into the building.

Charley why didn't you leave and go call the police for heavens sake?

I don't know judge…probably the same reason you didn't call the police when I first told you this story.

Good point Charley but I had my reasons. Please continue with the story. I can't wait to hear what happens next.

Well…I wanted to go call the police but two things were stopping me, said Charley. I was on private property and I knew as soon as I tried to leave that big guy was going to be all over me.

I can understand your fear Charley but I'm not excusing it.

Well…Judge, I was so scared by now that I had dug a hole that would rival most fox holes dug by soldiers. I was feeling quite comfortable in that hole until," I heard someone crying."

I looked up and saw this short lady with red hair running down the road toward the gate. "I never saw anyone with such short legs run so fast." She kept looking back over her shoulder as if expecting someone to be behind her.

She made her way to the gate and disappeared. I was now sure that something awfully bad was happening inside that lab.

This is an incredible story Charley. If anyone else was telling me this I'd find it very hard to believe. What did you do next?

It had gotten dark and I just set there like a kid waiting for the next movie feature to start.

"I didn't have to wait long."

***

There was a splash in the lake.

I crept along the wood line to get a better look. It was difficult to see anything at first, especially with these old eyes.

There was another splash and I quickly pinpointed where it was coming from.

Standing on the side of the lake closest to the lab was a man with the large grey bag. He was tossing something into the lake and each time he did he let out a terrible little laugh that sounded like a demon.

What was he tossing into the lake? Charley….what was he tossing into the lake!

"I heard you the first time Judge."

This is where the story gets crazy and it's always where the nightmares began, said Charley. This is where I wished I had never picked up my fishing pole that day and entered that fence.

"Charley are you ok?"

You're starting to sweat and breathe heavy. Here have something to drink.

Thank you Judge.

I'm ok now.

Charley…are you going to tell me what he was tossing in the lake?

I'll tell you but you're not going to believe me.

"Just tell me Charley!"

He was tossing body parts into the lake. He was tossing human body parts into the lake Judge.

What did you say Charley?

"You heard me Judge."

"There's no need to repeat myself."

Dear God Charley. Please tell me that I heard you wrong.

"You heard correctly."

Charley you must be mistaken. I wish I was but I can remember it like it happen two minutes ago.

"I'm so sorry Charley."

I wish I had listened to you when you first tried to tell me.

"It's not your fault Judge."

I was drunk that night Judge. "I don't blame you for not believing me." Besides, I wasn't ready to talk about it that night, "I just thought I was."

What you have to understand Judge is that I've been drinking all my life.

My father shared a drink with me when I was nine years old. "It was my first drink." I don't even remember what it was. All I can remember is him laughing at me, when I started choking on what ever it was.

How can a father give his nine year old son a drink and then laugh at him when he starts to choke on it?

I don't know old man, I just don't know.

Funny thing is, I've been drinking ever since. I've tried to stop on several occasions but never with any success.

Since that night at the lab, I've only had one drink and it made me so sick that I haven't touched the stuff again.

My therapist says that I'm much better for quitting but he still can't seem to help me with the nightmares one little bit.

Hey Judge I think you've got one, it's a little one though, "you should throw that one back."

Charley have you told anyone else this story?

Just my wife but I tell her everything.

"I can't blame her for not believing this story." What about when the story about the lab hit the newspapers and the TV, said Leon?

We live out here in the hills Judge. We don't really concern ourselves with what going on beyond our piece of land.

We don't read the newspaper and we hardly ever watch the news. It's just too depressing Judge.

Well...Judge that's about it for the story.

Do you believe me?

Yes old man, yes I do. "There is not enough alcohol in the world to help you make up a story like that."

Before this trial is over I might have to ask you to tell this story in front of a court room full of people.

Judge you know I can't come around that court house. "I can't do it." I just can't. I understand my friend...trust me I do.

I have two more questions Charley and then I'm afraid I have to go. Which one of the men was tossing those things into the lake?

"They weren't things Judge," they were body parts I tell you. I even saw a head. Come on Charley, it was dark how can you be sure it was a head?

Because that little monster held it just inches in front of his face and stared at it as though he was trying to look into its soul or something before he threw it into the lake.

"That little monster was the only one that I saw leave the building Judge." I never did see the big guy leave.

"I think he killed him Charley."

Why would he do that? I don't know, said Leon. Something must have happened once they were inside the building. Maybe...."the big guy called him stupid again." That would have done it Judge.

I'm curious why the woman that you saw running out of the building didn't go to the police?

I can answer that Judge. She's scared of that little monster.

That little monster as you call him made a very serious mistake. He allowed a witness to escape and that makes no sense at all. It's been almost a year. I wonder where she is.

She's hiding somewhere Judge, I can promise you that.

Charley, according to the news reports there were five bodies inside that building but they were all burned beyond recognition. The spokesperson for the lab verified that they had five employees working late that night.

How do you know all this?

Because I watch TV and I read the newspaper. I suggest that in the future you do the same.

See what I mean Judge, the news is just full of depressing stuff, said Charley.

Charley something about your story and the police report doesn't make sense about that night. It's true that the bodies were burned beyond recognition but there was no mention of any heads missing. Someone would have had to go through a lot of trouble to cover that up.

Now...I'm confused Judge. How did the bodies burn?

The lab burned to the ground Charley? Didn't you know that?

Yes but I thought that was much later. I finally got up my nerves to go fishing out there after a couple of months had passed. I was told that there had been an electrical storm and the place caught on fire.

You didn't see a fire that night?

No, I was there at least an hour after the little monster left and I didn't see any fire.

Why did you wait so long?

I was scared and I also wanted to make sure they were gone. So how did the fire start? Maybe he set off some type of delay device Judge.

Maybe…. or just maybe someone else did, said Leon.

An electrical storm was blamed for the fire Charley but supposedly it happened the same night you were there. After hearing your story, I'm not sure that is what really happened.

Charley when is your next therapist appointment?

I have to see that idiot next week at two o'clock. If you ask me I should be the one getting paid to help him.

Don't go Charley, if you need to talk, call me. I'll listen to whatever you need to talk about and I won't charge you one red cent, said Leon. Thank you Judge, it's like you're saving my life all over again.

You have the good Lord to thank for that Charley "not me.

"Old man," do you ever miss that small town in Alabama?

After what they almost did to me, no I don't. "I feel much safer here."

Even after what you saw at the lab?

Yes…Judge even after seeing that.

Here you go old man; you know I don't eat these damn things. My God Judge! When did you catch this one? I snagged it while you were talking about the little monster standing beside the lake. I was in the fight of my life with this fish. I would have asked for your help but you were so into that story that you were telling, I didn't want to interrupt.

This is the biggest fish I've ever seen, said Charley! I believe this is the one I've been looking for. You go ahead and take it my friend. Show it to your wife, she'll have to believe you now. You can even take credit for catching it.

Judge there's just one more thing. What is it? I can't come around that court house. I just can't.

I know Charley and I understand. Take care of yourself my friend. I'll talk to you later.

Good bye Judge and thanks for listening. Good bye my friend and maybe you can sleep better now that you've told this story to someone who believes you.

No judge, "you are a very wise man but you are wrong about that." I'm afraid that as long as that little monster's out there somewhere, "I'll never be able to have a good night's rest."

CHAPTER 3
(Two months earlier)

Good morning Peaches. Hello Darius, "I didn't realize that you had an appointment today." I don't but I really need to talk to William. I'll let him know that you are here.

William...yes Peaches. Mr. Pollard is here. Darius...is here? Yes he is sir. Did he say what he wanted? Only that he really needs to speak to you. Send him in. You may go in. Thanks Peaches, by the way that's a real nice dress you're wearing. Thanks Darius.

You've also lost weight haven't you? Yes...I have lost a few pounds. Thanks for noticing.

It would be hard not to notice Peaches. Call my wife and let her in on whatever it is that you are doing.

"I'm not doing anything special." Really...well call her anyway; I'm sure she'd be happy to hear from you.

***

Darius, what do I owe the pleasure of this little surprise visit? How you doing William? I'm doing just fine.

May I have a seat? Sure, make yourself comfortable. I see you have a new desk. It's beautiful isn't it? It's nice but I like the older one better, "it had character." What character? The damn thing was full of nicks and scratches.

"That's what gave it character William."

Come in the boardroom for a second. I want to show you something.

"Take a look at that my friend."

Amazing, this whole room has been remodeled. You even had the floor redone. If I stare at it another second, I think the shine will make me go blind.

Nice isn't it? What do you think about this table? It is magnificent William, simply magnificent.

"This had to cost a fortune."

I was just tired of the old stuff. Things are looking up for the company lately and I thought we deserved to flaunt it a little.

Well William...I can assure you that any visitors will be impressed. I agree, I can't wait to hold our first meeting in here.

"I get the feeling that won't be very long after I leave."

"Why do you say that?"

Let's go back to your office.

***

I know how busy you guys at the FDA can be. So is this little visit business or pleasure?

"It's business."

I was afraid you would say that. Would you like a cup of coffee? I could have Peaches make you a cup in two seconds flat. How ya like it? Cream and sugar I bet. I don't have time. Maybe coffee is not the kind of drink that you need. I've got a new bottle of Brandy in the cabinet. I also have a few other drinks that you might be interested in.

"I'm trying to stay away from the stuff since I developed an ulcer." I've gotten so skinny that every time the wind blows I have to grab onto something.

Darius, I can't see where you've lost any weight. "You've always been a bit of a runt but if you say you have lost weight," I guess I have to believe you.

"I only wish I could lose some weight." I've been as big as a horse since I was born. Can you imagine how much I have to pay my tailor to make my suits? These damn Italian suits are expensive enough without the added cost for being a big guy.

"Oh stop your crying William." I can only dream of someday making the kind of money this company is paying you. You have that twenty room mansion in Manhattan of all places and that fancy Yacht that you hardly step foot on. What's the name of it again?

I call it, "The Ink."

"How did you decide on such a weird name?"

Damn it Darius, you are starting to give me a headache. Give me a few seconds while I take a couple of these aspirins.

You're still popping those aspirins aren't you William.

Stop beating around the bush Darius and tell me what you are doing here!

I'm here about Advernox William. I've learned that there is a problem with the formulation.

"You're kidding me right?"

I wouldn't joke about something like this William. I would hope that you wouldn't Darius. That drug saved this company! I don't disagree with you on that but Advernox is unsafe William, "it may even be fatal".

None of our tests have shown any indications of this. Don't bullshit me William. We both know that there weren't sufficient tests done before it was released to the market!

"Darius please lower your voice before Peaches hears you." Ok, Darius we can both agree that we took some short cuts in that area.

You're damn right you did.

How am I supposed to know that this isn't a trick to get more money out of us?

This isn't a trick William and it pisses me off that you would suggest such a thing!

I don't give a rat's ass about how pissed you are Darius. Do you think you can just stroll your little short skinny ass in here and drop a bomb like this on me and expect me not to be the least bit suspicious! Advernox will be this company's most profitable product ever and not you or anyone else is going to get in the way!

Listen to me William and you listen good because I'm not going to repeat myself. You have a serious problem here and it needs to be dealt with accordingly.

If what you say is true what do you recommend? We have a ton of this stuff on the market and please don't start talking to me about a freaking recall. No a recall will only get us both sent to jail, me faster than you, said Darius.

"You know I had to pull a lot of strings to get it through our system so fast." You were paid very well for that if I remember correctly, said William. Yes I was but that money isn't going to do me a bit of good if I'm locked away in prison.

There is only one thing that can make this nightmare go away William.

"I'm listening."

I recommend a complete reformulation and the sooner you do it the better. It's not that easy Darius. Reformulating can take a very long time and can be very, very expensive. There are so many things that I would have to get approved and these things would take time.

"Time, is not a luxury you have William."

"I'm suddenly very aware of that Darius!" However, certain things have to be done. A budget would have to be approved. After that I would have to assemble a team of scientists to work on this project and given the delicate nature at hand, "it would have to be someone who knows how to keep their mouth shut.

William you've been in this business over twenty-five years. "I'm sure you know someone that you can trust to handle this. I can only think of one person Darius but I'll never be able to convince him to work for me again.

Who is he, said Darius?

"His name is Richard Naylor."

In my opinion he's the best damn scientist that ever walked the face of this earth. "He's also the only one that can handle the type of team that it's going to take to work on this project."

"If he's that good William, you better find a way to get him back here." "He may be the only thing standing between us and prison."

How much time do I have Darius?

I'd say a couple of months at the most and that's probably a month too many.

So what you're saying is I have less than four weeks to make this happen. Darius you are indeed living in the land of make believe.

Darius no product can be reformulated in that short of a time unless you know exactly what the problem is. Furthermore, like I said earlier, reformulating can be awfully risky even under the best of circumstances. Most products don't work at all after they are reformulated, you should know that Darius.

"Well then William we have a problem don't we."

I suggest that you contact Mr. Naylor right away.

You don't understand. It's not going to be easy to convince him to come back.

Why won't he come back William?

He won't come back Darius because I made a terrible mistake. You ever hear of the Chester Project? Of course, who hasn't? That was a huge story. It stayed in the news for over two months.

It was my assignment and when things went wrong I made Richard Naylor the fall guy. The truth of the matter is, "he was only following my orders."

You're right William...

"He won't be back."

Darius how bad is this problem?

Some of the women are only getting sick William but some are losing their unborn babies and if our instincts are correct some of these women themselves might be dying.

That is how bad things are.

William maybe you should open that bottle of Brandy.

We can have a drink together, like we did on that glorious day that I marched in here and told you that I got you the approval to put Advernox on the market.

"Remember that day William?" We were both pretty happy then weren't we?

Happy is not the word, we were more like two sharecroppers who had just won the lottery. "Yes we were," what a difference a few months make.

It appears that your miracle drug is anything but a miracle William, fix it or we'll both be....

"You don't have to say it Darius, I know."

Let me walk you out.

Peaches please call John and tell him to meet me at the Diner in one hour. I'm heading there now.

***

That rain is really coming down out there, said Betty. This is the eighth day in a row. Will it ever stop Mr. Winters?

That's God's work child. When he's ready for it to stop, it will.

Of course you're right about that Mr. Winters. I'm not trying to question God's will; I just hope it stops by the time I get off work. Five blocks is a long way to walk in this freezing rain. Besides, I just had my hair done.

Your hair looks great Betty. I can understand your concern but maybe next time you should consider the fact that it's been raining for over a week before you waste your money.

What can I get you today Mr. Winters? Just coffee right now, I'm expecting company in about ten minutes. Can you come back then?

"Sure I can big guy."

***

William knew that the last place that he should be was this diner. His doctor had warned him that if he didn't cut back on his cholesterol intake and lose some weight his heart would soon give out on him.

"William knew his doctor was right."

He could no longer ignore the burning sensation in his chest. It wasn't heartburn and he had to stop pretending that it was.

Mr. Winters wasn't even six feet tall and he weighed close to three hundred pounds. He had always been a big person. When he was young the kids at school would tease him about his weight but he didn't care. He would eat the large meals that his mother had prepared for him every day and ignore them because he loved food. Over the past year he had been feeling a tight pain in his chest. He knew it was his heart warning him.

When you are approaching sixty some things seem more important that others. He had never been married and he could count the number of women he had been with on one hand. Not something that he was proud of or shared with anyone. What's even worst is they were all one night stands that he had to pay for and they never returned, even when he offered to double and triple their fee. He accounted most of his bad luck with women to his premature balding, his enormous belly and the fact that he wasn't well endowed in the penis area. So food was his only joy, that and the power that comes with being the CEO of one of the most powerful and admired pharmaceutical companies in America.

***

Hello William, I hope you haven't been waiting long.

Hello J.T. I've only been here a few minutes.

"Are you hungry?"

Yes, "I am starving", said John. Betty we will order now. I'll have a large bowl of beef stew for starters with a lot of crackers. What about you J.T.? I'll have the special of the day.

Can I get you gentlemen something to drink while you wait for your food? I'll have a Dark beer, said William. Can you make mine a Michelob, said John? Sure, I'll be back in a moment.

I don't know how you do it William. Do what?

You're still drinking that damn dark German beer, said J.T.

It's good stuff J.T. Do you remember the first time we had it, said William? How could I forget? We were stationed in Bamberg, Germany with the 1st Armored Division.

It was the worst beer I had ever tasted. It reminded me of what it must be like to drink water straight out of a sewer, said John.

I agree with you on that but remember how the old German bartender kept saying it was an acquired taste and once you got past the first couple you wouldn't want anything else, said William.

Yes, I remember him saying that and it appears that he was right at least in your case, me I couldn't get past the first one.

It's pretty crowded in here today, said John. Are people seeking shelter from the rain? This old diner has been a meeting place for a lot of people through the years, said William. "I'm sure it has William." When do you think they'll tear it down?

Have you lost your mind John? You shouldn't even think such thoughts! "These old diners are a part of American history," "more so than apple pie."

Come on William, from the outside it looks like it belongs in a redneck trailer park. On the inside the floor is falling apart and the walls are paper thin. I'm surprised a strong wind hasn't picked this thing up and dropped it somewhere near the Verrazano Bridge.

That's because it's not God's will.

This old diner will be here long after we're both dead and gone J.T., nothing on this earth goes before the good Lord is ready for it. That includes me and you. Besides, this Diner was built back in the fifties when they built things to last unlike this new stuff that they put up over night.

Back up just a minute said John. When did you become an expert on the works of the good Lord? I'm no expert. Good, because for a moment there, I thought an alien had abducted your body as well as your mind.

Screw you J.T. I have my religious belief as well as the next guy.

William, I've known you almost thirty years and I've never heard you mention the Holy name. You do it twice in less than two minutes and I'm not supposed to think that's a little strange.

Do you realize how many meals we've eaten at this place over the years, said William? Oh I get it, time to change the subject right. The answer to your question is no William, I lost count a long time ago but my wife hasn't.

She believes this place is responsible for my cholesterol problems. She just might be right about that John but the food taste great doesn't it.

Amen to that and at our age does it really matter?

Yes it matters, "I don't know about you John but I'm not ready to meet my maker yet," "hell I may never be." Yeah, you're right again William; we both have a lot of stuff to set right before that glorious day.

In the mean time J.T. just follow up every meal with a glass of Brandy or Scotch like I do and you won't have any problems. I didn't realize they sold hard liquor here. They don't, I keep the stuff in my car. Now, how long do you intend to bore me with this small talk John?

"It's time to talk about business."

It's been over a week since we've talked. I hope you have some good new for me. I hate to disappoint you William but

I don't. We tried every trick in the book but we couldn't get our man in. What's the problem J.T.? I thought your guy was highly qualified. He is but Warrenton Pharmaceutical are some picky son of a bitches.

Do you realize everyone on that damn project was hand selected by Brian Gatewood? Then we have no choice John, we have to move to the alternate plan.

"I strongly advise against it William."

"Listen to me you chicken shit ass hole." We have no choice now, we've already wasted too much valuable time. For two months now I've been patience. For two months, I've tried it your way and what do we have to show for it John? I'll tell you said William; we have nothing, not a damn thing!

Here are your beers gentlemen. Thanks Betty.

Tomorrow I'm contacting an associate that I've worked with in the past and moving forward with my plan.

You don't mean Cliff do you? Yes, J.T., that's exactly who I mean.

There has to be another way William, there just has to be!

Has old age made you soft John? In the old days you wouldn't have given this a second thought. It's cold-blooded murder and I want no part of it William. Let's find another way.

There is no other way John and at the rate you are going, we might as well just pick up the damn phone right now, call the got damn police and ask them to kindly escort us to prison straight from here!

John don't you understand if we don't do something soon, this whole thing is going to blow up in our face. I'm not going to just sit back and do nothing, said William!

You are in this just as deep as I am J.T. and we both know you don't have the appetite for poverty or prison any more than I do.

I realize we have to do something William but not this! There just has to be a better way.

We've been friends for a long time J.T.

I'll give you 72 hours to come up with a better plan. For God's sake William, "that's not enough time".

It's all you have and if I were you I'd get started right now. I'll tell Betty that you had to hurry away on business.

Can I at least eat my lunch first? There is no time for such luxuries and don't worry about the special of the day. I've had it before, said William. There's really nothing special about it.

It's very hard being your friend William.

This is business. It has nothing to do with friendship J.T.; you better go now, the clocks ticking.

(Present)

"All rise."

Please be seated. Gentleman this case really intrigues me, said Judge Kenton. It is with the greatest amount of curiosity that I have made my decision today.

First, let me tell you that I do not appreciate being rushed into making any decision; however, I do feel that I have enough information to make a fair ruling.

It is the ruling of this court that a trial should commence two weeks from today to get to the bottom of these allegations. That date will be August 11th at nine a.m. Mr. Legitt, I sincerely hope this gives you enough time to meet with your other clients.

"This hearing is adjourned."

***

Thank you so much Mr. Legitt, I was afraid that it wouldn't go good for us if we had to wait until tomorrow morning.

You can kiss my ass Vonhart! You and that rag tag firm of yours don't have a leg to stand on. My client will be filing a counter suit. We will win and bankrupt that small ass company that you are representing. It only figures a small outfit like WPP would go with a small time law firm like Vonhart and Associates.

How many partners do you have over there now, said Jackson? Oops my bad, you don't have any partners, do you? It's just you and that two bit P.I., what's his name.

"You know his name," said Vonhart. You're just still pissed that he wouldn't come and work for you.

That's not true but I could have paid him a hell of a lot more money than he's making with you.

It's always about money with you isn't it Jackson? We all need money said Vonhart, that's just a fact of life but some people have to be able to look at themselves in the mirror without the guilt that I'm sure much be eating you up inside Mr. Legitt.

"I don't feel any guilt about anything," said Jackson.

I'm sure you don't and that's even worse. BMX definitely picked the right man to represent them, said Vonhart. Your only mistake up to this point was rushing the judge to make his decision and your client's first mistake was retaining you to represent them, said Vonhart. No scratch my last statement; their first mistake was stealing my client's drug. You were their second mistake. Why didn't they check you out first?

Screw you Vonhart. We both know that you don't have a chance in hell of winning this case. If it were any other attorney I would agree but since you are the attorney for the defense, I think I have a great chance, said Vonhart.

I was in the court room during your last case. Your act is getting weak. I admit it was very cleaver ten years ago for you to use your handicap to get all those juries to feel sorry for you but there are so many attorneys out there with similar handicaps as yours that it's no longer a big deal.

That patch that you wear over your eye has gotten to be a bit much and that cane is a little dated also. Do us all a favor and drop both of them. There have been numerous conversations amongst your colleagues about you being seen on several occasions outside of this courthouse without that cane.

"No one feels sorry for you any more." All this jury is going to care about is the truth and the cold hard facts. I'll make sure of that!

First of all, I have never used my handicap to help me win a case. Secondly, no one has ever seen me without this cane. I can't even walk from here to that door over there without it. Thirdly, I'm going to make you wish you had never taken this case.

"You...can't...beat me...Vonhart!"

You're wrong Jackson and I'll tell you why. You always make a mistake in your cases but you always manage to cover it up somehow because that's what you're best at but not this time.

All I have to do is make sure I'm around when you make that one fatal mistake that's going to lose you this case. Your only mistake up to this point was rushing the Judge to make a ruling. I promise to be right there when you make your next one.

"There won't be any more mistakes," Vonhart.

"We'll see about that Jackson." It will be interesting to see who pays your expensive salary when this is all said and done.

I'll see you in two weeks Jackson. Don't worry we'll be ready!

Why are you still standing here talking to me? I thought you had other clients that need your help.

"That's true Vonhart." How many are waiting for you?

Let me see if I can help you understand something Mr. Jackson Legitt. I've been waiting the better part of eight years to get a case against you and now that I have one, I'm terrified that you are going to try to settle before we go to court.

I have never settled a case in my life and I'm not about to start with you!

"Don't be stupid!" As much as I dislike you as a person Jackson, I realize that you have the potential to be a very competent attorney when you listen to reason. Do what's right for once in your life Jackson.

"You can accept my client's settlement now and save the people their hard earned tax dollars and your client the embarrassment that's headed their way." Besides, a settlement would only make them appear to be guilty, I'm sure you and those idiots that sit on the board at BMX Pharmaceutical can come up with a statement that doesn't make them look so bad.

"All you guys have to do is remind the public of all the good the company has done in the past." Soon everyone will forget all about this. However, if you insist on going to trial and you lose this case, "which I'm sure you will," your career and your client's company is history.

Are you really willing to throw everything away just to prove that you can beat me?

Take the deal Jackson before I pull it off the table!

Excuse me; I have work to do, said Jackson. I don't have the luxury of hanging out in court rooms all day like you do.

Ten billion dollars right now Mr. Legitt and this nightmare goes away, right here, right now.

No deal Mr. Vonhart but I'd pay twice that amount just to make you go away. Very well then Jackson, have it your way but when I walk out that door so does any chance of a settlement.

"Good in that case Vonhart," let me get the door for you.

***

Hello Mr. Winters, this is Mr. Legitt. Hello Jackson, how did it go today? Not good at all, the case is going to trial in two weeks sir. Warrenton Pharmaceutical is asking for twenty billion dollars but they are willing to settle for ten billion, if you offer seven billion, I think they will take it. What would you like me to do?

Jackson what are our chances of winning, said William? That depends on how honest you have been with me.

I know their attorney very well and I can handle him. What I can't handle is any surprises. If there is anything that you have forgotten to tell me or if there is something that you haven't told me, "now is the time to come clean."

Well… there is this one thing….

***

Good morning Tracy, this is Peaches from Mr. Winter's office.

Hello Peaches how have you been?

Good and how about yourself? Just fine, William has scheduled an emergency board meeting for one o'clock this afternoon. He would like for Mr. Randolph to be there.

I'm sorry Peaches but Mr. Randolph should be boarding a plane to Chicago as we speak. Tracy it's very important that Mr. Randolph is not on that plane when it takes off.

I'll try to reach him but I can't make any promises.

***

Sir I just got an urgent call from Mr. Winter's office. He has scheduled an emergency board meeting for one o'clock today and he wants you to be there.

I've been waiting three months to take this trip and I'm not about to miss it because Mr. High and Mighty William Winters has scheduled another of his stupid, emergency board meetings.

It's almost noon now and I'm about to board the plane. Wait until about twelve thirty, then call his secretary and tell her that you couldn't reach me. I'll call you once I land in Chicago.

Have a safe trip sir. Thank you.

***

Excuse me sir, are you Mr. Randolph?
"Yes I am."
There is an emergency call for you.
"Thank you."
Hello... hello Randolph, huh... hi William.
I hear you are on a plane headed to Chicago.
"Yes that's correct."
"Has the plane left the ground yet," said William? Oh how silly of me, if it had left the ground we wouldn't be talking right now would we?

I need you at this meeting Randolph.

William I really need to get to Chicago, it's important. Is it more important than your job Randolph?

"It's pretty important William."

You didn't answer my question Randolph. The answer is no Mr. Winters, it's not more important than my job.

Good, I sent a driver to pick you up fifteen minutes ago. He should be there any second now.

I have to tell you William your timing sucks! What's so damn important this time? Did your secretary break her freaking nail or something?

Very funny Randolph but maybe you should save your jokes for now. You might need them when you are looking for a new job. There are decisions that need to be made today and you are one of the key voters, now get your ass off that plane now, or consider yourself fired! Do I make myself clear!

Yeah William… painfully clear!

Stewardess, I need to get off the plane.

Is everything Ok sir?

No it isn't. My boss is an asshole!

"They all are sir."

***

Well William, we're all here. What's so damn important this time?

How about your got damn pension?

What about our pension?

Good, "I see I finally have your attention."

With the exception of J.T. each of you morons gave me a hard time when I called you to come in for this meeting today. I admit that in the past I might have jumped the gun a little with these emergency meetings but I think that once you've heard what I have to say, you'll agree that this one is very necessary.

"Excuse me William," said Randolph, who is the gentleman sitting to your right?

I'll explain who he is later. For now just know that he is a very important man to us. Now, if someone would kindly turn out the lights I'll begin....

CHAPTER 4

Richard Naylor stared out the window of his plush New York penthouse apartment that overlooked the Hudson River. He had just finished working out in the gym down stairs and had worked up quite an appetite.

He really didn't enjoy working out but it was necessary if he wanted to keep his six foot, four inch lean frame in shape. He knew that old age has a way of creeping up on you if you're not careful.

He'd seen it happen too many of his friends.

He noticed a gray hair in his beard as he was shaving this morning. This discovery led to a search for more but that was the only one. It would only be a matter of time and the gray hair would take over. That's if he was lucky.

Most of his child hood friends were already bald or half gray.

Since birth he had been blessed with a half dollar size gray spot directly in the middle of his head. Since grade school, his friends had teased him that it was going to grow toward the back and he would look like a skunk. Fortunately, it had hardly grown at all.

It was always a conversation piece with men and women alike. Most people thought he put it there and were amazed to find out he was born with it. He was amazed himself that at the age of thirty-five, it was still the only gray in his entire head.

Rick continued to stare out at the rain soaked night. It was such an awesome view from the seventh floor. Even in the rain the view was magnificent.

There was just so much to like about this huge penthouse apartment. It had wood floors that seem to make the place even larger than it was. The cleaning service made sure the floor shined. The kitchen was a dream, especially for someone like Rick, who spent a lot of time there. He especially liked the fact that the stainless steel refrigerator had a small TV mounted where most had the ice maker. This made it easy for him to watch sports center while he prepared his meals.

The master bedroom was indeed the masterpiece of the entire penthouse. The thing that set it off was the huge fireplace that was smack dab in the center of the room.

Unfortunately it was the dead of summer and he was in the fourth month of a six-month temporary housing allowance.

He knew he would never get to use that fireplace.

There were times that he wanted to turn the air conditioner to its lowest setting, just to have an excuse to light that fireplace.

The awesome view seemed such a waste without someone to share it with. Stacey would love this view and would have gotten a kick out of a cleaning lady coming twice a week. The linen is always fresh and the place always smelled great.

Yes, all this and rent free for the first six months. Bartell Pharmaceutical really knows how to treat their people.

Moving to New York had been a very difficult decision for him. He had left all his family, friends and Stacey Morrow his fiancée and childhood sweetheart.

He rarely allowed himself to think about her anymore but it was hard to get her five foot, eight inch hour glass frame out of his mind. He knew she was probably out there somewhere jogging right now.

Running had always been her passion.

He'd hate to imagine what she would do without it. Although he tried not to think about it, he had imagined a thousand times seeing those long beautiful legs running across the country to be with him in New York.

He would never forget the day she passed him that note in fifth grade English class. The words were simple but the meaning was earth shattering. He read it once and then over and over again. Could his eyes be deceiving him he thought?

He looked across the classroom at her smiling face and he knew his life would never be the same again. For that he was grateful.

He looked back down at the note and read it one more time. I like you do you like me? Check yes or check no. With trembling hands he quickly checked yes and sent the note back across the room to her. Unfortunately as the note was making it's way back to her, it was intercepted by their English teacher.

Miss Gantry opened the note and for the first time in seemingly forever, "she managed to smile". She handed the note to Stacey and continued with her lecture on adjectives and adverbs.

At the end of class he walked over to Stacey's desk. She seemed to be waiting for everyone else to leave the room.

He asked, Stacey if he could carry her books. Her response was, "I can carry them".

Just look at you two said Miss Gantry, is there a classroom romance going on here? Stacy said, "I'll see you at basketball practice and ran from the room," leaving him alone with the lady that until today was known as the teacher with a smile turned upside down.

When he finally escaped from Miss Gantry and made his way into the hallway, there was a group of girls crowded around the lockers and they were giggling that crazy laughter that can only come from 13 year old girls.

In the center of that crowd was Stacey with the note. Rick was so embarrassed that he started to turn around but this was the only way to get to his next class.

As he walked past the group, they stopped giggling and watched him until he turned the corner. Then the giggling started up again.

I like you. Do you like me?

With that magical phrase a twenty-two year love affair began. Even after a failed marriage to another woman and several kids later. Stacy was the one he truly loved.

Fate had found a way to bring them back together and things had been great until now. He begged her to come with him but she wouldn't, "she simply couldn't". "Who would take care of mom," she said?

***

How could he get mad at her for wanting to take care of their mother? Her mom didn't need her around as much as she pretended.

He even said bring your mom, she can live with us but Stacey knew that her mom would never leave Memphis. It was the only place that's she'd ever called home.

Rick understood that her mother was getting old and set in her ways. He also knew she would never be able to adjust to living in someone else's home. The poor old lady is just afraid of being alone and he knew it.

Who wants to be alone?

Unfortunately for Rick, Stacy did not believe in long distant relationships. She gave back the engagement ring that he had given her two years ago. She swore on the night that he gave it to her that she would never take it off. It was the only lie that she had ever told him. He knew he should have married her a long time ago.

In his mind he had tried to let her go a million and one times but his heart wouldn't allow it.

The kiss that she gave him before he got on the plane heading to New York had convinced him that it wasn't over for her either.

He thought back on that moment and could hear her pain in her voice as she wiped a tear from her eye and said, "I'm proud of you Rick". This is what you've always wanted and now you have it.

Her eyes filled with tears as she said, "don't worry you'll have lots of women to choose from in New York". Then she turned and ran out of the airport like she was being chased by a herd of will buffalo.

"She never looked back."

Rick stared at the picture on the bedside table. The two people seemed so happy together. Was this new job really worth taking a chance of losing her?

What a silly question he thought.

There are millions of jobs out there but there is only one Stacey.

He had to put her out of his mind and he knew she was right about one thing". There truly are lots of women in New York but his choice was made in that old cold English classroom many years ago and he would find a way to get her back.

This was the first time in his life that he didn't follow his heart. Of course he realized his mistake by now. It was simple he got greedy. He wanted both, the great job and the great woman and why shouldn't he have both, he thought?

Four months had passed since she ran out of that airport and left him wishing things were different. Time had showed him that having both would be short of impossible. For now he would have to hope that he had made the right choice but he still prayed that Stacey would realize her mistake and come back to him someday.

***

For most people reaching the top at thirty-five would have been a great accomplishment, however, Richard Naylor had tasted success very early in life so this made thirty-five seem like a century but he had finally made it.

One thing he was sure of, "they would have never given him this opportunity at his previous job". Besides, that company was heading no where until they stumbled onto that new wonder drug. It seems that things turned around for them overnight.

"How could one product have such a huge impact in such a short time," he thought?

It didn't matter, "he was just glad to be out of there."

***

Is that the phone? Hello...hello, may I speak to Richard? This is he.

Hi Rick, this is Peaches from William Winter's office. How have you been doing? I'm doing just fine Peaches. Why are you calling me?

Mr. Winter's asked me too, said Peaches.

"What in the world makes him think that I would ever speak to him again?" Please Rick, "I realize you are probably still upset but it's been almost six months now." Can I put you through to him?

"Hell no Peaches!"

Please Rick, don't be so hasty until you've heard what he has to say. I've known William for a long time and I can feel that something is very, very wrong, said Peaches.

Rick, "you know he is a proud man."

"I'm sure it took a lot for him to ask for your help."

He's not the one asking Peaches, "you are". I have always liked you Peaches and I realize what happened to me there had nothing to do with you but please don't call here again. Click...

***

William, "I'm afraid things went just as you predicted."

Ok Peaches, "I guess I'll have to make that trip to New York after all.

What makes you think he'll talk to you if you go there, said Peaches? Curiosity mostly, "that's what makes him so damn good at what he does." Call the tower and tell them to get the company jet ready to depart first thing tomorrow morning, said William. After that, contact the three scientists on this list and set up a telephone conference with them for three o'clock this afternoon. I must speak to them before I leave for New York tomorrow.

William, "why is this so urgent?"

Will you stop asking so damn many questions and just do it Peaches!

Yes sir...

***

Why on earth is William Winter's trying to reach me, said Rick?

I'm too sleepy to even think about it now. I can still remember being summoned to his office that day. I have gone over that meeting in my mind a thousand times since leaving his office that day and it still doesn't make any sense.

"How could they do that to me?"

That's in the past now and I will not waste another second of my life thinking about the "Chester Project" or Mr. William Winters but I will call Peaches back and apologize.

***

Hello... BMX Pharmaceuticals.

Hello Peaches, "I just wanted to apologize." I realize you are just trying to do your job.

Don't worry Rick; you have reason to be upset. I forgive you, now will you please do me a personal favor and meet with William. Peaches you are asking an awful lot.

'It's important Rick."

What's it about Peaches? I can't really say Rick.

So...you don't know do you? I could never lie to you. I really don't have a clue but I've never seen William so worried.

Peaches for you, "I'll meet with him but I'm not making any promises." Thank you Rick, "you are a saint."

I'll call him now and tell him that you'll see him. What's a good time for you? You better make it soon before I change my mind. I'll talk to you later Peaches and again I'm sorry.

***

Hello William this is Peaches, I just got off the phone with Richard Naylor, he has agreed to meet with you but he wants to do it soon. Please call me when you get this message and don't forget that I will not be in until late tomorrow because I'm going to attend my nephew Timothy's graduation.

***

Cliff I need you to pack an overnight bag, I have a new assignment for you, said William.

"Who do you need me to kill this time?"

I don't want this person killed; I just want you to bring him to me unharmed. Who is it, said Cliff?

"It's Richard Naylor," said William.

The Richard Naylor that use to work for you?

Yes that's the one.

What did he do?

"It's what he won't do that's the problem," said William. Isn't he somewhere in New York, said Cliff? Yes...his new employer has him set up in a fancy high rise penthouse apartment over looking the Hudson River. I was going to leave tomorrow morning but I changed my mind, "we need to deal with this tonight."

We are headed there in two hours, so get whatever you need and meet me at the tower.

"William this is kind of short notice."

For the kind of money I'm paying you, you don't need a freaking notice, "just be ready to go in two hours."

Alright...what's the plan?

I want you to go to his apartment and kindly ask him to meet me at a location in New York that I'll give you later. William what if he doesn't want to come?

"I'm sure he won't." you idiot. That's why I'm sending you!

***

Mr. Naylor, how are you doing today sir?

"I'm just fine Ralph." How are you? I'm fine sir. There is a messenger here with a package at the front desk for you. Would you like me to send him up?

I was just about to jump in the shower but send him up.

Good evening sir. Are you Richard Naylor?

"Yes I am."

Here you go Mr. Naylor. Wow, this is really a nice penthouse.

"Thank you."

I'll just need you to sign here for your package.

Sure but who sent this?

It's from a Mr. William Winters.

What...I don't believe you!

Here check for yourself. You're right it is from William. Why would he send me anything? Well thanks; excuse me sir.... no tip?

"Oh how rude of me." I'm just a little shocked to be getting a package from this person. It's probably a bomb. Just one second, let me get my wallet.

That won't be necessary Mr. Naylor. I need you to come with me.

Come with you...where?

"Who are you?" Let's just say that I work part time for Mr. Winters.

I don't care who you work for I'm not going anywhere with you.

You can either come peacefully or we can do this my way with my gun. The choice is yours Mr. Naylor.

What's this about?

Mr. Winters will explain that when we see him tonight. Why didn't he come himself, instead of sending you? He pays me to do as he says. I don't waste his time by asking stupid questions. Now don't force me to use this, Mr. Naylor because I'm very good with it.

Now listen closely Richard. We will be leaving the building to meet Mr. Winters very shortly. I'll be following directly behind you but not close enough for it to appear that we are together. Once you get outside the building there will be a brown panel van parked across the street. Get in and wait for me. I'm very accurate with this gun so no funny business when you get to the front desk.

***

Hello Mr. Naylor. Did you receive your package?

"Yes I did Ralph and there was a wonderful surprise inside. When I see your boss I'm going to recommend that he give you a raise for doing such a fine job.

Oh shucks Mr. Naylor that won't be necessary. I'm just doing my job like the other doormen. No Ralph, I think you're doing a far better job than they are and he should be made aware of it as soon as possible. Who knows Ralph, "there might even be a raise in it for you."

Are you really going to speak to him Mr. Naylor?

Yes Ralph, "I promise you I'm going to speak to him".

***

What were you and the Doorman talking about?

I just mentioned to him how great a job he is doing.

Oh yeah…"he's an idiot."

Where are you taking me? I'm not sure, said Cliff but I'm about to find out. Do you ever go anywhere without that gun? Never! That's too bad; I was hoping that I might catch you without it, so I could kick your ass, said Rick!

Seat back and shut up, said Cliff! I better call Mr. Winters before I do something that he might not like. Go ahead and call him, all of a sudden I can't wait to speak to that ass hole!

***

William I have Mr. Naylor with me. He's not being very cooperative. I'm not sure I'm going to be able to deliver him to you unharmed.

If you touch one hair on his head Cliff your ass belongs to me! Let me speak to him.

Here Richie, he wants to speak to you.

What the hell is going on William?

I knew you were into a lot of shady dealings but I didn't know kidnapping was one of them.

Relax Rick, it's not as bad as it seems. I just need to talk to you. Well this is a hell of a way to do it! I'm sorry, I didn't get Peaches message until several minutes ago. I now see all this wasn't necessary.

"You're damn right this wasn't necessary!"

Please just try to remain calm until you get here and then we'll talk. Give the phone back to Cliff. "William where the hell are you?"

Do you know where the old fisherman's pier is just off of Steeplechase Way? Yes, isn't that where they found that fishing boat full of dead bodies a couple of years ago?

That's correct Cliff.

We'll be there in less than ten minutes.

We are almost there, Mr. Naylor. I must warn you that any attempt to escape will not end in your favor. You're a pretty big man with that gun in your hand aren't you?

Just keep your mouth shut unless someone speaks to you, said Cliff. Ok Rick we are here, watch your step when we enter the building. I think the walkway might be a little tricky

***

William what's going on? Why have you dragged me out to God only knows where with this little midget with the big gun?

Please Rick, Cliff has a very bad temper, he gets upset very easily. I'm pretty upset myself right now. If he were a real man, he'd put down his big gun, so I could show both of you just how upset I am. There's no need for that kind of talk, said William.

Cliff, please wait in the other room.

Rick I want to apologize to you. Forget it William an apology is not necessary. I've moved on and I'm happy. I only agreed to meet with you as a favor to Peaches and this is the thanks I get. Rick, I made a mistake. I didn't get the message from Peaches in time.

Rick we both know that the boys over at Bartell won't challenge your mind. What the hell does Bartell have to do with you kidnapping me?

Besides at least I know that I can trust them.

Trust is very important to you isn't it?

I shouldn't have to answer that William. I know Rick and I understand how you must feel and I'm trying to make it right. Please William just get to the bottom of why you drug me here so I can go.

"Rick you are owed an apology," so please let me say my piece.

***

I listened to what he had to say but the words meant nothing to me. A million sorry would have done him no good. After the apologies were finally over he went into this big spill about what was going on at BMX Pharmaceutical. I couldn't put my finger on it but something in his demeanor just wasn't right. His conversation didn't match his body language. It was as if he was also trying to convince himself that what he was saying was true. Yes, something was terribly wrong and a hunch told me that I was about to get caught up in it.

***

Rick are you familiar with our drug called Advernox? Yes, I am William, "I think everyone has heard of your new block buster, wonder drug." Well, I'm afraid that there might be a problem, a very serious problem. Do you mean the kind of problem where the FDA gets involved? You guessed it Rick.

Right now there's only one little FDA fart that's thinking about making any noise but he's being as quiet as a mouse for his own reasons.

Not that I care but what's the problem with it?

Side effects partner. What kind of side effects are you talking about William? If what I'm being told is true, it's the worst kind. William the worst kind of side effect would be death.

Is that what you're telling me?

That's one of the reasons why I hired you Rick because you catch on fast. I don't know how we let you get away from us. The answer to your question is yes. I'm afraid that death is a possibility but we are on top of this. Do you want to hear my game plan Rick?

Not really but it doesn't look like I have a choice.

We are bringing in three new scientists to work on this project and we want you to be the lead. They will report directly to you.

What on earth makes you think I'd come back to work for you?

'You will because you care about people." William, you really have some nerve. What about my old team, said Rick? When they were put together we only chose the best. I'm sure they could handle anything this drug can throw at them.

I realize you are proud of that team Rick and you should be.

In the small time that you were together your team managed to accomplish some wonderful things, however, this project is very delicate and requires a different shall we say, level of expertise.

You are barking up the wrong tree *partner*. You need a new game plan because I won't be the quarterback for this one.

Women and their unborn babies are dying Rick! We need you.

"Damn it William," isn't there someone else?

I'm afraid not, "it's you or no one."

When are you pulling the crap off the shelves?

We're not, we can not.

My God I don't believe you just said that!

We can't Rick! It would do more harm than good.

You money hungry ass hole yelled Rick! Something is wrong with this picture and I think I know what it is. You're trying to save your own skin, aren't you William? You knew there was a problem with Advernox all along didn't you?

Please Rick, people are dying and if we don't act fast more will. We need your help, besides, you owe me.

I don't owe you anything! My debt was paid on the day that you made me the fall guy on The Chester Project!

Is that how you see it Rick?

How could I see it any other way?

I was simply following your orders. I had no idea that you would turn out to be the kind of man that you are. Rick you know that I had no choice. Now for the sake of God man please forget about the "Chester Project" and help us! I know you have a good heart, please try to forgive me but if you can't please don't turn you back on these poor helpless women.

"Damn you to hell William Winters!"

If the devil ever needs a partner, I'll highly recommend you!

Sit down Rick and calm down. I'm afraid that you really have no choice. Make it easy on yourself and cooperate with us.

Damn...who are these scientists?

They are the best that this world has to offer in this field, said William. First you have Etienne (Steven) Batiste from France. He came so highly recommended that I couldn't say no. There is also Evan Blair from Eastern Europe. I'm told he's a little strange but in a pleasant way. The last and probably the smartest member of the team is our very own Candis Lockhart from Burlington, New Jersey. She works at our research center that's five miles from here.

That's strange, I would think that someone who is considered the best in the world, name would ring a bell, especially working so close to us but it doesn't and where in the heck is Burlington, New Jersey?

Well...I think Burlington is about fifteen miles north of Philadelphia, Pennsylvania. Now the story on Miss Lockhart is that she is somewhat of a loner and a little hard to work with at times but she is dedicated to the company and she is very good at what she does.

"Which is what?"

She solves the problems that other scientists say can't be solved. How do her co-workers feel about that? They hate her but when there's a problem, "she is the one they call."

Just remember that each of these scientists is considered the tops in their fields; so there may be a time when egos get in the way. This is when you get to assert that God given talent that you have. I didn't know I had a God given talent, said Rick.

Come on Rick no one is a better people person than you are. I have personally seen you work your magic on your subordinates. They all agree that you are the best Manager they have ever met and they would do anything that you ask because they know you have their back. "You have a gift man and you know it."

There is just one small detail that I forgot to mention.

What is it William?

Miss Lockhart was the front runner for the lead position and if memory serves me correct she was very disappointed when she didn't get it, no, let me rephrase my last comment. Candis Lockhart wasn't disappointed, "she was pissed."

"Oh that's just great."

Don't worry about her Rick. "I'm sure once you put on the charm," she'll melt in your arms just like all the others.

"Now listen *partner*," because this is important.

In the briefcase on the chair next to you is information on each of them, said William. I want you to look it over and contact them within the next twenty-four hours. Then schedule a group meeting with them in four days and contact me shortly after that.

Now that you know who will be working with you, "lets talk about where you will be working." I have leased the IOC Tower which is located downtown. That's a very unique facility, said Rick. I went there on a tour once. It's state of the art.

Yes it is, said William, you and your team should be very comfortable there.

"I hate to say this William but I'm impressed."

It's not going to be a picnic Rick, so don't get too excited. You and your group will be required to put in a lot of hours because you only have about four weeks to make this happen.

Ha, ha…"You really are living in a fantasy world aren't you William?" No I'm not! You are not the first group to look into this problem. The last group was unsuccessful that's why this time we have assembled the best team that we could find. Their mistake was they believed that the problem couldn't be solved from the very beginning. Don't let this thought creep into your teams' head, once it does, it will never get out.

What about the other teams notes?

They don't exist.

William is that official or unofficial?

Does it really matter?

"Yes it matters William!"

There might be something in their notes that could help. Their notes don't exist Rick and neither will yours if you fail. Just keep an eye out for anything that doesn't seem right with the current formulation. Hell I don't know what to tell you, I'm not a scientist, that's why I called you.

I'm not your man William but whoever does this for you could probably start by breaking down the formulations into two sections and then examine each active ingredient for starters but even that could take months. We don't have months. We need this problem to go away now! So will you help us or not?

I wouldn't help you if God himself asked me! You are the Devil, William, not his helper but the Devil himself and we all know how tricky and underhanded the Devil can be.

What am I suppose to do take a leave of absence from Bartell. That would not only be stupid, it would be crazy. I've only been there four months.

A leave of absence sounds like a great ideal when you consider the alternative Rick.

"Which is?"

"Don't make me say it Rick."

William you always get your way but not this time. I'm walking out of here right now and there's not a damn thing that you can do about it.

I'm afraid that I can't let you do that Rick.

William...just try to stop me! I'm walking out the door now.

***

Crack.... oh shit Cliff; you didn't have to hit him that hard. What else was I going to do yelled Cliff, "he was trying to leave!" He doesn't look good, said William and I think he's out cold. I see a little blood but he has a pulse, said Cliff. My God Cliff, "you could have killed him!"

"Help me put him on the sofa." Go get some ice Cliff and hurry up.

Rick are you Ok?

Here's some ice but I'm afraid it's not very much.

Well go get some Cliff!

Aren't you afraid of what he's going to do if he wakes up before I get back? No, it looks like it will be hours before that happens. You screwed up good this time Cliff.

"Go get some ice!"

***

What happened? My head feels like I ran into a brick wall.

I'm sorry about that but I asked you not to leave. Cliff hit you over the head with the butt of his gun, you've been out for several hours and I'm afraid that you have a rather large lump on your head. "So you won't be going anywhere for quite

79

a while." Just relax and we'll talk more when you are feeling better.

"I want to go now William!"

I promise I'll let you go as soon as you are strong enough Rick.

Damn you to hell William Winters! Can I at least use the bathroom?

Sure Rick, "it's right this way."

Wait a minute, I can't walk and the room is spinning.

You better lay back down Rick. I don't like the look of that bruise.

William if I lay back down, "I'll piss on myself."

Ok, "I'll help you to the bathroom but you have to hold your own penis."

Here Rick drink this, "it should help."

What is it William?

It's just a little something to make you feel better.

Well…it tastes terrible.

I know it does but it will ease the pain and let you sleep for a while. I want do go now, said Rick, I think I should go to the emergency room.

Just calm down Rick and try to relax. You should be getting very sleepy any second now. When you wake up we'll talk some more and then I'll let you go. Trust me; you will feel much better when you wake up.

Ha-ha…What a joke, "trust William Winters."

What are you hiding from me William? What did you say Rick? I said, what are you hiding from…..

***

He's been sleep for over two hours now, said Cliff. How much of that stuff did you give him William?

Enough to ease his pain and allow him to rest comfortable but I think the trauma of the hit to the head is keeping him out longer than the medication. He seems to be coming around a little, said Cliff.

Let him sleep for a little while longer Cliff. "We need him healthy." Without him, The Advernox Project is doomed to fail.

William, it will be light outside in a couple of hours. You better wake him soon because we have to be out of here before day break. Yeah, I know. I need to talk to him when he wakes up, said William but if we run out of time just make sure he gets back to his fancy Penthouse safely.

***

How did I let him talk me into getting involved with BMX again? That hit on the head must have really knocked something loose. What is he hiding? What is William Winters not telling me?

I spent all day gathering information on Advernox. Except for a few mild side effects everything looked great. I still needed to get one more report before I made my finally assessment. It was time to contact these scientists.

Since Miss Lockhart was the closest I decided to contact her first. However, she was giving a very good impression of someone who didn't want to be found. I had to contact personnel for additional phone numbers because apparently the information in her folder was out dated. By the time I finally reached her two days had passed. I had already held a telephone conference with Steve and Evan. I wanted to meet with each of them privately before our first group meeting but time would not allow it because they had to travel but I would try to meet with Miss Lockhart.

***

Candis is a Harvard graduate and finished number one in her class.

BMX wasted no time recruiting her. She has been with the company for almost seven years now and it was true that she had been considered the front-runner for the job that I now held. I asked around and according to her co-workers, if she had been friendlier with her former boss the job would have been handed to her on a silver platter.

However, that was not her style according to Mark Tucker the departments go to guy. He had a crush on her from day one and didn't mind telling the world.

Mark wore dark rimmed glasses that were two sizes to big for his face. It was rumored that he had been seen following Miss Lockhart when she would leave for the day. She put an end to that by driving him straight to the police department one day.

Her other co-workers were very eager to offer information. She was said to be a loner and a snob who hit the bottle heavy on occasions, with the preference being Seagram's gin with a smidgen of orange juice.

This was not the only rumor to attach itself to the lovely lady that was called Miss America behind her back but it was probably the one closest to the truth. Since her female co-workers started most of these rumors it was hard to give credibility to any of them.

If you asked the men, they simply thought she was the best looking woman that ever walked the face of the earth. Unfortunately for Miss Lockhart, this only led to other rumors.

***

It's funny the things that you can find out about a person by looking at a sheet of paper or listening to idle gossip. I've never given either of these much weigh because I liked to form my own opinions about people.

It was very hard convincing her to come over tonight, I think, "it would have been easier to build a rocket out of tin cans." I had spent almost an hour earlier in the day explaining who I was and why I needed to meet with her as soon as possible. She kept insisting that whatever it was could wait. I promised that it was business and we needed somewhere that we could talk without being interrupted.

After checking to make sure that I really worked for the company she finally, agreed to meet with me for one hour. I still wasn't sure she would show but at 9:00 p.m. the doorbell rang.

***

When I opened the door I couldn't believe the woman that was standing before me. I looked her up and down twice before I could utter a single word. "Is it possible for a woman this beautiful to exist," I thought?

"She's can't be human," I thought.

"Is she an Angel?"

No I thought, "not even an angel could possess this kind of beauty."

***

Are you going to invite me in Mr. Naylor?

Hello Miss Lockhart, it's nice to finally meet you, please come in.

Please, call me Rick. May I get you something to drink? No thank you, all I need from you is an explanation about why I had to rush over here at this time of night.

Are you sure you wouldn't like something to drink first, said Rick?

"Yes, I'm sure."

Now, what's so important that you felt that you needed to drag me half way across town at this time of night? Well try not to get upset until you've heard everything that I have to say.

I can't make you any promises on that one, said Candis.

"I guess that's fair." Please have a seat Miss Lockhart. The reason that I needed to see you so soon is mostly a hunch that I have about something.

Did you say a hunch Mr. Naylor?

"Yes, I did."

I'm afraid that I'll need you to be a little more specific than that.

You've heard of a little wonder drug called Advernox, haven't you? Did you say Advernox Mr. Naylor?

Yes, I'm afraid that I did. How much do you know about it?

I know that it's the hottest thing going right now in the pharmaceutical industry. I know that it has made a lot of pregnant women extremely happy because it takes away the occasional dizziness, stomach pains and their fatigue. It works fast and most of them think it's worth the price even if there are a few side effects and last but not least, Mr. Naylor, "it's making our company a ton of money."

Yes the money is rolling in Candis but my concern with money is that it tends to cloud the issue sometimes.

"What exactly are you getting at Mr. Naylor?"

Have you been watching channel 12 this week Candis?

Mr. Naylor...no one watches channel 12 anymore.

Well, maybe it's time that someone started.

Why should they do that?

There is a reporter named Veronica Taylor. For the past three weeks she has been reporting on a problem that pregnant women are having across the country.

So what do her reports have to do with Advernox?

Miss Lockhart, "I believe that Advernox is involved some how." You mentioned earlier that pregnant women love Advernox even though there are side effects. What kind of side effects were you referring to?

Look, Mr. Naylor, I hope you are not trying to waste my time. "You are a scientist aren't you?" Any good scientist knows that every drug has some type of side effect. "Advernox is no different from any other drug in that respect!"

I'm sorry, Miss Lockhart, "I didn't realize you were so passionate about this drug."

"You are not qualified to say what I'm passionate about sir." Advernox is a product that's been needed for a very long time and as I have said before women don't mind the few side effects because it makes them feel better and that's the bottom line.

I have to disagree with you. Although women love this drug today, "I fear somewhere in the near future that will hate the name Advernox." What I have learned about this drug in just the past two days sends shivers though my spines. I've done my homework on this and I tell you that something is not right with this drug.

"You are serious, aren't you Mr. Naylor?"

Listen, you are new here, "let me give you some friendly advice". You have a job that most people would kill for. It would probably be in the best interest of everyone if you minded your own business.

Candis, I think the company is hiding something from the public and now they are asking us to find a way to cover it up.

Cover up what, said Candis?

"I'm not sure yet," I told you it's, "just a hunch."

Well...Mr. Naylor I don't know many people stupid enough to risk their job on a stupid hunch!

"What if I'm right," said Rick?

Mr. Naylor, where are you from?

What does that have to do with anything Miss Lockhart?

"You just don't get it do you?" I realize that you probably think you are doing the right thing so I won't beat you up over it.

"Just keep me out of it."

It's already too late for that Candis. I'm sure you can see by them assigning you to my team that you are already a part of it?

Listen to me man!

I got my orders just this morning and frankly I haven't had time to read past the first page.

Well, Miss Lockhart "I suggest that you do that as soon as you get home". "I realize that you are probably the best that there is in your field." I also realize, *"that maybe,"* the job that I have should have gone to you but those are not the cards that we were dealt and it's to late in the game to ask for a new deck.

Maybe after you have read the information that I have you will understand my hunch better. I'm taking a big chance by even sharing this information with you so soon, so I need you to promise me that you will not tell anyone. Why don't you fix yourself a drink while I go to my study and get the papers? You should find every thing that you need behind the bar. "I'll be right back."

Why do you keep insisting that I have something to drink, yelled Candis? I probably should be leaving now anyway.

"Wait just a minute, Miss Lockhart."

You promised me an hour, "it's only been twenty minutes". I would hope that you are a woman of your word.

I am a woman of my word but if I have to spend another forty minutes listening to you, "I should probably have that drink," yelled Candis!

Please Miss Lockhart; I only need a few more minutes of your time. After you read my report you may go.

I'll stay and read your report but it had better be worth my time.

"Thank you." I have to go to my study; I'll be right back.

Where are your wine glasses?

They are right behind the bar with everything else that you might need. You just help yourself. This apartment came fully stocked, "there's no way I could drink all that by myself." I'm not really that much of a drinker.

Mr. Naylor..."I thought you were going to get the information."

***

This is all the information that I have gathered in the past couple days. Most of the information looks good but this last report is troubling. Take your time and read it carefully. That drink looks good. Is that gin and juice?

Yes it is Mr. Naylor.

I think I'll make myself one, said Rick.

***

As I was making my drink I took time to observe Miss Lockhart as she read my report. At first she was pacing back and forth reading with the drink in her hand. Then she suddenly stopped and sat down on the couch.

The outfit she was wearing seemed as though it had been painted onto her body. I can hardly blame Mark for being so obsessed with her.

I finally made myself a drink and returned to the living room. I sat silently in the love seat opposite her and for the next five minutes watched the color slowly drain from her face, "which is quite a feat for a woman of color".

She was sitting there rereading the entire report. I didn't mind though because it gave me a chance to check her out. She is a beautiful woman. "If only she would smile," I could only imagine the beauty that would radiate from her face and fill this entire room.

As I continued to watch her I suddenly felt myself getting aroused. I quickly finished my drink and made myself another drink but that only seemed to make matters worst.

"I was suddenly in a trance." Who is the lucky man that making love to her I wondered?

I tried to stop staring at her but I couldn't. It was as though she held me under a spell and I couldn't take my eyes off her breath taking body. Her full lips are a perfect match for the fullness of her breast and buttocks. Her long legs can only be measured by the long skirt that wrapped itself tightly around them.

She must really like her drink because she licked her beautiful full lips twice after each sip she took from her glass. If she only knew how much licking her lips was driving me insane.

"Please stop I prayed." *Yet...her beauty still held me in a trance until...I heard someone yelling my name.*

Mr. Naylor....Mr. Naylor!

I'm having trouble concentrating on this report with you gawking at me like that. Do you think it might be possible for you to stop?

"You're making me very uncomfortable."

***

Ten minutes later she put the papers down. She had long ago put down her drink. She looked at me as if I was the grim reaper himself. When she finally spoke, it was not with the hate or spite that had dominated our conversation up to this point. It was simply fear and disbelief.

Is this true, she asked? "I'm afraid it might be Candis." However, "I'm not sure." that's why I need your help.

Mr. Naylor the only way to do what you are suggesting would be to do our own private investigation because BMX is not going to allow us to do what you are suggesting.

I realize that and I also asked you to call me Rick.

Well...Mr. Naylor, "do you also realize how much a project like this would cost?"

Yes, I estimate somewhere in the neighborhood of two hundred thousand dollars.

That sounds about right sir, "so you have done your home work after all." Are you also telling me that you have that kind of money just lying around?

"Whether I do or don't is not the issue Miss Lockhart."

The fact is I have a close associate who does. He would spend the money in a heartbeat if I can convince him that it's worth his money and his time.

Is he also a BMX employee Mr. Naylor?

"He was once."

Oh I see....said Candis.

Mr. Naylor, "if what's in these papers are true," why should we be the ones to try and bring down our own company?

I don't look at it as bringing BMX down, said Rick; I'm just trying to save peoples lives. If I'm correct then it is fair to assume that BMX is already aware of this deadly side effect.

Wouldn't you agree Miss Lockhart?

Your report does have a couple of hair-raising points but I'm still not convinced.

What else will it take to convince you?

Proof would convince me, Mr. Naylor. Where is your proof man?

You can't make a claim like this without proof. So far all you have is a report with assumptions that are unproven and although I can clearly see your point of view in this matter. There has to be proof!

Then help me get the proof Candis!

No way...not only are you are basing everything on a stupid hunch sir but you are also going up against a company that is worth billions. BMX has a proud history and a clean background.

"They are probably untouchable."

I'm not an idiot and before I could even dream of helping you. I would need something more concrete or the life of my parents would have to be at stake. All you're going to accomplish is getting us fired or killed!

I understand your concerns and I can agree with you in theory Candis but my experience tells me that there is much more going on here than we are being told.

I need time to think Mr. Naylor.

No, "what am I saying." I'd just rather be left out of it completely. You've only been with this company a few months. I've worked for this company for almost seven years and in that time I've never known them to do anything but try to make people live more comfortable lives. I believe with all my heart that this is a good company and although your report does have a few eye raising points, it does nothing to change my mind about this company and what it stands for. I must insist that I be left out of your mess.

Candis I..."The name is Miss Lockhart!"

Very well...Miss Lockhart, please think about how many lives are going to be impacted by this if we don't do something.

"We are not the law or the FDA Mr. Naylor!" Find someone else; it shouldn't be that hard to replace me.

We don't have time to look for a replacement.

"You are the best and we need you."

Our first team meeting is tomorrow morning. We need you there.

"I want you to listen to me Mr. Naylor and I want you to listen well." I won't be there and there is nothing that you can do to make me. Have you got it!

"You are making a terrible mistake Candis!"

This meeting is over Mr. Naylor. I have given you the hour I promised; now it's time for me to go home!

"Well...go home then!"

Maybe you are not the right person for this job after all. I must admit that you are more stubborn than I was led to believe, said Rick.

"Who said that I was stubborn?"

That's not important but if by some miracle you should change your mind here is the address where we'll be meeting tomorrow. Do you know how to get to the IOC Tower down town?

They have you set up in the IOC Tower?

That's a great facility, said Candis.

The meeting is scheduled for 9:00 a.m., if you are not sure how to get there my driver can pick you up at your apartment. Here's my driver's number.

They gave you a Limo driver?

"Who are you really Mr. Naylor?"

I'm just a man who wants to do the right thing but I realize I can't do it alone. Please help us. You don't give up do you?

Thanks for the drink, "I really must be on my way but before I do I want you to remember something."

"I don't like being bullied and I'm not afraid of anyone!"

Miss Lockhart, "I'm not trying to bully you and I sincerely apologize if that's how you feel." I just know how much we need you on this team. You just read the report; you know that lives are at stake here. How can you just turn you back on these innocent people Miss Lockhart?

You are the best scientist in your field and we need you.

"What part of no don't you understand, Mr. Naylor?"

"Find someone else Mr. Naylor!"

I hope that after you sleep on it, you'll change your mind. It will be a chance for you to work with a team instead of solo, said Rick. I'll be expecting you tomorrow morning at 9:00a. m.

"Please don't let us down."

May I leave now, said Candis?

Sure let me get your coat. Good night Miss Lockhart and drive safely.

***

She left without saying another word but the look on her face said it all. I stood in the doorway and watched her walk to the elevator. She looked just as good going as she did coming. A woman like that would definitely be worth chasing any other time but not now. "There was no time for those kinds of foolish thoughts." I had to find a way to convince her to be on this team. What would it take to win her over? Never mind that's just wishful thinking, besides; it's time for the news. So no one watches channel 12 but me. How can they afford to stay on the air?

***

Good afternoon, I'm Veronica Taylor, reporting for channel 12 news. We are at John Thompson hospital in Atlanta, Georgia where this morning eight pregnant women were admitted after reporting to the emergency room complaining of extreme labor pains.

"The irony of this is that all are about four months pregnant." I have spoken to members of the hospital staff and they say, "they have never seen anything like this before."

It appears that all these women are in danger of losing their baby. At this point, the doctors don't know what to think. They have refused to comment until they have performed all of the necessary tests. Hopefully there will be more on this story tonight at eleven.

I'm Veronica Taylor reporting for channel 12 news... goodbye.

CHAPTER 5

Clifford Miller slammed down the phone. "Why am I surrounded by so many idiots," he said?

***

Not only was Cliff annoyed that he was surrounded by idiots but he was also feeling the pain of an old war injury to his leg.

The highly decorated fifty-five year old war hero had been shot in the leg when his patrol was ambushed. Since that day he has had to live with the never-ending pain.

He didn't take his pain medication anymore because his body had grown immune to it. The pain seemed worse when it rained and the cold East Coast winters were not helping. The only thing that seemed to provide any comfort at all was his expensive twenty-four year old mistress and a bottle of Jack Daniels whiskey.

Cliff had seen countless doctors but they all said the same thing. He would just have to accept the fact that he would be walking with a limp for the rest of his life.

Some days Cliff would just sit at his desk all day long because of the pain but he never missed work because of it. He would just sit there and long for his old bayonet and rifle. This he thought would be the proper way to clear this place of all the idiots. He pressed the intercom. Donna please bring me a glass of water.

Like a robot...Yes sir, was always her response.

Being the head of Internal Affairs for BMX Pharmaceutical had not always been easy but in five short weeks it would all be over because Cliff would be able to retire and with full benefits.

He had been here through the good times as well as the bad. The last three years had been the worst. Thank God for Advernox. Without it his retirement pension would definitely have been in jeopardy.

Yes, it was time to turn the reins over to someone else. All he wanted to do now was make it five more weeks. There would be a lot of changes in his life after retirement. He had chosen Florida as the place to retire. Two months ago he purchased a home there. His old body needed the warmth of the Florida sun. It had been a dream of his for a long time. He had been so deep in thought that he didn't notice when Donna brought him his water.

***

Donna please cancel all my appointments for tomorrow, I'm taking a day off. Excuse me sir, for a moment I thought you said you were taking a day off. You heard correct.

Are you Ok sir? You never take a day off.

I'm fine, "now please cancel the got damn appointments!"

Yes sir...

***

What Donna didn't know is that Cliff was not fine. For the past six months Mr. Miller had been seeing a very expensive doctor. He was seeing the kind of doctor that a person needs to see when leading a double life starts to catch up with you.

You see not only was Clifford cheating on his wife of twenty-five years, he was also a murderer for hire. He was very good at the latter and was paid accordingly.

However, old age and a guilty conscious were starting to get the best of him. He had killed more people than he cared to remember and he had done it without a second thought or any remorse. So why couldn't he shake his last job? It had almost been a year now and it was as though it happened yesterday.

Would the rest of his life be haunted by this one job? Every time he closed his eyes at night he was visited by the ghost of Lilly Cantrell. The nightmare was always the same. The words would echo throughout the night and they were always the same, "please don't kill me", over and over again. As if that wasn't bad enough, every time he looked in the mirror the eyes staring back at him belonged to her.

Why won't her ghost leave me alone, he thought?

He knew he would burn in hell for what he did that night almost a year ago. Only God could forgive him now but that was not likely because he knew even God could only forgive so much. His only hope was if God didn't exist. The way he reasoned it, if God didn't exist, then neither did the Devil. For some strange reason this gave him comfort.

***

Cliff, I've called you several times said Donna are you sure you are Ok? I'm fine, what is it?

Your wife is on line two.

Hello Mary…hello Cliff. What do I owe the pleasure of this call, said Cliff? You never call me at work.

I've decided to head down to Florida tonight and get a head start on things, said Mary. Why do you need to do that? I'm bored and you never have time for me any way. I don't think it's a good idea Mary but you never listen to me anyway.

Cliff darling, I do listen to you on those rare occasions when you have something intelligent to say.

Don't start with me woman! How long are you going to be gone?

Not long enough, thought Mary.

Will you be back in time for my retirement party? I wouldn't miss it for the world. I'll see you when you get back then. Sure Cliff and you stay out of trouble.

***

Mary knew that telling Cliff to stay out of trouble was like giving a kid candy before dinner and expecting them not to eat it. The real reason that Mary was leaving should have been clearer to Cliff.

Rumors of Cliff affairs were running rampart around the company and Mary had heard enough. She needed to get away from it all and decide what to do about her cheating husband. She knew she should have left him fifteen years ago when she caught him in the guest bedroom with a girl young enough to be his granddaughter. She thought…for some crazy reason I forgave him for that. Probably because I would never do what that young lady was doing to him. I'm sure the Lord will forgive me for divorcing him because the part of our vows that said for better or worst didn't mean your husband could have as many women on the side as he wants. I've had enough and I am no longer in a forgiving mood. This time he will pay!

***

Donna order a dozen roses and have them delivered pronto. You know whom and you know where.

Should I send a card?

No card but hurry before she leaves work for the day. Donna there's just one more thing.

What is it sir?

You look very nice today. Well… thank you Cliff.

***

When Mary arrived at the Florida home she felt a renewed sense of life. It was time to move on without Cliff and take care of me. She ran a shower to wash away the harshness of the East Coast winter. Then she got a blanket and headed to her favorite spot on the beach. As she started to walk though the sand, twenty-five years of memories hit her hard and the grief was surprisingly unbearable. Starting over at her age was almost unthinkable. The reality of this was too much for her and she collapsed in the sand and cried herself to sleep.

When she awoke two hours later there was a young boy sitting at her feet playing with a toy. He had covered her feet with sand. When she spoke, it startled him and he took off running. I even scare the small one away she thought.

There was only one man that she hadn't scared away. His name was Ralph Goodwin, a painter from Chicago. They had met nine years ago at an art gallery. He did not try to hide his affection for her. He took it very hard when she finally told him that she was married. It was only a little secret that she kept from him the first couple of days while he showed her around the windy city. She knew that she had to tell him the truth before she left Chicago.

She told him while they were having diner her last night there. He looked at her for about ten seconds and took out his wallet. He placed the money on the table and rushed out of the room. Several weeks later he forgave her and they became the best of friends. They both wanted it to be more.

It was his voice that was such a comfort on those long lonely nights when Cliff was supposedly working late. She needed to hear his voice now. She picked up her cell phone and called his number, after the fourth ring he picked up.

Hello Mary. How are you?

I'm fine Ralph and how are you?

I'm doing well. I haven't heard from you in a while, said Ralph. That doesn't mean that I haven't been thinking about you.

Mary I have company right now. Oh I'm so sorry Ralph, please go back to your company, I'll talk to you later.

"Mary are you alright?"

Sure I am Ralph, "now go back to you company. I'll talk to you later."

"I'm such a stupid woman," thought Mary.

Is that the phone? Hello Mary, it's me, "now tell me what's wrong." I thought I told you to go back to your company. I sent her home. Now talk to me.

"I'm leaving Cliff."

Oh is that it, said Ralph? I've heard that before. "I'm really going to do it this time Ralph." I'm afraid to ask why but tell me anyway.

Why don't you come see me and I can tell you all about it in person. Where are you?

"I'm at the beach house in Florida."

Where's Cliff?

He's in New York.

Are you coming?

"I'm on my way," said Ralph.

***

Driver please let me out at the next light. I think I'll walk the next two blocks. What time would you like me to pick you up today? Three o'clock should be fine. What was your name again?

My name is Darryl, Mr. Naylor.

I'll see you at three o'clock Darryl.

"I'll be here Mr. Naylor."

***

I really needed to stretch my legs and get my blood circulating before meeting my new team. If what the CEO says is correct I need to impress Steven and Evan at this meeting. It's probably too late to impress Candis.

As I approach the door to the boardroom I notice a short man in a wrinkled suit standing across the hall opposite the entrance. As I put the key in the door he said are you Mr. Naylor?

Yes, how may I help you? No, my friend, I'm here to help you.

"Excuse me."

Please allow me to introduce myself Mr. Naylor.

"I am Evan Blair."

Well Mr. Blair it's nice to meet you. You are a little early aren't you?

I don't like to be late.

"Why are you looking at me like that Mr. Naylor?

I was just wondering if you slept in your suit.

Why do you say that?

Never mind Evan just come on in. "Don't worry about me Mr. Naylor," you won't even know I'm here.

"Please call me Rick."

Ok Rick…"I'll just sit here and get a quick nap before we start the meeting."

Ten minutes later the door swung open and in walked a man nearly 7 feet tall. He was wearing a white tee shirt, blue jeans and had an old school Walkman attached to his side with the music blasting.

Please I thought; let this guy be in the wrong room. My hopes were crushed when the giant stuck out his hand and yelled hello Mr. Naylor.

He obviously didn't realize that he was yelling, "a common mistake made by people wearing a headset with music blasting out of it." This entrance captured the attention of Mr. Blair and we both knew that his nap was over.

***

You must be Mr. Batiste.

Yes but please call me Steven and may I call you Richard?

Rick will be fine. Ok then Rick it is.

I hope you don't mind me showing up a little early. No Steven, "actually I like it." Please turn down your music just a bit and have a seat. "I'm trying to prepare for our meeting."

Sure thing Rick, "don't worry about me," you won't even know I'm here.

Twenty minutes after 8:00 and two-thirds of my team is present and accounted for. I was surprised at how quiet the two of them were able to be. Evan had taken a pencil and pad out and was busy writing down something. Steven was sleeping but I could still hear the faint sound of music coming out of his headphones. It was ten minutes to nine before I was ready. There was a knock on the door and in entered two guys carrying breakfast with coffee and fresh orange juice. Evan and Steven both leaped out of their seats and dug in.

It was ten minutes after nine now and there was no Candis in sight.

"It was time to begin."

Good morning gentlemen, the other member of our team seems to be running late, so we'll have to start without her.

The first thing on our agenda today is the introduction. I think it will be good if we each told a little about ourselves and maybe shared with the group how we chose our current profession.

Who would like to go first? Come on don't be bashful. Neither of you would like to speak?

Rick, I think I should let my food digest a little first.

"I agree with Evan," said Steven.

Ok…I guess I can see your point. You guys really did pile it on.

I'll guess that means I get to go first.

***

I attended the University of Michigan where I received a degree in Psychology. After that I immediately applied to Princeton and spent five hard years working my way through college.

As luck would have it I found out that I was fascinated with chemistry. It was not something that I was rushing to take when I was in high school but I found it to be very interesting once I started to understand it better.

"Which is a story all its own." I fell in love with a freshman named Sharon Fisher. Her major was pediatrics, which meant a lot of chemistry. She got straight A's in all her classes.

I got involved with her because she was so damn good looking and the fact that she was a virgin didn't hurt. She was one of those cute country girls who didn't fool around but she always had to touch you when she was talking to you.

"Boy talk about sending mixed signals."

She would invite me over to help her study. We would study for hours. I just knew one day I was going to come over and she would open up the door and be in her birthday suit and tell me that we would not need the books tonight. I held onto that dream for nearly a year but I never got pass first base with her.

The following year I gave up on her. There were a lot of pretty women in my other classes." I knew by now that nothing was going to happened between me and Miss Fisher, "so I decided to start dating."

What I didn't realize at the time was what a huge favor she had done for me by introducing me to the, "world of chemistry." I had spent so many hours helping her do her research that I knew as much about it as she did. So I enrolled the following semester and aced the class.

I'll never forget the last time I saw Miss Fisher. I actually walked right past her. She looked so different. When she spoke to me, I stopped dead in my tracks because although I didn't recognize the person, "I recognized the voice."

I turned around and couldn't believe what I was seeing. It had been over five months since I'd seen her and it was so obvious that she was no longer a virgin. She had a small suitcase in her hand and her transcript.

I didn't know what to say. I walked over to her and asked her how have she had been doing? She said, "are you just going to pretend not to notice I'm pregnant?"

Before I could say anything, she started crying and said, "I don't even know who the father is." I got bored one night and they were having a party on the next floor and I went down. I had one drink and woke up the next morning (sob) pregnant. That's all I remember.

So where are you headed now I asked? Home, the baby is due in two months, the Dean says I have to leave.

I had always hoped to be a mother someday but not this soon. I had hoped that you would be the father of my kids; however, you just couldn't wait for me could you? I knew you had feeling for me but I guess they weren't strong enough for you to wait. It destroyed me when I saw you with that cheerleader but that only lasted a few months and I got my hopes up again until I saw you with that girl from Alpha Beta.

I'm sorry Sharon; I never knew you cared so much. You should have known Rick; we were studying chemistry for goodness sakes. I'm so sorry Sharon, is there anything I can do? There is nothing that you can do now Rick.

She took a long look at my face as though she was taking a picture of it. I noticed a tear forming in her right eye as she turned and walked out the door and out of my life.

***

So there you have it. Maybe that was a little too much information for you gentlemen but that young lady changed the course of my entire life. Otherwise I'd be sitting somewhere in a small office with a worn out couch listening to people talk about their problems.

Well…that's it for me. Now who would like to go next?

Neither of you have anything you'd like to say about yourself? Well after hearing that story Rick, it would probably be better if we just heard your presentation, said Steven.

Unless Evan has something that he'd like to say. No thanks, I agree with Steven on this. It's probably best if we just heard your presentation.

Very well gentlemen if that's how you feel. I was hoping to stall long enough for the other member of our team to get here. However, I should get started because I have a lot of information to go over with you.

***

Given the complexity of this project it will be necessary for us to work in teams of two, said Rick. I realize that working individually would be faster, however, I'm not willing to take the chance that one of us might miss something. Everything we do will be double-checked by the other team.

I realize that this will take more time, which is something that we have little of. We will be spending a lot of time in the lab. I'm sure Mr. Winters explained this to you when he gave you that nice bonus check for joining this team.

Now let's talk about the formulation. I know you gentlemen are familiar with class 100 ISO5 conditions correct.

Yes of course, said Evan. That's the highest level of sterility when dealing with Aseptic manufacturing.

"That's correct Evan."

"I know what you are both thinking." What does Aseptic manufacturing have to do with a drug like Advernox? To answer your question, it has nothing to do with it directly, however indirectly it has everything to do with it.

I have put together a small slide presentation that will show you some of the equipment that we will be using. As you will see on the first slide here I have listed several components of Aseptic manufacturing.

This list includes, swab testing, contact plates, peristaltic pumps, a unidirectional flow cabinet, tri-clove fittings, sterile tweezers, sterile forceps and a biological safety cabinet.

Have I confused anyone yet?

Yes, "I'm confused," said Evan and from the look on Steven's face, so is he.

Rick what does Aseptic manufacturing have to do with a product like Advernox, said Steven? That's a good question. Let me see if I can give you a good answer.

Excuse me Rick but I think I now understand. Can I try to explain this to Steven? Sure Evan "be my guest."

Well…Steven, I think what Rick is getting at is Advernox was manufactured in a class one hundred thousand environment, which means the manufacturing environment is clean but not sterile. Compared to Aseptic manufacturing which is performed in a class one hundred environment. These rooms are not just clean but also sterile, "which is the highest form of clean."

This class of production is normally reserved for products like Flu viruses and so on, not for over the counter products or solid dose medications.

***

You are exactly right Evan.

"I couldn't have explained it better myself."

Excuse me Mr. Naylor, said Steven.

'Please call me Rick."

I thought we were here to just check the product for any informality.

That is correct Steven but only to the point of exclusivity.

You see, there are some people that believe Advernox can only be effective in its current form. I just happen to be one of those people.

However, as a scientist I have to put my objectivity aside and nipple at the corners of this great drug and hope that whatever we find wrong with it doesn't disturb the molecular structure that makes Advernox so effective but at the same time solve the terrible side effect problem.

There are also some concerns that the problem that we face is directly related to the incubation period of one of the ingredients in Advernox. That ingredient my friends is what I plan to make the focal point of our investigation. Once we have determined the root cause analysis we will be able to recommend corrective actions and preventive actions but until we get to this point it may be necessary for us to manipulate certain salient elements to qualitatively assess our findings.

Do you both understand what that means?

Yes, "I think we do," said Evan.

Good but remember gentlemen, we must also document any simulations and certifications that we make along the way, said Rick. I will also be implementing new ways of analyzing any new growth that is found in the supporting media once we have move into the lab.

Are there any other questions at this time?

Come on guys, there has to be some questions...

***

Now let's talk about the findings as I know them today, said Rick. Advernox works great for pregnant women until around the fourth or sixth month. This is when many of the complaints have started.

Several doctors have reported a small number of cases of miscarriages during this time. The one alarming thing that all these women have in common is that they are taking Advernox. With that said there is also a very large number of women that currently take Advernox and they don't seem to be affected at all.

Excuse me Rick but I have a question.

Finally...What is your question Evan?

What percentages of these women have had problem free deliveries?

Unfortunately Evan, Advernox has only been on the market for about seven months, so we don't have that data yet.

What about the women that were used in case studies, said Evan? Were there any documented cases of side effects involving them?

I'm afraid that I don't have any such data.

Well...who has it, said Steven?

I don't know and to be perfectly honest, I'm not even sure it exists.

"You must be kidding me," said Steven!

I agree, said Evan. How do they expect us to solve anything without that type of information?

Gentlemen, please calm down.

Listen Mr. Naylor, I'm starting to get an uneasy feeling about all of this, said Steven. Please tell me that there were case studies done before this stuff was sent to the market.

Steven in order to receive FDA's approval there had to be proven success with this drug, said Rick.

We are aware of the protocol my friend but where is the proof that this happened with Advernox," said Evan?

All I can tell you at this point gentlemen is that there was a team that tried to figure out this problem long before they asked us. It should be obvious that they were not successful.

If they had been, there would be no reason for us to be here today. I have asked for their notes but I was told that they would not be made available to us. As a matter of fact, we will not be allowed to use any of the information that was gathered by that team.

Why is that, said Steven?

"There are two reasons that jump into my mind," said Rick. First of all they don't want us to be influenced by someone's work that was a failure and secondly gentlemen, "I'm sure you've been brief by Mr. William Winters himself about the top secrecy of this project." That alone should have been reason to let you know that something is terribly wrong here.

***

I have to admit Rick that this is a little mind bogging. I'll need time to digest what I'm now learning, said Evan. I agree with Evan, I have never heard of any thing so crazy, unless it was in a horror movie and I'm sorry said Steven but I think I might have to remove myself from this project unless things start to make a little more sense.

I have to agree, said Evan, I'm also starting to get the feeling that we aren't being told everything and it's starting to send off alarms in my head that something is seriously wrong here.

What is troubling you gentlemen the most, said Rick? Is it the sudden rush? Well...yes, said Evan, it could take years to dissect all of this information.

Did you voice these concerns when Mr. Winters talked to you about this? Rick, I'm afraid that he painted a rosier picture than the one I'm seeing now.

" That definitely sounds like William."

Rick why does it really need to be fixed so soon, said Steven?"

I'm afraid that's an easy question to answer. The reason is that lives could be at stake here gentlemen.

As the leader of this team I feel I have to do a better job of getting you the answers to the questions that you have but make no mistake gentlemen, we are involved in something that will not follow the proper avenues that we have all grown accustomed to in our profession. This project will require a lot of our time and we need to solve this puzzle yesterday.

Where is our other team member, said Evan? Once again you have given me a question for which I have no answer.

I spoke with Candis Lockhart last night. "I'm afraid that she was even more concerned than you are." I can assure you that Miss Lockhart is in a league of her own in her field. She will be a very valuable member of this team.

If there are no more questions, that's going to be it for today.

Oh...I have plenty of questions Rick but I think I'll hold off until tomorrow, said Evan.

"I appreciate that Evan."

***

Now let's talk about a more cheerful topic. Tonight we will be dining at a place called Lemur's Catania. The driver will pick you up a seven and take you there.

The company's picking up the tab for this one; however, any freebies in the future will probably depend on how successful we are with this project. It's a quarter to three are there any questions about dinner?

I have one question Rick. What is your question Evan?

Will there be women there? I was hoping for a nice American blond about five feet, eleven inches tall with a nice golden beach tan on my first night here.

If I were you Evan I'd concentrate more on a nice pressed suit, said Rick. Blond women like for their men to look neat also.

Yeah Evan, did you sleep in that thing?

That's very funny Steven, "I see you are a comedian as well as a scientist."

If that's it, "I'll see you gentlemen later tonight."

There's just one thing Rick, I don't think the Limo will be necessary. I heard of this really nice club that I would like to check out and I'm hoping my new friend Evan will join me. Don't worry we'll be at Lemur's Catania before you get there.

Alright, "I'll see you both later then."

***

Good afternoon Rick, hi Darryl, you're right on time.

Yes sir, that's how I roll, never be late, my father taught me years ago that in this business a late man is a broke man.

Well, "I can definitely relate to that." Where would you like to go? Please take me to BMX headquarters.

Sit back Mr. Naylor and enjoy the ride, "it'll take about twenty minutes."

Darryl seemed to know his way around very well and in almost twenty minutes exactly we were pulling up to security gate at BMX. The guard waved us through without checking I.D.

Darryl I'm not sure how long this is going to take but I'm hoping no more than fifteen minutes. Can you wait for me?

Sure, I can wait.

***

Stepping inside of BMX headquarters was like going to a museum. This place was suddenly a marvel to the eyes. Everything looked so fresh. It was five o'clock in the afternoon and the floors looked like they had just been waxed. There was also a slight hint of paint in the air. One look at the walls told me they had recently received a fresh coat of paint and I even hear that the old conference room had been redone. I can't wait to see what it looks like. I'm sure all of this was because of the success of Advernox.

The receptionist was a very attractive Latino woman who spoke perfect English. I couldn't decide if her breast were fighting to stay in her blouse or struggling to get back in. As soon as she saw me she immediately picked up the phone and announced my arrival. I guess Peaches had the day off.

"He said to send you right in Mr. Nadar."

"Thank you…Anna and I like the way you pronounce my name.

***

"Good afternoon William."

Hello Rick, "well how did it go?"

Well sir…"I have great concerns about this team."

"What do you mean?"

Well for starters Miss Lockhart didn't show today.

"I told you she would be difficult." Do you want to replace her?

Yes I do, however after meeting the other two members of my team I'm afraid of what I might end up with.

Ha ha, "Rick you need her on this team."

"Yes I know."

I have a plan but I'll need your approval.

Ok, we can discuss that later. Tell me about your concerns with the other members. Why don't you start with the positive stuff first.

They were both on time, "actually they were extremely early."

What else?

"That's about it."

Give them some time they might just surprise you. They came highly recommended.

"I'll try to keep an open mind." They did share my same concerns about this project. "Good then at least you have that to build on."

Are you still meeting for diner tonight?

"Yes we are."

Rick use that time to win them over.

Now lets discuss Candis Lockhart. "

She's a knock out isn't she?"

Yes she's a knock out William but she's also very stubborn. A stubborn woman, "I never heard of one of those...*Ha, ha.*

You do have a plan to deal with her, right?

"Yes I do."

Well what is it? No on second thought don't tell me, just make it happen. Are you sure you don't want to know? Yes Rick, "I'm very sure." The less I know about some things the better.

By the way I asked personnel to start interviews for you an administrative assistant. Do I really need one? Sure you do, besides it's in the budget. You know what they say; use the budget, or lose the budget. They should contact you in a day or two. Now get out of here it's almost time for me to go home.

"Enjoy tonight's dinner."

***

Hello may I speak to Miss Lockhart?

Who's calling? Never mind, "I know who this is." What do you want Mr. Naylor?

We missed you at the meeting today Candis. It was very important to the team that you be there. Why weren't you there?

I was there! Your presentation was unbelievable and I don't mean in a good way. I was listening outside the door until I couldn't take it any more. I got pissed off and left.

'Why didn't you just come in?' We could all have gotten pissed off together! Mr. Naylor, I've told you that I want no part of this mess. Then why were you there?

"Curiosity mostly," I also wanted to meet the other members. "I'm afraid they don't seem too bright." You have a wrinkled suit wearing bum and a giant infant that can't go anywhere without music blasting out of his ear. I guess you were there but how could you see all that from listening outside the door.

"I have my ways." It would have been better for everyone if you had just come in.

I called to remind you that we are meeting for dinner tonight. There will be free drinks and all the food you can eat. I think it's the company way of spoiling us before they work us to death. So, if your curiosity hasn't gotten the best of you, I'll have my driver pick you up after he picks me up. "Let's say a quarter after six." I personally want to make sure you are there.

Ok Mr. Naylor, it's been quite a while since I've had a good meal but I'm not promising that I will help you or your team of misfits. That's fair but I still don't understand. From what I know about you I thought that you would be eager to help save people lives.

Who says that people lives are at stake here?

It's obvious that this is where we have a difference of opinion. How about this Candis...instead of helping me prove that there is a problem with Advernox join my team and prove that there isn't a problem with it.

What should I wear? It's informal but you can wear anything you want. My driver will pick you up at 6:30.

CHAPTER 6

*L*emur's Catania was a magnificent place. I was just a little irritated because the trip to Miss Lockhart's apartment had been for nothing. I rang her doorbell several times but she didn't answer.

At least Steven and Evan were there when I arrived. Both were standing outside smoking a cigarette. I went to greet them and five minutes later we were being shown to our table.

Just as we were about to order I smelled a sweet aroma fill the air. I glanced to my right and standing next to me was Candis and she was looking great.

She walked to a seat at the far end of the table and just stood there.

Gentlemen this is Miss Candis Lockhart...Miss Lockhart, please meet Steven Batiste and Evan Blair.

Both men seemed to be stunned at first, then they both made a mad dash to get the chair for her. It was quite a hilarious scene.

Thank you, it's nice to know that there are still a few gentlemen left in the world, said Candis.

It's a pleasure to have you join us Miss Lockhart.

Thank you Mr. Naylor now lets order I'm starving.

Does any one have any suggestions? I do the lamb is to die for Miss Lockhart; you may call me Candis, Evan. How about a nice white wine to go with that?

White wine with lamb, said Candis?

Try it pretty lady, "you might be pleasantly surprised." I'm sure I will be Steven. Now your last name is Batiste.

Is that French?

Yes it is but I was born in Hamburg, Germany, "my parents were immigrants." They were poor sharecroppers living off the land. We barely had enough to eat from day to day.

I learned at a young age that I wanted no part of that kind of life. My mother went to the market every single day and my father went to look for work every single day. When he was lucky enough to find work, "it paid very little." Fortunately, I had a rich aunt who lived in the small town of Polaris, France. She could not have children, so one day out of the blue my father tells me that I was going to spend the summer with her. The next thing I knew ten years had past and I was graduating from high school and heading for college.

My Aunt took very good care of me. She made sure that I studied hard. There were times that I wanted to play with my friends and she would say no, you study now. I hated her for that then but no longer do I hate her. If not for her who knows what would have become of me. She made sure that I had the best of everything. God bless her soul. That's a beautiful story Steven. No Candis, it's a good story, beautiful is what you are.

"Thank you Steven."

What about you Evan? Blair is English isn't it?

"That's correct Candis." You are not only gorgeous but intelligent as well. Where did you grow up?

Right down the road in New Jersey I'm afraid. We were a simple family, living a simple existence.

Yes from what I've learned of New Jersey it is considered the country correct? What is it that they are called by their New York neighbors? I think the term is country bumpkins Evan.

Thank you Steven that is precisely the word I was looking for. What does a country bumpkin look like Evan?

I've never seen one in person Seven but in the books and the movies they always seem to be wearing a straw hat, dirty blue jeans or coveralls with holes in them. However, I believe someone has been pulling my leg because Candis doesn't look like any country bumpkin.

Thank you gentleman, you are both so kind but I'm starving can we please order now?

Mr. Naylor, "would you please order the wine?" Sure Miss Lockhart, your preference would be? "

"Surprise me."

Very well, excuse me waiter, we are ready to order. First we'll have three tall Budweisers for the gentlemen and a Chere Patier' for the lady.

"That's an excellent choice sir."

Excuse me waiter, said Candis but what exactly is a Chere Patier'?

It's a delicious soft red wine my lady. Ordered by men who only what the best for their lady, it is indeed an excellent choice. Someone really knows their wines.

Thank you Mr. Naylor, "I'm impressed,"

You're welcome Miss Lockhart.

Why are you two so formal, said Evan? Candis and Rick sound so much better. Amen to that brother Evan, yeah what are you two lovers or something?

Boy are you two way off, said Rick.

It was just a guess so loosen up you two.

"That will be just fine with me Evan if it's ok with her."

Is that the real reason you ordered the Pateir'?

What do you mean?

You know too loosen her up a little.

I assure you that was not my intent. I just wanted the lady to enjoy her meal and it has been my experience that nothing compliments a meal better than a great bottle of wine.

"Well thank you Mr. Naylor, I mean Rick and thanks for inviting me." You're very welcome Miss Lockhart.

You may call me Candis.

Thank God we finally got the formalities out of the way, said Steven.

Amen to that brother Steven, said Evan, "amen to that."

***

Is there something wrong Steven?

Not really Candis, I was just thinking about this crazy project.

Lets all put that out of our mind tonight, said Rick. Let's all agree, tonight we wine and dine tomorrow we work, agreed, yes agreed.

Let's toast to it then, said Steven.

"Candis are you with us?"

Does what we discussed earlier today still go Rick? Yes Candis, it does, said Rick. Alright then, said Candis, I'm in.

Great then I propose a toast to us, said Candis. We are the Advernox Team, working on "The Advernox Project."

Great name said Steven. Yeah, "I like it, said Evan. Now let's eat, I'm starving someone get that waiter back over here, Amen to that sister Candis.

Mr. Naylor...what's your story, said Candis?

There's not a lot to tell I'm afraid. I don't have any rich relatives, I grew up in the south, where everything is cheaper and most people grow their own food. It's a good life if you're raised the right way. I had wonderful parents. They are deceased now.

"I'm so sorry to hear that."

"Thank you."

I have eight siblings, six sisters and two brothers, both brothers are deceased also.

Life has been rough on your family hasn't it? Yes Evan, "it has thrown us a couple of curves but we are a strong, loving family."

Do you have kids Rick?

"Yes Candis I do." I have five wonderful kids, two girls and three boys, two of which I adopted. Are you married said Candis? We divorced a long, long time ago.

"I'm sorry to hear that," said Candis.

Thank you Candis but it wasn't working from the very beginning. She was much younger than I was and we had problems from the very first day of our marriage.

"It was mostly my fault."

You had three kids together so there must have been something working right, said Steven.

Well…Steven like I said she was young and she loved to climb on top of me at night when we went to bed, sometimes I would fall asleep with her up there and when I'd wake up in the morning she'd still be at it.

Absolutely incredible said Evan. It sounds like that part of your marriage was very good, my friend.

Wow Rick, "most men would love to have a wife like that," said Steven. Let's just say that I will forever be thankful to her for giving me my wonderful, loving kids but every damn thing else about that marriage has been locked in a sealed vault marked lies and deceit.

"I'm sorry to hear that Rick."

It's Ok Candis, "like I said, it was mostly my fault," besides, how could it have worked, "I never bought her a bottle of Patier'." Ha ha, our leader has a sense of humor doesn't he, said Evan?

"It sounds like that's not all that he has," thought Candis.

***

Waiter, "I think we are ready for dessert and coffee," said Steven. Ok sir, I strongly recommend the chocolate or the strawberry cheesecake. The cheesecake sounds good, I'll have that also, said Rick. Looks like cheesecake for everyone. This has been a great meal, said Evan. Yes, the lamb was really good.

It was a good idea to get together like this, said Candis. I agree, in my country this would be unheard of, said Evan. Well thank God we are not in your country right now or any other time for that matter, said Steven.

"What is everyone doing after dinner, said Rick?"

Evan and I are going to check out this club down the street, said Steven. What about you Candis? I've had a long day; I'm going home and climb into my hot tub. Rick do you want to join Evan and me at the club? Not this time Steven, I have work to do but have fun. I'll see you gentlemen tomorrow.

Candis may I walk you to your car, said Rick? I didn't bring my car. How did you get here? I caught a taxi. Can my chauffeur drop you off at home? Sure if it's not too much trouble, said Candis. It's not a problem, I'll call him now.

Darryl...yes Mr. Naylor, please bring the car around.

Rick that really was an excellent meal and the wine was to die for. I've got to get me a bottle of that. Good luck, it's hard to find, it's also three hundred dollars a bottle, said Rick. Well that's just a little too expensive for me but I'm glad you talked me into coming. I'm glad you enjoyed it. Here comes the car.

Miss Lockhart meet Darryl, Hello Darryl, hello Miss Lockhart, it's a pleasure to meet you. The pleasure is all mine Darryl and you may call me Candis.

We are giving her a ride home. What's the address, said Darryl? It's 312 Park Avenue, said Rick. We'll be there in about twenty minutes. Hey you knew my address. It's part of my job to know. I guess so but it seems unfair that you know so much about me and I hardly know anything about you. Trust me there's not that much to know.

"It's been a pretty boring life so far," said Rick. Still, I'd like to know more than I do, said Candis. Can we stop a few blocks before we get to my apartment? "I need to get some fresh air." Sure, Candis, "if you consider the air in New York fresh."

Darryl, "please stop about three blocks before we get to Candis's apartment."

***

It appeared that Candis was a couple of sips away from being stoned. I some how got the feeling that she'd had a couple of drinks before dinner or maybe Chere Patier' didn't agree with her. She talked the entire three blocks and I still have no idea what she was talking about. She was talking some gibberish about wanting more excitement in her life. When we finally reached her apartment she was starting to make a little more sense but not much.

"Good night Candis."

"Rick what's the hurry?" I think I might need a little help getting up these stairs. If Evan or Steven had bought me home

I wouldn't have had to beg them to help me up these steps. You're right, "those two were laying it on a little thick don't you think." Maybe they just don't have your coolness when they are in the presence of a beautiful woman. Oh you think I'm cool? Yes…I do Ricky, "in a strange sort of way." "No one has called me Ricky in twenty years." I like calling you Ricky. You are starting to sound like you've had a little too much to drink Candis. "That's nonsense Mr. Naylor."

Candis I want to apologize about what I said about my ex-wife tonight. What exactly are you referring to Mr. Naylor? Come on Miss Lockhart, "don't make me repeat it." Oh…you must mean the part about her riding you all night into the early morning. Yes, "that's what I'm referring too." Was that really true Rick? "Yes it's true." I'm sorry Ricky, "I just thought you made that up."

"Why would I do that?"

"Too impress the guys."

No Candis, "it was like that almost every night for eight years," the only break I got was her…never mind. I see…so you had a little freak on your hands didn't you Ricky. She wasn't a freak; she just enjoyed sex and she had a bad habit of not wanting to stop once we got started. I bet you miss that don't you…Ricky.

"No comment Candis."

I have this great coffee that was imported from Italy. Would you like to come up for a nightcap? I'd love to but we have a busy day tomorrow, I should probably get going; besides I'd hate to leave Darryl waiting in the car. Oh he'll be fine, I bet this happens to him all the time. Its part of his job, said Candis. Maybe next time Candis.

I can't believe you are going to leave me hanging like this Rick. Candis I think you've had a little too much to drink. I don't want us to do anything that we'll regret tomorrow.

"What exactly do you mean Ricky?"

Do you think that I'm offering you the comfort of my bed? Only in your wildest dreams would that happen Mr. Naylor. Just because I invited you up for coffee doesn't mean I'm trying to sleep with you. I'm afraid that the only riding that you will be doing tonight is back to your apartment with your Limo driver!

"I'm sorry Candis but what did you expect me to think?"

Mr. Naylor, you are impossible and to think I was just starting to like you but it must be the wine. Good night Mr. Naylor, screamed Candis.

Wait a minute Candis, "I'm sorry." It's Miss Lockhart to you, stupid man, she hissed!

***

Is everything Ok Mr. Naylor, said Darryl? Just women, said Rick. I understand no need to say any more. Rick I hope you don't mind me saying this but she's very pretty. Yes Darryl I know. I should probably have my head examined for not going upstairs to her apartment.

She asked you to go upstairs with her? "Yes she did." So what are you doing in this car? She's drunk; I couldn't take advantage of her like that. Besides something tells me that she is a wolf in sheep's clothing.

Someone once told me that everything that glitters is not gold Mr. Naylor. Yeah, I've heard that a time or two myself. However, I wouldn't mind digging a little deeper to find out if she's the real thing or just fool's gold.

I can't say that I blame you for that Mr. Naylor. I must confess, "I though I'd be out here in the car alone for most of the night. Did you really? Yes, it is so obvious that you two like each other.

Darryl that woman doesn't like me.

"Sure she does." Are you sure you don't want to go ring her doorbell Mr. Naylor? I'm sure and Darryl please call me Rick. So you're telling me that you going to leave that beautiful, sexy, woman all alone tonight…Rick.

Just take me home.

Are you sure that is what you want?

Yes Darryl I think I am, besides, "she is probably passed out in her bed or on her floor by now." Ok, Rick but you're going to hate yourself in the morning.

"I hate myself now." Let's just go Darryl.

"I'll have you there in twenty minutes."

***

Good morning, 'I hope everyone got a good night sleep," said Rick.

Here are today's assignments. Steven and Evan you have the Febor formulations. Candis and I will tackle the Canto formulations. Lunch is being catered in so take it at your own leisure. We will meet back here at the end of the day and discuss our finding.

Are there any questions? Good let's get to work.

What are you doing? I can't believe you put us together! What's wrong? I think it will be better if I worked with either Steven or Evan. Is this about last night?

What happened last night?

Never mind, come with me to my office. Please have a seat.

I'll stand if you don't mind.

Fine, just keep your voice down. Neither of them wants to work with you.

What are you talking about?

Well, for some strange reason you have a reputation for being hard to work with.

"That's absurd."

Is it really Candis? Let's think about this for a moment.

You have been at BMX for almost seven years now. In all that time how many assignments have you been on?

More than I can remember at the moment Mr. Naylor, "what's your point?" My point is, of all those assignments Candis; how many were solo assignments?

"A few were," I guess.

Ha, more than a few. How does the number seventeen sound? How do you know that? I have information on everyone on this team Candis. You have had a total of 22 assignments since becoming employed here.

"No one wants to work with you."

That's why you keep drawing the solo assignments. Management knows it, hell… everyone knows. Let's not forget the fact that you are considered and I quote "a witch to work with," according to your co-workers.

The only reason that you are allowed to work on this team is because you are the best at what you do and I only work with the best, "so shut up and do your damn job," like the rest of us.

I don't have to take that kind of talk from you or anyone else!

That's right Miss Lockhart you don't.

Women and their babies are dying while you are complaining about who you have to work with. You should be thanking God for giving you such a gift to help others. Now if you are not willing to help us, "please step aside now," so I can find someone who will.

I'll stay Rick but don't you ever talk to me like that again! If you are staying, "I suggest that you get to work." Our assignments are in the folder on your desk. "I don't want to have this conversation again!" Do you understand me Miss Lockhart? Yes, Mr. Naylor, "I understand you better than you think."

***

"Everyone please have a seat." I realize that this was only our first day and there may be nothing that really jumps out at you as being important but you'll be surprised at what the smallest clue can lead us. First let's hear from Evan and Steven.

Well Rick, you are absolutely correct, we spent the entire day working and dissecting these formations and we have absolutely nothing to show for it. Everything that we have tried so far only leads to a dead end. The only suggestion that I can make at this point is to completely reformulate Advernox. Is there anything that you would like to add Evan?

As Steven just stated we have nothing to report of any substance. A reformulation does indeed look like the best approach at this point.

"Is there anything else?" No Rick, "that's it for now."

Candis would you like to brief the group on our finding? Sure, Mr. Naylor.

The majority of the morning Mr. Naylor and I wasted just setting up our research area. I might add though, "it is a great place to work." When we were finally set up, we began with the first level of the Canto formulations. What we learned right away was that it appears that Advernox can only be effective in its current form. If it is altered even by the smallest degree, "it will be ineffective."

We are hoping that we will have better luck tomorrow as we research more into the second level of the Canto formulations, which I might add, "I feel is completely unnecessary." It has been my experience that level one through four is so elementary that they can be skipped all together, however, Mr. Naylor is the boss and we will proceed as he wishes.

Thank you Miss Lockhart. As you can all see this is not going to be a walk in the park. It is very important that we don't get ahead of ourselves on this project. I realize that we are on a time line but we cannot afford to over look anything. Take nothing for granite; you'll be glad in the end. I have to report our finding every single day. I do not wish to make that journey to the CEO's office every day with nothing new to report. So, "if we have to set up camp in this lab," we will do just that.

I suggest that anyone who has personal business takes care of it ASAP, because for the next week, month or however long it takes us to solve this problem we belong to BMX and nothing and no one else exists.

Do I make myself clear?

Oh yes Rick..."Clear as day my friend."

Miss Lockhart.... Yes, Mr. Naylor? Do I make myself clear?

Yes sir, "very clear."

Good, I want everyone to get a good night's sleep tonight. Today is our last short work day. I'll see everyone back here tomorrow morning at 6:00 a.m.

"Did you say 6:00 a.m. Rick?"

Yes Steven, "I did."

I'll be in my office for the next thirty minutes getting my report ready for the CEO. After I stop and see him, I'll be heading home for the day. If anyone has any ideas or suggestions feel free to call me at home at any time, day or night, no matter how insignificant it may seem.

"Everyone have a good day."

***

Rick can I talk to you a minute?

Come in Evan.

Can I close the door?

Sure, what's wrong?

I don't know how to say this but I believe that Steven might have a different game plan than we do.

Why do you say that?

It's a gut feeling mostly but I hope I'm wrong.

Thanks for bringing your concerns to my attention. Please don't mention to him, "that I said anything," my friend. I realize how important this project is but if we are not working together we will fail.

Evan it makes me feel good that you feel that way. I'll keep an eye on our friend Steven. You have a good night my friend, I'll see you tomorrow.

***

Hello BMX Headquarters how may I direct your call? Hi Peaches it's me. Oh hello Rick. Peaches I need a favor.

"Just name it Rick."

I want Trenise Clinton and Patricia Winslow from my old team transferred to my new project right away.

Rick I get the feeling that William doesn't know about this.

No he doesn't but I plan to tell him when we meet tonight. He's not going to like this, said Peaches. I know but they are necessary for the success of this project.

Ok, I'll call H.R. now. When do you want their start dated to be? I need them as soon as possible. I'm sorry Rick but four days is as quick as this can happen. Thank you Peaches, four days will have to do.

You are a sweetheart Peaches. I might be a fired sweetheart if you don't smooth this over with William.

***

Hello Mr. Naylor my name is Isabella Kemp. I'm the head of personnel here at BMX. It's nice to meet you Miss Kemp. William told me that someone would be in touch with me soon.

Please have a seat Miss Kemp.

"Thank you Mr. Naylor."

I just wanted to let you know that we will be interviewing candidates for your administrative assistant on Wednesday from 1:00pm to 4:00pm. I'm hoping that this doesn't interfere with your schedule. I'm afraid that it does Miss Kemp, every spare minute that I have needs to be spent in the research facility.

Please call me Issee, "everyone else does."

Alright Issee, I'm up to my elbows in work right now. Can you handle it for me?

"Are you sure that's what you want?" Most men in your position want to pick their own assistant. They seem to get some sick thrill from lining up a group of normally attractive women and fantasizing about which one will be easiest to get into bed.

"You're kidding me right Issee?"

Not at all Mr. Naylor, I've been in the business over twenty years and I've seen it happen over and over again.

Well...Issee, let's just shoot for the one who's the most qualified this time shall we.

Mr. Naylor are you saying that you don't care about how perky her breasts are or if she has a nice round butt? What about her age? Most men prefer the young ones.

Miss Kemp is there a hidden camera in here? You are just pulling my leg aren't you?

No, 'I'm very serious Mr. Naylor."

Issee. I could care less about her breasts, age or any of that other stuff you mentioned. Just pick me someone that can handle the job.

Very well, "I will handle it," Mr. Naylor this has been a very enlightening conversation.

I agree Issee, "it definitely has."

***

William I just off the phone with Mr. Naylor. He has asked me to pick an assistant for him. That's great, Issee, this is going to be easier than I thought. Go ahead with the plans as we discussed yesterday. Do I need to refresh your memory?

No William that will not be necessary, "you want me to wait two days and call him with our selection.

William it was so refreshing to speak to a man who doesn't seem to look at women as a piece of meat but please don't ask me to do anything like this again. There is just something unethical about this whole thing, pouted Issee.

"Oh relax Issee," it's no more unethical than sleeping with a married man. You don't seem to have an ethics issue when it comes to that, smirked William.

"Oh how I hate you William!"

You don't hate me woman, now get in touch with Mercedes. I don't want to miss a thing that goes on in that office. You really think your niece can handle this?

"Of course she can," William said.

One more thing William…can she type? I have no idea. Well if she can't, it's going to look very suspicious to Mr. Naylor don't you think? Yeah, I guess you're right but I think she can type. You call her today Issee!

William why do you need to monitor Rick's team anyway, isn't he briefing you daily? Those were his instructions. However, I know Rick very well and as good as he is at what he does he has a weak spot for doing the right thing, said William.

I guess that means he could never do your job, laughed Issee. Ha, ha you are such the comedian woman.

What about this weekend woman, I've asked you three times already. What about your wife William? I'm working on that, I need a little more time.

You've had five years William. How much longer do you think I can wait? Is that your way of saying no to this weekend?

Take your wife, you never take her anywhere. I'm sure she'd enjoy a trip to Vegas.

I'll see you later William.

Come back here woman!

"Take you wife William!"

***

Rick please we've been at this all night, said Evan. We are completely exhausted! Drink some coffee everyone or do some jumping jacks but we have to continue, said Rick, we have no choice.

Rick, "I'm so tired, I can't see my hands in front of my face," said Steven, besides you might as well face it. There is no cure, there is no antidote and there is no hope!

Does anyone else feel like Steven does? If you do we are finished as a team. We have to remain positive or there is no way that we can be successful. We don't agree with Steven on everything but he is right about us being exhausted.

Listen to me, I don't care if we have to sleep here, eat here, or shit here, we are not going anywhere! Now take a ten-minute break and then let's get back to work!

***

Rick, "why are you pushing them so hard?" Why are you pushing yourself so hard? We aren't going to accomplish anything without some rest, "sweetheart."

What did you call me?

Forget I said that, I must be getting exhausted myself.

Everyone is exhausted, they need rest and so do you. Let them go home and get some rest, "we've been at this for four straight fourteen hours days now and we have very little to show for it." We need some rest and a fresh start.

"Candis there just isn't time for rest."

There is always time. You just have to be willing to take it. Just look at them. Don't they remind you of zombies? We are not going to solve anything without rest.

"Maybe you have a point."

Go tell everyone to go home but they need to be back here at two o'clock. Great but I think you should be the one to tell them, "after all they are your team."

No I have some more tests to run. If I go into that break room I might lose my focus.

What you need to focus on is getting to your car and driving home like the rest of us. "I'm not leaving," said Rick, besides I live too far away. By the time I get home, take a shower and grab an hour of sleep it will be time for me to fight the lunch traffic to get back out here.

"I'll just catch a few hours sleep on the cot in the lounge area."

"You will do no such thing mister!" See..."that is exactly what I'm talking about." You're so tired you're not thinking straight. What do you mean? "I mean sleeping on that cot is a terrible idea." "You won't get five good minutes of sleep on that thing all night."

"I have a better idea."

My apartment is only fifteen minutes away. You can stay with me tonight. I can't do that. What will everyone think? First of all, they don't have to know. Besides it's not like anything is going on between us, "everyone knows you can't stand me." Oh really..."Is that what they think?" I thought it was the other way around.

Whatever Rick but if you really want to solve this whole Advernox mess as badly as you say you do then you'll accept my offer. You need a good night's sleep just like the rest of us. Besides, I seriously doubt you're going to get a better offer this late on a Thursday night.

Are you sure you can tolerate being in the same place with me overnight? Sure I can. As long as you stay on your side of the bed, "it shouldn't be a problem." What? "I'm just kidding Mr. Naylor."

"You need to loosen up."

Ok Candis, "you win this one." Go tell them to be back here at two o'clock. It'll take me about twenty more minutes to finish this last series of tests. Everyone else should be gone by then and you can lead the way to your apartment.

***

Mr. Naylor I'm going to stop at the store on the corner just before we get to my apartment. I need to get some milk. Why can't you call me Rick like everyone else? I'll try. Would you like me to get anything else? I really don't have much to eat at my place. In that case, I better come in with you.

Candis what is all this junk that you are getting? Are you having a sugar attack? Why do you say that? Everything that you have in that buggy is full of sugar. Aren't you worried about your blood glucose?

No, I've been eating sweets like this all my life. I'll pay for it later in the gym. I didn't know you worked out. I have to; otherwise I couldn't eat like this.

Why don't you get another quart of milk, I'll pay for it. Oh you don't have to do that. Please Candis it's the least I can do but make it chocolate milk.

Hello Candis, I see you have a friend with you tonight. I've never seen you with a man before. Who is this handsome fellow and where have you been hiding him?

Please stop Cindy...you're embarrassing me.

Don't be embarrassed child, just introduce me. Cindy this is my boss. Oh really...your boss at this time of night. Who do you think you're fooling?

Mr. Naylor please tell her. Hi, you can call me Rick but yes I am her boss. Oh shit honey, I thought you had finally nabbed yourself a man. It just doesn't make a lick of sense to me. A woman as beautiful as you and you can't get a man.

"Who said I was looking for a man Cindy?" Oh you're looking...every woman in the world is looking honey. Some are looking even if they have a man. Men are the same way. Every time they leave home they are looking, sometimes their wife or girlfriend will be standing right beside them and their eyes will wonder because..."they are still looking."

"You understand what I'm saying," don't you Rick? You might be her boss but you understand don't you?

Just ring these items up for us Cindy. Sure honey but if you ask me, it looks like you two are more than just boss and employee. It's also obvious that someone has," the munches". Is there anything going on that I might want to be a part of? Goodnight Cindy.

Don't mind her Rick. I've been coming here for over two years, "she doesn't mean any harm," besides, "I've never seen her with a man either."

It's Ok, "I thought she was funny." Really…"what part was funny?" The part about us smoking pot.

Good, I thought you meant the part about her never seeing me with a man. What would be funny about that Candis?

Is she your friend?

I don't have any friends Rick.

"That's sad Candis."

My apartment is just a few minutes away.

"I'm right behind you."

***

As I tried to keep up with the crazy woman driver as she swirled from side to side to avoid the pot holes, I thought about what Cindy had just said.

I agree, why is a woman a beautiful as Candis alone? Even tonight when she must be just as exhausted as everyone else she still looks beautiful. I want her; there is no denying that but what can I do about it.

There is something about her that goes far beyond the beauty of her body and that beautiful golden brown skin of hers. I've noticed lately that she has stopped wearing her clothes so snug but she has one of those bodies where it doesn't matter what she wears, she still looks great.

I have to find a way to deal with what I'm starting to feel for her. It would help if she hadn't called me sweetheart earlier and the remark about me staying on my side of the bed...really got my blood to boiling. I'm sure those remarks don't mean anything. I must concentrate on what's important. Oh good she's stopping.

I feel so guilty Stacey. Are we together or not...

***

Well here it is, "home sweet home."

Candis you have a nice apartment.

You're so nice but this is a dump and we both know it. You saw that crummy parking lot, the chipped paint on the walls inside the wall and doesn't the painting on the elevator remind you of the show "Good Times".

I never noticed the elevator on Good Times but if you don't like it why don't you move? I make a good salary Rick but things are very expensive in New York, I help my parents and I'm saving up to buy a house. Another year and I plan to purchase a nice two bedroom on the eastside of Long Island. That will be a long commute Candis but it sounds like you've got it all planned out. Well Rick, "you know what they say about the best-laid plans."

Follow me, "I'll show you where you'll be sleeping." This is a nice bed Candis, "now that you are right about." It definitely beats that old cot back at the lab doesn't it? "Yes it does."

What time should I set the alarm for? I think 5:00a.m. will be fine for me. Rick that's barely seven hours from now, "I'm sorry but that's not enough rest." How about I make it 9:00a.m.? That will give us four hours to relax here before we have to head back and the morning rush hour traffic will be over. I'll even make us some breakfast.

"Can you cook Candis?"

"Who can't cook breakfast Rick?" I know a lot of people who can't even boil water, besides, "I just never pictured you slaving away over a hot stove." Really...so how do you picture me?

Trust me Candis, "you don't want to know," thought Rick.

Breakfast does sound like a good idea and thanks again for talking me into coming over. You're welcome Rick and if you need anything, just call, "I'll be in here on the couch."

You're sleeping on the couch? Now I feel bad. Don't feel bad this is where I spend most of my nights. Don't worry Mr. Naylor, "it's a very comfortable couch." Even if you weren't here, "I'd probably be sleeping on the couch." Are you sure about this? I'm sure, "now good night Rick." Goodnight...Candis.

***

"Good evening everyone." "Are we ready to get started on today's assignments," said Rick? You guys look rested but you don't sound motivated. Anyway, before we get started, "I want to apologize for pushing you so hard." I realize how much of a workload this has been on everyone. That's why I have asked for some help. Two members of my former team will be joining us in a couple of days. They are not scientists. They are chemists and they are very good at their jobs. They should be able to help us move along easier. I'm assigning one to you Steven and the other to Evan.

"Well that's a start Rick," said Evan. Now all we need is about twenty more people. Sorry...I had to practically guarantee William Winters that we would be successful if he gave us these two. "There will be no more help I'm afraid."

Now I don't like too lie so let's make it work. Are there any questions?

No questions Rick but thanks for the help my friend. You are welcome Evan. I want everyone to understand that I'm proud of the way you all have worked together. We will make this happen. Does everyone understand me? We understand Rick. Thank you for saying that. I'm going to order dinner at six. Are there any requests? I have a suggestion Rick. What is it Candis? I think we should just have finger food. What is finger food, said Evan?

A delicacy better know as cold cuts. Oh you mean small sandwiches. Yes, that's what cold cuts are. That way we can eat at our desks if we need to, also it won't make us sleepy afterwards.

How does every one else feel about that idea? That works for me, yeah me to.

Rick what's wrong?

Well, it's always been a rule of mine not to allow eating while we work. If you are not careful the food particles can interfere with the tests. However, I'll allow it this one time but be careful.

Candis here's my credit card. What am I suppose to do with this? Since it's you're idea, you get to place the orders. Thanks Rick and just when I thought you and I were making progress. We are making progress Miss Lockhart….

Candis…"Yes Evan." I don't know what you did to Rick last night but keep it up. "He seems so much more relaxed." He might even let up on us a little.

What makes you think I did anything to him last night? I noticed him following you in his car last night. It's none of my business of course and I will respect your privacy.

"There is nothing going on between Rick and I Evan."

"I didn't say that there was Candis I'm just thanking you for making a difference," that's all.

Evan if you must know, "I asked him to follow me home so he could get a good night's rest." The poor idiot was going to sleep on one of those terrible cots in the break room. "He didn't want to go home because it was too far."

No need to explain Candis, "that's between the two of you." You are right about those cots. I didn't get five good minutes of sleep on that thing last night.

You slept here last night?

"Yes, I did."

I'm sorry about the idiot comment Evan. Don't be sorry, "you're right," it was an idiotic thing to do. Do you have any pain medication? My back is killing me. I think I have something in my desk. Follow me.

Why would you sleep here?

It's a long story...

CHAPTER 7

Rick please tell us that we are not dreaming, said Trenise. Ok, ladies you are not dreaming. We are so honored to be working with you again.

We never got to say goodbye. Yeah, we came in one day and they said you were gone. Everyone was so shocked and we never did find out what happened.

"It's very simple ladies." I had not been happy at BMX for quite a while. William and I didn't see eye to eye on a couple of things. "I had another opportunity and I took it." Well you could have said goodbye. "You're right about that," I'm sorry.

Have both of you read the information that I forwarded to you?

Yes, "we both have," said Pat. Do you understand what's being asked of you? Yes Rick, "it seemed very strange at first but we understand." Good, "it is indeed a pleasure to be working with the two of you again."

The pleasure is all ours Rick.

We'll see how you feel about that statement after you spend fourteen straight hours here. Oh shoot, "is that all we have to do," said Trenise. I can do fourteen hours no problem. Good, "that's what I needed to hear."

Now let's go meet the other members of your team. Miss Lockhart isn't here at the moment but the two gentlemen that you'll be working closely with are. Please follow me ladies and I'll give you a quick tour of the place.

The ladies rest rooms are down the corridor to the right.

The break room is the third door to your left. Unfortunately, "you won't be spending much time there." These are the door that's lead to the lab.

Please take a few minute to look around and familiarize yourself with the equipment in this room. I'll be back in ten minutes at which time I will introduce you to Steven Batiste and Evan Blair.

***

Trenise...yes Pat. "You trust Rick right." What a crazy question Patricia. Yes "I trust him." So do I...but something about this assignment doesn't seem right. I know what you mean but I'm sure Mr. Naylor is aware of our concerns.

Pat, "we are being asked to assist him with something extremely important and I'm honored that he would ask us to help him.

I feel the same way Trenise but I think we better pay close attention to what's going on around here. Fine...I spy, "you take notes and solve the mystery surrounding the Advernox Project," while you are doing that, "I'll try to make sure Rick doesn't regret asking us to help out on this assignment."

Now shut up, "here he comes"

Well what do you ladies think about your new work area? It will do fine Rick. Good. If there is anything else that you need, don't hesitate to ask.

Are there any questions? No said Pat, "everything is fine." Ok, ladies let me introduce you to two of the finest scientist that this world has to offer. Please follow me.

***

Excuse me gentlemen, "I hate to interrupt you but the Calvary has arrived." Evan Blair and Steven Batiste please welcome our newest team members, Patricia Winslow and Trenise Brite. "They are two of the finest chemist that you will ever meet."

"Hello ladies," said Steven "it is indeed a pleasure to meet you".

"Watch out for him ladies, he's a tiger."

Thanks for the warning Rick.

Trenise will be working with Evan. That means you will be working with me Pat. Ok Steven, show me what you got so far. I like that, straight to work. "Isn't that's why we're here Steven?"

Good Pat, "you'll have him broke in, in not time." "He's not going to be a problem Rick." Great, "I'll leave you guys to your work."

CHAPTER 8

I'm sorry Miss but this card has been declined. "You're joking right."
No I'm not.

Can you run it through again?

Ok...I'm sorry, it was declined again.

This can't be happening. Here try this one.

I'm sorry but it's declined also.

There must be something wrong with your machine.

The machine is fine Miss, now the line is getting very long, either pay for these items with cash or return them to the shelf. "I don't carry cash with me." May I please speak to your manager?

The manager's on break right now. She should be back in about an hour. Miss where are you going? You need to return these items. Return them yourself!

Hello, may I speak to someone in customer service? This is customer service. How may I help you? I just tried to use my credit card and it was declined. Can you give me your account number? Yes it's 2228600346.

Are you Miss Candis Lockhart?

"Yes I am."

What is your pin? I never give out my pin. Very well, it's totally up to you; however, "I can't help you without it." I could look it up in the system but it will take a while or you can call back in thirty minutes, but there is no guarantee that you'll get me again and you'll just have to explain everything to someone else. Alright it's 500055. Thank you.

Now let's see what's going on with your account. Did you have an account with Chase Bank?

Yes I do have an account with them.

Well here's your problem. Your account was closed this morning. That's impossible.

I haven't closed my account.

Well, the system shows that it was closed at 11:17 this morning.

Does anyone else have access to your account Miss Lockhart?

No one does.

Are you sure? In the past I have known this problem to come up when a boy friend or girl friend has had access and they get upset for any number of reasons and decide to take the money out of their partners account.

I can assure you that is not the case here lady! For the last time, no one has access to my account but me. There has to be a problem with your system.

The system is operating fine Miss Lockhart. I suggest that you go to the bank right away so they can straighten this out for you. I can't do that because it's after seven and the banks are closed. Well I'd get there first thing Monday morning if I were you.

I can't wait until then! I don't have any money! Is there someone else that can help me? Sure but I'll have to put you on hold.

***

I've been on hold now for twenty minutes. I don't think I'm getting any help from these people today. As soon as I get this straighten out I'm going to cancel that card. It's probably a stupid computer glitch. I can't wait until Monday so I can give those people at the bank a piece of my mind right after I withdraw all my money and close my account. What will I do in the mean time? I have only two choices. Call my parents or just rob my piggy bank. I know I can't call my parents there will be too many questions.

I can't wait to get into my tub and take a nice long hot bath. I'll take the stairs so I can burn off some of this steam that I've built up. It's only six flights. I should have tried my credit card somewhere else. But based on what that lady was saying that would not have done any good.

Where are my keys? I just had them. Here they are but oh shit, I left the door unlocked again! I was sure that I locked it this time. Well it looks like everything is still here. I've been in New York almost seven years now. One would think that the last thing I would forget to do is lock the door.

I'll start my bath and then make a cup of tea. Rick is becoming a slave driver. Something has to be done about these long hours.

I have do admit that I am, "utterly confused by his tactics but I'm impressed with the results," "he is good at his job". Some of the things that he has discovered so far I might have overlooked because of their simplicity.

I guess, "I have been wrong about him all along." Tomorrow when I go in to work, I'll try not to be such a pain in the ass. After all he is a man and they can't be expected to be perfect.

What is that smell? I know that smell, it smells like...but it can't be. Is the room starting to spin? I'm getting dizzy. What is happening to me?

***

Hello Miss Lockhart.

Who are you and what the hell are you doing in my apartment? Who I am is not important lady but the fact that you've been out over an hour, is important.

What happened to me? You hit your head on the side of the chair when you fell. "I've never seen it work that fast before."

What did you do to me? I gave you a dose of knock out gas and it really, "knocked you out". I didn't know it could work that fast.

Why are you doing this to me?

You have a lot of questions don't you? First let me say that who I am is not important Candis but the reason I'm here is.

Mister you have ten seconds to get out of here before I call the police. I wouldn't do that if I were you. On second thought...where is your telephone? Oh, there it is.

Now who was it that you wanted to call again? I think you said the police but we should probably call 911, they normally respond quicker than the neighborhood police.

You're probably still a little dizzy, aren't you Miss Lockhart. I'll dial the number for you.

***

Hello, this is 911 operator Lydia Evans. What's your emergency?

Hello my name is....click.

Where did you get those pictures? Candis do you know these people? Yes, you stupid deranged ape! They are my parents. If you've harmed them in any way, "I'll kill you."

Your phone is ringing. That's probably the 911 operator. You should answer it Candis. Kiss my ass you crazy idiot!

Lady I'd love to kiss that beautiful round ass of yours but I'm afraid that this just isn't a good time for me. "Now answer your damn phone!"

What do you want me to say? Tell them that your kid accidentally hit the speed dial button. "I suggest that you be very convincing."

***

Hello...may I help you? We just got a call from this number. Oh I'm sorry, "my son must have accidentally hit the speed dial button."

Miss the voice I heard was not a child's voice, "it sounded a lot like your voice". Are you sure everything is Ok? Yes I'm sure; the only emergency we are going to have here is when I get my hands on my son. "I warned him about playing on the phone."

Miss Lockhart..."have a good evening."

Thank you for calling Lydia.

***

That was very good Candis. What is it that you want and how did you get in here? Slow down Candis one question at a time.

How do you know my name? Now that's three questions in a row, unfortunately I don't have time to answer all your questions because I don't trust those idiots at 911. They are probably sending someone to this address as we speak, so just shut up and listen.

***

You are part of a team that's testing the formulations for Advernox. I need everything; all notes all conversations and anything else that you can get me.

"Is that what this is all about?" Apparently lady you have no clue about what you have gotten yourself into. So shut up and just listen!

The days of Advernox making millions of dollars for your company are almost over. Unless it is reformulated, it will be worthless, except on the black market where it will be renamed and worth millions again.

What makes you think it's going to be reformulated? Because I know those greedy bastards that sit on the board at BMX Pharmaceutical and once they see that there is no other way, the reformulation will take place.

As soon as the reformulation takes place you are to contact me or the next picture you see of your parents might not be as nice as this one. It was very easy to get them to pose for it.

"Old people just love to hear that something is free."

Please leave my parents out of this. "I'm not asking you," I'm telling you!

Sorry doll, "I can't do that."

They are the only people important in your life. You don't have any friends, not even a boyfriend, which I really find odd as sexy as you are. You're not a dike are you?

Screw you! There you go again, can I get a rain check on that one. Mister you are all messed up in the head!

Please no more sex talk, "now Candis…I want you too listen closely." There are two things that you need to remember. First thing is, "I was never here," the second thing is, "I'll be back."

How will I get in touch with you, said Candis? You silly woman, you don't contact me, I contact you. Oh there's just one more thing Candis, you should change that lock on your door. "It's not safe to live here."

***

Evan and Trenise, I need to see you in the office before you get started, said Rick. Oh shit what have we done? Who said that you did anything? Just follow me. Now have a seat. I need to know how late you two can stay tonight. We will work as late as you need us to work Rick. We work as a team, if one of us stays so does the other. Good, just try to pace yourselves so that you don't burn out to fast. We can do that. Ok, get out of here and go to work. Is that all you wanted? Yes, now send Steven and Pat in.

You wanted to see us Rick. Yes come in and have a seat. I was looking over your report and I'm having a little difficulty reading what you're saying on pages 27-29 and 42-44. Can you please tell me what you are talking about because it's not making much sense?

Pat, I believe this is your handwriting. Can you read it for me?

Sure Rick, let me have it. Oh I see what you mean, said Patricia. I'm sorry there appears to be some type of oil all over the pages. I think it's from that salad that we had a few nights ago. We're sorry Rick, we can redo this, and I'll have it back on your desk in less than twenty minutes.

You two know how I feel about you eating in the work area. We don't have time to be doing our work over again. Don't let this happen again.

Actually Rick we weren't in the work area. That's right Rick we were in the break area. I see, so that's supposed to make it Ok. No sir, I guess it doesn't. We were just trying to get some work done while we were on break.

This isn't the first time that I've had sloppy work from you Steven but I'm surprised at you Pat. "Now get out of here and fix it!" I have to go over that report with Mr. Winters in about two hours.

***

Rick here's the report. I'm really sorry; I don't know how that happened. I normally don't hand in sloppy work. I should have noticed that. I agree Pat. Close the door and sit down for a minute.

What do you think about your partner? He's a bit of a flirt but he's good at his job. Does he seem dedicated to his work? Yes he does, I think he works just as hard if not harder than everyone else.

Keep an eye on him for me Pat.

I realize he's working hard, there's no doubt about that, and "I just hope he's working hard for us." I'm sorry to ask and it may be none of my business but why do you say that Rick? Let's just say it's a hunch for now and leave it at that. I guess that means I should get back to work. That's right young lady.

***

I don't know how much longer I can keep up at this pace. All I have time to do is go to my apartment, take a shower, go to bed and come right back here, said Evan. "Someone has got to talk to Rick."

All this work and no play is making me sick, said Steven. I had no idea that this project would require so much of my time and be so draining.

Why did he give Pat and Trenise the day off? He's never given us a day off. I don't know said Evan but I'm sure he has a good reason. Maybe we can ask Candis to talk to him, said Steven.

Don't be crazy man; those two hate each other's guts. No, I don't think Rick hates her but she sure despises him. Yeah she sure does, I wonder why that is, said Evan?

You haven't heard? The word on the street is that she was the front runner for the job Rick has. It was all but done then out of no where Rick appeared.

The entire department was shocked, said Steven. They just knew the job was hers. You mean we could be working for Candis instead of Rick, said Evan. I'm not sure I would like that, me either but things would definitely be different.

Hey Evan, "come over here for a second, "I want you to see something." Look into the microscope and don't look away, "not even for a second!" What is it Steven?

"Just do as I say."

Ok, "I'm looking but I don't see anything."

"Just keep looking!"

Hey, I do see something. Wow, "is this what I think it is?"

Oh my God Steven, I think we might finally have something to report!

Yes my friend, "I think you are right."

***

You have eight unheard messages; message one, hello Rick this is Stacey, remember me; how is New York? Call Me. Message two: Congratulations Mr. Naylor we have chosen you an assistant. Her name is Mercedes Johnson. She is twenty-eight years old, a graduate of Millsap College; she can type sixty words per minute. She has a wonderful personality. We think you will like her. She's looking forward to meeting you. She can start first thing Monday morning. Give me a call if you have any questions. Message three: Hello Mr. Naylor this is Charles A. Davis, please give me a call as soon as you are back in your office, the number is 435-1987. Message four: Hello Rick, its Stacey again, please call me... I miss you. Message five: Mr. Naylor this is Ken from Verizon Wireless. We didn't receive your August payment. Please send it in soon to avoid an interruption to your service, thank you. Message six: Mr. Naylor this Mr. Davis again, there has been a change of plans; we need to stop by your apartment tonight, let's say eight o'clock sharp. Message seven: Hi Daddy its Brittany; my stupid car won't start again, I love you. Message nine: Hello Mr. Naylor, its Candis Lockhart. I really need to talk to you. Can I come over around nine o'clock tonight? Please call me to confirm.

Hello Brittany, hi Daddy, how are you?

I'm fine but it doesn't sound like you are. Are you finally ready to get rid of that car? No but I think I have too. Honey, I understand that you love that old car but it has seen its best days. Why don't you go out tomorrow and look for a new car? When you find one that you like call me and we can talk about it. Ok Daddy.... I love you. I love you to sweetheart. By the way how is that new photography job going? It's going fine Daddy. I really love it. That's just great, maybe when I come to visit for the holidays you can take a photo of the entire family. That's a great idea Daddy. I have to go now so I can catch the bus.

***

Candis, I just got your message. Is everything Ok? Not Really, I realize it's late but I need to talk. Can I come over? Sure, do you remember how to get to my penthouse? Of course I do. Is nine o'clock Ok? Sure that will be fine.

Would you like some dinner?

No thanks, "it's too late for me to eat."

Ok Candis, "I'll see you at nine."

I don't know any Mr. Davis? It really doesn't matter because whoever you are you will have to reschedule. On second thought maybe I should call this guy. He doesn't need to be here when Candis gets here. I wonder what she wants anyway. She sounded a little stressed. I hope everything's Ok.

Hello…"may I speak to Mr. Davis?"

I'm sorry, "he's not in at the moment." May I take a message?

Yes, my name is Rick Naylor. He called and said he needed to stop by my apartment tonight. Can you tell him that tonight is not a good time?

"Who is he anyway?"

Mr. Davis will answer all your questions sir. I will give him your message but if I were you I'd make myself available tonight. He normally doesn't take very long with his appointments.

"I didn't schedule an appointment with him!"

I realize that sir but he did schedule an appointment with you. "If I were you I'd keep it." Now I'm very busy Mr. Naylor, "please have a good day."

"Who the hell is this guy?"

It's almost six o'clock. I think I'll take a shower, no a dip in the Jacuzzi will be even better but first, I'll throw those steaks in the oven *and cook them on low heat. They have been marinating since I left for work this morning.*

I learned a long time ago to always have food when a woman is coming over. I wonder what she wants. Hopefully, she has some news about the formulations. We are getting nowhere with them.

What we really need is someone who worked on the original formulation. All we are doing is wasting a lot of valuable time. There has to be something that we are over looking.

I'm starting to talk to myself again. That's not good. I'll take the phone with me to the Jacuzzi. I'll call Stacey while I'm in there but I better set the timer on the oven so my steaks don't burn.

***

Hello Miss Carter, how have you been?

Is this Rick?

"Yes it is."

How have you been son? It's always nice to hear from you.

May I speak to Stacy? Oh honey I'm sorry, she's not here. She went to a movie with little Shorty from up the street. He's been after my baby since you left. Sending her flowers and stopping by all the time.

Oh my, "I probably shouldn't have said anything." Don't tell Stacy that I told you. She'll be mad at me for weeks. But it serves you right for leaving my baby behind like you did. You know how much she loves you. I don't guess that matters now with you being up there in the big city. "You probably have a hundred girlfriends by now"...don't you?

"That's not true Mrs. Carter."

Well just the same...I hear there are a lot of crazy people up there in New York City.

Yes Mrs. Carter you are right about that but there are crazy people everywhere. I have to go now Mrs. Carter, please tell Stacy that I called.

I will tell her son but if I were you, "I wouldn't be waiting by the phone." Ha, ha. Click…

I can't believe Stacy is that woman's daughter. She must be adopted. I wonder how she would feel if she knew Stacy stayed behind because of her. Mrs. Carter's not stupid. She knows why her daughter didn't come with me. I think she enjoyed giving me that message about Stacy being out with Shorty. Did Stacy hit her head or something? How can she be on a date with that gangster Shorty? This just can't be happening.

"I need a drink."

So the rumors are true. The poor girl has lost her mind. He is definitely not her type. I will not feel sorry for myself; after all I brought this on myself. Stacy, I will say a prayer for you before I go to bed, I promise.

***

"After dinner there was a knock on the door."

I looked at the clock it was exactly eight o'clock. I walked over to the door and looked out the peephole. There were two women and a rather large man. They were all dressed in very nice suits. For the first time I noticed that my hands were shaking a little.

"Who is it?"

My name is Franklin Davis. May I come in Mr. Naylor? What do you want? I'll explain once I'm inside. Please open the door.

Come in. Ladies wait here this won't take long.

Hello Mr. Naylor. This is a very nice apartment.

What do you want sir?

Ok, I won't waste you time. I understand that you are in charge of the Advernox Project.

How do you know about that? It's my job to know certain things. Word on the street is that you have a small team of specialist working with you. What exactly do you want Mr. Davis?

"I want information Mr. Naylor."

What type of information?

Are you going to offer me a seat Mr. Naylor?

No I don't think that will be necessary. Very well then, I will need all information that you have. I can't do that. You can and you will!

Give me one good reason why I should give you anything! I'll give you four. Here, these pictures are for you. Just consider them a gift from me. Do I have your attention now?

These are pictures of my kids. Where did you get them? I had an associate of mine take them this morning, just in case you were not willing to cooperate.

What exactly do you want? It's simple Mr. Naylor. I want a weekly report of the finding during your investigation of the Advernox. If anything unusual comes up you are too contact me right away. You contact me before you contact anyone including the CEO of BMX. "Do you understand?" I need you to be more specific with what you want.

Rick you are trying my patience. I should have been gone by now. "I'll say this one more time and you better get it." If you find anything wrong I want to be the first to know or say good-bye to your kids now.

How do I know that you won't harm them anyway? You don't but the best way to keep them safe is to cooperate with me. I normally keep my word, unless someone really pisses me off. So do you understand now? Yes, I understand but you better understand this. If anything happens to my kids, "you will pay dearly."

Ha…you are threatening me? Call it what you want, now get out of my house! Mr. Naylor you are a very funny man. I knew you were a scientist but I never imagined you as a comedian.

I hope you are as good a scientist as you are a comedian. I'm going to leave now before you say something else funny and I'll die from laughing so much. I've got to tell the girls what you just said.

"Get out of my house!"

I stood there with the door opened and watched them walk to the elevator. The idiot was stilling laughing but I didn't see a damn thing funny. He whispered something to the ladies. They looked back at me and also started laughing. One woman was directly in front of him the other was directly behind him. They reminded me of high priced hookers that had seen better days.

***

I slammed the door, picked up the phone and called my kids. Derrick answered the phone. I only needed to know one thing. After beating around the bushes a little, I asked him what he wore to school today. He said a pair of khaki shorts and a black tee shirt.

Is everything going Ok in school? Sure Dad, I made the football team. That's great, "I can't wait to see you play." I have to go now but I'll be in touch later. Tell the girls I said hi. Ok, dad, "I'll tell them."

I looked at the picture in my hand. My son was wearing, "khaki shorts and a black tee shirt."

"I needed another drink."

After I finally calmed down enough to sit down the phone rang and sent my heart to racing again.

My hands were shaking so bad I couldn't lift the receiver so I simply pressed the speaker button and said hello.

Hello replied a very sexy voice. Is this Rick?

"Yes it is."

I left a little something for you under your couch. Open it now and follow the instructions. "I'll call you later sweetheart."

"I could hear Mr. Davis's voice in the background." He was still laughing.

I looked under the couch and there was a small brown box with my name on it. I slowly opened it. There was a phone number and a long series of numbers that looked like a bank account. The instructions were simple. Call this number as soon as you open this box.

I called the number and got an overseas operator. When she finally connected me it was to a bank in Switzerland.

"Hello may I help you?"

Yes, my name is Richard Naylor and I have instructions to call this number. Please hold one moment sir.

Hello, my name is Linaska Alison; I'm the bank manager here. How may I help you? I was instructed to call this number. Are you calling for your account balance? I don't have an account with your bank.

"Sure you do sir."

Can you give me your account number? "I just told you that I don't have an account with you."

Sir, let me ask you something. Were you given a set of numbers on a piece of paper?

"Yes I was."

Well that's your account number. Please read me the numbers.

The numbers are 70859349-5592.

Very well give me a few seconds to look it up. Ahh...there it is. Are you Mr. Richard Naylor?

"I just told you my name!"

Calm down sir, "I'm just trying to do my job." Now I need to ask you a few questions to verify that you are indeed who you say you are.

Very well Mr. Alison..."I guess I can play along." What's the first question? What was your first car? You're kidding me aren't you? No sir, I assure you I'm not. Now will you please answer the question? It was an Opel. "That is correct."

What color was it? It was yellow. That is also correct Mr. Naylor

Where was your first child born? In Germany, I need you to be a little more specific. Can you tell me the name of the hospital? It was a German hospital, I can't remember name but the town was Bamberg. That's close enough, it was Bamberg General Hospital.

What was your daughter's weight at birth? How the hell do you expect me to remember that? It should be easy Mr. Naylor. Wasn't she your first born? Most parents can remember the weight of all their kids. We're only asking you for the weight of one. "It's important that you remember."

Listen to me you stupid prick! I don't care who you are or anything about this silly game. It's hard to remember because she was born in a German hospital and they recorded the weight in grams. Her mother might remember but I don't have a clue. Now if you are willing to allow me time to call her maybe I can get the answer for you otherwise...

Wait a second...I think I do remember....Brittany weighed nine pounds, three ounces. That's correct Mr. Naylor. Your daughter was a big baby.

Only one more question. What is going to happen to your daughter if you don't deliver what Mr. Davis wants? What? I said...

"I heard what you said!"

Well please answer the question Mr. Naylor, you must understand that I'm only the bank manager by no means am I saying that I agree with Mr. Davis's business tactics. Now please answer the question sir, "I do have other customers to attend to." What is the answer?

He..."will kill her."

That's the correct answer.

"I'm satisfied that you are Mr. Naylor."

Your current balance is $750, 000 dollars.

This can't be true, "there must be a mistake." I'm sorry Mr. Naylor, "were you expecting more?" No, I wasn't expecting more, "I wasn't expecting anything."

Who set up this account and who deposited that money? "Why...you did Mr. Naylor." Have a good day Mr. Naylor and if you need any more assistance please don't hesitate to call.

***

Is that the telephone again? Please let it be Stacy this time. Hello...hello Mr. Naylor it's Candis. I'll be there in about ten minutes. There is one small request Mr. Naylor. What is it? Please make sure there is plenty to drink.

Before Candis got there I had already consumed my second drink and was well into the third one, which was definitely a record for me. What a day, I was strangely $750,000 dollars richer: money that I knew I couldn't touch.

My kid's lives were being threatened; my former fiancée was on a date with the neighborhood drug dealer and in less than ten minutes the sexiest woman I had ever met was coming to see me late on a Friday night. This would be great if she didn't hate my guts. So why is she coming and what other surprises would this night bring?

That must be her at the door now. Come in it's open.

Do you always leave your door open? I knew you were coming....my goodness Candis what happened to you? I didn't think I'd ever say this but you look terrible!

Thanks Mr. Naylor because that's just how I feel.

Have you been crying?

Yes (sob) you are not going to believe my day.

Sure I will Candis, "there is not much that you can say that will surprise me today." Here, have a seat.

May I use your bathroom first?

Sure, it's the first door on the left. What kind of drink would you like? The same as last time only make it bigger.

***

Here's your drink, "now tell me about your day." I need a few minutes to catch my breath first. Sure take your time.

What smells so delicious?

That delicious smell is a couple of steaks that I cooked. There's plenty if you'd like some. There is also a potato and a salad. It smells so good I can't say no. Well you sit right there and I'll make you a plate.

Mr. Naylor you don't seem like the typical bachelor.

Why do you say that?

Cooking is not something that a lot of bachelors do.

Well, I haven't always been a bachelor. There was a time in my life when I had to cook for four small kids. They are always telling me that my cooking is what they miss the most. Here you go and there's more where that came from.

Hmm...this is good. I'm really impressed.

"I'm glad you like it."

So tell me about your day Candis.

When I came home tonight there was a man in my apartment. What's so odd about that? I'm sure there are a lot of men trying to get into your apartment.

I knew it was a mistake coming here! Why did I ever think I could confide in you?

Wait, I'm sorry Candis, I truly am. Please sit back down and finish your dinner. I guess this is more serious than I thought. One more wisecrack Mr. Naylor and I'm walking out that door.

"I'm sorry Candis." How did he get into the apartment?

Apparently he picked my lock. What did he want? After I came to he said that if you scream I'll kill you. He didn't have to worry about that because I was so scared that I couldn't speak.

What do you mean after you came to?

He had used some type of gas to knock me unconscious. Oh my God, did he harm you in any way?

No he didn't. Well...how did you get away? What did he want Candis? He said that he wanted information about Advernox.

Are you kidding me?

"I'm afraid not."

I think I better make myself another drink. What kind of information? He said that if we found any problems with the original formulation I was to contact him immediately.

What did you tell him? I didn't tell him anything, "I don't know anything." I told him that if he didn't leave immediately I was calling the police. He then walked over to the phone, dialed 911 and handed me the phone. As soon as the operator came on he showed me a picture and I almost fainted.

"It was a picture of my parents."

Was it a recent picture?

Yes my father was wearing the scarf that I knitted him for his birthday two weeks ago. I dropped the phone on the floor. It started the ring almost immediately. It was the 911 operator. He made me tell the operator that my son had accidentally dialed the number.

He left directly after that. But not before warning me that he would be back and I was not to tell anyone that he had been there. He also said that I have lovely parents and that he would hate to see anything happen to them.

Candis are you sure you have never seen this man before? Rick, I'm sure. I don't know what I'd do if he harmed my parents. What should I do? Have you talked to them? No I haven't. I think the first thing that you should do is call your parents and make sure they are Ok. I can't do that, my father always knows when something is wrong with me.

Alright give me the number; I'll call them and ask for you. That way we'll know if they are Ok. Thanks Rick, "that sounds like a good idea."

Hello...hello my name is Rick Naylor. I'm an old friend of Candis's. I was hoping that I could get her home phone number. How do you know my daughter son?

We went to school together. What school was that son? Harvard...that's not a school son, "that's a university." There's a big difference you know.

Yes sir, "you are right."

Look son, maybe you did go to college with my daughter and you might even be a friend but we don't give out her phone number. I understand that sir but can you take mine and tell her to call me? I can do that. What's the number? It's 631-555-9812.

That's a New York number isn't it? Yes sir. When she calls I'll give it to her but son don't ever call here this late again.

Yes sir, "I'm sorry."

Well Candis your parents are fine. Who did you speak to? I spoke to your dad. "He reminds me of you." Why do you say that? Never mind it's nothing. Finish telling me about your day.

Well before all this happened I had gone to the grocery store to get a few things for dinner tonight. When I tried to pay for them with my credit card it was declined.

"It was so embarrassing." I don't carry cash on me, so I just left the things on the counter and walked out. I went straight to an ATM but it wouldn't let me get any money. I called customer service and they claimed that I had closed my accounts earlier in the day but I didn't.

"What is going on Rick?" I remember that man saying that I have no idea what I have gotten myself into. He claims that before this is all over we are going to have to reformulate Advernox and it's going to be worth millions on the black market. That tells me that he must be connected to the mob or something.

"I'm afraid that you might be right about that Candis." After hearing your story, it makes me wonder if anyone has tried to contact Evan or Steven.

What am I going to do Rick? I suddenly have no money and I'm afraid to go back to my apartment. That's not a problem Candis. You can stay here tonight if you like. I can give you a small loan until you get things straighten out. Actually, you can stay here as long as you need to.

I have a spare room and you are welcome to it. I do recommend that we go to you apartment tomorrow and get you some clothes. After that just make yourself at home here until you are ready to leave.

Are you sure Rick?

"Yes Candis, I'm sure?"

I've been so mean to you. Forget about it Candis. The important thing is that you are Ok.

I'm so sorry that I've been so mean to you Rick. It's just that men look at me and they only see one thing.

"Was I that obvious?"

I'm afraid so but that wasn't the only reason. I just used it to keep me from getting mad at the real reason. You mean the job right? You knew about the job? "I just found out recently."

He wanted me to sleep with him and I wasn't willing to do that even if he could have given me the world.

"I'm just not that kind of girl."

I'm sorry Candis, "that's a terrible thing to have to experience." I realize now Rick that it's not your fault, if they hadn't given the job to you, "it would have been someone else."

As far as men looking at me as if I was a juicy piece of steak, I'm used to it but I do wish you would work on that. I'll try Candis, I really will. I'm sorry for making you feel so uncomfortable.

Like I said, I'm use to it. There is one thing though, just because you are helping me, don't expect anything in return. Do you understand? I understand Miss Lockhart. Please...call me Candis.

Come with me, "I'll show you to your room." I slept in this room once. "It was very comfortable." I'm sure you'll be fine here. There are fresh towels in the cabinet to your right and the bath and shower is the door to your left. I want you to get a good night's sleep. We can talk about this tomorrow at breakfast.

Rick what time are you going to work? Tomorrow's Sunday, "I'm not going to work." I just thought I'd do some research from here at home. Oh no that's a mistake, especially now that this man is threatening my parents, please Rick.

We should be working everyday. Call Evan, Steve and the girls also. Calm down Candis, we can go in late tomorrow afternoon but you can probably forget about Steve and Evan they are probably out at a club right now trying to pick up women.

Why aren't you doing the same thing? Oh that's simple Candis, I had a good woman and I lost her. I let this stupid job get in the way. There's nothing out there for me.

Do you want to talk about it?

Yes, I think I need to but not now. We both need some rest; maybe we can talk about it after we figure out all this other stuff that's going on.

CHAPTER 9

Wake up J.T., William is that you? Good grief man do you have any idea what time it is? Yeah, I know exactly what time it is. It's time to move forward with my plan. Is that what you called me at two o'clock in the morning for? Can't we talk about this tomorrow morning? Sure J.T., let's just talk about it tomorrow when we are both sitting in a five by ten cell with a dirty urinal staring us in the face. Alright, "I think I'm awake now."

What's the problem this time? I just heard from the attorney, we are going to trial. Oh no William, this is not good news. Why don't we just pay the son of bitches to drop the case?

Are you crazy John?

Where are we going to get ten billion dollars? We don't have it do we? Yes we have it but it would bankrupt the company. So we really don't have a choice.

No, "I'm afraid we don't."

I'm contacting Cliff as soon as I get in the office this morning. Do I have your support J.T.? Yeah William, and may God have mercy on our souls.

***

Good morning Peaches.

Good morning Mr. Winters. How are you today? Get me Cliff Miller on the line ASAP. Yes sir.

Hello Cliff. How ya doing partner? I can't complain William. How you been? Cliff you know I'm no good at beating around the bush. I know that, I figured if you're calling me, "then someone's about to die."

What's the problem this time?

It's Advernox, "someone's getting just a little too close for comfort." Do you know who it is?

"Yes we do."

How do you want it handled? I want it handled very quickly and very cleanly. Make sure that nothing can be traced back to you. Have you ever had that problem with me before? No, and I want to keep it that way. There's just one thing William. I'll need twenty-five thousand plus the normal fee.

Damn Cliff, "you are becoming an expensive son of a bitch." Hey you want the best; you have to pay for it. Fine just make it happen quickly.

Is this weekend quick enough? That will be fine. Good send me over the name and the location and I'll handle it. My messenger is already on the way. He should be there any minute.

***

This is the room. Can you pick the lock? Wait a second, let me see. No it has a silent alarm sensor on it. Let's try the windows. No good, we're on the 20th floor. Besides if the door has a sensor on it, I'm sure the windows do also.

Do you have any other suggestions? How about we just knock on the door? That's just stupid enough that it might work, except for the fact that he'll probably open the door with a got damn gun in his hand!

"Are you saying that I'm stupid?"

Of course not Cliff, "I just meant…"

I know what you meant asshole. Never call me stupid, "you freaking idiot" or I promise I'll make you regret it.

I have an idea follow me, Cliff said. Look for the fire alarm. Why? I think that might be a good way to get him out of the room. Cliff you are a genius, "that just might work." There's the fire alarm Cliff. Good, now you go stand at the door and wait for him to open the door.

What are you going to be doing?

Idiot, "I have to pull the fire alarm."

Remember once were inside he's all yours. I know, "that's why you're paying me ten thousand dollars." I should be getting at least twenty-five for a job like this.

Well it's ten or nothing so make up your mind. I agreed to ten so that's what I'm sticking with. It's good to know you are a man of your word, besides; I have to see how you operate under pressure before I can even consider paying you more. You mess this up and there won't be a next time.

Now go stand by the door. I'm pulling the alarm in ten seconds. When he opens the door deal with him.

Hey what the hell is going on! Is there a fire? No, I'm afraid not. Who are you? My name is Cliff Miller. What do you want? I want your life idiot. What? Can you fly? Can I fly? That's what I said. Get the hell out of my room! No you get out and take the express. What express?

***

Let's go Cliff. Did you take care of him? Yes I did, now let's go. I got the feeling that this place will be swarming with cops in a few minutes. What did you do to him? I tossed his ass out the window. Well I guess that's one way to find out if the window was armed.

Was it? Yes it was.

What did you say to him before you threw him out? I told him that I was Cliff Miller. That was brilliant. I know, "I thought you'd like that." Did he say anything before you threw him out? He said please don't kill me but they all say that. Yeah..."I know."

***

Come in Mercedes.

Hello Uncle William. How are you? I'm just fine come over here and give me a hug. You look great young lady. Well, "I'm still struggling with this weight."

Don't be silly, "you look great." That's why you're my favorite uncle.

So what's this new assignment that you've lined up for me? I hope it's nothing like the last one. Don't you worry yourself; it's nothing like that one. Good because I'm still having nightmares about that one. Don't worry; this is simply an administrative assignment.

You will be working for a fellow named Richard Naylor. Is he cute?

Never mind that Mercedes.

He's our new research manager. I need you to keep an eye on him. That will be easy if he's cute.

Will you just listen?

There will be a lot of important document coming across his desk, "duplicate everything but don't get caught." He might have lunches or dinners with important people. I'll need to know who they are. I want to know everything that goes on in that office no matter how insignificant it might seem. Even the phone calls, the ones going out and coming in. The most important thing is he can never know that you are my niece. Do you think you can handle this?

Sure I can Uncle. Now let's talk about my salary, "you know I got Williams."

***

Hi, Douglas I've got a situation here and I'm going to need a private investigator. Is there anyone that you can recommend? How long will you need him William?

It depends on how good he is. I've got someone in mind. Give me about an hour and I'll call you back. Thanks Doug and tell that beautiful wife of yours I said hi. I would if I could William but she left me about a month ago. She hasn't spoken to me since.

I'm sorry to hear that Doug. Oh it's Ok, "I'm getting use to doing things for myself." The funny thing is she hired one of the guys that I use to employ on a regular basis to catch me with my red head down in Atlantic City. It served me right though I'd been cheating on her for years.

Well you have had quite a handful of ladies on the side haven't you? Twenty women would be the exact number. They were all one night stands. Guess how many it's been since she left me? I have no idea, I'd guess about three. Wrong William, you never were good at guessing. I haven't been with anyone since she left me.

"Ain't that a...?"

It's as though it's no fun unless there's a chance of getting caught.

That's not the first time I've heard someone say that. We've talked enough about me. How's Margaret doing?

She's doing just fine, hasn't caught me yet, (ha, ha) at least I don't think so. Well you can never be too careful. I'll talk to you later buddy. Alright Doug, once again I'm sorry, maybe she'll come back, you never know.

Oh hell, "it's Ok William." She wasn't any good in bed anyway.

***

Are all the pieces in place Jeff?

"Yes sir they are." I need to make one more stop at Mr. Naylor's apartment and we will be all set. I hope you are right Jeff. I will not tolerate one more mistake or delay!

"What about the girl?" She wasn't at her apartment last night.

"Jeff she is important to us!"

"I want someone watching her at all times!" Do you understand me? Why is she is so important to us? You are not paid to understand things Jeff. You are paid to execute orders, specifically my orders! Do you at least understand that?

Yes sir "that I do understand."

Now put a guy on her and stop trying to play Dick Tracey. I want to know her every move. If she has a damn headache, "I want to know how many aspirins she takes." Got it!

Yes Sir, I've got it. Good, "now get the hell out of here and do your job!"

***

Stacey call Mark Jackson.
Yes sir.
Mark's on line two.

Hello Mark, how are you? I'm just fine William, what's up? I'm just checking in on the progress at the lab. I'm sorry but there's not much to report William. We are having no luck with the Advernox reformulations. We are running out of time Mark.

I'm well aware of that sir. What we need is a miracle.

No, what we need is one of the original chemists that worked on the original formulation. Well that's not going to happen. When you ask Cliff Miller to do a job, it gets done. You're right I just wish we hadn't asked him to kill all the chemists.

Well, no one knew about these damn side effects. Wrong Mark, WPP knew. That's why they pulled the plug on the entire operation. We just got greedy thinking about all the money that we would make. "At least we were right about that sir."

Yes but it might end up costing us more than we can afford.

I'm going up to the lab in a few hours Mark but I need to talk to Cliff first. William do you think he's told his wife that he's leaving her yet? No of course not. That would be a stupid thing to do right before retirement. Cliff is a lot of things Mark but stupid is not one of them. "I wouldn't be so sure about that William." Sometimes a man can get too comfortable when he's been cheating on his wife as long as Cliff has.

They tend to get a little sloppy William. Well that wouldn't surprise me. What does surprise me is that young girl hasn't given his old ass a heart attack, said William. How old is she?

She's twenty-five William and they say she takes after her mother. I've only seen her once but she left a lasting impression. Apparently she's also a gold digger and she has a body that makes digging for gold easy. Interesting, sounds like her mother taught her well.

You can teach your kids a lot of things but only Mother Nature can create a body as fine as hers. That reminds me, I need to give her mother a call later. I've taken up enough of your time Mark; I'll see you in a couple of hours at the lab "don't be late."

***

Stacey get Cliff Miller on the line. Yes Sir, Mr. Winters
Hello may I speak to Mr. Miller. This is he.
Mr. Winters would like to speak to you.
Please hold on while I connect you.
Hello Cliff how ya doing partner?
Good William, how about yourself?
Same old shit different day. I'm still dealing with this Advernox mess. It's going to be the death of me yet, said William. I understand, said Cliff, maybe you should think about retirement? No way partner but that's why I'm calling. Are you still going through with this retirement party that people keep talking about?

Oh it's not just talk William, it a done deal. I'm giving it up and moving to Florida so I can warm up these old aching bones.

Really...I bet Mary's pretty excited about that, she has always complained about the East Coast.

Well...uhh, "yes she's excited."

Wait just a minute Cliff...what was that hesitation about old partner? You are taking her with you aren't you?

Of course I am William.

"You big liar!"

You've never been able to lie to me boy. What ya think ya gonna do, ride off into the Florida sunset with that twenty-four year old mistress of yours? Mary gonna kick both ya asses if you try that but hey that's your funeral, said William.

Cliff, old partner, "you are aware that 70% of the people that retire at your age die within four years." Where you getting you information from William? Just thought I'll let you know partner.

"Don't you worry about me William boy."

I've got a lot of years left in this body.

Not if you keep riding that twenty-five year old. You might be right about that but on the other hand she might be what keeps me alive. Who would want to die and leave her? She takes after her mom you know. Yeah Cliff, "that's what I've heard."

Are you coming to my retirement party?

Are you kidding me?

I wouldn't miss it for the world. Besides the only way I'll believe it, is if I see it for myself. There is one more thing Cliff.

What is it William?

You will remain available for me if I need you in the future right.

Sorry William, "I've lost my edge." I just don't have the stomach for it any more. That's a shame partner. They don't make them like you any more.

"You were the best and I mean that."

Thanks William that means a lot coming from you. Well, I've got to head to the lab and kick our chemist in their butt. You take care of yourself partner. I will William and you do the same.

Maybe he has lost his edge, other wise his wife wouldn't be in Florida with another man. None of my business though at least not yet. He is wrong about one thing. Nobody quits on me, not even the great Mr. Clifford Miller. If I need him he had better be ready.

***

Good afternoon sir. Hello Phil, Where to sir? The lab is where we are heading. How are things going out there? Less talk and more driving would be appreciated Phillip. Very well sir. Get me Walter on the phone. Yes sir. No one is answering his home phone. Then try his mobile phone idiot.

Hello is this Mr. O'Brien? It depends on who's calling. I'm Mr. Winters Limo driver. What does he want? You'll have to ask him sir. Sir, Mr. O'Brien is on line one.

Hello Walter, hello William. I need you to meet me at the lab in twenty minutes. I'm afraid that's impossible. I'm in Chicago at the moment.

What the hell are you doing in the freaking windy city? Peaches and I are attending a couple of Broadway plays. Don't we have that crap in New York? Sure but we wanted to get out of that rotten apple for a minute.

When ya heading back?

In two days.

Cancel that *partner,* I need you back tomorrow morning at the latest.

I can't do that William, Harriet has been waiting for this play for five months, Well let me put it to you this way, if you are not here tomorrow morning consider your ass skinned alive.

I guess you have left me no choice William. I can either get my ass skinned alive by you tomorrow or by Harriet today. Since tomorrow's not promised to any of us I guess you know my decision.

Click….

Honey is everything Ok? Who was that? It was nobody sweetheart. Lets get something to eat before we go to the play.

Walter, Walter! That ass hole hung up on me. Get me Stacey on the line right now. This is Stacy sir. Put in the paper work to terminate Walter O'Brien right now. Excuse me sir but did you say Walter O'Brien?

"Yes I did."

"Sir are you sure about that?"

"Yes I'm sure." It's just that you put him in charge of the Tempol project. He knows information that I'm sure he's not going to keep to himself if he's fired. Damn it, you're right Stacey, "I wasn't thinking." I'll have to handle him another way.

Sir we are approaching the lab. Would you prefer the front or back entrance. The front entrance will be fine. Philip one more call before I get out. Who sir? Please call Mr. Cliff Miller.

***

Darryl, please stop at that doughnut shop just before we get to work. Which one? It's the one on the corner of 34th and Grand.

Are you in the mood for some doughnuts, Mr. Naylor? No, actually, I'm hoping to get a cup of their coffee.

Do they have good coffee? The best, you should try it, I'll get you a cup. How do you like yours? Cream and sugar my man, cream and sugar. Let me out here and circle around the block. If I'm not out when you get back please circle around one more time.

***

Hey where's the coffee? Man that line was too long. I guess we have to get here earlier next time. Just drop me off at work.

Alright Rick but I was looking forward to that coffee. So was I Darryl.

I know I might be out of line here Rick but is everything going Ok?

What do you mean?

Hey I'm not as stupid as I look my man. This company doesn't just hire a chauffeur for anyone and they don't put just anybody up at the Palace for six months either.

Well BMX isn't doing that. I wish I could answer your question Darryl I really do but I'm sworn to keep my mouth shut. Nothing personal, it's just the way things are around here right now.

I understand Rick but just so you know, I can always tell when you didn't have a good day at that research facility. I think you need to do something to help you unwind a little my man. You know what I mean right? I think so Darryl but trust me when I say I don't have the luxury of taking time to unwind.

Hey Rick now you listen to me. There is nothing in the

world better than getting with your lady friend and forgetting about all your worries, even if it's only for a couple of hours.

I may just be a chauffeur but I'm a man to and I have problems just like anyone else. Listen to me; I know what I'm talking about. At least think about it, who knows it might even help you figure out whatever has you so puzzled. What makes you think that I'm puzzled about something?

Well we've been sitting in front of your office building for over two minutes now and you haven't even tried to get out of the car. Normally five seconds after I pull up you are out the car and half way up the stairs. I didn't realize we were here already.

See that's what I mean Rick. You need to unwind a little. Call your lady friend that we took home. She likes you. Invite her to dinner tonight. You never know it might be just what the doctor ordered. Thanks Darryl, I'll think about it.

***

Good morning Mr. Naylor. Hello….you must be Miss Joyner. Yes I am. It's a pleasure to meet you. What smells so good? That smell Mr. Naylor is fresh coffee and Danish rolls. Really, that's great; I see you've done your homework. I love Danish rolls and I've wanted a good cup of coffee all morning.

Have a seat and I'll get some for you.

How do you like your coffee? Let me guess. You probably take one cream and two sugars right. That's very good Miss Joyner. How did you know that? Well sir… let's just say I have a hunch about these things.

One more thing we are going to be working together for a long time so you might as well get use to calling me Mercedes.

Ok, Mercedes it is. That sounds much better; now let me get that coffee for you.

Here you go sir. Be careful it's hot. What's with this sir stuff? You made the rules so live by them. You're funny Rick I can tell I'm going to enjoy working for you. Are you ready for your first assignment? I hope so. I definitely don't want to disappoint you. Your first assignment is to have a seat and tell me about yourself. That's easy talking about myself is my favorite topic.

I'm the oldest of three kids. I have one brother and one sister. I attended Millsap College for six years to get a four-year degree. I attended too many parties that first year.

I understand, that happens to a lot of people their first year. Tell me about your hobbies. Well, I love reading books and listening to music, I don't know what I'd do without either of them. So what's your favorite song? Three times a lady by the commodores. Have you ever heard it? Yes I have, I think everyone has. I hope some day to meet a man that says that to me.

Are you telling me that no one has already? Oh, that's sweet of you to say Rick but unfortunately it hasn't happened yet. I've been struggling with this weight so long, I'm not exactly the shapeliest women in the world and that's what men look at first I'm afraid. You look just fine, don't worry some man is going to look at you someday and know that you are the one. Trust me it will happen

Hello Mr. Naylor's office.

Hi Mercedes don't you sound professional. Well I take my job very serious Miss Kemp. Good for you, now may I speak to Mr. Naylor?

Miss Kemp is on line one. Hello Mr. Naylor, I was just calling to see how Miss Joyner was working out but it seems that you are on first name basis already. It doesn't sound professional though. Don't worry Miss Kemp; I think that she is going to work out just fine. Very well but don't hesitate to call if she doesn't. There is a long line of qualified ladies waiting to be your assistant. I'll keep that in mind. Have a good day Miss Kemp. Please call me Issee, everyone else does. Very well Issee, have a good day, I'll talk to you later.

Mercedes the coffee and Danish rolls were great. I'm heading to the lab now. I'll probably be there most of the day. Here are a few things to keep you busy while I'm gone. Also here's my cell number just in case you need to reach me. Is there anything you need from me before I go? No Rick I don't think so. Alright I'll see you later.

Good morning Candis.

Morning Rick, how are you today?

I'm just fine. Where is Evan and Steven? They are not here yet but they did call. They said they are got caught in traffic. Really...their hotel is only ten blocks from here. That's what I'm thinking but this is New York City. You're right about that.

Well we can't worry about them right now. Is Pat and Trenise here? Yes they are. Good we have a lot of work to do. Let's start where we left off last night. This is going to be another long day.

***

Hello may I speak to Mr. Naylor?
This is he. Who's calling?

Is this a secure line?

Who is this?

I'm sorry but I can't give you my name just yet. Ok, so why are you calling then? I would like to meet with you. I have some very valuable information. What information? I'm afraid to talk about it over the phone. If you could meet me in a secure location I'll tell you everything.

Listen lady, this has been a very hectic week for me and the last thing I need to do is go on a wild goose chase. I do understand Mr. Naylor, really I do. I'll call back next week, maybe you will feel differently then.

Why do I seem to attract the crazy ones? Is that the phone again?

Hello Rick how are you doing? Who is this? It's Marcus; I've got a slight cold. Oh hi Marcus, I didn't recognize your voice at first. Look Rick what are you doing tonight? Nothing really, thing's have been a little rough lately. I've got just the thing to cheer you up old buddy. How does a couple of hot dogs and a couple of beers at the Garden sound? You've got tickets to the game? Yep, interested? You bet I am! What time does it start? The start time is 7:00p.m. In that case I better hurry. Come to gate C-19, I'll be waiting for you but you better hurry I don't want to miss a second of this game. I'm on my way.

How was that lady? That was great. Then give me my twenty bucks. I hope he doesn't really want to see that game.

***

I realize that I'm taking a big chance but this has to be done. What is taking him so long; he should have been here by now. I'm not even sure how he looks but how many men can there be showing up late for a game at gate C-19. I'm just worrying too much; no I'm not worried I'm scared. I've got to stop talking to myself. Hiding in Canada has not been good for me. Where is he?

"This is just great."

A flat tire I can't believe this, these tires are brand new. I guess I won't be making the game after all. No I'll make it; I guess I'll just be even later. What a waste of good tickets but I better call Marcus, so he won't be waiting. Hello this is Marcus, please leave a message. Marcus I have a flat tire but I'll be there as soon as I can. Don't wait for me go enjoy the game.

Well I hope I remember how to change a tire. It's been over ten years since I've done this. I just hope the spare is Ok. First let me take off this jacket. My watch has 7:05pm. It will take me about fifteen minutes to change this tire. That will make it 7:20pm. I'm fifteen minutes from the arena, which puts my arrival roughly 7:35pm, which means the first quarter will be over. Great the spare is ok.

***

Where is he? It's almost 7:30 p.m. I'm about too lose my nerves. I hope I haven't over estimated this man's heart. From what I've been told about him he is the only person that can help me. Are those lights coming this way? Is he driving that black BMW...? Oh that's not a bimmer, that's an Audi; I see he has expensive taste.

I'm shaking like a leaf. Lord please give me strength. I hope I can recognize him from his picture in Manchester's Who's Who. I think that's him all he has to do now is walk toward gate C-19. Here he comes.

Excuse me sir, can you help me? Sure lady what seems to be the problem? It's my car, it won't start. I called AAA thirty minutes ago but they are not here yet. I understand they have always been over rated. Lead the way to your car. I can't promise you that I'll be able to help because I'm not a mechanic.

Oh thank you. My name is Jennifer, hello Jennifer my name is Rick. Are you Rick Naylor? Yes I am. How did you know that? Thank God, Mr. Naylor please don't be upset with me.

My real name is Katherine Levens. What's this all about? Give me a few minutes and I'll explain. I'm waiting. I called you earlier today but you wouldn't talk to me. I thought your voice sounded familiar. What is it you want?

Please I can tell you are starting to get upset. It took a lot of courage for me to do this. I even approached a bum and paid him twenty dollars to get you to come here.

You mean to trick me to come here. Well I'm sorry about that, but after you hear what I have to say I'm sure you'll understand. Start talking Lady.

As I've already said my name is Kathy Levens and until a year ago I was a chemist for WPP. Are you talking about Warrenton Pharmaceutical? Yes I am.

This is starting to get interesting. Go on. I understand that you are the new research manager for BMX and that you have a team of specialist working on a drug called Advernox. You seem to know an awful lot about me lady. Get to what this is about.

Are you aware of the fire that destroyed their lab late last year?

Yes, "I remember reading about that in the paper." It was a terrible tragedy. They lost five of their best chemist in that accident. Two corrections Mr. Naylor, first it wasn't an accident and they only lost four of their chemist. How do you know this?

Because I was there, "I'm the fifth chemist."

You've completely lost me now. What you're saying can't be true. As much as I would like for it to be it just can't. It is true Mr. Naylor. Please trust me; I have no reason to lie to you.

I've been hiding in Canada for the past year. Why haven't you gone to the police? Because he threatened to kill my family if I didn't disappear. Now I'm starting to believe you. Do you know who these people are? I know one of them. Who is he? I don't know his name but I'll never forget his face.

Is there somewhere else that we can talk?

We can go to my apartment.

Is it safe there? I think so. Why do you say that?

Mr. Naylor you have no idea how much trouble you and your team are really in do you? I'm not completely unaware of that Miss Levens. Get me out of here and I'll tell you everything I know. However, it's probably not a good idea for us to go walking into your apartment together.

Let's go, 'we'll talk about it on the way."

You had better get in the back and lie down. We'll be there in twenty-five minutes. When we get there you stay in the car for about twenty minutes. If anyone is watching me they are probably not watching my car unless I'm in it. After twenty minutes you come up to the seventh floor, penthouse number 719. The door will be closed but it will be unlocked. Take the hallway all the way down to the room at the end. That will be my bedroom. Stay in there and be quiet until I get there.

Why do I have to be quiet? I have a temporary roommate. She is part of my team. I'll probably have to distract her until you're safely in my room. Once I've heard what you have to say I'll decide at that time if I want to share what you've told me with her. You just might be the miracle that I've been praying for.

Mr. Naylor please don't get your hopes up about that. Lady we need a miracle and I'm starting to believe you are it. Here take this key. You'll need it to get into the lobby.

You did work on the project didn't you? It wasn't called Advernox then. You don't steal someone's product and keep their name too.

No, "I guess you don't."

I was told that the Warrenton chemists worked with BMX chemists to develop Advernox and that they sold all rights to BMX.

"Well that's a lie."

BMX never worked with us. They stole the formulation for our drug and named it Advernox. This is incredible. What was it called? Once we were sure that we would have to scrap the entire project due to the horrific side effects, we just never decided on a name.

Do you have any proof that there was a drug Miss Levens? No, I'm afraid not. All I have is just my word.

I was there when the theft took place. That's what the fire at the lab was all about.

Are you saying that BMX Pharmaceutical would kill innocent people to get their hands on your drug?

Yes, "that is precisely what I'm saying,' except they have already killed.

Why would they do that?

All you have to do is look at the state of BMX at the time they stole the formulation. I did some research and I found out they were close to bankruptcy. They are almost in the clear now. Just look at the money it has made them since being dumped on the market.

The greedy idiots were not even smart enough or patience enough to complete the final tests on it. They just rushed it to FDA for approval. Well as far as I'm concerned Kathy that's another issue that puzzles me. Why would the FDA approve it, if there was a problem with it?

How do you know that they didn't do the final tests? I know because people are dying. We knew this would happen unless it was reformulated. That's why we had canceled the entire project.

Those bastards at BMX stole it and (sob) killed my friends.

"I'm sorry about your friends Miss Levens." Forgive me for being harsh with you earlier. I believe everything that you are saying. My God we are in trouble. I had a hunch that something wasn't right when they assigned me to this project but nothing like this. "This is incredible news."

We are approaching my apartment just remember what I said. It doesn't look like we were followed but be careful anyway. Remember wait twenty minutes and then come up.

***

Candis, "I'm home." What smells so good?

Hello Rick. What's going on in here Candis? I made you dinner to express my gratitude to you for being so nice to me. Have a seat dinner will be served is a few minutes. Do you mind if I wash my hands first? Of course I don't mind. Washing your hands is always a good idea, especially in your line of work. Can you also get that bottle of wine out the refrigerator? You got wine also? Yes I did. I think you'll like it.

Hey this is Patier'. This stuff is hard to find. Where did you find this? Oh I have my ways. I guess that means none of my business. Well that's not what I meant but I think I like the way it sounded coming from you. Does this mean that you were able to get things straighten out at your bank? Yes that's exactly what it means. That's great; I can't wait to hear about it. That's if you want to talk about it. Sure I do. But I was hoping that you'd let me stay here a little while longer. I'm still nervous about going back to my apartment. As soon as I can I'm moving. I'll never feel safe in that place again.

Like I said you can stay here as long as you like. Thanks Rick, how could I be so wrong about you? I don't know.

Creak. Did you hear that? Here what? It sounded like the front door. I closed the door when I came in. Are you sure you locked it? I'll go check if it'll put your mind at ease.

Would you please?

Sure just stay right here and guard the food, it's the only thing in this apartment worth stealing. I can go with you. No need for that. I'll be right back; you just continue what you're doing.

I checked and everything is secure. I'm sorry; I guess I'm just a little paranoid. I understand anyone who went through what you did has a right to be. Do you mind if we use the table in the dining room? Whatever you want boss, it's your pad. I'm going to my room and change clothes, I'll be right back.

Oh by the way someone has been calling here all day and hanging up. What was the number? It's on the caller ID, it was definitely long distance. I think it started with area code 863. Did you say 863? Yes, you should probably put a block on your phone.

THE ADVERNOX PROJECT

That's not a number that I want to block. How many times did she call? How do you know it was a woman? That's my ex-fiancée's number.

Oh really, well like I said it was all day. I got tired of answering the phone but she didn't get tired of calling. Remind me to check my messages after dinner. OK, I will. I'll go change for dinner now. Don't take to long.

Kathy where are you? I'm in here. What are you doing in the closet? I heard someone coming, so I hid in the closet. How did you hear me? I wasn't making any noise. When you've been hiding as long as I have you hear things that you normally wouldn't. Candis heard the door open. So you have to be very careful, I don't think she's going to buy the old wind theory again.

That food sure does smell good. Are you hungry? No, I'm starving. Well I'm sorry but you'll have to wait until we're finished I'm afraid. Excuse me I need to get my robe. Can you turn around while I put it on? I'll sneak you something in after we're done. Now lock the door when I leave and try to be quiet.

That's a nice robe. Thank you, I like to be comfortable when I'm dining at home. The food smells so good. Does that mean you're finally ready to eat? Yes, "suddenly I'm starving." Well as soon as you bless the food we can began.

Dear heavenly father thank you for this food we are about to receive may it strengthen us spiritually as well as physically, amen.

Amen, that was very nice Rick. Thank you, I've been saying that since I was a kid. All right what would you like first? I'm not sure everything looks so good, just pile it on. Here taste a spoonful of this first.

Hmm that's good.

I thought you'd like that. What is it?

Can't tell you it's a secret family recipe. Come on give it up. I can't do that mister. If I give it to you, you'll just end up fixing it for one of your lady friends. Ha, now that's funny. I don't have any lady friends. Well you just managed to hurt my feeling mister. Don't you consider me your friend Rick? Of course I do but when you said lady friend I thought you meant…well you know what I thought. Yeah, "I'm afraid I do."

Candis are you going to tell me about your day or should I start guessing? Just let me take one more sip of this wine, it taste so good.

Well, the first thing I did was go to the bank this morning. According to them my account had indeed been closed. I almost lost it when they said that. But by some miracle I was able to remain calm. I calmly asked to speak to the manager but it took him so long that I was starting to boil again. By the time he got there I was ready to scream.

After what seemed an eternity, he finally waved for me to come into his office. He reached out his hand to shake mine but his eyes were glued to my breast. After he came back to reality, he smiled a big crooked teeth smile and asked me to have a seat. He said, I'm Mr. Goodwin, how may I help you Candis? There seems to be a problem with my account. Everyone is telling me that my account is closed but I never closed it. Do you have your account number and signature card? Yes I do. Here it is. Give me a moment, I'll be right back. After I had been sitting there about ten minutes he returned with a coke, which he offered me but I said no thanks.

Miss Lockhart on behalf of Greater Chase Bank I want to sincerely apologize to you for this screw up. Apparently some one with an account very similar to yours did close their account on Friday morning.

There must have been some sort of computer glitch, because their account remained open while yours I'm afraid was closed. So has my account been reinstated? "

"Yes it has."

What is my balance?

Here look for yourself. Does that appear to be the correct amount?

"Yes it does."

Do you think I'll have to worry about anything like this happening again? No Candis I give you my word. Well, I'm afraid your words not going to be good enough. I would like to with draw all my money at this time. But Candis I assure you that...

The name is Miss Lockhart and I would appreciate it very much if you gave me my money right now Mr. Goodwin. Very well, let me get someone to assist you.

"It will be just a moment."

***

So did you open an account at another bank? No way, I took that money and put it in the safest place I know of. Where is that? It's under the mattress in the bedroom of your apartment. But Candis (ha, ha) you won't collect any interest that way. I know but I will be able to get to it when I need it. (Ha, ha) I'll drink to that.

Pass the rolls please.

Are these home made Candis?

Yes, Rick they are.

You are going to make some man a happy husband some day. Oh Rick that's the nicest thing that anyone has ever said to me. Well let's drink to that too. (Ha, ha) Ok.

"Oh I'm stuffed."

Candis that was the best meal that I think I have ever had. "I'm glad you enjoyed it." Should we open another bottle of wine? I'd love too but I've got to get to bed. There is a lot of work to be done tomorrow.

We missed you in the lab today. I didn't have any luck today with those stupid Canto Formations but Steven and Evan were really excited at the beginning of the day. They said that they finally had something to report, however, I stared into the microscope for nearly twenty minutes and nothing happened. They were very disappointed. So they're hoping to show it to us tomorrow.

What is it that they want you to see? They said they weren't sure about it themselves. I'm pretty excited about whatever it is. It will be refreshing to see anything.

"I agree with you boss."

Stop calling me boss. Ok Rick, I'll do these dishes and take a shower so I can hit the hay myself.

Don't worry about the dishes, "I'll do them."

Are you sure?

It's the least I can do. Alright, you'll get no argument from me. Thanks again for everything Rick. You're welcome. Hey have you talked to your parents lately? Actually I had just got off the phone with my mom when you came. She sounded a little tired. I wish I could make a quick trip to see them. Then why don't you? But you just said that I was really missed today in the lab. Go see your parents; you'll probably be able to focus better when you get back. Take your notes with you. Are you sure about this? Yes I am.

Rick I'm confused, didn't you say it wasn't a good idea to be around our family with these lunatics out there. I know what I said but I'm thinking about going to see my kids in a couple of days and it's not a good idea for both of us to be gone at the same time.

Alright you've talked me into it. I'll call the airline right now and see if I can get a flight out first thing tomorrow morning, that way I can be back by Monday afternoon, if that's Ok. That will be fine. Do you want to finish off the last of this wine? No thanks. Fine, I'm not going to beg you. I'll just take it with me to my bedroom while I call the airline.

***

Are you finished with the dishes already? Yep and I put the left overs in the refrigerator, so you should have plenty to eat tomorrow. Thank you but it won't be as much fun without you.

That's a nice thing to say Rick, thank you. I got a flight but it's very early, can you give me a lift to the airport? Sure, what time, said Rick? It leaves at 7:45am but I have to be there no later than 6:00am.

That's fine I need to get to the office early any way. Thanks Rick, I'm going to take my shower now. "I'll see you in the morning." Ok, Candis good night and don't forget to set your alarm. Are you Ok Candis; you look like you are having a little difficulty walking. I'm fine Rick just point me toward the bedroom.

***

Here you go Kathy, "I'm sorry that it took so long."

No need to apologize Mr. Naylor I understand. It sounded like you and your girlfriend was having too good of a time to be worrying about little old me. She's not my girlfriend.

She was just showing her appreciation for me letting her stay here the last couple of days. If you don't mind I'll stay here while you eat. Sure that's fine, said Kathy.

What are you thinking about Mr. Naylor? Please it's Rick, remember. I was just thinking about sleeping arrangements for tonight. Please don't take this the wrong way. I know it's your home but I sleep alone.

Why don't you sleep in the room with Candis? I've told you it's not like that.

Sure it's not, "that's why you just had that great dinner together." I bet you probably had wine too, didn't you? Well.... yes we did but.... What is she doing now, said Kathy? She's taking a shower...

You're going to let her take a shower alone after drinking. Maybe you're right about that. I'll check on her after you finish your food. No Mr. Naylor, I think you should go check on her now! Besides, "I don't like being rushed when I eat." Ok but I wasn't rushing you, "I'll be right back."

***

Candis are you Ok in there? Candis, I'm coming in, I hope you're decent.

Where are you? Are you in the shower?

Oh my God Candis!

Get up. What are you doing on the shower floor? Let me help you to bed. What happened, said Rick? I don't know but I've got a pretty good idea that it had something to do with that wine, said Candis.

I'm sorry Candis I don't know what I was thinking; I shouldn't have let you go into the shower alone after drinking. So you would have come in there with me if I had asked? Candis you've obviously have had too much to drink. Come on let me help you to bed.

Rick will you lay down in bed with me? I don't think that's a good idea Candis. What's wrong, don't you like me? Sure I do but you're drunk. I am not said Candis! Can you just get in bed and hold me. I better find you something to sleep in first. I don't sleep with anything on. Oh I see. Well at least let me get you something to dry off with.

No...get in this bed right now mister, I know if you leave this room you won't be coming back. Alright then, just remember this was your idea, said Rick. I'll remember, said Candis. I can't believe this is happening. Will you hand me a pillow? Candis please hand me a pillow. Are you sleep Candis? You are sleep and you're snoring. This is just great; I never pictured you as a snorer.

I better cover you up. I don't know which is worst, your snoring or that fact that seeing you naked has me aroused beyond belief. How am I supposed to sleep now?

***

Good morning Rick.

Wait a minute! What are you doing in here? Did you sleep in here?

Yes, I did Candis. Why? You asked me to. Did we do anything, said Candis? No, I'm afraid not, said Rick. You were a little drunk last night Candis, so as much as I wanted to, I couldn't.

Thank you Rick, I don't remember a thing about last night. I wish I didn't remember anything said Rick. What does that mean Rick? It means that I saw you naked Candis. I'm sorry Rick, I'm sure that must have been a terrible thing for you to witness. I disagree with you strongly on that issue Candis. You are so kind Mr. Naylor.

***

So how do you feel Candis? I have a slight headache. Let me get you some aspirins, said Rick. I never touch those things. I just meditate it away, said Candis. Are you sure you don't remember anything about last night? I don't remember a thing and I'm afraid to ask but go ahead and tell me any way. Well Candis it was a pretty strange night from the minute I came home. What happened?

Well for starters you cooked me dinner and it was a terrific. Also there was wine chilling if the fridge. You can only imagine what was going through my head. I can't imagine what was going through your head, Mr. Naylor, so you'll just have to enlighten me.

Well normally dinner and wine means someone is heading to bed and I don't mean for a nap.

I was only trying to thank you for being so nice to me, said Candis. I had been so mean to you and I wanted to make it up to you but not by having sex.

Why do men always think it's about sex? Never mind don't answer that, said Candis. Just for the record Mr. Naylor the next time I make love to a man, it will be after we have said our vows. I see...said Rick. Now would you be kind enough to continue with the story about last night.

Certainly Miss Lockhart, we had dinner and some wine. We finished off one bottle and was about to start on the next but I decided that I shouldn't because I had a busy day the following day. Then I kissed you on the cheek, thanked you for a wonderful dinner and went to my room. Then you took a shower and went to sleep.

What's so strange about that?

Well you went to sleep on the floor of the shower.

I did what!

Oh this is so embarrassing. How much did I have to drink? I'm so embarrassed, said Candis. So, how did I get to bed? I carried you, said Rick. All right but that still doesn't explain how you ended up in my bed this morning. Well technically Candis it's my bed. You know what I mean.

So you carry me to bed? Yes I did. How long was I in the shower? I'm not sure, it had to be less than ten minutes from the time we finished dinner to the time I found you. I'm confused about something Rick. What is it Candis? Why were you in the shower, in the first place? Good question let's just say that I had a hunch that I needed to check on you. I knocked on the door and called your name several times but you didn't answer. I got worried and went into the room. I didn't see you in the bed so I checked the shower and there you were lying on the floor with the water running. Really, I don't remember any of it. I just wonder what would have happened to me if you hadn't been there.

Listen pretty lady things have been very stressful for both of us lately and last night thanks to you we were able to relax a little. Yeah but I relaxed just a little too much, wouldn't you say? Oh forget it, besides like I said dinner was great.

***

What time are you leaving? Leaving for where? You really don't remember anything about last night do you? You are going to see your parents today. I'll drive you to the airport when you're ready. Is it just my imagination or are you trying to get rid of me? Trust me after last night the last thing on my mind is getting rid of you. So something did happen between us. For the last time nothing happened but it was nice to hold you in my arms while you slept.

So you are telling me that we slept in the same bed, I slept in your arms, I was naked and nothing happened. That's right. Are you gay Mr. Naylor? Hell no, I'm not gay! I just didn't want to take advantage of you while you were drunk, said Rick.

That would not have stopped most men I know. Well, "I'm not those men."

Just one more question Mr. Naylor.

"I'm listening."

Did I ask you to sleep with me? Well…yes you did. Your exact words were Rick will you stay with me? You went on to say please don't make me beg, I thought you wanted me and finally get in this bed and hold me. I think I've heard enough.

Can you close your eyes? I need to go to the bathroom. Go right ahead Candis. I won't see anything that I haven't already seen. Mr. Naylor its one thing for you to see me when I'm drunk, naked and oblivious to my surroundings but it's a different ball game when I'm sober.

I think it's time for me to go to my room Candis.

Good I'm going to try that shower thing again. I'll try to be out in less than ten minutes. If I'm not, please come get me again. You're upset with me aren't you? Maybe I am just a little Rick. Why are you mad at me, I didn't do anything. Maybe that's why I'm mad, said Candis. What…but you just said…? I know what I said man.

***

Come in, said Kathy. Good morning how did you sleep? It's the first time in a long time that I had a good night rest Mr. Naylor. I'm glad to hear that Kathy. How is your girlfriend this morning? She is not my girlfriend.

I seem to recall you telling me that you'd be right back, that was about nine hours ago? Well let's just say that you were right about it not being wise for her to take a shower after drinking. I went in there and found her on the floor of the shower.

Candis is leaving this morning to go visit her parents for a couple of days. We will be free to talk after she's gone. I'll fix us some breakfast while she's taking a shower. She's taking another shower? I guess things went well last night.

I'm making breakfast do you want any? Sure whatever you can sneak in will be fine but I'm really hungry, so could you hurry. Lady you've never tasted my cooking you might not want me too hurry. I'm sure it will be fine.

Rick one more thing, could you run down stairs and get the morning paper. Will there be anything else Kathy? No, breakfast and a paper, what more could a girl ask for, except maybe what you gave your girlfriend last night. You are hopeless aren't you? I wouldn't say that, said Kathy. Well it seems to me that once you get an idea in your head, it stays there, said Rick. Would you please go make the breakfast Rick? "I really am starving."

***

Candis do you want some breakfast, said Rick? No thanks, I'll just grab something at the airport, maybe by then I can keep something on my stomach. I'll be ready to go in a few minutes but we have to hurry, if I miss this plane I'll have to wait until late tonight or tomorrow morning to get another one. Don't worry we'll get you there on time, said Rick.

Wow, Candis you have a lot of bags. Are you coming back? I'm not taking all of them Rick. I was hoping that we could drop these two off at my apartment. It's kind of on the way. I thought you had to leave in thirty minutes, said Rick. I added in time for the stop at my apartment, I'm afraid to go there alone, said Candis. I understand, so exactly how much time do we have?

The plane leaves in two hours, it takes about twenty minutes to get from here to my apartment at this time of the morning and about thirty minutes to get to the airport from there. Add the check in time and we are running about five minutes late. In that case we had better go. Just let me get something out of my bedroom and we'll be on our way.

***

Mr. Naylor, I'm impressed, this is a beautiful Audi and it's so big. Can I drive it? Have you ever driven a 400 horse power German sports sedan before Candis? No but how hard could it be? Ok but this is my baby, you get one scratch on her and we've got problems. My goodness, Rick, you really do need a woman don't you. Here are the keys; the first thing that you need to know is Ahhhh…

Sorry Rick, I had no idea it was so fast. Just slow down, before you kill us!

***

Mr. Barrows, it appears that Miss Lockhart is heading to the airport. Is she alone? No, Mr. Naylor is with her. How do you know she's the only one catching a flight? Because all the luggage looks like a lady's luggage. I'm following them now but it doesn't look like they are heading to the airport. Well don't lose them.

CHAPTER 10

Well Kathy, I see you have made yourself at home. Are you ready to talk? Yes, I'm ready, I think, said Kathy. Rick can you promise me that whatever happens in the next several weeks that you will make them pay for what they did to my friends. I can't promise that Kathy after all I'm not the law. I realize that Rick but after I tell you my story you will have the power to make things happen. I promise you Kathy that I will do what I can.

After I tell you this story, I'll probably have to disappear again. I'm sorry that you feel that way Kathy, I guess these people really have you scared don't they. Yes they do. I have so much to say but I'm not sure where I should start. Why don't you start with the murders at the lab? I'll try but it's still painful. I understand it must be a hard thing to remember. Please take all the time you need.

***

We were about to end for the day when these two men burst through the door and told us to get on the floor. We were so startled that they had to tell us again. After that everything started to move very fast. Before I knew it, two people were dead. Did they say what they wanted? No, they were just yelling and throwing people around.

How did you manage to escape? I guess I owe it mostly to Henry, he was our chief chemist, while all this was going on he was in the bathroom. When he flushed the toilet it startled the two men and one of them went to the bathroom. A few seconds later Henry was dead. During the brief struggle in the bathroom I managed to hide in a cabinet.

They didn't notice that you were missing? No, like I said it had gotten very hectic. What did the man in charge look like? He was a white man probably in his late fifties. He was mean and walked with a slight limp.

After they shot Henry, Lilly Cantrell started screaming and pleading with them not to kill her, I have three little girls, please don't kill me, I'll do anything you say just please don't kill me, pleaded poor Lilly.

This unfortunately only seemed to make the little man more furious. He told her to shut up, but I don't think she heard him because she had completely lost it. Not only was Henry a very good friend of hers that were rumored to be lovers. Any way she would not shut up so the little man picked her up off the floor and started choking her.

I remember thinking how can someone so little be so strong? His choking her did no good. She was still able to get out the words please don't kill me.

He then took out his knife and looked her straight in the eyes and (sob) slit her throat. Are you kidding me?

I wish I were, said Kathy. Lilly let out one last scream before her body went limp as she fell to the floor. She lay there like a (sob) rag doll. It took everything in me not to scream to the top of my lungs.

What an amazing story! I haven't even gotten to the amazing part yet, said Kathy. After they had killed everyone the little guy told his partner to go to the truck and get the explosives and an ax.

While he was gone the little man started crying, he got on his knees and prayed to God that he never allow him to kill another person.

I was so shocked by the sincerity of his pray that I accidentally knocked over a glass and it crashed to the floor. He didn't seem too startled. He got on his feet and walked over to where I was and snatched open the cabinet door.

He was pointing the gun directly at my face and his hands were trembling very badly. It was like he wanted to pull the trigger but he couldn't. He seemed only mildly shocked to find me there.

He calmly said, so there you are. I was afraid that I had miss counted. I thought there were suppose to be five of you. Please come out from your little hiding place he said.

What is your name he asked?

"I was too scared to say anything."

He then said, "you must be Katherine Levens." I nodded in agreement. If I were you Miss Levens, I'd leave the country before nightfall. If you ever come back, I will kill every member of your family. I would not try to contact anyone by phone either. Do you understand?

I was too terrified to speak, so I nodded my head again. What did his partner think about him letting you go? I don't know, I took off running as fast as my short legs would carry me. I never saw his partner again.

***

Kathy shhh…. I think someone's at the door. I'll go see who it is. Oh shit, it's Mr. Davis. Quick hide in here and don't make a sound.

Mr. Naylor open the damn door!

What do you want?

Let me in. Looks like I caught you in your little jimmies. What do you want? I was about to take a shower and go to bed.

Where is my new information? I don't have any new information. There hasn't been any new development since my last report. You and that team of yours had better get off your asses and deal with this problem.

I need results; I don't know how many times I'm going to have to say that before you get it. I'll give you what I have but it's not much. Wait here and I'll go get it, it's in my bedroom.

Do you mind if I accompany you? Sure whatever makes you happy I don't have anything to hide.

Here you go, Mr. Davis. This doesn't seem like much, Mr. Naylor. Isn't that what I just told you? I need more, this isn't anything. I'll be back at the end of the week I'll expect something more concrete by then.

You can have this back; it's not worth the paper it's written on. Before I forget I have some more pictures for you.

Keep your got damn pictures! I don't want or need them.

You better watch you language boy! Don't you ever raise your voice at me again. Now take your damn pictures. You really must see them. I'll show myself out. These are some pretty impressive locks on your door. Are they new?

***

Kathy you can come out now. I said you can come out now. Where are you? Kathy! Did you just disappear into thin air? I only left the room for a minute and she couldn't have walked out of here with Davis and his lesbian bodyguards posted at the door. So where is she?

Was that the phone? Hello.... Hi Rick...

Kathy where are you?

I'm sorry for leaving like that but that man's voice sounded very familiar and I wasn't going to stick around to see what he wanted. How did you get out of here without being seen?

Rick I've been hiding for over a year now. I've become very good at not being seen when I don't want too. When are you coming back, said Rick? I'm not, said Kathy. Why not? I've just got a bad feeling that they are watching you too close and I don't want to get caught up in it.

Just tell me where you are and I'll come get you. You don't have to come back here. I'll get you a hotel or something. I can't tell you where I am. Besides, it's probably best if I just disappear again.

Don't do that Kathy! We need you.

Remember you said that you had information that could help us with the reformulation. Do you even have money for food? I'll be just fine, said Kathy. Don't worry about me Rick. You have enough to worry about. I have to go now but I'll contact you when I'm somewhere safe. Goodbye Rick and good luck. Don't hang up Kathy. Kathy.....

***

For your sake you better hope you convinced him, said Mr. Davis.

What are you going to do with me?

I haven't decided yet but I can promise you I'll do a better job than Cliff Miller did. You should have stayed in Canada. It would have been better for everyone, especially you. How did you know where I was? Nothing goes on in that apartment that I don't know about. So it is bugged. That's not the least of it.

Lillie put her in the trunk, said Mr. Davis.

Please don't put me in there, said Kathy. Don't worry your pretty little red head, if he wanted to kill you, you'd be dead already. Yeah carrot top just take small breaths and you should be Ok, (ha, ha). Now get in!

***

Rick my flight was delayed, so I'll be about an hour late getting to work. How was your trip Candis? It was nice. My dad told me that some gentleman from the New York area called claiming to be an old friend of mine but he wasn't sure the guy was telling the truth, other than that he seemed like a nice person. Did you tell him who I am? Yes, I said that you were a dear friend and I couldn't wait to call you back.

Rick one more thing. I'm sorry; I can't believe I forgot this. The day before I left you got a call from someone named Stacey. She called several times and she seemed pissed that I was there.

How could you forget to give me a message from a pissed off woman? Who is she, said Candis? She's my ex-fiancée but it's been over now for a couple months.

A couple of months is that all? I hate to tell you this Mr. Naylor but it's not over until she says it's over. I think you had better call her. I will call her and I hope you got plenty of rest, said Rick; we need to put in a lot of hours this week. I'm ready Rick.

Hello Rick, hello Steven, how are you? I'm fine. Well you look like shit Steven. I'll be fine once I get some coffee in me. Where's Evan, said Rick? He's at the coffee machine. If you think I look bad wait until you see him.

Good morning Rick, hello Evan, what the heck happened to you? Nothing, I just haven't had much sleep. What did you guys do last night? Never mind but I bet it had something to do with blondes. Not me but that does sound like Steven's typical weeknight. Well at least I have a good excuse for looking the way I do Evan. What's yours?

Let's just drop it. Good idea gentleman...we have a lot of work to do this week and I expect each of you to put in some extra hours even if it means sleeping here.

Where is Candis, said Steven? She went to visit her parents and her flight got delayed on her return. Speaking of delays, have you laid that yet Rick?

What did you say Evan? I expect that kind of question from Steven but not from you. Come on Rick your secret is safe with us, my friend. There is something's going on between the two of you, it's so obvious.

Why are you looking at me Rick? Evan is the one that asked the question. I know that but you want to know the answer as bad as he does don't you? Hey that's your business; it has nothing to do with me, said Steven.

It's becoming clear to me that you both have been concentrating on the wrong thing. No wonder we can't solve this damn formulation problem, said Rick.

Steven do you think you can stay out of the bars for the next four days? Sure Rick, not a problem. I'll hold you to that. Evan whatever you have planned for this week put it on hold. We have too much to do. Do I make myself clear? Sure Rick we understand. Good now let's get to work gentlemen and you had better have something to report at the end of the day.

Do I make myself clear?

Yes Rick…crystal clear.

Good and by the way the answer to your question is no. I'm not banging Miss Lockhart. Now close the door on your way out gentlemen.

***

So Evan how did it go Friday night? How did what go?

Don't you remember? You threaten to take my life if I didn't get you to the lab at warp speed. Oh that, it was just a hunch that didn't pan out. Really but you seemed so sure. Like I said Steven it was a hunch that didn't pan out, now drop it!

Evan I'm tired of staring at these same formulations. Nothing has changed in three weeks and I doubt anything will change in the next three weeks. I agree Steven but we have to keep looking. Forget that man, let's quit early and go have a drink at that nice little bar on 17th Street. That sounds great Steven but Rick would have a fit if he knew we left early.

Where were you this morning when he said he wanted us to put in over time on this project? Just how pissed off are you trying to make the man.

"You worry to much my friend."

He has his head so far up Candis's skirt that he can't see straight, let alone keep tabs on us.

That may be true but you know either of us would gladly take his place, said Steven. You are wrong again my friend. I admit she is a beautiful woman but she has a nasty mouth, said Evan. She's too much of a witch for my taste, also said Steven.

Well…there you have it, "finally something that we both agree on."

***

Well you can sit here and stare into that thing all night if you want too but I'm leaving, said Steven. Where are you going? Any where but here, I was thinking about that gentleman's club down town.

Have fun, I'll see you tomorrow but Rick's not going to like you ditching work to go gawk at naked women. You mean you're really not coming? No, I'm not but hey more blondes for you right.

Fine Evan stay here all night, I'm shutting this thing down right now...hey what the heck was that, said Steven! There it is again. Hey come over here Evan, "you've got to see this."

What is it?

It's that same formation that we saw before only it's different this time.

"Just come see for yourself." Look into the microscope and don't take your eyes away. Do you see it? I don't see anything Steven. Wait a minute, I do see something. Now it's gone. What was that? I'm not sure Evan but I have an idea.

Evan bring the high-resolution scope over here. Where did it go? Just keep looking, said Steven, it'll be back, it always comes back. There it is, said Evan! Focus on the cell formation on the left Evan.

Steven, "this is unbelievable."

How long have you known about this?

"Only about a week now."

Why haven't you said anything? Because I've only seen it twice before tonight and I didn't think anyone would believe me unless they saw it for themselves. Well.... congratulations my friend, we finally have something to show Rick.

Not so fast Evan, you just saw it with your own eyes and the first thing out of your mouth was I don't believe it. So how are we going to convince Rick if we can't show it to him when it happens? We have already tried to show him once and it was a failure. I will not look like an idiot before Rick again.

We probably won't see it again for days. It disappears for a couple of days and then it comes back for just a few minutes and it's gone again. It was pure luck that it happened tonight. If it had been a few seconds later, I'd be half way to the bar by now. I haven't been able to pin point when this happens.

Well I think instead of running to some stupid bar tonight this is what we should be focusing on. I couldn't agree with you more Evan; however before we bring this to any ones attention will have to pinpoint when it happens. But Steven this is the break that we've been waiting for.

We should tell Candis and Rick, four heads might be able to figure this out quicker than two; maybe the four of us can set up shifts around the clock and wait for this phenomenon to happen again.

No Evan! I'm not ready to show this to them yet. Let's just say it's a way of giving them a dose of their own medicine.

What do you mean? I've got a hunch that they are hiding something from us. Why would they do that? Because they are bloody Americans, said Steven. History has shown that all they care about is the glory. That's why they put so much stock in sports. Take sports from that country and what would they do with themselves?

I'm sorry Steven but that is probably the stupidest reason I've ever heard. We should report these finding immediately!

That's exactly why your country is in the shape that it is today Evan. You like your countrymen don't know how to take advantage of a good thing when it's staring you in the face.

You listen to me my friend. My country is full of God fearing people who abide by the law and help each other through hard times. So until you learn more about the people of my country, I'd appreciate it if you keep your lame comments to yourself.

That was very touching Evan but I live in the real world, where real people have to make real decisions and some are a lot tougher than others. So I really don't give a rat's ass about how you feel about me at this moment.

Very well then Steven, it's starting to become obvious to me that you had a hidden agenda all along.

"I'm highly disappointed in you my friend."

Will you please stop saying that! It's driving me crazy!

Stop saying what?

"My Friend" you call the bartender, my friend, you call Rick my friend. You call every freaking person you meet, my friend. Well guess what Evan everyone is not you freaking friend and it's time that you realized that. Now hear this, "my friend," I'm not reporting a damn thing to Rick or anyone else until I'm ready!

You have three days, "my friend", and then I go to Rick!

CHAPTER 11

Rick you have an emergency call on line one, said Mercedes. Thanks Mercedes. Hello...hello is this Rick? Yes Miss Carter it's me.

Son please come quick its Stacey, she's been shot.

Oh my God. Is she Ok Miss Carter?

What happened? Where is she? Can I talk to her?

Now calm down son, I'm afraid you can't talk to her, no one can Rick. She's still in surgery.

Dear God, what happened Mrs. Carter?

That Shorty fellow came by again. I should have known he'd be involved. We were eating dinner when he came by. Just so you know son she only went out with him that one time. She realized that it was a mistake; she was just confused, missing you and all.

She had asked him not to come by anymore but he wouldn't take no for an answer. Today he was drunk. When Stacey answered the door she told him that he couldn't come in. He grabbed her by the arm and pulled her outside under the tree.

Then everything happened so fast. He was shouting at the top of his lungs, begging her to give him another chance but she said no and started walking back to the house. That's when I heard gunshots and saw my (sob) baby fall to the ground.

He shot her, said Rick!

No, there was a blue car parked near the maple tree at the corner, that's where the shots came from I think. You mean a drive by? The police say it was drug related. I'm sure it was Mrs. Carter.

They killed Shorty and now my baby is (sob) fighting for her life. How long have they been in surgery? I don't know Rick, "it's been at least an hour." They have removed one bullet but the other one is close to her spinal cord.

"Oh my God!"

The doctors say she may never (sob) walk again. Oh dear God, "I'll be there as soon as I can Mrs. Carter." Is it St. Johns hospital? No, it's Memphis General. Please hurry son, "she needs you."

***

Hello Candis. Hi Rick what's up?

I'm going to be catching a flight to Memphis in a couple of hours. I'm going to leave you in charge until I get back. What's wrong Rick? You sound agitated.

Stacey was shot today and it's not looking good.

Oh Rick I'm so sorry. What happened?

I'm sorry Candis; I can't go into that right now, I'll have to tell you later.

Can I count on you to take care of things until I get back?

Sure but why me?

Because I don't think I have to worry about you sitting around in a bar all night getting drunk and trying to pick up blondes.

"Is that the only reason Rick?"

No there are several but I can't go into that right now. Let's just say you are the most qualified and I trust you.

Ok Rick, "I'll do it."

Good, I have some information that I need to drop off on my way.

Why don't I take you, that way you don't have to pay those outrageous airport-parking fees.

Are you sure you can get me there on time?

Sure, I can pick you up in thirty minutes.

Ok thanks Candis, that'll give me enough time to take a shower. Just come on up when you get here, the door will be open.

***

Hello.... hi William, it's Rick. I'm catching a flight to Memphis tonight. What for, said William. Stacey's was shot today. Stacey...hmm why does that name sound familiar? Oh I remember now, she's your fiancée.

Is it serious Rick?

Yes it is William; she's been in surgery for an hour already. They have to remove two bullets; one is very close to her spinal cord. I'm sorry Rick that is serious. Who are you leaving in charge?

Candis...I mean Miss Lockhart.

You better watch out for her she might not want to give it up when you get back. Maybe she shouldn't have too, said Rick. What does that mean? Let's just say that she's not as bad as people are making her out to be.

Rick, I'm sure she knows how important this project is.

Don't worry William if any one knows how important this project is, it's her. My assistant will be delivering a report to you first thing tomorrow morning.

How long will you be gone?

I'm not sure right now but I'll be in touch.

I don't want too sound insensitive but I need you back here as soon as possible.

I know that William.

Good...I hope your friend is Ok.

Thanks William, "you're not as bad as people say either."

***

Here's your gate.

Rick, I know we haven't always seen eye to eye but I do respect you.

Thank you for saying that.

Can you call me when you land?

I sure will Candis.

I hope your fiancée is ok.

We are no longer engaged. I told you that she gave me back the ring. That doesn't matter right now, you'll see. She's a lucky woman to have you in her life Rick. Now give me a hug before you go.

Thanks Candis; I needed that but why are you being so nice to me?

You should try to get some rest while you're on the plane.

I'll try.

Cheer up Rick and don't worry, "she'll be just fine."

***

I get on the plane and my only thought is the embrace that Candis and I just shared. It has been almost six months since I've held a woman in my arms. At a time like this I should only be thinking about Stacey but its hard not too think about that hug.

When I find my seat I collapse in it and immediately fall asleep. I dream that the three of us are walking down the isle. At the end of the isle is a minister. The church is crowded with people I've never seen before. Cameras are flashing all around us. Candis is on my right arm and Stacey is on my left arm. Just as we approach the minister Stacey stumbles and falls. I bend down to help her up and notice that her legs are missing. She cries out, Rick please help me I can't move. I stand there in shock as Candis whispers in my ear," leave her you belong to me now". She then pulls me toward the minister.

I look back over my shoulders unable to turn and go help her. I see two men in blue suits snatch her body up and rush out the door with her but they forget to take her legs. Then her legs slowly get up and wobble down the aisle behind them.

I start screaming but no one seems to hear me. The minister is speaking but his voice sounds like a woman's voice. When I finally understand what he is saying, he's asking me if I would like a glass of water. I turn and look at Candis and she's suddenly wearing a stewardess's uniform. She whispers would you like a glass of water Rick? I look back at the minister and he says take the water son it will cleanse you of your sins. You know it's your fault the young lady's legs fell off. Drink the water and you will be forgiven. I start screaming again.

***

I hear another voice saying, wake up sir, wake up sir, we are about to land. Please bring your seat to the upright position. I look around me and notice people staring at me. Someone has placed a blanket on me. I guess it was one of the stewardesses. Another stewardess walks toward me with a glass of water and a concerned look on her face. I take the water and quickly drink it.

Would you like another sir, she says?

Yes I would.

Ok, I'll be right back. Here you go sir.

Thank you.

That was some nightmare you were having.

You could tell I was having a nightmare?

We all could sir. Who is Stacey?

She's my fiancée. Well…. who is Candis? She's just a co-worker.

I see…. Well, I hope you enjoyed your flight.

***

I waited until almost everyone had left the plane before I moved. I could feel their eyes on me as they slowly walked pass my seat. I'm afraid to think what that dream meant. As I approached the rental car counter I called Mrs. Carter.

How's Stacey? She's out of surgery; they were able to get both bullets out. She's in recovery right now. Good I'm so glad to hear that. Have the said anything else? If you mean can she walk, they say it's too soon to tell. They gave her medication for the pain. She'll sleep for hours. Let's just be thankful for one blessing at a time. Yes indeed Miss Carter, you are right about that. I should be there in about an hour. Here comes that police officer again. He asks so many questions. I'll talk to you later son.

***

Candis I arrived safely. How was your flight Rick? I slept through the whole flight. Good you needed the rest. Well, it wasn't a peaceful sleep. Please remind me to tell you about it when I get back. Ok I will.

Where will you be staying? That depends on how Stacey is doing. I'll either be at the hospital or at her mom's house. Well I'll just call you on your cell if I need you. Cell phones aren't allowed in the hospitals Candis.

Oh I guess I didn't know that. Fortunately for me I haven't had to visit one. You are very fortunate Candis. You can call the hospital and have me paged. It's Memphis General.

Have you had a chance to go over any of the information that I left you? I'm going over it right now. I'll call you later tonight and you can tell me what you think. I can tell you now that William's probably not going to be happy with it, said Rick.

My assistant is delivering a copy of it to him tomorrow. Don't be surprised if he wants to talk it over with you. Don't you think he'll want to wait until you get back? No William Winters is a man that acts right away, unfortunately most of the time he over reacts and he loves meetings.

I'm at the rental counter now, I'll talk to you later. Rick, there is just one more thing before you go. I feel awful for even mentioning this right now but I really enjoyed that hug.

Rick...did you hear what I said?

Yes, "I heard you." I have to go Candis.

***

Everyone have a seat. I've been reading Rick's report and I must say that I'm very disappointed in the team's progress up to this point. I realized that this was going to be a difficult assignment that's why we selected you. Is there anything at all that I can do to help you?

Mr. Winters we have gone over the formulations a thousand times and we can't find anything wrong with Advernox. We've tested the active ingredients and they check out. We've tested the inactive ingredients and they check out. At this point the only thing that makes sense is that nothing makes sense.

Are you sure that there is a problem with this drug, said Candis?

Yes I'm sure that there is a problem, said William.

When Rick returns I'm going to suggest that we consider reformulating. Not so fast Candis. That is not an option, said William. Advernox only works in its current form and I'm sure Rick will agree with me or I've chosen the wrong man to lead this team.

Can I at least explain why I feel this way? I don't guess that can hurt, go ahead and enlighten me.

It appears that in its current form Advernox only affects women negatively in their third or fourth month of pregnancy. It is because of this that I feel that reformulation is the key.

I have to agree with her on this William because without case studies to compare with our findings we are like blind men being led by other blind men. Why do you say that Evan?

Mr. Winters what we have found and agreed upon is that there is something similar in the genetic make up of every woman that is key here. Reformulating is not only the best thing to do it's also the smartest.

What about you Steven?

I haven't heard from you yet.

Mr. Winters, if Advernox is not reformulated then we are going to have to consider one of two things; either admit to the public that there is a problem or figure out the mystery of the fourth trimester and for that sir you will need an Army of specialists. Well I don't have an army so you guys will have to do

***

Hi, my name is Rick Naylor. I reserved a black Audi A8L sedan.

May I see some I.D. sir?

New York City huh? What's got you down here with us country folks?

I just recently moved to New York.

I'm originally from this part of the country.

Have you hooked up with one of those East Coast women yet?

Huh...no I haven't.

What's wrong with those women up there? A good-looking man like you wouldn't last five minutes in this town without being swept away by some fine ass sista. Shucks, if I wasn't married, "I'd give you a shot myself". I'll make you trade in that damn Big Apple for some of Mildred's southern fried chicken.

Do you talk to everyone like this?

Hell no, I'd lose my job if I did that. You're just so fine a sista kind of lost her mind for a few seconds. Watch out for us southern women mister, we take what we want.

I'll keep that in mind.

Here's your I.D. honey and here are the keys to that fine ride. It's a beautiful car and you will make it look even better. Don't forget sir, an apple is just a snack but my southern fried chicken is a meal. The next time you come back this way, holla at a sista, I'll hook you up with some. It'll make you forget all about that damn Big Apple.

Thanks Mildred, "I'll remember that."

***

Mom...

I'm right here sweetheart.

Where am I? What's going on, I can't see.

You are at Memphis General Hospital and the doctor

has wrapped your eyes. Why did he do that? Don't you worry yourself about that honey. They told me to get the nurse as soon as you woke up.

"I'll be right back."

Nurse Kimberly, my daughter is awake.

I'll be right there Mrs. Carter.

Stacey, I'm back and the nurse is on her way.

Mom what happened? You don't remember honey? I remember Shorty pulling me outside under the tree and a lot of shouting. I told him that I never wanted to see him again.

Well honey you don't….. What else do you remember?

I was walking toward the house when I felt a sharp pain in my back and then everything went black. Then I woke up here.

Mom I want Rick. Can you please call Rick for me? I really need to see him. Honey Rick has been right here at your bedside all night. It's funny that as soon as he leaves the room you wake up. He just stepped out to make a phone call. I'm sure he'll be right back.

**

Stacy you're awake. Thank you Jesus, said Rick. Come here mister, I'm surprised you were able to tear yourself away from the big city. Stacey nothing would have kept me away from you. Same old Rick, always know what to say don't you but how can I be sure that it's really you? I know it sounds like you but I have these bandages on my eyes and I can't be sure unless you come over here and give me a kiss. It will be my pleasure.

Should I leave the room said Mrs. Carter?

Excuse me sir but we are about to remove the bandages we'll need you to step outside. No please can't he stay? I need him and my mom to be here.

It's up to the doctor, said Kimberly. What do you think doctor?

I think we can make an exception this time.

Hello Miss Carter, I'm Doctor Grant. Hello doctor how are you, said Stacey? I'm just fine; you are a very lucky young lady. You gave us all quite a scare.

Now listen to me very carefully. We removed two bullets from your back. One of those bullets was very close to your spinal cord. This could have affected you in two very important ways. One is your sight and the other is your legs.

Is that why I can't feel my legs?

Yes I'm afraid so but we'll discuss that later.

Now the first thing that we are going to do is remove the bandages from your eyes. Once this has been done I need you to keep your eyes closed, count to ten and then slowly open them. It's very important that you follow my instructions precisely.

"Can you do that Stacey?"

Yes doctor, keep my eyes closed, count to ten and then slowly open my eyes.

That's right...are you ready?

Yes doctor...I'm ready.

Kimberly please hand me the scissors. Ok Miss Carter... slowly open your eyes.

Mom...I'm right here honey.

Please do me a big favor. What is it honey?

Clean that ketchup stain off Rick's' tie. Honey Rick's not wearing a tie. I know I'm looking right at him but there is a tie on that chair in the corner over there.

You can see that, I can't even see that.

She's right Mrs. Carter, I had a hamburger and I did get some ketchup and mustard on my tie.

Oh thank you Jesus, "my baby can see."

Yes praise the Lord, said Rick.

***

Now let's have a look at your legs, said Doctor Grant.

Can you feel this?

No, I can't doctor.

What about this? (sob) no, I can't. So I wasn't dreaming when I was in the operating room and I overheard the surgeons saying that I may never walk again.

Is that what you heard? Yes I thought I had dreamed it but now I know I didn't. First of all young lady you shouldn't have been able to hear anything. It looks like I've got to have a long conversation with our anesthetist department.

Nurse Kimberly, schedule her for a cat scan as soon as possible.

Now Stacey, "I want you to listen very carefully to me."

I have had dozens of patients with injuries similar to yours. Some of those patients are walking just fine today but initially they could not feel a thing either. We are going to do some more tests as soon as you are strong enough. Your body has been traumatized and it needs time to recover. However, a big part of your recovery will depend on you.

Do you understand me?

Yes, I do doctor but what about the other half of your patients? I won't lie to you Miss Carter. Some need assistance walking, by that I mean a cane or a walker, others I'm afraid have never walked again.

Let's never forget how lucky you are. Another inch to the left young lady and we wouldn't be having this conversation. I'm going to do everything in my power to help you but I'll need nothing less than a hundred and ten percent from you. Now I want you to get some rest. I'll be back later today.

"Thank you doctor," said Mrs. Carter.

Rick I could really (sob) use a hug right now.

Ok sweetheart, now don't worry, I'm right here.

"I know but for how long?" I'll be here as long as it takes Stacy. I (sob) love you Rick. I love you too Stacey.

Let's give them some privacy, said Mrs. Carter.

***

Peaches get Mr. Batiste on the line for me, after that order some food and drinks. Tell him to drop whatever he's doing. I need to see him right now.

Yes sir.

William...Mr. Steven Batiste is on line one.

Hello, Steven. Hello Mr. Winters. Please Steven call me William.

Ok, what can I do for you William? I'm getting the board together. Are you ready for your presentation? I've been ready for the last two days William. Good, how soon can you get here? I can be there in one hour.

***

Gentlemen it's time that I introduced you to Mr. Steven Batiste.

Many of you will remember him from our meeting that we had several weeks ago. I didn't want to introduce him at that time for my own reasons. Now I think it's time for us to hear what this fine scientist has to say. However before he begins, I'd like to tell you a little about him.

For the past four weeks Mr. Batiste has been working with Richard Naylor, Evan Blair and Candis Lockhart. None of his team members is aware that he has approached me with this information mainly because they don't know it exist.

Mr. Batiste seems to feel that he alone has discovered the problem with Advernox. He also feels that he knows the key to reformulating it. Are there any questions before he begins his presentation?

Mr. Batiste, my name is Samuel Randolph; we hope that you are not trying to pull a fast one on us. I agree with Randolph, said J.T. we also hope that you have proof that your reformulation works.

I have the proof gentlemen. You just make sure you have the money. Now if someone would kindly dim the lights I'll begin.

***

First let me say that I'm sure you are not going to like what I'm about to show you. I have put together a small side presentation to show you what I have discovered.

I'll try to keep it as simple as I can for those of you that might have trouble keeping up. On the left is the formulation for Advernox and on my right is the formulation of a drug to be named at the end of my presentation.

Let's go over the facts as we know them. It appears that only women in their fourth month of pregnancy are having these side effects. I ask you gentlemen does this seem odd to anyone? Well judging from your response I guess not.

As you are well aware Advernox has been on the market almost seven months now. Until two months ago there wasn't a single case reported. So why are women just now starting to get sick?

Here's the question that I kept asking myself. Why weren't women getting sick, six or seven months ago?

Finally, I have someone attention. You with your hand up go ahead, what's your question? Maybe they were getting sick but they were not being reported. Not likely from what I've gathered in my reports the pain is so bad that the women always seek medical attention and just as many were taking this medication then as they are now.

Would anyone else like to add anything before I continue?

Yes J.T. what is your comment? Maybe someone changed our formulation after the first couple of months. Now that's an interesting theory but no, that's not it either.

Are the any more theories or guesses?

Very well then, it's time that I revealed the correct answer but before I do I want you to know that I have done every possible experiment to rule out my finding and I came up empty.

Let's review; you know what the formulation on the left is; now it's time to learn what the formulation on the right is. This popular medication is administered to pregnant women normally in their second month. It is a drug that has been used since the beginning of modern medicine. Behold gentlemen this is the drug that is aiding in your nightmare.

Is this your idea of a joke?

I'm afraid not William.

What the heck does this medication have to do with the Advernox problems?

Listen and I will explain. This medication produced right here at BMX has been a steady cash cow for this company for a very long time.

Would anyone like to guess what ten percent of Advernox is? Yes, it's the medication that you are looking at on your right. Now what is the one medication that pregnant women should not take during her first three months of pregnancy?

Before you answer remember Advernox is for stomach cramps, fatigue and nausea. If a woman takes this medication several time a day...well let's just say it's not going to be good for her or her baby because It triggers a cationic effect in the uterus, causing it to contract, giving the woman false signs of labor.

This gentleman is the problem with your great drug. Someone can turn on turn lights now.

You expect us to believe that silly explanation?

Calm down J.T., I agree it sounds fishy but let's not be so hasty with our comments.

Now Mr. Batiste you must admit this theory of yours is just a little far fetched. We are going to need some time to talk this over with the other members of the board.

Sure William, I can understand that but you understand this, I delivered as promised, and I expect you to do the same with my money.

We'll be in touch with you tomorrow afternoon Steven. Please see yourself out.

I was afraid that you wouldn't be convinced, said Steven. That's why I have someone out side waiting to speak to you. Can you ask your secretary to show the lady waiting outside in? Hopefully, "she will be more convincing than I was."

Peaches is there anyone waiting out there, said William?

There is a lady sir.

Please send her in, said William.

You may go in now Miss Williams.

Hello Cynthia...hello Steven.

Gentlemen let me introduce you to Miss Cynthia Williams; she has been helping me with the reformulation.

Are you a chemist or scientist, said William?

No sir, "I'm afraid not." I did take some courses at the junior college but that was years ago.

Why is she here, said J.T.?

I'm getting to that J.T.

Five weeks ago Miss Williams was pregnant. She was in a hospital in Chicago along with several other women. Unfortunately she lost her baby.

We're very sorry to hear that Miss Williams.

Thank you.

Gentleman because the hospital was so crowded, she had to share a room with another pregnant lady. During their time there they had a very interesting revelation.

Miss Williams, please tell these gentlemen about your stay with Mrs. Parkman.

We were both admitted on the same night. Through out the night we were both in a lot of pain. The stomach pain was horrific. Once when they were giving us pain medication we over heard one of the nurses say that our charts had been switched. When we asked them about it they said that it wasn't a problem. However, when we told the doctor of our concern it turned out to be a huge problem.

They immediately put Mrs. Parkman on a saline IV drip. Ten minutes later she started screaming that she was in pain.

It turned out that Mrs. Parkman had a family history of high blood pressure, although she didn't have it herself, there was a good chance that her baby did. The saline drip combined with her pain medication almost sent her into labor. The doctor told them to immediately remove the saline drip and to flush her system. A few hours later, she was fine. When I asked her about it, she said it was like she was going into labor.

It was a good thing she was in the hospital so they could act fast.

Thank you Miss Williams you may leave now.

Good bye Steven, I hope my story helped.

Yes your story has been a great help. I'll be in touch.

There you have it gentlemen. The combination of these two medications can be deadly. Someone needs to talk to that doctor before he pieces this together.

What's the name of the doctor again? Her name is Dr. Janice Edwards. J.T. call our friend and go take care of this!

***

Hello, we are looking for Dr. Edwards. I'm sorry the doctor isn't here at the moment. When will she be back?

What is this in reference to gentlemen?

We just want to get her opinion about something.

Give me your names and phone number and I'll give her the message when she comes back.

When will that be Nurse Betty? I'm not sure; she had to make an emergency trip out of town.

Are you sure you don't know when she'll be back?

That's what I said. Now please gentlemen, I'm very busy.

We understand, sorry to have bothered you. Let's go Cliff. What do you think her emergency was? I'm not sure but I willing to bet that it won't be good for BMX when she returns.

Damn, "I better call William."

***

Honey can you get the door? Who is it? Just some vacuum cleaner salesman. You're kidding right. No I'm not. I thought they stopped doing that. The last time one came by Candis was ten years old.

"Send him away."

Can we just see what he wants? Sure if you want to but I can tell you now that we're not buying.

Good morning young man.

Hello, would you like a free demonstration?

I'm sorry but we are not looking to buy. I understand but maybe you'll change your mind after you see how good this baby works.

Send him to the den and let him work on that spot where I spilled the wine but I'm not buying no freaking vacuum. Come on in son. My husband says that he is not buying anything but if you still want to do a free demonstration, follow me.

This is the den, please be careful in here young man. I'll never hear the end of it if you break something. I promise to be careful.

Honey as soon as he's finish let's go to the market. Now you know the game is on. Don't you ever get tired of those stupid games?

No woman I don't.

Fine you just stay here and watch your stupid games; I'll just go by myself.

Now you know you can't go alone, as soon as your little vacuum cleaner salesman is finished, we'll go.

***

Mr. Davis this is Samuel. I'm inside of the home. Do you want me to continue with your instructions?

Yes I do Samuel and be careful, "we need those bugs hidden well." That's not a problem sir. "I'll be out of here in ten minutes."

I'm finished with your free cleaning.

You're finished already, "that didn't take long."

Would you like to look at it?

I sure would. The rug looks great young man. You did a good job and I didn't hear anything break. Here's a little something for you. I'm sorry lady this is twenty dollars. I can't take this.

"It's the least I can do son." Now you take it and get out of here before my husband finds out.

"Thank you Mrs. Lockhart."

***

I'm out of the house sir. You said that you had one more job for me.

"Who is it?"

Does the name Leon Kenton ring a bell?

You've got to be kidding me sir!

Do I sound like I'm joking?

No, I can't say that I've ever heard you tell a joke.

"That's going to be a tricky one."

Ricks' apartment and office was easy enough and the Lockhart's home was a breeze but Judge Leon Kenton, "I'm just not sure about."

Are you saying you refuse to do it?

No, I'm not but I have to think this one through. They will put me under the jail if I get caught. I have to really think this one through. Well don't think to long! You only have three hours to make it happen.

I might as well have three years. That place will be like Fort Knox. I don't have to think about it any longer. You better find someone else. I'm not stupid enough to mess with Judge Kenton.

***

Hello Candis, it's your mom (sob). Mom what's wrong?
"It's your father."
What's wrong with dad? We are at the hospital.
Your dad's arm is broken. How did that happen? We were on our way to the market when these two men jumped out of their car and threw your father to the ground. We told them that we didn't have any money. They said they didn't want our money. Before your father (sob) could get off the ground they grabbed him by the arm and broke it. Honey, it was terrible, "I actually heard it snap."
Dear God, mom did you call the police? No sweetheart we couldn't.
"For Christ's sake why not?"
They said not to Candis. One of them said he just wanted to teach someone a lesson.
Teach who a lesson?
You Candis.
The man said that they were trying to send you a message. What's going on Candis? We've never (sob) hurt anyone. Why would they do this to us?
Oh mom…. I'm so sorry. Are you sure he said my name?
Yes I'm sure. Is dad Ok? Yes he's resting now; they gave him a sedative for the pain.
"I'm scared Candis." When can you be here? I won't be able to get a flight until tomorrow morning mom but I promise to be there by noon.

Candis how did they know your name?
I'll explain everything when I get there.
Please be careful honey. "I love you mom."

***

Hello you have reached the voice mail for Richard Naylor, please leave a message. Rick this is Candis, I'm not sure if you are back yet. Please call me when you get this message. It's important (sob) very important.

***

Candis I was in the shower. What's going on?

Rick are you back yet?

Yes I got back a couple of hours ago but I plan to go back in a couple of days. What's wrong Candis, you sounded like you were crying.

"Its my parents Rick." Those stupid idiots are (sob) messing with my parents!

Calm down Candis. Tell me what happened.

Someone broke my dad's arm.

You've got to be joking!

Why on earth would I joke about something like this?

He and my mom were on the way to the market and two men jumped out of a car and threw my father to the ground.

Were they trying to rob them?

No they said that they were just trying to teach someone a lesson.

Who were they trying to teach a lesson?

Me Rick, they (sob) said me. They even called me by my name. What am I going to do?

Candis, I'm so sorry about all of this but don't worry, we'll figure out something.

How's your dad?

He's alive if that's what you mean.

Where are they now?

They are at the hospital.

Did they call the police?

No, they were told not too. They did all of this in front of my mom and in broad daylight. I'm surprised it didn't give her a heart attack.

When are you going down there? I can't get a flight until 10:00a.m. tomorrow. They don't deserve to be going through anything like this and it's my fault. Rick (sob) what have we gotten our selves into? Do you think it was the guy that broke into your apartment? I don't know. I haven't seen or heard from him since that night.

There is only one person that I can think of that would do something like this. I'll try to contact him from my cell phone once I get to your apartment. He's not the easiest person to get in touch with.

You are coming over?

Of course I am. I can't let you go though this alone.

Thank (sob) you Rick.

Don't worry Candis, everything's going to be fine, trust me on this. I'm so sorry about all this Candis. I feel so responsible. If I just hadn't talked you into joining this team.

Are you going to be Ok until I get there?

Sure I have to be.

Well remember you are not in this alone. I'm sorry Candis; I should have asked if you felt like having company. Yes, please come over, I can't do this by myself.

My new apartment is a mess; I haven't had time to straighten up since I moved in. That's fine, I won't even notice. I'll be there as soon as I can.

Would you like me to bring something to drink? It's probably not a good idea for me to be drinking right now. I might try to kill somebody, if only I knew who.

I understand. Make sure your door is locked.

I've already checked it. It's locked.

Good, I'm on my way.

***

Who is it?

It's Rick.

Thank you for coming so soon. I see you bought something to drink anyway. Don't worry I'm not going to force you to drink it but I thought it might be a good idea to have it around just in case.

Well I think it's time for me to return a favor. What favor, said Candis? Last week, I was the one who needed a hug. Now I think you do.

Oh yes Rick, a hug would be so nice.

I think (sob) I'm going to be Ok now.

Hey that hug was supposed to make you feel better.

It did but I wasn't ready for you to let go. Please hold me again. I'll hold you to the end of eternity if that's what you want.

Let's sit down on the couch and talk (ha, ha). First you're crying now you're laughing. What's so funny Candis?

Four weeks ago we acted as though we hated each other. Now look at us. Who would have ever imagined that we would end up like this?

"I guess I did."

Really…when?

The day you first came to my apartment. I thought too myself she looks just as good going as she does coming. But I pushed those thought out of my head.

I remember wishing that things were different.

Different how? Not so much business and more pleasure.

Why Mr. Naylor…are you flirting with me?

Yes, "I am Miss Lockhart."

There's chemistry between us and I'm tired of pretending there isn't". When ever we are alone together I can't keep my eyes off you. When ever we are in a room with a group of people I can't keep my eyes of you. Every since the first day I laid eyes on you I've had to fight this burning desire that I have for you.

Tonight I can no longer fight my desire for you Miss Lockhart. Tonight I must have you. You are so damn sexy and so damn beautiful. I have to hold you in my arms tonight so that I know you are real.

I don't know what to say Mr. Naylor. I didn't know that you felt this way…but now that I know, "what are you waiting for mister?"

Kiss me…

***

"Good morning sleepy head."

"Good morning Candis."

What time is it?

It's early and I have a plane to catch remember, but first I was hoping for a little more of what I had last night. Candis are you sure you have time?

Yes I have time. That's if you're up to it.

Are you up for it Ricky?

Come over here and check for yourself.

Oh yes baby, "you are definitely up for it." I want all of that. Then climb your sexy self up here and take it.

Please be gentle Ricky.

I'm a little sore from last night.

"I'll be gentle sweetheart."

We did get a little carried away last night, didn't we? Yes we did Ricky but it was so damn good and it had been such a long time for me. Now stop talking so much and make love to me.

There's just one problem Candis. I'm afraid that I don't have any more condoms.

Baby, that's not a problem. Look inside the bottom drawer of the night stand.

Damn Candis; you have a ton of these things. It looks like you've been very sexually active.

Just because I have a drawer fun of condoms doesn't mean I'm sexually active. I shouldn't be telling you this but I've only been with one man my entire life and that was nine years ago. Now get a couple of condoms and come on.

Candis, I hope this is not a dream.

It's not a dream Ricky.

Last night was real and so is this moment.

Why are you staring at my breasts like that?

"Because they are magnificent Candis."

Oh thank you Ricky.

"Do you want to taste them?"

Do they taste like candy?

I don't know Ricky, I've never tasted them. Don't you want to taste them and see?

Yes, "I want to taste them again and again and again.

I want to suck and caress them."

Take them and do as you will with them my love but be gentle, yes...oh yes...just like that.

"Oh my...that feels so good." You are going to make me fall in Love with you Mr. Naylor.

Why Miss Lockhart..."I thought you already were."

I'm ready...

Oh yes Rick, it feels so good. Oh my...oh my goodness Mr. Naylor. I can see why your ex-wife was on you all the time.

You feel so good inside me.

Do I feel good to you Ricky?

No Candis; you feel great, you are so hot and tight. I want you so much. You have me Ricky. I'm yours from this day until the end of eternity. Oh yes Rick; you feel so good. It's been so long...so very long

"Slow down a little Candis." I thought you said you were sore. I can't Rick, your penis feel so good to me. Oh Ricky, oh Ricky it's so good...I'm coming. Already...yes Ricky...I'm coming but don't stop, "keep giving it to me just like that." It feels so good, I want this all the time.

Can I have you all the time Ricky?

Yes Candis, "you can have me all the time."

I'm coming again Rick...oh yes, it's good; it's so...so good.

Candis lets try a different position.

No Rick; I don't want to move, it feels so good right here.

Don't worry sweetheart, "it will feel good no matter what position we are in."

Ok Ricky. How do you want it?

Lay on your stomach baby. Ok.

How does that feel to you? It feels great Ricky...oh it feels great! Baby it's better than I ever dreamed it could be! Yes Candis...it feels good to me also. I feel like I've struck gold and I'm not talking about fools gold either.

Why are you stopping Rick? Please Rick, don't stop.

Candis the condom just burst. I'll have to get another one.

No Rick; I want to feel you without the condom.

I'm sorry Candis; I never have sex without a condom. You big liar, how did you get those four kids? That's was different, I was married to her. Beside there was no need to practice safe sex back then.

I can respect the fact that you practice safe sex Ricky but I'm the only woman that you'll ever be with for the rest of your life. So forget the freaking condom and give me what I'm asking for.

Candis sweetheart are you sure about this?

Yes I'm sure...please Rick!

Ok but if I get you pregnant...but Rick I want to be pregnant by you.

You don't know what you're saying Candis.

Rick if you don't climb back on me then I'm going to take what I want!

Ok baby, I just hate it when a woman begs for Mr. Ricky.

Here you go. Take all of me if you can. Oh yes baby, that's it. I can feel your hot rod and it's making me so horny. Do I feel good to you Mr. Ricky? Oh yes woman you feel great. You have the most beautiful ass that I have ever seen. I didn't know an ass could look and feel this damn good.

Candis what are you doing....oh damn...you're gonna make me scream if you keep doing that to me!

"You like it when I do that Mr. Ricky."

"Oh hell yes, I like that!"

Well you just go ahead and scream baby because I'm not going to stop doing it...you scream as loud as you want to Ricky..."it'll be our little secret darling." Oh Candis it feels so wonderful...please stop...please stop...oh, it's simply wonderful!

Miss Lockhart...yes...Mr. Naylor...I think I love you...

"You don't love me man, you're just horny. You're only saying that because I'm so hot inside." Now keep making love to me but don't tell me that you love me. I don't need to hear that bull shit!

You are like and inferno Candis now shut up before you make me come. But Ricky...I want you to come. Oh baby, please come inside of me. No Candis that's not a good idea. Please...I want you to come inside of me. I want to have you children.

"You don't mean that Candis."

Yes I do Ricky...oh yes I do! I want to make love you every night and I want us to have a hundred children.

That would really be something Candis.

Oh Rick, I'm about to come again...here is comes...oh Candis I'm coming also...it feels so damn good doesn't it...yes it does Ricky...yes it does. I love you man! What did you say?

Got damn, I said that I love you so (sob) so much Richard Naylor.

Candis why are you crying? I'm crying because I've never felt so good before. You really know how to make love to me Mr. Naylor. Last night was so wonderful and this morning was too. I wish I had time to make love to you all day.

Candis you are a hell of a woman. You are so beautiful and I don't just mean your outward beauty. You are a special lady and I love being with you but there is no way in hell that I can make love to you all day.

"Did I please you Rick?"

Lady you have been pleasing me every since the day I opened that door to my penthouse and saw you standing there.

Do you want to do it again? That would be nice but I have to take a shower now so I can go. Do you want me to shower with you? I'd love for you to shower with me but I think you better stay in bed. I'll never get out of here if you come in there with me.

I feel so good right now. Thank you so much Mr. Naylor, no...thank you Miss Lockhart. Can I touch your grey spot? Sure close your eyes and touch it. Why do I have to close my eyes? Because I asked you to. Ok my eyes are closed.

Ok you can open them now.

What was that all about?

Just a little insurance Candis. Now do you want to touch the other one?

What other one?

Oh my Rick, I didn't know about that one.

"Touch it Candis."

"I can't Rick," I have to go but I promise to touch it when I get back...as soon as I get back...my love.

CHAPTER 12

Thank you for being there for me all those years Ralph. It has been my pleasure Mary. You are the most understanding man that I have ever known and there will always be a special place in my heart for you. I hope Jennifer realizes how lucky she is. Thank you. She knows how I feel about you Mary.

Mary are you sure that you want to go through with your plans tonight? Yes Ralph, I've never been so sure about anything in my life. This is something that I have to do for myself. Damn that Jennifer, "how could one woman be so lucky."

"I'm the lucky one Mary."

I have two wonderful women that love me. Shut up Ralph and give me a hug before you make me cry. They are calling my flight I better go. I love you Ralph.

As Ralph watched the plane take off, he felt as though a part of him had just died. You deserve the best Mary and I hope that someday you find it.

Ring….hello Ralph, hello Jennifer, how is your friend doing? I think she is going to be just fine. I love you Ralph. When are you coming home? I love you too Jen and I'm on my way.

***

Clifford I don't think it's a good idea for me to attend your retirement party. Please sweetheart I want you there. I have waited over thirty years for this night. That's longer than you've been alive. Now, I won't accept no for an answer.

Wear that nice brown dress that I like so much and come help celebrate old Cliff's grand farewell. There will be a lot of people there, "no one will even notice you."

I've got to go home now and get ready. People will expect Mary and me to arrive together. Is she back from Florida yet? Her plane should have arrived several hours ago.

"You are a terrible husband Cliff." You should have met her at the airport. Come on Karen, I can't be in two places at once. No I guess you can't and if you ever call me Mary when we're making love again, I'll cut your nuts off. I did not call you Mary.

Yes, you did old man and that wasn't the first time. It's getting a little weird old man, so watch yourself. Why haven't you said anything before? I told you in the very beginning that I didn't love you. That hasn't changed. I'm only in this for one reason that has never been a secret. But Karen I thought you had started to feel something for me. Oh that was just to make sure the checks kept coming.

You do realize that no other woman my age would put up with that little limp penis of yours. You should probably invest in some type of sexual enhancement or something. I would like to feel something every now and then myself. Karen are you saying that I don't satisfy you? Of course you do Cliff, every time you open your wallet but the sex I'm afraid, "is terrible."

The only time you even make me feel a little something is when you call me Mary. I know you're joking aren't you? No, "I think you love her Cliff." I do not.

Well why haven't you divorced her then?

It's complicated Karen.

Whatever Cliff, "just remember that I want that house in Florida old man." "It's as good as yours sweetheart," just be patient a few more weeks.

I have to go now.

***

As Cliff left the hotel that he had shared once a week for the past three years with his mistress, a strange thought crept into his mind for the first time. Do I really want to divorce Mary, he thought? Of course I do, don't I?

He reached under the seat and pulled out a bottle of gin. After a couple of swallows he had his answer and the answer was yes but why hadn't she left me when she found out about my first affair he thought? That really wasn't the question that he needed an answer too. He needed a quick calculation of all the money that he had spent on all the other women.

He had wasted a small fortune on them and they had all eventually left him, except for Karen. She was the real thing, "he was sure of that". She had been with me longer than any of the others, ironically though she was the most expensive by far. None of them had been as expensive as she is but one Karen was worth all of them combined. So what if she doesn't love me, I don't care. What I do care about is her nice young vibrant body keeping these old bones warm on cold nights.

Yes, it's time to divorce Mary. I'll give her a nice divorce settlement but the Florida home is mine. Why do I keep calling her name when I'm making love to Karen? I haven't been with Mary in over five years, so why would I be calling her name when I'm with a woman as sexy as Karen?

***

When Cliff arrived home Mary was there. She met him at the front door. They shared an awkward hug and Cliff was off to get dressed without a single word about how nice she looked.

Mary paced the hallway for a few minutes and then went upstairs to confront her cheating husband.

Where have you been Cliff?

Don't you start with me woman! How was Florida?

You smell like her tonight Cliff.

What did you say?

I said that you smell like her. You've smelled like her for a long time now.

"You must really like this one."

I don't have time for this crap tonight Mary!

How much is this one costing you?

"How old is she?"

Listen to me Mary, "you are not going to ruin this night for me". Do you understand me!

Take your hands off me Cliff, you take your hands off me right now or I swear to God in heaven that you will never make it to your damn retirement party!

This is my night Mary and I will not let your stupid jealous remarks ruin it for me.

"Did you ever love me Cliff?"

You don't have to answer that question. I've always known that it was my family's money that you were after.

"Now tell me the truth." Who is she?

There is no one Mary, "I promise you there is no one else". Your imagination has just gotten the best of you.

There was a time Cliff when you cared enough to at least tell me a good lie. You can't even do that anymore can you?

Mary, I'm telling you for the last time there is no one else!

Why do you smell like a woman then?

I was down at the bar with a couple of guys from the job. "Which guys?"

You know how crowded those places can be sometimes. Someone probably just rubbed against me by accident. Are you really telling me the truth? Yes I promise, now wipe those tears from those pretty little eyes and let's go celebrate my retirement.

The Limo will be here in less than thirty minutes Cliff.

"I'll be waiting down stairs."

Ok, sweetheart, "I'll be right down."

***

Cliff made sure that he arrived in style. He rented a white limo and had the red carpet rolled out as he arrived. This was almost too much for her but she grinned and bared it. She thought, "I knew I should have stayed at home".

At the party were some of Cliff's closest friends and Mary was actually surprised at the large turn out. She thought, the poor fools, "they don't even know the real Clifford Miller," if so they would have skipped this little party. She watched as her husband made the rounds to each and everyone of them and for a moment she was sure that he had just won the presidency of the United States.

Two hours later it was finally time to toast the great man and this toast could only belong to one woman.

As Mary made her way to the podium, she was slightly surprised at the amount of satisfaction that she felt when she finally reached the podium and looked out at the smiling faces awaiting this heartfelt toast from Mrs. Margaret Miller. What she was about to do next was the easiest thing that she had every done in her life. She had everyone's attention and it was time to toast Cliff.

***

I would like to thank each and every one of you for attending my husband's retirement party tonight. He has talked of nothing else but this day for the past two years. (Ha, ha)

Congratulations my dear Cliff, your day has finally arrived. So please everyone lift your glasses and join me in a toast to my husband and your friend, Mr. Clifford Miller. He is a man that I have been married to for the past twenty-five years. During that time I have faithfully stood by his side as our vows say for better or worst. Sadly, most of you know him better than I do.

You probably know what he likes to eat and what his favorite movies are better than I do and let us not forget what kind of women he likes. Some of you would say that it takes a special kind of woman to be married to a man like Cliff. The kind of woman that knows how to hide her shame and her pain in the mist of affair, after affair, after affair.

So tonight not only do we all celebrate his retirement from BMX, we should also celebrate his retirement from our marriage. Don't feel sorry for him though because this is what he wants.

Isn't that right Cliff?

"Mary what are you saying," yelled Cliff!

"Shut up Cliff!"

"Everyone here knows that you are an adulterer!"

Why would you want me when he can pay for any woman you want? I only hope that the young lady sitting at table five in the nice brown dress realizes that one woman will never be enough for the great lover, Mr. Clifford Miller.

"Cliff my love," please enjoy this night because you have truly earned it. Tomorrow, I start divorce preceding. Then you can be free to chase women until your penis falls off!

"That's if it hasn't already."

***

The stunned crowd just sat there in silence until they were able to comprehend what they had just heard. Then they got out of their seats and slowly walked toward the exit.

The first one to leave was Issee Kemp, who was followed closely by her beautiful daughter, Karen Kemp. It was true what people said, she truly did take after her mother.

Cliff sat there speechless and unable to move. Only one thought filled his head," God please give me the strength to kill again".

***

Mary had the Limo driver take her back home. On the way she called Ralph but all she got was his answering machine. "It's done Ralph." Cliff had a retirement party that he will never forget and neither will his friends.

Cliff's cell phone started to ring.

Please let this be Karen he thought.

***

Hello…How are you doing Cliff?
Oh it's you, 'I've been better."

Look Cliff I need you to stop by the house for a couple of minutes. Not tonight, can we do this tomorrow? "I'm afraid not Cliff." This is just too important. "I'll see you in ten minutes."

Come in Cliff, I'm sorry for having to bring you in here after the kind of night you just had. Mary is a hell of a woman isn't she, said William? I wonder how long she'd been planning that little toast.

"So you heard about it."

Heck no Cliff, I was there. I told you last month the only way I'd believe you were retiring was to see it with my own two eyes. I never expected it to be such an unforgettable occasion though.

"Mary really shocked us all." Especially your mistress but she did look gorgeous in that damn brown dress. If I hadn't been sleeping with her mother for the past five years, I'd give that girl a shot myself.

"Screw you to hell William." "Why am I here?

Does the name Katherine Levens mean anything to you? I don't think it does. Are you sure?

What's this about William? I just said the name doesn't ring a bell. Well you are getting older Cliff; maybe your memory is starting to slip a little. My memory is fine. I just don't know any damn Katherine Levens! Very well Cliff. I was beginning to think that Miss Kemp had been taking more than just semen from your old ass.

"What does Karen have to do with this?"

Not a damn thing Cliff, not a damn thing!

Look William, "I don't have to sit here and take this shit!"

Yes Cliff, you do!

See the brief case in the chair next to you? Open it. Inside you will find an array of pictures. Do any of them look familiar to you?

This is the lab that we blew up a year ago. These are the chemists that we killed. What about the lady on the final picture? She looks familiar.

Oh shit...she was also at the Lab.

Where is she now Cliff?

Well...I think she's in Canada.

We told you to kill everyone at the lab! How is it that she survived?

How did she survive Cliff!

I was getting tired of killing people. I thought we had killed everybody but then I found her hiding in a cabinet. I tried to pull the trigger but I couldn't.

So I told her to leave the country and never come back. I told her if she did I would kill her family.

Well Cliff...either she doesn't believe you or she doesn't give a crap about her family. "Either way it doesn't matter now because she's in protective custody."

Before I kill you Cliff, let me ask you a very important question. When you decided to defy my orders and let this woman run off to Canada did you search her first?

What...?

"I said did you search her!"

"No I didn't."

You idiot, yelled William! Do you know what this means? This woman claims to have a tape recording of the entire murder at the lab.

What...?

"Is that all you can say!"

She claims that she has a tape of the entire murders.

That's impossible. Well if she's telling the truth this tape is in police custody now.

I don't believe her; I never saw any damn tape recorder. That doesn't mean there isn't one, because you never searched her, shouted William!

Cliff…"I hope you realize what this means." They are coming for you Cliff. I asked you here tonight because I wanted to kill you. However, I think the thought of you rotting away in prison makes me happier.

I just need to know one thing before I let you walk out that door. When they question you tomorrow will this company's name or my name be mentioned? What makes you think they are coming after me! They are Cliff and you might as well face it now. If you are lucky they will take it easy on you and just lock you up for life.

No one is locking me up anywhere. "I kill myself before I allow that to happen."

No you won't Cliff; you've lost your edge.

"You'll never kill again."

It's actually a little sad that you would go out like this Cliff. Now I ask you again, "will my name or the company's name be mentioned when they pick you up?"

No William, I give you my word that your name will not be mentioned.

You realize that I have to trust you on this one don't you Cliff. Because if I didn't I'd have to put a bullet in your head right there where you sit.

Pull the trigger William Winter! We both know you don't have the guts to kill anyone. That's why you hire people like me!

You're not worth it Cliff, besides the maid would have a hell of a time cleaning up the mess. If I were you I don't think I'd go home tonight. I hear Canada's a good place to hide out for a while.

"Screw you William."

I'm not running and I'm not going to spend one day of my life locked behind bars. William this conversation is giving me a headache. Here asshole take a couple of these aspirin, they should do the trick.

I'll need more than a couple for this headache, just let me have the bottle William, I'll take some with me for later. Here take the bottle Cliff.

"What happened to you?"

Do you really want to know William? Do you really want to know?

"Yeah I want to know," that's the least you could do.

You are what happened to me! You and your got damn assignments!

Do you know how many people I've killed for you? I bet you don't have a clue do you? "The sad part is neither do I.

Most of the people that you wanted me to kill didn't deserve to die.

Tell me one who didn't.

Do you remember Marvin Edwards? Why did he have to die?

Marvin was becoming too powerful Cliff. He was getting in my way and he had to be stopped!

He didn't have to die William! How was he getting in your way, he worked for a completely different company. I guess I can tell you now. There was a rumor that they were going to ask him to replace me. Besides his wife Suzanne was a....

That's the last time I wish to hear the name Marvin Edwards, said William. Who else do you think didn't deserve to die?

There are several but the one that didn't deserve to die the most was Lilly Cantrell.

"Who the heck is she?"

That's right asshole; you wouldn't know who she is. She was a chemist at that lab, said Cliff.

When I slit that woman's throat as she begged for her life a part of me died with her. Her ghost has haunted me every single day since I killed her. I don't understand what happened, it's as though her soul entered my body with her last breath.

Every time I look in the mirror the eyes staring back at me belong to her. I haven't had a good night's sleep in over a year. The only time I don't think about her is when I'm with Karen and now she's been taken away from me. So if you think I'm worried about you or the stupid police you need to think again.

"You really have lost it Cliff."

I had no idea that you were going through all this. It's sad, only God can help you now. You should consider my idea about you moving to Canada.

"Wait a minute Cliff." If you couldn't kill any more then who killed Justin Beavers?

If you're talking about the asshole that broke into Candis Lockhart's apartment, I paid someone to toss his ass out the window of his apartment but if it makes you feel any better William, "he thought it was me."

Good bye Cliff...You know the way out.

***

The following morning Cliff was awaken by loud sirens but he realized that it was only a dream. William Winter's voice kept echoing through his mind. You know they are coming for you Cliff. He couldn't take it any more. So Mr. William Winters thinks I'll never kill again. I'll show him, his next headache will be his last. Cliff went to his closet and took out a large black box. Inside the box was his prize 45 caliber revolver.

He went to the hallway and called Mary but there was no answer. He knew there wouldn't be. She wasn't there and never would be again. She was probably in Florida.

He heard the sirens again. Was he still dreaming he thought? The sirens were getting louder. They were not on his street yet but they were close. He went into the bathroom and looked into the mirror. Yes, he thought, they were still there; staring at him, begging and pleading for him to let her live. I have kids was repeated over and over again in his nightmares. Please don't kill me. I'll do anything just please don't kill me, please, please. Cliff couldn't take it any more.

He raised the 45 to his head and said God thank you for giving me the strength to kill again. He pulled the trigger but instead of the defying sound that a gun makes, he heard…"Freeze". In the reflection of the mirror he could see two police officers. In their hands and pointed directly at him were guns. Cliff knew they were not a dream, a nightmare maybe but not a dream. How could it end like this he thought? He knew he wouldn't let it end like this.

He heard one of them say, "you have the right to remain silent", "anything that you say can be used against you in a court of law". Do you understand, said the policeman?

Cliff didn't understand what was happening at that moment. He didn't understand the countless affairs, he didn't understand the murders and most of all he didn't understand why Mary had left him, however he did understand what he had to do next.

Clifford quickly turned while yelling no I don't understand and lunged at the officers with the "special edition" colt 45 in his hand.

The officers fired several shots into his chest. As he lay on the floor looking up at the officers, "he asked for a mirror."

When the stunned officers realized what he was saying they handed him a small mirror from the bathroom vanity table.

Cliff looked into the mirror and for the first time in almost a year he was able to smile because the eyes staring back at him were his own.

"He mumbled welcome home."

With his last breath of life he told the officers thank you. I finally have my eyes back. As Cliff drifted into the world of the unknown, "he thought he heard a soft voice."

"So soft and so sweet was the voice."

It was difficult to understand at first but with every second it was becoming stronger and stronger. Then the soft whisper became a scream which was easy for him to understand and he had no trouble hearing these words.

"Please don't kill me!"

One of the stunned officers took the colt 45 from Cliff's clenched fist and examined the gun. This is a nice gun he said to his partner. "He kept it in excellent shape." He had time to get off a shot. Why didn't he shot at us? Wait just a minute, I think I see the answer to my own question. "There are no bullets in this gun."

"This man...wanted to die."

***

Hello Judge how are you doing today?
I'm fine Charley, how about you?

I'm sorry to be calling because I know you are a busy man. It's not a problem my friend. You can call me anytime.

What's on your mind?

Well…a few weeks ago at the lake when you said if I needed to talk just give you a call. Did you really mean that? Of course I did Charley. That's good because I really need to talk now. Ok Charley, I'm listening go ahead and talk. Well, I'd like to talk face to face. Where would you like to talk? How about the lake? When? I need to talk right this minute but I suppose I can hold it until you get here but no fishing this time. My wife hasn't cooked the last mess of fish we caught. How does five o'clock sound? "I'll be there Judge."

***

Nora can you come in here for a minute?

Yes Leon…I need you to file these. After that I want you to take the rest of the day off. Do you really mean it? Sure I do. I'll be here about two more hours and then I'm also leaving early. Thank you Judge. Your welcome, tell that lucky husband of yours that I said to take you and the kids out for dinner tonight. "I'll definitely tell him."

Have fun Nora, I'll see you tomorrow.

***

Sorry, I'm late Charley but the traffic leaving Stalin Island was terrible. I almost thought you had forgotten about me Judge. Another ten more minutes and I would have lost my nerve to talk about this.

Well now Charley if you had a cell phone, I could have called you and let you know that I was running late. Those things give people cancer Judge. Oh Charley, "that's just a rumor." Well rumor or not I'm not taking any chances Judge.

Don't you think it's time that you started calling me by my name? I like calling you Judge.

Here I bought you some lunch but it won't hurt my feeling if you don't eat it. My wife, she ain't the best cook, "as you already know." Thanks Charley, I've already eaten but if it's Ok with you I'll take it with me.

So what are we here to talk about today? Judge...it wasn't my fault. What wasn't your fault? I'm talking about that terrible accident at the courthouse. I know it was four years ago but to me it feels like it just happened. Are you telling me that you are finally ready to talk about that Charley? Yes, "I think I am Judge."

Good Charley, "this is definitely a step in the right direction."

She just came out of no where. One second the street was clear the next second she was standing directly in front of my car. By the time I hit the brakes (sob) it was too late. I'll never forget the look on her mothers' face afterwards. I felt so helpless.

Now Charley there were witnesses and they all said that there was nothing you could have done. Her mother should have been watching her.

I know that Judge but I looked directly into that little girl's eyes just as I hit her, "she was laughing and seemed so full of life." She never knew what hit her. I wasn't even going that fast.

There hasn't been a day that I haven't thought about her.

I know it must be a hard thing for you Charley but you have to try to put it behind you. It was an accident and it could have happened to anyone. I know that Judge but it didn't happen to just anyone, "it happened to me".

Why are things always happening to me?

That's a good question old man, I'm afraid that I don't have a good answer.

"I think God is mad at me Judge."

God is not angry with you because he has allowed you to live this long. Oh I think he is mad Judge, "that's why I've lived so long."

"It's his way of punishing me."

Nonsense Charley, "here I bought us a couple of beers?" You have beer Judge? I didn't even know you drank. I drink like a fish Charley but mostly behind doors so I can sleep it off afterwards. It wouldn't look good if the public saw me drinking all the time now would it? No not a man in your position, "no Judge that wouldn't look good at all."

A beer seems like a great idea Judge. Ok but don't let it drive you back to the hard liquor. Do you think the Lord will ever forgive me for taking that young girl's life?

"He already has Charley," now it's time for you to forgive yourself.

CHAPTER 13

Good morning sexy. Who is this? Oh stop playing games mister. You know who this is.

Is this Deborah? No it's not! How about Angela?

You get one more guess, "if I were you I'd try to get it right this time". Well in that case my final guess is Candis?

Good for you Mr. Naylor, "now I don't have to kill you and have my friends feed you to the fishes."

Good morning Candis, "I was just thinking about you."

"Yeah, I could tell."

I probably won't be in the office when you get here. Mercedes has a report that I need you and Evan to go over as soon as you get here. Also I was hoping that you would have dinner with me tonight. I'd love to Rick but only if it's my treat. I don't have a problem with that.

Do you know how to get to Fredica's on 19ᵗʰ and Elm Street? Sure that's just a block over from Macy's, said Candis. I have to run some errands when I get off work at six. That's if my slave driver of a boss doesn't make me stay late but I should be finished by seven. How does seven-thirty sound, said Rick? That's cutting it close but I think I can make it.

What about dessert? I mean Italian is great for dinner but I'd like to go somewhere else for dessert. Where would you like to go? How about your place, said Candis? Why my place? Oh…you mean that kind of dessert! Very good choice, we can do that. Great, I'll be thinking about dessert all day, said Candis. You are not the only one. I've got a meeting in less than an hour so I better get out of here. Ok, I'll see you tonight Rick.

"Mercedes, I'm heading out." I'll be back in a couple of hours. You have a call on line one Rick. Would you like me to take a message? No, "I'll take it." Transfer it to my office.

Hello..."Good morning Mr. Naylor." I said good morning Mr. Naylor! You act like you're not happy to hear my voice. What do you want Mr. Davis and why are you calling me at work? I just want you to know that we are raising the stakes. What does that mean? It means that we expect more out of you. We think you should be spending more time at work. I'm doing all I can, and I'm also working from home.

"That's bullshit Rick!" I believe that your personal life is interfering with our chances for success.

What the hell are you talking about Davis!

Mr. Naylor is there any truth to the rumor that you and Miss Lockhart have become involved in a little office romance?

Now wait just a damn minute Mr. Davis! I have cooperated with you in every way that I can. There is only so much that one person can do. Find a way Mr. Naylor and I suggest that you start spending more time at work and less time with your little playmate.

I really can't be mad at you; anyone can clearly see why you'd want to play with her. She is a knock out. I've never seen a woman like her before. Not only does she have a prefect body but she has a beautiful face also. What is she about six feet tall? It's rare to find a woman with all three of those qualities, "most only have one if they are lucky". I'm thinking about trying to recruit her to work with me when this is all over.

That confirms it for me you are crazy. Maybe I am a little crazy Mr. Naylor but at least I know it.

Now put your little office romance on hold until you give us what we want. After that you and Candis Lockhart will be free to do whatever you please! Don't let me have to warn you again! Click.....

"Damn it!"

He seems to know everything about my life. How does he know about us? It's as though he was listening to our conversation just now. "

"Oh shit that's it."

I bet he has a tap on my phones and if he has a bug on this phone he probably has one on my house number. Wait...am I jumping to conclusions? I need to just calm down and think for a minute. How can I find out for sure? I think I know what I need to do.

Mercedes are you still working on the Advernox report? Yes I am but I'm almost finished. Good, come in here when you finish. I need you to do something for me. I'll be there in a couple of minutes.

I have no idea what a bugging device looks like anyway. On second thought, it's probably not a good idea to get Mercedes involved in this either. Mercedes, yes Rick, I'm almost finished. Just take your time. I've changed my mind. Rick what's wrong? You sound a little agitated.

"I'm fine." Would you like a cup of coffee? Sure that sounds good but no cream or sugar this time.

Here you go Rick, now be careful it's hot. Would you like to look over the report before I put it in final draft? Just leave it on my desk; I'm sure it's fine. Are you sure there's nothing wrong? It's just life Mercedes; you're probably too young to understand.

People have made that mistake about me all my life. I would hope that you were different. I'm sorry Mercedes, "I didn't mean that the way it sounded."

I know that you are under a lot of pressure Rick. Just remember if you need someone to talk to, "you can always call me". Thanks Mercedes, I'm really glad you're here. I'm glad I'm here to Rick.

Can you make sure that I'm not disturbed for the next thirty minutes? Sure I can. Would you also lock the door behind you? Ok...but what about your meeting?

"I'm going to be late."

**

Hello Uncle, "how are you this morning?"

Hi Mercedes, it's kind of early to be hearing from you isn't it? It may be nothing but Mr. Naylor seems very agitated this morning. Really...what happened? He received a phone call just as he was heading to a meeting a few minutes ago. He was very upset when he got off the phone.

Who was it? The number came up blocked. "Where is he now?" He's in his office. He asked not to be disturbed for the next thirty minutes and also told me to lock the door on my way out.

So something is going on. "I would love to know who that call was from."

I'm sorry uncle it might not be anything at all. No sweetheart, something is going on "you did the right thing by calling me." That's why you're there. Are all calls coming through your desk now? Yes as soon as he said he didn't want to be disturbed, I redirected all calls through my line. You are becoming quite the little administrative assistant aren't you? I love you uncle. I love you to...call me if there are any more developments.

***

Sir you wanted to see us. Yes, have a seat. I had a talk with Mr. Naylor this morning and it appears that he is more stubborn than I thought. I've been thinking and I decided that there is a better way to get his attention.

What do you mean boss?

Candis Lockhart seems to be the only thing he can concentrate on right now. I want you fellows to bring her to me.

Are you talking about the babe with the nice butt? Yeah, you noticed that too. Who wouldn't, said Robert?

I think I'll use her to send him a message. I thought we were using his kids to get him to do what you wanted.

Robert how long have you worked for me? "I've been with you almost fifteen years sir." In fifteen years have you ever known me to harm anyone's kids? No sir I haven't, I just meant. I know what you meant, and I'm not about to start now. Miss Lockhart is here and the impact of kidnapping her will be felt immediately.

When would you like us to do this?

Do it when she gets off work today. She's supposed to run a couple of errands before meeting him for dinner at 7:30 to night.

Where are they meeting for dinner, said Luke? Fredica's on 19th and Elm but I need you to follow her as soon as she gets off work because you'll have to wait for the right moment to grab her.

Mr. Davis, "it seems to me that the best place to get her would be as she enters the restaurant," said Luke. It's gets dark around seven, so that should make it easier. No, too many things could go wrong, besides we can't take the chance that they might change their plans at the last minute.

What would you like us to do with her after we get her? The first thing you need to do is call me, after that take her to the warehouse. The warehouse is starting to get mighty crowded boss. Yes it is and when are going to move out of that dreary place? I wouldn't wish that place on my worst enemy.

I think there might be snakes in that damn place. There are no freaking snakes in there Luke. Yes there is Robert, "I've seen them on the dock sitting out in the sun." Snakes love dark, dreary places and that damn warehouse is one dreary ass place.

Shut up you two and listen. I only plan to keep her there long enough to get Mr. Naylor's attention. I'm guessing that should take less than one day. Don't harm her. Now get out of here you two and make it happen. Yes Sir.

***

Robert have you ever wondered what goes on in Mr. Davis head sometimes? I know exactly what you mean Luke. When I first started working for the man I thought he was a lunatic. "The stories I could tell you."

Don't you worry my brother, as crazy as he seems, "the man is actually a genius". After we finish this little caper, lets grab a couple of beers down at Lillie's Tavern and I'll tell you all about the good ole days. Ok, that sounds good. I know it does. I'll supply the stories and you my brother can supply the beer.

"I should have known this would cost me."

There she is now. Wow, she is beautiful isn't she? We don't need to be thinking about that right now. She's getting in her car. Follow her but don't get too close. It looks like she stopping at the dry cleaners. Should we try it here? We can't, too many people around besides this location is not good, "we'll have to wait." Here she comes, I wonder where she's headed now? It looks like she's heading into Macy's parking lot. Damn this is not good either. That store has more security guards than Fort Knox. I know but it's a quarter to seven, this might be her last stop before the restaurant. I'll follow her in and see if an opportunity presents itself. Keep your phone on so I can hear.

Robert what's going on? It's been almost ten minutes. She's in the lingerie department. It looks like she has big plans for tonight. That Mr. Naylor is one lucky man. Not tonight he isn't.

She just looked at her watch and is heading toward the check out. Do you have that picture with you? Relax, I got it, now shut up, I'm about to make my move. Listen and pay attention so you'll understand how a professional does it.

Hello pretty lady. Excuse me but I'm in a hurry. I'm sorry; I'm not trying to upset the pretty lady. I was just wondering if you could help me. I have misplaced my daughter. One second she was here standing beside me and the next second she was gone. I'm sorry to hear that but shouldn't you be talking to security about this? Please if you could just tell me if you've seen her. I have a picture of her right here. Look I'll show you.

See why I can't show her picture to security.

Oh no...Who are you?

Relax, I wouldn't dream of hurting you but I do need you to come with me Miss Lockhart. I'm not going anywhere with you until I know my parents are Ok. Your parents are just fine but if you want them to stay that way I suggest you come quietly with me.

Where are you taking me? Please be quiet Miss Lockhart. Luke can you bring the car to the north entrance? Ok Robert, "I'll meet you there." See why you must cooperate. If my partner hears anything go wrong, it won't be good for your parents. Why can't you people just leave us alone?

We've been instructed to deliver you unharmed and that's what we intend to do, so don't try anything funny. I hate to say this Candis but you are going to have to leave the lingerie here until another time.

I'm starving, said Robert. Candis, I'm going to stop at that hotdog stand and get a couple of dogs for me and my friend. Would you like one? Screw you ass hole! I'll love to but this isn't a good time for me. I'd be glad to take a rain check on your offer. Well mister as soon as it starts raining in hell, "I'm your girl."

You really need to work on your people skills Candis, besides I wouldn't expect to find you in a place like hell but I guess you are right about me being there. Oh I'll be there mister because after I kill all of you, "that's where I'm headed."

Excuse me may we have a couple of hotdogs? Hey Robert... yes Luke. Do they have bratwurst? On second thought make it a couple of bratwurst and heavy on the sauerkraut, said Robert.

"That will be eleven dollars sir."

Please pay the man Candis. What? I said pay the man. I will do no such thing!

Don't even pretend that you don't have any money. I saw the expensive price tags on the lingerie that you were about to purchase.

Pay for your own food ass hole.

Excuse us for a second. Look...I just remembered I don't have a cent on me, said Robert. Don't worry your next meal is on us. Now kindly pay the man, Candis and add two large sodas.

Your total is now fourteen dollars lady.

Thanks for the food, Candis, now lets go to the car. My partner is waiting for us. There he is. Watch your head when you get in, said Luke. Hey Robert she's even more beautiful up close.

Hello Candis, I'm sorry that this car is not as nice as yours but we are on a strict budget. This is my new partner Luke. Luke this is Candis. The name is Miss Lockhart! Here's your bratwurst, compliments of Candis..."I mean Miss Lockhart."

Sir we have her in custody, said Robert. Very good, let me speak to her.

Here Candis, the boss wants to speak to you. Hello Miss Lockhart, how are you? Who is this? That's not important right now, "we'll meet later today." I just called because I wanted to put your mind at ease.

You can't possibly think a freaking phone call is going to put my mind at ease right now. Well I'm afraid that you are not going to be able to make your little dinner date tonight. How do you know about that? I know everything.

Your boyfriend is a very stubborn man. It's because of him that you are in the situation that you are right now. What do you mean? I mean that he can't seem to keep his hands off your goodies long enough to concentrate on his job. You seem to be the only thing he cares about lately. As sweet as that might be for you, it's pissing me off royally but I think this should get him to refocus on what's important.

We are doing everything we can to give you what you want. Explain exactly how having dinner at Fredica's and shopping for lingerie at Macy's helps me get what I want?

The problem is what you're asking for might not exist. Oh but it does exist Candis and the sooner the two of you get your heads back on straight the sooner you will realize that. Now, I probably shouldn't be telling you this but I'm only keeping you for one day because I need you to get back to work.

When this is all over I want you to come work for me. Not in your wildest, craziest dreams, Mr. Davis. "So you do know who I am."

"I hate all of you yelled Candis!"

Give the phone back to Robert.

Do you see what I mean about her, said Davis? Yes I do. Watch her like a hawk, "she's dangerous". Yes sir, "I will watch her".

"I promise not to take my eyes off her."

CHAPTER 14

Hello stranger, I haven't heard from you in a while, how's everything? Everything is good. What was that strange message you left on my cell a while back. It was nothing. Let's go out for some drinks tonight and catch up on old times. Sure that sounds great. What time, said Marcus? How about six o'clock at Ralph's bar?

Isn't that kind of early to be hanging out at a bar? Yes it is but I have plans for later. Oh really and what's her name? Marcus are you coming? I'll be there Rick.

***

Hello Marcus I almost didn't recognize you in that suit. Hi Rick, I'm just trying to change my image. Well I like it my friend. I'm sure the ladies will like it also. So what going on Rick and by the way I didn't buy that let's get together and talk over old times bit at all.

Well Marcus, I think I better order you a drink first. Otherwise you're not going to believe a word of what I'm about to say. You make it sound as though the world's coming to an end Rick. It just might be, for me. Don't beat around the bush with me spit it out. Just one second Marcus, bartender can we have two Heinekens please?

Marcus have you ever known me to lie to you about anything? Not to my knowledge. Well I haven't and I'm not about to start now. What I'm about to tell you is going to sound just a little bizarre. You mean stupid don't you, said Marcus? Alright stupid might even be a better word.

"I'm in some deep shit Marcus."

I think my phone at work and at home have been bugged. You mean like a wiretap or something? That's precisely what I mean. Rick my friend you are definitely working too hard? Who'd want to put a tap on your line?

I've got a couple of ideas Marcus but I can't act on them until I know for sure. Rick why would anyone care about what you have to talk about? I'm doing research on a new wonder drug called Advernox. However, there seems to be a problem with the formulation and there are a lot of people who stand to lose a lot of money if it isn't reformulated right away.

Most of these idiots don't realize that any reformulation will off set the chemical balance and the drug will be useless. So you're saying that it only works in its current form? Yes that's what I'm saying and it works great but there are side effects that weren't known when it was released. Maybe my last statement is incorrect but the truth is hard to understand and no one is talking.

Why doesn't the company that made it just take it off the shelf? That would be way too easy Marcus not too mention that it would also be the right thing to do but I'm afraid that we are not dealing with self righteous people. Oh yeah Rick, I see your point. So what's the plan?

There are a couple of reasons that I asked you here tonight. I knew that talk about old times sounded just a little fishy. Here Marcus this is for you. What is this? It's a pre-paid cell phone. What am I suppose to do with a prepaid phone? Now, I know you're joking old friend. This is no joking matter Marcus.

As advanced as technology is today, it's still impossible to tap a pre-paid phone. What am I going to do with this? Listen to my plan and you'll know.

I can't wait to hear this Rick but just to be on the safe side, I think I'll need another Heineken first. Marcus, in about ten minutes a lady is going to approach us. I'm going to offer her a drink and then basically forget that you are sitting here. You are going to appear to get pissed and leave after a few minutes but you need to wait until she leans over and whispers in my ear. That will be your clue to leave and go to your car and wait for us to leave. Why am I doing this? If someone follows me I want you to call me and give me a description of them.

"That's your plan?"

You really do think someone is following you?

Yes, "I do Marcus and they are not nice people." I can't prove it but I know they have already killed for this drug.

What...are they in here now?

Don't look around like that Marcus! I'm not sure if they are in here or if they are waiting outside but if they are this little plan will draw them out and I can stop being so paranoid because I'll know the truth.. I don't know about this Rick, this seems really dangerous. I think you should eighty-six this plan and go to the police. Besides, Rick you are a scientist not James Bond or 007. Damn it Marcus...James Bond is 007.

What.., really?

Now listen, I've thought this through and it can work, but I need your help. Oh crap, there you go again. What are you talking about Rick? I'm talking about your eyes. The way they always dart around in your head when you are scared. I'm not scared just cautious. Marcus you are the scariest person I've ever met. I must have been crazy asking you to help me.

You were this way when we were kids, said Rick. I had hoped that you had grown out of it by now. I can still remember of all the kids in the old gang you were the only one who wouldn't take a piece of candy from old man Buckley's store. Everyone knew he was blind as a bat. I wasn't scared, "I just knew it was stealing."

Yeah…unfortunately you were right about that. My mom wasn't too happy when he finally caught us. I guess that was a bad example.

How long do I have to wait in the car? Only a few minutes, five at the most. My car is parked just across the street. I noticed your expensive German car when I came in. Don't start with that again. Just think about buying an American car once Rick. "I've thought about it Marcus."

Excuse me gentlemen would one of you like to buy a lady a drink?

Sorry but we're waiting for someone. It's your loss boys.

That wasn't her? No…that's not her.

Good because that lady was a prostitute.

So is the one we're waiting for.

What, you almost made me choke on my beer. Have you lost your freaking mind? Hey, where else was I going to get a woman on such short notice. How about an escort service? I thought about that, too unreliable. Besides if I'm being followed or if my phone is taped they would have found out because escort services have you checked out and they like to call you to confirm your appointment.

Rick later we are going to discuss this prostitute matter.

Hello, gentlemen. Hello…would you like to have a seat? Sure if someone is buying me a drink. Sit right here honey; I'll buy you a drink. My name is Rick, this is my friend Marcus.

Are you two together? What do you mean together? I mean like a couple. Oh hell no woman! We are just old friends. I'm sorry but you two seem to be sitting awfully close to just be friends.

We can fix that, Why don't you sit down between us.

Oh baby, now I like the sound of that. Are you boys going to make a sandwich out of me?

No I'm afraid my friend isn't into that kind of thing.

Are you Marcus? Me however, I can go for just about anything.

Good then order me that drink and we can talk about it.

Bartender please get the lady whatever she wants. Hey why don't we lose your friend? I'm sorry what did you say? Lean over so I can whisper in your ear. Lets get out of here baby so I can really get to know you better. Ouch, woman, you bit me. I just wanted to taste you.

Hey Marcus where are you going? Rick you are crazy. I'm leaving…three's a crowd. "I'll see you later."

Lady you did very good. Thank you, I aim to please but I wasn't joking about getting to know you better. Can we get out of here and go to your place? No, "I'm afraid tonight is not a good time."

Finish your drink and let's go for a ride. Can I have one more drink first? Sure, bartender another drink for the lady. Yes sir, I see you changed drinking partners. She's much sexier than your last partner. You mean my friend that just left? I'm only joking. This drinks on the house. "Well thank you."

He likes you. Maybe after this little game is over you can come back here and hook up with him. Him no way, he's gay. No he isn't. Honey when you've been in this profession as long as I have, you can tell. He's gay and so is your friend Damascus. His name is Marcus and he's not gay. Whatever you say honey. Are you sure we can't go to your place? I'm sure.

The truth is I'm seeing someone.

Don't let that stop the show, "she is welcome to join us."

I'm afraid that's a terrible idea. She would never go for that.

You might be surprised what a woman will do if the right opportunity came alone. How long have you two been together?

About four days.

Oh is that all...you two probably think the sex is great right now but you'll get tired of her soon. When you do Derrick give me a call. Thanks for the drink.

Can you drop me off on 111th and Market Street?

Isn't that clear across town?

Yes it is but that's my next stop. Can I have the rest of my money now? I'll give it to you in the car. On second thought I will give it to you now.

Aren't you going to count it? No honey I trust you. I want you to count it. Ok honey if you insist. See it's all here just as I thought. Good lets go.

My car is the black one parked across the street.

"Sweet ride man."

Thank you. Let me get the door for you.

Hey stop it, you're being too nice. A girl can get use to a thing like that. I can't remember the last time a man opened a car door for me?

"Watch you head."

"Wow this is a beautiful car inside." What is it?

It's an Audi A8L. This is an Audi? Boy have they come a long way. Yes they have, back in the day the largest engine they made was a turbo 5 cylinder. It was a beautiful car even back then but it did have its issues. The only issue with this car now is the price. It's very expensive but worth it.

Step on it baby, let me see what it can do.

Alright but you had better put your seat belt on.

Screech...go baby go.

***

Rick you took off pretty fast didn't you.

Yes Marcus I did, my lady friend wanted to see what this thing would do.

Well you might want to slow down just a little. It might make it easier for the ladies following you in the brown sedan to keep up. You're kidding me right? No and from where I was sitting they could follow me anywhere at any time. Thanks Marcus, I think I know who those two are.

I'm going to head home now Mr. 007, if that's Ok with you. Thanks, Marcus and don't lose that cell phone. Rick just one more thing before you go. What is it? You're not fooling me one bit my friend. I want to hear all about your night with the prostitute.

"She's actually not bad looking." She'll probably do things to you that you've only dreamed about.

Marcus, I think you've had one too many Heinekens.

Rick, "promise me that you'll be careful."

I will Marcus and that's a promise.

***

So who's following us honey? Just a couple of gambling buddies. That's funny I must be slipping, I had you pegged as the white-collar type. The gambling is just a hobby baby. I love the rush it gives me.

Hey isn't there a police precinct around here somewhere? Yes but why would you want to go there? I think it might be a good way to lose our friends back there. Take Monroe over to 42nd Street and you're there. You seem to know your way around pretty well.

Unfortunately, "I know where all the precincts are." In my profession they are like a second home. Well I'm going to speed up a little and head in that direction. Let's see how bad they want to follow me.

***

Mr. Barrow, this is Jackie.

We are tailing Mr. Naylor. He just left the bar. It looks like he has picked up some entertainment for the night.

What kind of entertainment?

She looks like a hooker sir.

You've got to be kidding me. That doesn't sound like him. Keep an eye on them. Well there's a slight problem sir.

What's the problem? Well, for one he's speeding and the other is he's heading toward the 42nd precinct.

"You're kidding me." Pull back he must be up to something or he's drunk. He did have several drinks. Maybe that explains the speeding but it doesn't explain why anyone would pick up a hooker and head toward the police station. Right…something smells rotten. Pull back and go to your next post. You can wait for him there. Yes sir.

"Thanks for the lift honey." You're welcome.

Do you promise that we are going to get together soon?

I'm sorry, I can't make that promise but I've got your number.

Well…don't lose it, I can't wait to see you again and next time I'm going to run my fingers through that sexy gray spot of yours.

You don't really want to do that.

Why honey? It might be more than you can handle.

Sugar, I haven't met a man yet that I can't handle. I'm sure you haven't. Goodbye Jasmine, I'm running late

***

Excuse me sir. Would you like me to freshen up your coffee?

Yes I would, thank you.

She'll probably be here any minute now.

I hope so. I can't believe she would stand me up.

"I can't believe that either honey."

"Maybe I should give her another call."

Hello this is Candis, please leave a message and I'll return your call as soon as possible. Hi Candis it's me again. "It's a quarter to eight." "I'm starting to feel pretty silly sitting here by myself."

It's eight o'clock you must be starving. Would you like to order?

Sure I'll have the steak and mushrooms with the house salad.

Are you sure you wouldn't like to order from the Italian menu?

No, I'm afraid she's the one who loves Italian.

I see...well pardon me for saying this but any woman that would stand you up is crazy and you're better off without her. Thank you that's a nice thing to say but I'm starting to get the feeling that something has gone wrong.

I apologize but I've lost my appetite. Can you please bring me the check?

Very well sir, "I'll be right back."

***

You have three messages. Message one; hello Rick, this is Evan. I was going over the report today with Candis and we both agree with your finding. I'm going to turn in early tonight. I'll see you at work tomorrow. Message two; hello Rick this is Stacey. Can you give me a call when you get in? It doesn't matter how late it is. I love you. Message three; hello this is Jackie from heritage resort. I am pleased to inform you that you have qualified for our couple's only retreat. All we need is your credit card number and we can get you started. Please call me back at 1-800-555-5252. You have no more messages.

Candis where are you?

CHAPTER 15

Mr. Davis, I'm starting to worry about Kathy. She was in pretty bad shape when we finally took her out of the trunk of that car. Have you given her anything to eat? I tried but she refuses to eat anything. Well, can you blame her? First we kidnap her, then we lock her in a trunk for three hours and now we push a plate of God knows what in front of her and expect her to eat right up. She probably thinks it's poisoned.

Think about it Lillie, "if you were her would you eat it?" No, "I guess not when you put it like that."

Now listen to me, we need her healthy, she is no good to us any other way. Make her take a shower and get her some fresh clothes. I'll be there in two hours

Kathy we are going to try this shower one more time. After that I want you to eat. Now you can do this the easy way or I can call Robert and Luke to assist you. I'm sure they would love to make sure you enjoy a nice long shower.

Fine, "I'll do it but I want to eat first."

See that wasn't so bad was it. Here are some fresh clothes, they might be a little big but they are clean. By the way Robert and Luke were disappointed to find out that you are cooperating. They should be here in less than an hour. In the mean time, "you be a good little chemist and take a nap."

***

Guess what Kathy, you have some company. Get in there Candis and don't you try any funny business. We've been told to watch you like a hawk.

You better watch me with both eyes or I just might slit your throat.

Very funny Miss America now shut up and get inside your new home.

Hello, what did they get you for?

Excuse me…these ass holes like to play games with peoples lives! I can't wait until I get out of here. What are you going to do? You don't want to know. They have messed with me for the last time. I'm tired of them threatening the people I care about and I can't believe this dump that they bought me too. I think I saw a freaking snake when we were walking through the damn warehouse.

Poor Rick, "he probably thinks I stood him up."

Who's Rick?

He is a very, very good friend.

I know someone named Rick.

I'm sure you do sweetheart, it's a pretty common name.

I know but there's nothing common about this man. He's a scientist and I hate the way I had to run out on him.

You said, "he's a scientist."

That's right, he works for BMX Pharmaceutical.

You've got to be kidding me. "That's my Rick!"

Your Rick…? Are you talking about a tall handsome man with eyes that make you just want to jump into his arms?

I wouldn't have described him exactly that way but yeah… "that sounds like him."

"How do you know him?"

"It's a long story."

Well I'd like to hear it!

Ok, "it looks like we have time don't we." Yes we do and I can't wait to hear this.

Well it's a strange story; I first met Rick when I tricked him to the Knicks basketball arena. I paid a bum on the street twenty dollars to call him and pretend to be one of his friends. "Wait just a minute."

This story already isn't making any sense. How would you know how to get in touch with him and further more how would you know the name of his friends?

Well first let me say that I tried the direct approach and asked him to meet me because I had some very important information for him. I told him that it needed to be a secluded location but he thought I might be some lunatic and said no. He went on to say that his life was very hectic right now and he wasn't about to complicate it any more by meeting some stranger. I admit that I probably sounded like some crazy person.

Well he was right about his life being hectic. Why did it need to be a secluded location?

I've been in hiding for almost a year. I couldn't take a chance that he would see me. You couldn't take a chance that who would see you? A man that walks with a limp, I don't know his name. He's a very bad person and so are the people that work for him.

That's too confusing for me to try and figure out right now. Maybe you can help me understand how you know Rick's friends. Heck, I don't even know the name of his friends and I'm his lover.

It was easy, all I had to do was get a copy of his phone records and see who he talks to the most. Unbelievable, "I can't even get my own phone records without a court order." How you were able to get his phone records? Let's just say I'm very resourceful and leave it at that.

"So it's obvious that you did meet with him." What happened next?

After I explained who I was and he got over me tricking him, he took me back to his house to continue our conversation. He took you to his house? Yes, but it wasn't a house it was an apartment, a marvelous apartment.

"When was this?" About two weeks ago. That's impossible, "I was there two weeks ago." I would have known about this.

Oh my, "are you Candis Lockhart?"

Yes as a matter of fact I am. How do you know my name?

You are the one who cooked him that great dinner the night I stayed at his apartment. This is unbelievable! Where were you?

"I was in his bedroom." This story is getting crazier by the minute lady. I was trying to believe you. Well maybe you'll believe this part.

You had a little incident in the shower. I think you had mistaken it for a bed and laid down in it after drinking all that wine.

I'm the one who told Rick that he should go check on you.

Oh my God, "you were there." I can't believe this. Why would he do this to me? He had another woman in the house, in his bedroom and I didn't know any thing about it.

"How stupid am I?" Oh just wait until I see him tomorrow!

What makes you think you are going to see him tomorrow?

They said that they we going to let me go tomorrow. "Who told you that?" Mr. Davis did.

Come on Candis you didn't believe him did you? Yes he said they were just trying to teach Rick a lesson. I see now that I'm going to have to teach him one also. I can tell that my little story has pissed you off honey but you really shouldn't be upset with Rick.

"Why shouldn't I be?" He had you in his bedroom while I was in the house. You don't even look like his type.

Let's get something straight. First of all I was only there one night and I was only there to try to help him with the information that I have about a drug that was stolen from my company. Further more, if I remember correctly he slept with you that night.

I think I even recall him saying that after he heard what I had to say he'd decide if he should mention it to you. I'm afraid that he didn't really trust you at that time but from what I can tell things have really changed between the two of you since then. Yes things have changed but apparently trust is something that we both might be having an issue with.

How long have they had you here? The best I can tell is five days but they have had me since the day you went to visit your parents.

That was over a week ago. What are they planning to do with you? I don't know…

**

You wanted to see me sir? Yes please bring Miss Levens to me now. Alright, should we tie her up? No, I don't think that will be necessary.

Here she is. Bring her over here and leave us. Are you sure about that boss?

Yes, "I'm sure." But she might try something.

I said bring her in here and leave us! Don't blame us if she tries to jump out the damn window or something. Don't worry about that if she does you'll be following closely behind her.

I can't believe you are talking to us like this. Well believe it! You girls are not doing your damn job and I'm not going to stand for it any longer! Now leave us! I don't have time for this chitchat right now but maybe I should be looking for new help once this is all over.

Sir we promise to do better, yeah boss we'll do better we promise. Besides, have we ever let you down? Just go outside and wait until I call you. Yes Sir.

Hello Miss Levens, please have a seat. How are you today?

So you don't feel like talking today. That's just fine because all I need you to do right now is listen. It's about time that I let you know what your role in this big mess will be. For now just continue to play the deaf mute part but later we will have to get down to business if you ever hope to get out of here alive. Do I have your attention now? What do I have to do?

"So you can talk." Well for starters let's talk about the last project you were working on when you were employed with Warrenton Pharmaceutical. What does that have to do with anything? "Don't play stupid Miss Levens." As you well know, there is a big investigation into the Advernox formulation right now.

I don't know anything about a drug with that name. It's the drug that BMX stole from your company. They simply renamed it.

So let's just get everything out in the open shall we. We all know that BMX stole the formulation from your company. However, in doing so they made one astronomical mistake.

"What was their mistake?"

Greed Miss Levens, it has always been the down fall of man and it always will be. How do I fit into this twisted horror? You Miss Levens hold the key to unlocking this puzzle. If that were true Mr. Davis wouldn't someone have gotten to me long before you? Good point Miss Levens, "may I call you Kathy." I don't care what you call me as long at you let me go. I plan to let you go Kathy but not before you've given me what I need.

Do you realize that everyone thinks you are dead? It would be better for me if I were. Come on now, "stop feeling sorry for yourself."

Can you just get to what it is that you want from me!

Sure I can understand your impatience. I'll make this as simple as I can. We need you to reformulate Advernox.

That's impossible Mr. Davis and I think you know it is.

I'm not convinced Kathy, before I learned that you were alive I might have agreed with that statement but not any more. I believe you might not even know yourself that you can solve this puzzle. It's my belief that your company was about to ditch the project because you found some type of side effect that couldn't be fixed.

"Am I right about that?"

You might be.

I also think that if given enough time your group would have figured out a way to make your drug safe.

Am I right about that?

"No, you're not."

We had been looking into the side effect for months and there was no way to fix it without a total reformulation. The problem was our drug only worked in it current form and any type of reformulation would have made it ineffective. The project was all but put to bed when those mad men broke into the lab and killed my friends. The stupid idiots had no idea what they were about to do.

Several months later I'm reading a Canadian newspaper and on the front page is a story about this wonder drug that BMX Pharmaceutical had developed. It claimed to do all the things that our drug did. It took me a few days too piece everything together but when I did I completely understood what had happened. That's when I decided that I had to come out of hiding.

Well it's a good thing for us that you did. I have a hunch about you which tells me that you are on the verge of saving a lot of people lives. Believe me, if I knew of any way to help save these people lives I would not hesitate to do it.

What do you think it might take to help you remember? I don't think there's anything wrong with my memory. I just don't know what the solution is. I can say that this is too much of a problem for just one person to handle.

What if I got you some help? Who?

How about your new roommate? That poor woman thinks she's leaving tomorrow. Well maybe I've changed my mind about that. But didn't you give her your word? So what if I did, this is just too important to lose sleep over because I broke my word.

So you're telling me that if you ever give me your word on something, "it really means nothing right."

"Don't play games with me Katherine!" This project is just too important and we are running out of time. Do you think Candis can help you?

I don't know her background Mr. Davis.

What do your instincts tell you? Do you really want too know what I think about her? I think she's going to kill you once she hears this news.

"Well that's a chance I'm willing to take."

Tell me one thing Mr. Davis. How does any of this benefit you? What are you going to do with this information if we can solve the puzzle with the formulation?

Sure I can share it with you. I'm going to sell it to the highest bidder. In a perfect world that would be BMX Pharmaceutical because all they would have to do is make the necessary changes to the formulation and continue selling it. Are you telling me that no one would ever know there was a problem?

The important thing here is that people are taking a safe product.

"You really are a monster!"

What good would it do to alarm people about the side effects? It's too late for most of those people any way but you can help the ones that it's not too late for. I still don't know if I can help but there are some things that I'm going to need. Like what?

Give me a pen and paper and I'll give you a list.

"It better be a short list."

Just remember I'm doing this for those innocent people out there not for you. I understand. No you don't, you don't understand a damn thing except money and death. Now give me a pen and a piece of paper. This will only take a few minutes. Here you go now start writing.

"Don't rush me!"

Girls come in here for a minute. While Kathy is composing her wish list I want one of you contact the guys and tell them to go out and get us some food. Tell them to go to that restaurant in the Bronx that serves those great steaks that I like so much. Order enough food for an army and get back here with it as soon as they can. I think it's time that we showed our two guests some good old fashion New York hospitality. Have them pick up a couple of bottles of wine also. Yes sir.

Here's my list. This is a big list. Where the hell are my glasses? Oh here they are. I thought I said for you too make it a short list. Have a seat while I look this over. I need to go to the bathroom. Just hold it for a few minutes.

What are you trying to do blackmail me?

No I'm not but the way I see it I have no choice, "so I might as well get paid for it." I admire your attempt but this is outrageous.

"You listen to me you fat lard ass!"

I'm tired of being pushed around and I'm tired of living the way that I do. That amount of money is a deal and you know it.

Besides we know I'll never live long enough to spend any of it. I give you my word that you will be able to walk away unharmed when this is all over. I don't want your word. It means nothing to me. I see how much good your word did Miss Lockhart.

"That's different." Explain to me how it's different? A man's word is his word; it's as simple as that. There aren't supposed to be any strings attached.

I want a third of the money up front or I'll do nothing. So you are trying to black mail me. Call it what you want. Do we have a deal or not?

I can only offer you your life. I don't think I'm going to leave this place alive. So if that's what you believe what good is the money going to do you? I'm going to open a trust fund for my parents, effective immediately. I'll give you fifty thousand. I want at least a hundred or forget it.

Damn it woman you are lucky that you have time on your side. What account do you want us to deposit the money in? I'll deposit the money myself tomorrow morning. Alright then, "so we have a deal."

You had better remember a couple of things Mr. Davis. First of all I'm not doing this for you. I'm doing it for all those sick people out there. Secondly, there is no guarantee that any of my knowledge is going to help solve the reformulation.

That's a chance I'm willing to take. Why? I'd say because your life depends on it. Are these more of you're lies or is this a real threat? You can be the judge of that lady but if I were you I'd take it as a threat.

You just have the money and a car to take me to the bank first thing tomorrow morning. I'll need a couple of days to get my hands on that kind of cash. Fine but the longer it takes you the more it's going to cost you and I'm not doing anything until I have the money. You surprise me Kathy. I didn't have you pegged as being such a hard nose. Never under estimate a woman Mr. Davis. We are more driven than you men will ever be.

"I'll have the money first thing tomorrow morning."

***

Lillie…Jackie, take Kathy back to her room and bring me Miss Lockhart.

He wants to see you next Miss America.

What does he want with me?

You'll have to ask him that.

Kathy you just spoke to him, what does he want? I'm afraid you're going to have to stay here longer than you expected. What are you talking about? It's complicated Candis. I'm sure Mr. Davis will explain everything sweetheart. You should have never believed he would let you go so soon.

"Take me to him now!"

Just hold on a minute Miss America. We have to tie your legs before we take you anywhere. You didn't tie her up. There was no need. She's just as gentle as a little pussycat. You on the other hand, might not be as gentle. We are not taking any chances with you.

Here she is Mr. Davis. Do you want us to stay in here? No just wait outside the door like you did the last time. Ok sir but you better watch this one. She's nothing but trouble. I got this, just wait outside.

Have a seat Miss Lockhart. What's this I'm hearing about you not letting me go? Who told you that? Don't worry about that. Now is it true or not? Well Candis, it all depends on how you look at it. I do plan to let you go but it won't be today.

"If not today then when!"

That's also a little complicated. I had planned to release you as I had promised but I have a feeling that you will be of more use to me here for the time being. What the hell for? Apparently Miss Livens is going to need assistance with a little project that I just assigned to her and you seem to be the most qualified person for the job.

"I demand that you release me now or you'll be sorry!" Sorry, pretty lady as much as it saddens me to have to break my word to you I must.

You big fat ass liar. "What is it that you want now?"

Try to calm down. I am calm you overweight lard ass. You think you can just play games with peoples lives. Well not any longer, those days are over with.

What is that!

Is that a gun Candis?

Call your girls in here! Don't force me to use this, said Candis.

Where in the hell did you get that gun?

Don't you worry about that lard ass, just get them in here now.

Girls come in here.

What's going on boss?

Some how this witch got her hands on a got damn gun, yelled Davis! Shut up all of you, screamed Candis! You two ladies get over there beside your boss.

I want you ladies to take this rope off my legs and wrap it around his neck and squeeze until the bastard chokes to death.

What?

You heard me do it now! I hate repeating myself. I have half a mind to shoot all three of you in the head right now because I know if I don't I'll have to deal with you later.

You'll never get away with this Miss America. Yeah besides I bet you don't even have the guts to pull the trigger. I've had about as much of you as I can stand. Now shut your big mouth and tie your boss to his chair. If you say another word to me I'll blow your head off your freaking shoulders. "

If you don't believe me try me." Now do what I said and hurry up!

Wait before you tie him up, "take off his clothes."

Take off his clothes?

"That's what I said!"

See boss I told you she was tricky.

Shut up! I still haven't figured out how you let her walk in her with a gun, didn't you search her?

No…we thought the guys did.

Now toss the clothes in the corner and tie his ugly fat ass to the chair.

Alright it's done.

Now you ladies strip and throw your clothes in the corner.

Why do we have to take our clothes off?

"Just do it!"

Now you with the big mouth tie up your lesbian friend.

Miss Lockhart, I really wish you would reconsider what you are doing. Have you thought about your parents? Yes, I have thought about them every single second since this twisted nightmare began. They are my inspiration and I give them all the credit for giving me the courage to blow your fat head off your shoulders!

I went to see my father a few days ago and when I saw him lying in that hospital with a broken arm I knew I had to fight fire with fire.

What happened to your father?

You sent your goons to rough him up. You nearly gave him and my mother a heart attack. Candis I swear to you that my people never touched your parents.

"Shut up you liar!"

You put up a good front Candis but you are not the violent type.

You have no idea how violent I can be when I'm backed into a corner. You started this mess, so deal with it.

What are you going to do now? You do realize that you can't call the police don't you. If you do your parents' life will belong to me! How will you be able to live with yourself knowing that you caused their death? Oh and please don't forget about the love of your life, "I'm afraid that we'll have to deal with him also."

Mr. Davis, I see death is the only thing that you understand. Tell me how you are going to give all these orders after I send several bullets through your heart? Oh forgive me...I forgot you don't have one. I'll just have to put these bullets in your head instead.

Woman you don't have the nerves! Just look at how your arms they are shaking. Here's the deal Candis, I'm willing to forget about this little crazy act of yours if you put down the gun right now and untie us. Don't get me wrong I admire the way you handle yourself under pressure, much better than these two idiots in the room with us right now. You are a smart lady. Don't do something that you're going to regret.

I already have Mr. Davis. I regret allowing you to get to the people I love. I realize now that the only way to protect them is remove myself from this earth.

What are you talking about?

This gun was never for you or your stupid tricks.

"It was for me." Without me around my parents and the man I love can go on living a peaceful life.

What are you saying Candis?

"Stop with the damn questions!" I'm in charge now. "I'll ask the damn questions."

I want you to write out a confession right now about your involvement with everything. I will do no such thing! Yes you will or I'll send a bullet though you head right now. Screw you witch!

Bang...oh my God, "you shot him."

That's right and you two are next.

You stupid, stupid woman, I can't believe you shot me.

Consider yourself lucky that I'm a little rusty. You were lucky this time. That shot only glazed your arm. Next time I guess I'll have to stand a little closer.

Give me the damn paper and pen.

Boss you're not going to sign that are you?

Shut up!

While he's writing his confession you two can start on yours. Here's a pen. I'm sure I won't have to convince you like I did him or will I? Oh no Candis, just give us the paper and pen. Just as a little insurance I had this little tape recorder. I didn't think you'd give in so easy. Let's take a few minutes to listen to it....

***

Have you heard enough Mr. Davis or should I let it play for a few more minutes? I guess I didn't really need a signed confession after all. Except I don't think tapes are admissible in court.

A tape recorder, now I'm really impressed. She has a gun and a tape recorder. How did you sorry ass ladies allow this to happen?

You're both fired!

I think they already know that.

I can make you a very rich lady Candis. Just name a price and it's yours. Really, Mr. Davis any price at all? Yes just name it and it's yours. Are you giving me your word that this is not a trick?

Yes, "I give you my word."

Let me just think about this for a second. Do you remember the last time you gave me your word? It shouldn't be that hard it was just a few hours ago. Based on how that turned out I'm afraid I'm going to have to decline your generous offer.

Please Candis, "this time I really mean it."

You know what, I actually believe you this time but something tells me that you might also have a little trick up your sleeve. Besides, I can't be bought. Now where's the telephone? It's about time I called the police.

Can we have our clothes back?

What would be the point? You girls won't need them where you're headed.....

***

Hello, Rick. Sweetheart where are you? I've been worried sick. You're not going to believe me but I'm at a snake-infested warehouse somewhere in New York.

What are you talking about?

No time to explain right now the police are on the way and I have to get out of here. What's this talk about the police? I'll explain everything when Karen and I get there.

You do remember Karen don't you....Rick?

Karen who?

Miss Katherine Levens honey. Don't you remember the names of women that sleep in your bed? Oh...that Karen but how do you know her? I'll be home in about an hour and she'll be with me. Make sure the guest bedroom is ready for her. This time I'll be the one in your bedroom.

Sweetheart, I was so worried about you, I can't wait to see you.

I can't wait to see you either Mr. Naylor.

I'm in a lot of trouble right…

Yes you are Ricky…unless you have a bottle of Chere Patier' and some soft music playing in your bedroom when I get there.

***

Hi Rick, this is Albert.

Hi Al, how are you?

I'm fine, I just heard about Franklin Davis. How much longer do you want us to watch your kids? For a little while longer I'm afraid. It's too early to tell what's going to happen. He has a lot of money and he might find a way to get out of this but I doubt it. Just to be on the safe side, increase the security at my kids' house as well as at their schools.

I can put two additional men at each location Mr. Naylor but I'm afraid that it's going to cost you.

Money is no object these are my kids that we are talking about. I understand. I'll make it happen as soon as I hang up the phone Mr. Naylor.

CHAPTER 16

Good morning Mr. Taylor. Good morning Mr. Legitt. Would you please tell the court how you know Judge Kenton? The Judge and I have been friends for over forty years. That's a long time. How did this friendship develop?

Well I was on trial for murder and was about to be convicted when our future Judge here came to my rescue. He was only eight years old at the time. You say he came to you rescue. How did he do that?

He was a witness to a murder that I was accused of. If it pleases the court we would like to hear what happened. Maybe you should let the judge tell it. I'd rather hear it from you. Judge is it ok? Sure it is Charley, you tell it better than I ever could.

I can remember it like it was yesterday. I had this field hand named Eddie. He was one of the nicest people you ever want to meet. The only thing about Eddie was that he was slow. He was deaf in one ear and he couldn't talk. When he was a kid, his master had his tongue cut out because he told his mother that he heard his sister crying behind the corn shed.

When Eddie went to see what was happening he found the master on top of his sister, it wasn't until Ed tried to pull him off that he understood what was happening. Any way he was a terrific worker and he was great with horses. The women folk didn't care for him to much though except for this young girl named Daria.

It was a Tuesday afternoon and I had asked Eddie to go to town and gather some supplies. Against my better judgment I allowed him to go alone. He had always done exactly as I had told him. Just as he was leaving my neighbor Miss Thomas asked if Daria could ride into town with him and do some washing for Mr. Williams. I didn't see any harm in it, so I said yes.

About an hour later Mr. Williams came by asking for Daria. Miss Thomas told him that she had caught a ride into town with Eddie. We became concerned because the trip into town only took about fifteen minutes. We searched the entire road into town but we saw no sign of them. We even checked Old Dawn's Fall Road, which lead to a famous swimming area for the kids when I was young. It was the back way to town and was hardly ever used because the road was to narrow for a buckboard. We didn't see any signs of them there either.

Mr. Williams bought me back to the house and told Miss Thomas that he wouldn't need Daria's services in the future. Miss Thomas and I knew that something had to be dreadfully wrong. She convinced me that I should go out and look again.

Mean while the Judge was on his way back from school that day. He knew all the short cuts and took them whenever he could even though he had been told by his parents to stay on the main road.

On this day he took his favorite shortcut that led him past a small pond where the catfish were always jumping out of the water. The Judge liked to stand there and count them. He thought this was a far better way to learn math than what was being taught to him in that old run down school. He had counted about ten when he thought he heard laughter coming from inside the wood line.

He walked in the direction of the laughter. When he got closer, he noticed a buckboard behind some trees. The buckboard was rocking back and forth. He heard the laughter again and noticed a man and a woman in the buckboard. A pretty girl was laughing as a man tickled her or at least that's what it looked like to an eight year old boy. After a few more minutes of laughter the girl climbed on top of the man and started to move up and down and continued to laugh.

The man however, wasn't laughing, instead he seemed to be getting madder and madder the more she laughed.

Suddenly she jumped off of him and out of the buckboard and said. We best get to town now Eddie. The man wasn't saying anything he just kept waving for her to get back in. No Eddie she shouted, we must get going now.

Eddie jumped down and grabbed the girl by the hair and started pulling her toward the buckboard. It must have hurt because she let out a loud scream. Suddenly the woods got very noisy as the birds started flying and shrieking like the world was coming to an end.

Some how she broke loose from Eddie and started running toward the dirt road but Eddie caught up to her very fast. He wrestled her to the ground and climbed on top of her but this time there was no laughing.

She was shouting," get off me Eddie", get off me! Ain't you never had a woman before?

This is not how it's done Eddie, (sob) I's sorry for playing with you before," now please get off me".

Eddie had pulled her dress up and was starting to pleasure himself. There was no more laughter. The poor girl was screaming to the top of her lungs.

Eddie knew he had to shut her up. So he put one hand over her mouth and took the other hand and put it around her neck to make her be still. By the time he realized what he was doing, "it was too late".

Daria had stopped fighting and her body had gone limp. Eddie stood over her body and let out an awful cry of grief. He reached down and picked up her limp body and stood her on her feet. When he let go her lifeless body fell to the ground. This confirmed his fear and he sat down on a stump and cried like a new born baby.

Suddenly there was movement coming from the road and Eddie's head snapped around and looked in that direction. He jumped up and took off running through the woods. What Eddie had heard was me. I had heard Daria when she was screaming.

When I got to the area where they were I could see Eddie at the end of the wood line looking at me. He took two steps in my direction but then stopped. He gave me this sad look and pointed to the spot where Daria lay. When I looked back at him he dropped his head. I ran over to where she was.

It was obvious what had taken place because her dress had been ripped. I looked back at the spot where I had seen Eddie but he was gone. I stood there in shock as the reality of what had happened hit me like a tidal wave. I was over come with grief for several minutes. I finally kneeled down beside her and checked for a pulse. As innocent as this was, it turned out to be a horrific mistake because I was not the only one who had heard the screams.

I heard a noise and quickly looked up. Staring at me were three men that I had seen many times before. They rushed me and wrestled me to the ground. You can only imagine what it looked like to them. My buckboard was there, my horse and my neighbors house maid Daria was lying dead on the ground next to me. How could you blame them for what they were thinking at that moment?

The men started beating me until they came to their senses and sent someone to get the sheriff. I told the sheriff my story but he didn't believe me. My attorney tried too hide it but he didn't believe me either and that jury…they couldn't put a rope around my neck fast enough.

The trial only lasted two days. The whole town was calling for my neck. Just as I was about to be sentenced this young man's father went to the Judge and told him the story that you just heard. They reluctantly accepted the story.

That's a very sad story Charley. I know it is and it gets worst Mr. Legitt. How did it get worst?

A few weeks after they let me go I was fishing on the river. It had been raining for several days and the river was high. It was a terrible day for fishing. Just as I was about to call it a day I noticed something caught in the rocks just around the river's bend. I couldn't get close enough to be sure but it looked like a body. I stood there and stared at it for about a minute and then I realized why it had caught my attention in the first place. What I was looking at started to take on a form. It was definitely a body. I recognized Eddie's maroon shirt. It was his favorite shirt.

I think he must have jumped off the top of Dawn's Fall and hit the rocks below....

Please Mr. Johnson I think we've heard enough. I simply wanted to know how you knew the Judge. Well I just told you. I had to start at the beginning and tell the whole story because no good story is told in bits and pieces.

He is your witness now Vonhart.

Hello Charley, Hello Mr. Vonhart.

It's still a bit of a mystery to me that you would volunteer to come here and testify about something that relates to this case. Why would you do that? Well I was watching the news the other night and there was a report on about the lab that burned to the ground last year. It went on to say that there was a trial going on. I just thought it would be a good idea for me to come and tell everyone what I saw that night. Are you telling me that you were there when the lab burned down?

"No that's not what I'm saying."

Well..."what are you saying?"

What I'm trying to say is, "I was outside the lab when those people were murdered." I don't know anything about a fire though.

Mr. Johnson are you telling this court that you witnessed a murder at the Warrenton Pharmaceutical Products Lab?

Objection Your Honor, Mr. Vonhart is leading the witness. You are overruled Mr. Legitt. Mr. Johnson, do I need to repeat my question? No Mr. Vonhart. This is what I saw but I have to start at the beginning. That will be just fine.

"This is what I saw"......Objection!!

CHAPTER 17

Rick thank God I finally got you. I've been trying to reach you all day.

Hello Candis, what's up?

Last night I couldn't sleep so I starting going over some of my old notes about the Advernox formulations. I can't believe what I found. I feel so stupid. You feel stupid about what? The information that we have been searching for the past two months is right here in my notes from five months ago.

Candis you are not making any sense. How could you have note from five months ago?

Rick get dressed and come over. I'll explain everything when you get here. What time is it? It's two a.m.

Can't this wait until later today? No it can't, we might both be dead by then. Ok now you've got my attention. I'll be there as soon as I can.

How am I going to tell Rick the truth? There is no easy way to do this but I must tell him tonight. I love him so much. I have to make him understand.

***

Hi Rick that was fast. So, what's going on?

Come into the study.

I was hoping for the bedroom.

This is no time for being funny mister. I've laid everything out on the desk for you to review. Would you like something to drink? Sure, what you got? I have several things but I recommend coffee. It's going to be a long day. We don't need alcohol clouding our mind.

"I agree with that Candis." Where do I start?

Like I said Rick, everything is laid out in order on my desk, just start reading. I'll be right back with the coffee. Do you want cream and sugar? Yes.

Wow, "that's a lot of papers." Can't you just tell me what's in them? I could but I think you'd better read it for yourself. Ok but you better hurry up with the coffee.

***

Well Rick, what do you think?

Candis, I'm confused about how you came to gather this information but I have an idea. You were part of the first team weren't you?

"Yes...I'm afraid I was."

Why didn't you tell me? We could have saved a lot of time.

Is that really what you believe Rick?

"Yes I do." I feel betrayed.

I'm sorry that you feel that way but this was the only way. If you had known from the beginning it would have clouded everything. So tell me what you think after reading these reports.

Candis from what I can gather, it appears that BMX was in such a rush too manufacture this product that they took a lot of short cuts. The one that seems to be the most costly is the fact that they use an old facility that had not been used in over five years to manufacture Advernox.

It would appear that they didn't do a good job of cleaning all of the equipment, thus causing cross-contamination issues. I believe that there may have been residue from those old products and that residue got into Advernox when it was being produced.

"That's right Rick." It would only take a small amount of this other drug to create this horrific side effect. What I don't understand Candis is that you had this information all along and you didn't share it with me. Why?

Rick I didn't make the connection about the old facility and cross-contamination until tonight. So I wasn't keeping that from you. I'm sure Mr. Winters doesn't even realize it himself, said Candis. The question is do we tell him now?

I can't answer that until I know something. I need you too confirm something for me Miss Lockhart. I will if I can…Mr. Naylor.

All this time I've been thinking that I was in charge but I wasn't.

I'm afraid not Rick. This has been my project for the past six months. I needed someone who could handle a team like the one we now have. You were that person. You were so highly recommended that I had no choice in the matter.

Why so many secrets Candis? I've fallen in love with you. Please tell me that this wasn't just part of the game also.

Rick, sweetheart, I promise you that it wasn't. Actually, I was really pissed at you in the beginning. Well you didn't try to hide that from me Candis.

I felt that I could handle this project with the team I had but William Winters had grown tired of our failures. He was looking for a miracle and we couldn't give it to him so he wanted a change. That's the real reason I was so angry in the beginning.

So why are you showing me all this now? Because I think we have solved the formulation mystery, said Candis. The first batches of Advernox were manufactured in a facility where microorganisms existed, which explains why the side effect isn't present in the newer batches.

That may be true Candis but that doesn't explain why WPP had concerns about their product.

"I think it does Rick." You see, Warrenton Pharmaceutical is a small company. They didn't have a facility to test the product. I believe that someone at WPP was working with someone at BMX and that old plant that BMX has in North Jersey is where the formulation was produced. It was then given to the people at WPP to study. How else can we explain the fact that BMX even knew about Advernox or whatever Warrenton Pharmaceutical was calling it back then.

Once BMX had stolen the formula they just started producing Advernox at that plant. So Candis what you are telling me is all these women and their babies have died because someone didn't clean their equipment properly?

Can it really be that simple Candis?

"Yes it can Rick."

Kathy said that to her knowledge there wasn't any dealing with BMX. Come on Rick! Kathy was just a chemist; they probably never allowed her to attend a board meeting. How could she know what was really happening? Ok, Candis, I see your point.

With what you and I have discovered combined with Evan and Steven fantastic discovery all we need now is to get into the lab and do the tests. If we get three matches, it probably means Advernox doesn't need to be reformulated at all.

The only thing that needs to happen now is to get all product that was manufactured at that facility pulled from the shelves. The only remaining questions are how much was manufactured at that facility and how much is still on the market? Rick sweetheart, isn't this an exciting discover?

Well of course it is but forgive me if I'm not jumping for joy at the moment. There are just too many unanswered questions in my mind, "too many lies". I don't know what to think.

There is another thing that's been bothering me.

What is it Rick?

Steven has been out of work now for three days. He said that he had a cold. When I called him last night there was no answer. So I called the front desk. They said that he checked out of his room two days ago.

Do you think he went back home?

I'm not sure but Evan had doubts about him from the very beginning. It looks like he was right.

"Forget about Steven for now." We have bigger problems

This company has so much too lose if word of this ever got out. You're damn right they do, said Candis and to think I've been defending them. Don't worry so much about that now Candis. What you should concern yourself with is what they are going to do once they find out we know the truth. Rick do you think they might take measures to get rid of us?

Why would they do that Candis? We are the only ones who know the truth and the only ones that can help send them to jail.

Rick your humor escapes me at this moment. Can you please try to be more serious?

Rick you can start by helping me find a way to make sure they don't try to make us disappear. How do I know that this is not just part of your original plan Candis? I guess that's a fair question. Do you want me to prove my loyalty to you? I don't know what I want at this point.

Come to bed with me now and I'll prove to you who I'm loyal too.

After all these lies, you think I'm just going to jump into bed with you?

Are you saying that you don't want me anymore? I'm saying that you had better come clean about everything and you had better start doing it right now!

On second thought, "I think I should go". I need to be alone.

Rick, I love you, please don't leave. I'll make it up to you, "I promise".

I love you too but I don't want to be in the same room with you right now. I can't believe you're leaving me tonight of all nights.

Well I can't believe you've been lying to me all this time either. Goodnight Candis....

***

Who is knocking at my door this early in the morning? Good morning Miss Lockhart my name is Darius Pollard. I know this may seem weird but I must speak to you right away, it's extremely important. May I come in? I don't let strangers into my house, especially someone that is carrying a suitcase.

What are you planning to do sir move in.

That's very cute Miss Lockhart but, I'm leaving town in a matter of hours. Would you feel better if Mr. Naylor was here?

What's this about?

It's about Advernox Miss Lockhart and if I were you, I'd listen to what I have to say or be prepared to spend the rest of your life behind bars. Well...Mr. Pollard you definitely have my attention but I still can't let you in.

Fine, how soon do you think you can have Mr. Naylor here? I'm afraid he is not speaking to me right now. He needs to hear what I have to say also. Call him and ask him to come over right away. Here is my cell number, I only have one hour to spare before I have to catch my flight. What I have to say will only take a few minutes.

"You call him now!" I'll be in the lobby waiting for your call.

Hello Rick, how are you? I'm busy Candis, what can I do for you? Please, you don't have to sound so cold. I don't mean to sound cold but I am busy. There is a man named Darius Pollard waiting for us in the lobby. Who is he? I don't know. Are you telling me the truth?

Yes Rick, before today I never met the man. He said that if I didn't want to spend the rest of my life behind bars, I should let him in. He wants to speak to us about Advernox. He even knew your name and suggested that I'd be more comfortable if you were here. Can you come over?

You don't know this guy Candis? No I don't Rick, I've never seen him before. I don't have time for this right now but as soon as I'm finished with this report for William I'll be right over. No Rick you need to come now! Forget about what's happened between us, I think we need to hear what he has to say.

It's weird, he showed up here with a suitcase. When I asked him about it he said that he was leaving town in a few hours. He also said that he can only wait one hour. I guess I should come right over then. Give me about thirty minutes but don't let him in if I'm not there when he returns. I don't like the sound of this one bit Candis.

***

Candis I got here as soon as I could. It wasn't easy getting past all the police in the lobby. There are police in the lobby? Yes, someone was stabbed down there.

What is going on?

I don't know.

Did the guy give you his phone number? Yes he did. He said to call him as soon as you got here. Ok, call him.

Hello, is this Mr. Pollard?

No Miss, I'm afraid it's not.

Well, I'm sure this is the number that he gave me. I'm sorry I must have dialed the wrong number. No I'm afraid that you have the right number. Who are you Miss? My name is Candis. Are you family? No I'm not. How do you know Mr. Pollard? I don't know him. I just met him less than an hour ago.

Mr. Pollard was stabbed to death fifteen minutes ago. You're kidding me! No I'm not. So tell me again how you know the deceased. I don't know him. I only met him when he showed up to my apartment. What did he want? I'm not sure. What's your apartment number? It's 45c. Ok, my name is Captain Lester. I'm sending someone up there to take a statement from you. He will be there in less than ten minutes.

Rick, you're not going to believe this but Mr. Pollard was stabbed in the lobby. He's dead! The police Captain is sending someone up here right now. Candis can this get any worse? Who was this Mr. Pollard? I don't know but someone didn't want him talking to us.

Oh Rick, I'm so scared. What are we going to do? The first thing we are going to do is tell the police whatever they want to know.

That must be them now. You have a seat sweetheart.

I'll get the door. Hello, my name is Sergeant Gatewood. My Captain sent me up to take a statement from a Miss Candis; we didn't get her last name.

Come on in Sergeant. My name is Rick Naylor; Miss Lockhart is in the living room. We are so shocked by these developments. I'm sure you are Mr. Naylor, I'm sure you are. Please follow me Sergeant.

Candis this is Sergeant Gatewood. Hello, can I get you something to drink? Thank you but that won't be necessary. I only have a few questions and then I'll be on my way.

How long have you known Mr. Pollard? Like I told your Captain, I just meet him today. All he said was that he needed to speak to me. I noticed he had a suitcase and I got concerned. I told him that I couldn't let him in. He said he understood and suggested that I call my boyfriend. He also said," that he could only wait an hour" because he was flying out of town today. He knew Rick's name which I thought was weird, given the fact that neither one of us knew him.

Did he say what he wanted to talk about? No, I'm afraid he never got that chance but he seemed very nervous. Well, now we know why....don't we.

Miss Lockhart, I see a lot of unopened boxes in here. Are you moving out? I just move in here a few weeks ago. How do you think he knew how to find you? I don't know. Are you sure you're telling me everything? Listen Sergeant, she said, "that she never meet the man!"

Well what about you Mr. Naylor?

What about me!

Did you know Mr. Pollard?

No I didn't, Sergeant.

This is very odd, said Sergeant Gatewood. Mr. Darius Pollard wasn't just leaving town, he was leaving the country. You expect me to believe that a man who's leaving the country and his wife in a matter of hours and who is obviously fleeing for his life would take time to stop and chat with perfect strangers.

Doesn't that seem odd to you. I'm sorry but that just seems a little odd to me.

Well Sergeant, said Candis I agree with you, it does seem strange but I promise you that we are telling you the truth. We never meet the man! Now we have been very cooperative with you but unless you have more questions, I think it's time for you to leave. Very well, I guess that will be all for now, said Sergeant Gatewood.

We might need to question both of you again at a later date. Mr. Naylor, what's your address? Here, it's on my business card but it's only good for about three more weeks. Oh, I'm sure we'll be in touch with you before then. I'll see myself out. Sergeant before you go, I have a question.

What is it, Mr. Naylor? You say this man was leaving the country. Yes, that's correct, "he had his passport in his suitcase," said Sergeant Gatewood. He also has his employee I.D. The little fellow worked for the FDA. You two have a good day. Goodbye Sergeant.

Why did someone from the FDA want to talk to us? I don't know but get your jacket and enough clothes for a couple of days. I think we need to stay at my place for a while.

Does this mean that you forgive me? I afraid not but I do love you and I can't bear the thought of anything happening to you. Oh Rick, "that's such a sweet thing to say." Are you hungry Candis? Yes, Rick, I'm starving. I haven't been able to eat anything since you stopped speaking to me.

Stop being so dramatic Candis; it's only been two days. Now let's go get something to eat before you die of hunger.

I'll have lunch with you but I'm coming back here. I'm tired of running from my home. If you come back here Candis, I'm staying with you tonight. You'll get no argument from me on that Mr. Naylor. Is the Italian restaurant on 22nd and Vine Ok?

Yes, my love, "that will do just fine."

***

Mr. Winters this is Sergeant Gatewood. Mr. Pollard wasn't able to speak to Rick and Candis. They don't seem to know anything.

Thank you Charles. I knew I could count on you. Your debt to me is finally paid and thanks again for taking care of that little FDA weasel. It was my pleasure sir but there is one thing.

"What is it?"

I took a letter off Mr. Pollard that has some very disturbing information on it. Ok bring it to me. "I will sir but be advised that this letter is obviously a copy." I see…. that could mean trouble. Bring it to me right away. "Yes sir."

***

J.T. this is William, hello William. I think I'm going to have to deal with Sergeant Gatewood. Why, what has he done?

"That idiot thinks I'm a fool," said William.

That's not a crime William, "a lot of people feel that way about you."

Screw you John; just find someone to take care of him. Damn William, when do you want this done? I have a meeting with him later today. Anytime after that will be fine.

Are you sure about this William? James has worked for you over ten years. Yes I'm sure but don't worry, I'll send a nice wreath to his family.

"You are one cold-blooded man" Mr. William Winters. I may be cold-blooded but I'm no ones fool.

***

Rick thanks for taking me to dinner. That was some of the best Italian food that I have ever had. You are welcome. Where is the box with those movies that you were talking about? You are in the mood for a movie.

Yes, "I need something to calm my mind." A good comedy should do the trick. I don't have many comedies. How about a back massage instead?

Candis is that the door bell? I think so, I'll get it? Hello, are you Miss Candis Lockhart? Yes I am. Who are you? That's not important. This is for you. You've been served. What is this? It's a summons. Have a good night.

Who was that Candis? It was a process server. I just got a summons. I'm being ordered to appear as a witness for the defense tomorrow morning at 9:00a.m. Case number

239076, Warrenton Pharmaceutical Products verses BMX Pharmaceutical.

"It looks like Warrenton Pharmaceutical Products is suing Bernstein Medicines and Xenobiotics."

Apparently WPP is saying that Advernox was stolen from them.

That's exactly what Kathy Levens was saying. I think we should try to contact her. Good luck with that Rick. Remember she left in the middle of the night after that little situation at the warehouse with Mr. Davis.

She doesn't want to be found. We'll just have to wait for her to contact us.

Candis if you don't mind my asking, what else does the summons say? Well…it looks like William Winters also got served along with a few other employees at BMX. This can't be good Candis.

No it isn't Rick and I'm afraid it gets worst. Your name is also on this list. "Let me see that." You're right Candis, this is unbelievable and it can't be good. A summons never is Rick. I better call William right now. What has he got me involved in this time?

***

Peaches, this is Rick, please put me through to William. He's not in Rick but I bet you're calling about the summons. "Yes I am Peaches." Well William won't be back for several days, some big meeting came up. I've been trying to reach him all day but he hasn't returned my call yet. Peaches when you reach him please have him call me right away. Ok, Rick I will. I'll talk to you later.

Well William, "that was Richard Naylor". He called just like you thought he would. I hate it when you make me lie to him. I don't care what you like as long as you work for me, you'll do as I say!

Don't forget where you were working before I hired you. I'd hate to see you back on the streets at your age. Most men are into the younger prostitutes. You can be so mean sometimes William. I admit I made some mistakes when I was younger but that was a long time ago.

"That's my point exactly Peaches."

***

Candis I just tried to call William but he's at a meeting somewhere. Did you talk to Peaches? Yes I did. She couldn't tell you where he was? She said she'd been trying to reach him all day. You didn't believe her did you? Sure I did, why would she lie to me? I'm not saying that she's lying but come on; his number one girl can't reach him when she needs too. I just think it sounds a little fishy.

Maybe you're right, it's getting late, let's take a shower and call it a day, said Rick. Call it a day? Rick it's only four o'clock in the afternoon. Woman, "I know what time it is." I've been waiting all day to get my hands on you Candis. Alright then big daddy, let's take that shower and make sure you bring that new body oil.

CHAPTER 18

"All rise."

Please be seated.

Good morning, Mr. Legitt you may call your next witness. The defense calls Mr. William Winters to the stand.

Rick I thought William was supposed to be out of town for a couple of days. That's what Peaches said but it looks like your theory might be correct Candis.

Mr. Winters do you swear to tell the truth the whole truth and nothing but the truth? I do. Please be seated. Mr. Winters, please tell the court what you do for a living.

I'm the CEO for BMX Pharmaceutical.

How long have you held your position? I've been the CEO for seven years now. I've been with the company for over twenty-five years. That's pretty impressive.

Thank you, I'm proud of it.

Can you give us an overview of what a CEO does? Sure, basically, I'm responsible for all the company decisions. I have a board of ten members throughout the company and we meet and discuss issues that affect the company. Occasionally we even vote on these issues but when it comes down to it I have the final say.

What can you tell us about Advernox?

I can tell you anything that you wish to know. Do you know how long it was in research before it was sent to FDA for approval, said Mr. Legitt? Yes as a matter of fact I do. I remember meeting with a gentleman named J.T. Barrows and he had an ideal about this new drug which would later be know to the public as Advernox, said Mr. Winters.

We meet on December 1999 and started research in February of 2000. Approximately 19 months later we sent it to FDA for approval. What did the FDA have to say about it? They were impressed with our finding and case studies and did not hesitate to recommend that it be released to the public because there is a huge need for a drug of this kind.

I see, so you're saying that it was in research for about nineteen months. That's correct Mr. Legitt. Do you have proof of this? We forwarded the proof to the court as soon as we became aware of WPP allegations, said Mr. Winters.

Your Honor what I have here is the full report on Advernox, said Mr. Legitt. It includes all research, development, case studies and tests on this drug. It is marked as exhibit one. I have no further questions for Mr. Winters.

Mr. Vonhart, your witness, said Mr. Legitt.

Good morning Mr. Winters, good morning Mr. Vonhart.

I have one problem with what you just told the court. Yes and what would that be, said Mr. Winters? Well correct me if I'm wrong but I thought you stated that a Mr. J.T. Barrows came to you with this idea about Advernox.

"You heard correct."

What is Mr. Barrow's position with your company? He is currently our CFO, said Mr. Winters. What other positions has he held at BMX? He has only held the position of CFO.

Can you explain to those of us who are not familiar with these terms what a CFO does? Sure I can do that. A CFO is a financial expert who is in charge of all the company's finances, said Mr. Winters.

Maybe it's just me Mr. Winters but it seems odd that a financial expert would come to you with an idea like this.

Are you calling me liar son?

No sir but remember, "I'm the one asking the questions."

I was just wondering if it was his idea or did someone approach him with the idea and then he brought it to your attention. It was solely Mr. Barrow's idea. Mr. Winters are you a hundred percent sure about that?

"So you are calling me a liar!"

No I'm not Mr. Winters, "I'm just saying that it seems odd."

No further questions for this witness at this time, however, Your Honor I would like to ask that Mr. Winters remains in the court area, just in case I need to recall him to the stand later.

Mr. Winters, please remain in the area until the end of this session today, said Judge Kenton. Do you understand what is being asked of you? Yes Your Honor, "I understand all too well."

Good, you may step down Mr. Winters.

***

Mr. Legitt, please call your next witness. The defense calls to the stand Miss Candis Lockhart.

Miss Lockhart please raise your right hand. Do you swear to tell the truth the whole truth and nothing but the truth?

"I do."

Please take a seat.

Good morning Miss Lockhart. How are you doing today? I have very important work that I need to be doing right now, said Candis. I understand and I realize that your job must be very important to you. Yes my job is very important to me Mr. Legitt. I won't hold you long but I'm not sure about Mr. Vonhart.

Objection! Sustained, Mr. Legitt stick to the proper line of questioning, said Judge Kenton.

"My apologies Your Honor."

Miss Lockhart what is your line of work? I'm a scientist. Who do you work for? I work for BMX Pharmaceuticals. How long have you worked for BMX Pharmaceuticals? I've worked there almost seven years now. In all that time have you ever known them to be involved in any shady dealings?

Objection Your Honor, he is asking for the witness to speculate on something that is not a known fact. I'll rephrase my question Your Honor.

Miss Lockhart in your seven years at BMX has there ever been any public knowledge of any wrong doings at your place of employment? No, not to my knowledge. As an employee of BMX do you feel that your company operates in the best interest of the public? Yes, I strongly believe that they do. Are you proud to be an employee of BMX? Yes, I'm extremely proud of the work we do there. Thank you Miss Lockhart, "I have no further questions for you."

Mr. Vonhart; she is now your witness.

I have no questions for her at this time. You are free to go Miss Lockhart but remember that you may be asked to return to the stand before this trial is concluded, said Judge Kenton.

Call your next witness Mr. Legitt. Your Honor, if it pleases the court I would like to ask for a ten minute recess. Mr. Legitt, "we just started." I know but I was just made aware of an extremely important issue and I need to confer with my associates.

Very well, everyone take a ten-minute recess, be back in your seats by 9:30a.m.

***

Well, don't just sit there Rick, said Candis, this is a great opportunity to ask Mr. Winters what the hell is going on. Thank you very much Candis but I do have a mind of my own and that's exactly what I was about to do.

Candis the more time we spend in bed together the pushier you become. It's funny that you would say that now. I don't recall having any problem getting you too listen to me last night, said Candis. That comment wasn't necessary, said Rick. Oh really and neither was your fourth organism last night, said Candis. I thought you were going to pound me through the got damn bed. Oh come on Candis; you know you liked that.

Yeah, you're right I did but shut up, I can't be thinking about that right now, it's making me horny, said Candis. You just go talk to William and find out what the hell is going on.

Hello William, I tried calling you yesterday but Peaches couldn't reach you. She told me that you called but I just got back in this morning. I was going to call you then I got this stupid summons and I had to rush over here. I knew I would see you here.

What's this trial really about William? You never said anything to me about any trial. Don't worry Richard; Warrenton Pharmaceutical doesn't have a leg to stand on. Everything that they are saying is just speculation. There's not a jury in the world that would rule in their favor. Why didn't you tell me about all this?

Well frankly Rick, I never thought it would go to trial. Is this going to be another Chester Project, said Rick? No not at all, WPP got lucky and drew Judge Kenton for the hearing, said William. Everyone knows he would put his own mother on trial. You should have told me about this William!

There are two many secrets around here. I don't know who to trust and I still can't believe I allowed myself to be suckered in by you again. Listen Rick, sometimes things have to be handled a certain way. Please don't take it personal, it's just business, now stop whining like a bitch and tell me how are things going at the lab? I'm not your bitch William and don't be trying to change the subject, now I need some answers and I want them now!

I'm not going to just sit on the sideline and let you throw me to the wolves like you did before with the Chester Project! Will you stop talking about that damn project! It's over and done with, said William. It will never be over for me William, not until my name has been cleared.

***

Court is back in session. Mr. Vonhart please call your next witness. We call Mr. Richard Naylor to the stand. Mr. Naylor please raise your right hand. Do you swear that the testimony that you are about to give is the truth the whole truth and nothing but the truth? I do.

Hello Mr. Naylor. Would you please tell the court what you do for a living? I'm a scientist. Do you currently work for BMX Pharmaceuticals? Yes but only temporary. I'm only assisting BMX with a special project right now. I currently work for Bartell Pharmaceuticals located on Long Island, New York. I've been with them for about four months now.

Are you telling me that you are not a permanent employee of BMX Pharmaceutical? That's correct, however, I did work for them for about seven months but I was let go. That's a very short time to work for a new employer, especially for someone with your excellent background. That's why I'm having trouble understanding how they could let you go. Can you enlighten the court on what happened? It just seems very odd to me that they would let you go after only seven months. Did you get in any kind of trouble when you were there?

Objection Your Honor, what is the relevance of this line of questions? Please Your Honor, I'm trying to understand why a company would fire an employee that's never been in trouble a day in their life. Mr. Naylor is not just your ordinary employee; he is a very successful scientist, who is thought by some to be one of the most brilliant scientists alive today.

He has done nothing but good things for this company since the day he arrived. Then for some strange reason out of the blue they call him into the office and say you are no longer a part of our future. What's even more mind boggling to me is the fact that less than five months later they beg him to return for a so-called special project. This just doesn't make any sense. You would think that a company with the great reputation that BMX has would have thousands of qualified scientists lined up at their door everyday trying to get a job there and I'm sure they do. So why rehire someone that you fired recently and put that person in charge of this extremely important special project? Something doesn't seem right about this Your Honor.

Someone is lying to this court and I must know who it is and why. Mr. Jackson your objection is overruled, said Judge Kenton, you may continue Mr. Vonhart.

Now Mr. Naylor what were the circumstances surrounding the termination of your employment with BMX? I'm still not sure but I'll tell you what they told me.

I was called into the office and told that I was being let go because the company wasn't doing well and they needed to rethink the direction that they were headed. So you're saying that you were let go because the company wasn't doing well? That's what I was told.

Well congratulations Mr. Naylor, it looks like that's a thing of the past now doesn't it? With the success of this new product called Advernox, it look's like BMX can once again afford your services. I have no further questions for Mr. Naylor. He's your witness Mr. Legit.

Mr. Legit....yes Your Honor. Are you day dreaming? Mr. Vonhart just said your witness. What are you waiting for?

I have no questions for Richard Naylor, Your Honor. You may step down Mr. Naylor. This court is in recess until 9:00a.m. tomorrow.

"All rise."

***

Excuse me Mr. Vonhart. Yes, Mr. Naylor, how might I assist you? I'm just curious, you seem to know a lot about me. Don't worry son, I always check out any witness.

Most attorneys don't do it because it can become quite expensive. I do it because I hate to be lied too but don't worry you haven't lied to me yet. Well I don't intend to, said Rick. Relax son, you're not the one I'm trying to catch in a lie. Oh by the way, if I were you and Miss Lockhart, I'd take the back exit, the front is swarming with reporters. You two really have no idea what you have gotten yourselves into do you? No, I guess not, said Rick. Well son, both of you need to be very careful. Now excuse me, I really have to go.

***

William, Mr. Jackson Legit is here but I don't see him on the calendar. Its ok Peaches, send him in. Mr. Jackson you may go in. Jackson come on in and make yourself comfortable. If you want me to be comfortable William you will start telling me the truth! What do you mean? I've been truthful with you.

Don't play games with me! Do you want to go to Jail! You were in court today; Rick Naylor made things look very bad for us, said Jackson. I didn't think things went so bad. If that's what you think, you are a bigger idiot than I thought. I'm not the Idiot and if you call me one again I'll fire your crippled ass, said William.

Well that means that all I'm faced with is getting fired but you Mr. William Winters are facing a fate far more serious. Vonhart will eat us alive if we are not careful. I thought you told me you could handle him, said William! I also told you that I needed to know the truth, said Jackson!

Now unless you want to spend the rest of your life in prison you had better come clean with me right now William or find yourself another attorney. You're afraid of Vonhart aren't you, said William? I'm not afraid of anyone except you and that's because you are going to make me lose this case, said Jackson. I cannot and will not lose to Vonhart!

Now I'm telling you that Judge Kenton is not a fool, he can smell a lie a hundred miles away. That jury is not full of idiots either. I see a very short trial Mr. Winters and a very long prison term at the end of it for you. So what's it going to be? Alright, you want the truth Jackson, I'll tell you but you better sit down for this.

When I was first approached about Advernox I was skeptical, however...

***

Candis would you like to go somewhere for dinner? No I'm feeling a little lazy tonight. I would like for you to come over though. I'm not sure I can. I have a lot of work that I must get done tonight. Ok, I understand but my bed is not going to feel the same without you in it. Don't you worry about that, I'll be there soon enough.

What did you think about court today? I'm confused about some things. I understand what you mean. At first it seemed as if this whole case came up out of the blue. Now I think that Warrenton Pharmaceutical has been planning their attack for quite some time. I'm also sure that William Winters has known about this for some time. I wasn't able to get much out of him today but it's so obvious that he's hiding something.

Rick do you remember our first meeting at your apartment? How could I forget, I thought you were an angel when I opened the door. Remember when I said that you were stupid for risking your job for some silly Hunch. Oh yes, my dear, I remember that very well but I don't think the word that you used was silly. You're right and I apologize for that.

So let me ask you. What does your hunch tell you now? I don't have a clue Candis. I'm just glad that we don't have to be in court tomorrow. Not me; I can't wait to hear what's revealed in court tomorrow.

***

"All rise"….please be seated. Mr. Legit please call your next witness, said Judge Kenton. We would like to recall Mr. William Winters back to the stand. Mr. Winters please remember that you are still under oath. I understand.

Mr. Winters we have heard a lot of testimony this past week and it would appear to me that someone at BMX

Pharmaceutical has been withholding information from us. I ask you to think very carefully before you answer my next question. Are you aware of any one that would have anything to gain by keeping this problem with Advernox a secret? It makes me very sad to say this but yes we suspect two of our very own scientist of misleading us.

Mr. Winters please tell the court who these people are. We suspect Richard Naylor and Candis Lockhart. Objection Your Honor!

Councils approach the bench, said Judge Kenton.

Your Honor this is outrageous, said Mr. Vonhart! I think Mr. Winters is trying to defer blame from himself. My client is doing no such thing, said Mr. Legitt. If that is true, then why are we just now hearing about these allegations, said Mr. Vonhart? When did your client become aware of this so called plot by Rick Naylor and Candis Lockhart, Mr. Legit? I'm not sure, Your Honor but if I'm allowed to continue, I'm sure he will tell us.

Gentlemen, I'm not comfortable with this series of questioning, however, I'm going to allow it to continue but Mr. Jackson you had better keep it professional. Do you understand me? Yes, Your Honor I understand and thank you.

Your Honor this is ludicrous, it's so obvious that he's lying, said Mr. Vonhart. Then handle it Mr. Vonhart with your cross-examination. You do still remember what a cross-examination is don't you?

"Yes of course I do."

Well, if you catch him in a lie, his ass belongs to me. Do you understand what I'm saying Jackson? Yes, Your Honor, I understand completely. Now return to your seat, Mr. Vonhart.

"You may continue Mr. Legit."

I have to admit Mr. Winters that your last statement has caught us all by surprise. Can you tell the court today why you suspect these two fine scientists?

When we released Advernox to the market we did so with the full knowledge that there were some minor side effects. My company prides itself in putting out the safest product possible. So we had been doing research for the past four months to see if we could eliminate these minor side effects.

Were you able to do this? Unfortunately we were not. I was growing tired of the recent failures and started questioning members of the team. This is when I was informed that Mr. Naylor didn't seem to be following up on some of the vital tests.

It seemed that Rick and Candis had started seeing each other after work. She even moved in with him for a while. They had completely lost focus on the project or at least that how it appeared to us.

I have no further questions.

"Your witness, Mr. Vonhart."

Mr. Winters how does having an office romance or falling in love make these two people guilty of anything? We have a strict policy at BMX Pharmaceutical about dating your subordinates. Basically what that meant is that Rick was not supposed to date anyone that worked for him. So you're telling us that Candis Lockhart works for Rick Naylor. That is correct, Mr. Vonhart.

My records show that Miss Lockhart recently moved to a new address. Were you aware of that? No I wasn't aware of that. Were you aware that someone broke into her apartment and that she was afraid to go back there? No I wasn't aware of that either. When did that happen? The same day she moved in with Mr. Naylor.

You don't seem to know a whole lot about the people working for you do you Mr. Winters? Objection, Mr. Winters is the CEO, not the baby sitter. Over ruled Mr. Jackson!

Which scientist came to you with his concerns about Rick not doing his job correctly? It was Steven Batiste. Mr. Winters, how long have you known Mr. Batiste? I've known him about two months. How long have you known Mr. Naylor? I've know him about five years. Is it fair for me to assume that since you rehired Mr. Naylor for this special project that you must really trust him. I guess that's a fair assumption, said Mr. Winters. So based on what you just said, you expect us to believe that you would take the word of someone you just recently meet over a man that you have known for five years?

I'm sorry but I find that very hard to believe. I have my reasons Mr. Vonhart. What are they Mr. Winters!

We found out that Mr. Naylor had been depositing very large sums of money into a Swiss bank account. Did you say a Swiss bank account? Yes that's what I said. Incredible, I'm sorry but your testimony is becoming more and more unbelievable by the second Mr. Winters!

Do you know the penalty for telling untruths in a court of law? Do you mean telling lies! Yes, that's precisely what I mean! Now how much money are you talking about? Almost three quarters of a million dollars. Who would pay him that kind of money? That we don't know.

We believe he was selling secrets about our formulation to someone and that was his pay off. So you are smart enough to figure out that he is selling your formulation but you can't figure out who would be willing to pay an astronomical amount of money for it?

I can't verify the person but I can verify the Swiss bank account. Can you humor us in this court room for just a moment? You see I thought it was illegal to gain access to someone's personal account unless you were the IRS. Do you work for the IRS Mr. Winters?

Objection! Never mind I with draw my last question, everyone in here already knows the answer to that one. So how were you able to get information about this mysterious account? I have my ways and I can assure you they are all perfectly legal. Did Mr. Batiste inform you of this also? No he didn't. Did you put the money there? Did I put the money where? In the Swiss bank account. I did no such thing! Sure you did! Objection! Sustained, Mr. Vonhart! I withdraw the question Your Honor.

Mr. Winters is Mr. Batiste also a member of the team that you put together to tackle these minor side effects? That would be a good assumption. Why would you do such a thing? Do what? Assemble this team of what appears to be elite scientists to tackle a problem that the FDA has said was fine. I wanted the best people that I could find. Were this people instructed to look for any other problems with Advernox! No they weren't.

Where is Mr. Steven Batiste? I don't know. Is he still employed on this project? No, I received a phone call from Mr. Naylor last week. He told me that Steven hadn't reported to work and that he had also checked out of his room. Have you heard from him? No I haven't. Was his assignment complete? No it wasn't.

Why do you think he would just leave without telling anyone? I don't know Mr. Vonhart but if I had to guess, I would say he had grown tired of Mr. Naylor's leadership.

Who hired Mr. Naylor? I did and that's why this whole thing is so disappointing. Was this the first project that you hired him for? No, I first hired him 11 months ago. How long did he work for you at that time? About 7 months.

Was he let go or did he quit? I'm afraid that we had to let him go. Why was that? We got caught up in a budget crunch. We weren't doing very well and we had to let some very good people go. Unfortunately for Mr. Naylor it was based on seniority.

How did he take the news of being let go? Not very well I'm afraid. Did he relocate here for this job? Yes he did.

Well one could understand why he would be upset. Who wouldn't be? You move to a new city for a new job and seven months later you get terminated due to no fault of your own.

Do you know what the most surprising thing to me is Mr. Winters? Mr. Vonhart, I'm afraid that I don't know. Well sir, let me tell you then. How do you get a man that has move on with his life and found a very good job in their chosen profession to return to work for someone who has shown them no loyalty?

The only person that can answer that question is Mr. Naylor. No he's not the only one but he is probably the only one willing to tell the truth.

"Are you calling me a liar," Mr. Vonhart?

Yes Mr. Winters, "that's exactly what I'm doing! Your whole testimony up to this point has been filled with lies. Objection! Objection Your Honor! Plaintiff is badgering the witness for God's sake. Overruled! Sit down and shut up Mr. Legit!

Admit it! You're lying aren't you Mr. Winters? No I am not! Well sir I don't believe you. I doubt anyone in this court room does.

Your attorney claims that he didn't know that Rick and Candis wouldn't be here today but we all know how prepared he is when he comes to into this court room. He knew they would not be here today and so did you.

It's easier for you to place blame on them when you don't have to look them in the face when you lie about them doesn't it? Objection! Over ruled!

I promise you that I will get to the bottom of this barrel of lies that you and Mr. Jackson Legit have swirling around in this court room Mr. Winters.

"I promise you that."

No further questions for this witness Your Honor! Wait, wait, I'm afraid that I do have one more question for the CEO of BMX Pharmaceutical Your Honor. Go ahead Mr. Vonhart, "he's still your witness."

Mr. Winters less than five minutes ago you told this court under oath that you had to let Mr. Naylor go because of budget restraints. Is that correct? I said is that correct Mr. Winters!

Yes that is what I said Mr. Vonhart and if you ask me that question a thousand times my answer will be the same each and every time!

"Is that so Mr. Winters?"

"Yes Mr. Vonhart, it is so."

I see…. so the Chester Project had nothing to do with Mr. Naylor being fired. Objection Your Honor, what is the relevance of this line of questioning? Mr. Legitt have you been paying attention to this witness for the past five minutes, said Judge Kenton? Never mind counsel you don't have to answer that question because apparently you are the only person in this court room that isn't aware of the game being played by the gentleman sitting in the witness chair.

Now answer the question that was asked of you by Mr. Vonhart, Mr. Winters. Can you repeat the question? Was Mr. Naylor fired because of circumstances surrounding the Chester

Project? Mr. Vonhart for the last time, Richard Naylor was not fired because of the Chester Project!

Is that your final answer Mr. Winters? Yes, "I stand by my answer."

That's just great Mr. Winters "you stand behind your answer"...just don't forget the penalty for perjury my friend. I have no more questions for this witness Your Honor.

Mr. Winters...

Yes, Your Honor.

Are you aware of the penalty for perjury? Yes I am Your Honor. Good I'm glad to hear that because if I find out that you are lying, it will make sentencing you much easier.

Mr. Legit do you have any questions for your client? No, "I think he's been through enough questioning for one day Your Honor."

You may step down from the witness box Mr. Winters. Court is adjourned until 9:00a.m. tomorrow morning.

"All rise."

***

Nora please file this for me. Also I need you to look up this information for me before you go home today. Ok, Judge but this is pretty old stuff. I'm not sure it's still in the database. I know but I hope it is. I'll have to go through it all tonight. There is something that's bothering me and I think the answer is in those files. Just leave it on my desk when you're finished. I'm going to get some dinner but I'll be back. I might have to sleep here tonight.

***

Hello Roxanne it's me. I'm afraid that I'm going to have to spend some time at the office tonight. What about dinner

Leon? That's why I'm calling sweetheart. I'd like for you to meet me at the Martha's Country Buffet tonight. Really...yes, I hear they have terrific steaks there. Not as good as yours of course but good none the less. Leon it will be nice to get out of the house for a while. How does 5:30 sound? I'll be there.

Nora I'm going to meet Roxanne for dinner. Oh really where you meeting her? Martha's Country Buffet. Good choice they have wonderful food there. I'll see you tomorrow. Ok Leon, have a great time.

***

As Leon bobbed and weaved his old Mercedes through the rush hour traffic his mind was flooded with dozens of cases from past years. He knew what he was about to tell Roxanne would forever change their lives. He just hoped it would be for the better. One thing he was sure of, no matter what her reaction was to his news, there was no turning back now.

Hello sweetheart. Are those flowers for me? Yes they are. This place is a little dark isn't it? Yes but don't be afraid I'll protect you, said Roxanne. I've already ordered for us because I know you have to get back to the office. This trial is taking a lot of your time. I've never known you to be so caught up in a trial like this before, "I'm not sure I like it."

Don't worry Roxy. That's what you always say. When are you going to give this up Leon? It's funny that you should mention that because that's part of the reason I asked you hear tonight.

Here you go, one T-bone well done and one porterhouse medium well. Would you like some wine with your dinner? I'd love some but I think I better pass. Me too, can you just bring us some ice tea instead? Sure not a problem, "I'll be right back."

They look good don't they? Yes they do. Now my dear if you'll bow your head so that I might say a silent prayer before we began. How do you say a silent prayer Leon? You know what I mean Roxy. I'm just playing, go ahead.

All right Mr. Leon Kenton, what's this little get together about? Well, sweetheart it's like this. I've been thinking lately that it's about time for me to retire. Oh Leon you almost made me choke on my steak! Do you really mean it? Yes my dear I do. I've been in the court room as an attorney or Judge for over twenty years now and I'm ready to let it go. But Leon twenty-years really isn't that long.

It depends on how you look at it sweetheart. For me all those nights that I had to leave your bedside because of a case that wouldn't let me rest or the late nights that I spent at the office for the same reason makes twenty years seem like fifty. I want to be in bed next to you all night long for the rest of my life.

Oh Leon that is so sweet but you are a great Judge and I'm proud of you and I know that you are thinking of me but you'll miss it sweetheart besides, what will you do with yourself? I'm sure I can find plenty to keep me busy. Leon I'm starting to believe you are serious.

"I am serious Roxy." You'll have to excuse me Leon while I take a second to catch my breath.

Are you saying that you don't like the idea? No, its just that I didn't think I'd hear you say those words for a long time. May I ask what brought this on so sudden? It's simple Roxy, "I want to spend more time with you." You've been such a wonderful wife and mother and I think it time that we started spending more time together. I'm sure you can think of plenty of things to keep us busy.

You mean like the cruise we keep talking about? Yes we can do that my dear and we can also visit your sisters down south. Oh Leon that would be great! Could we consider buying a home down there? Yes my dear if that's what you want.

Oh Leon (sob) I love you so much. Yes I know and I love you, my dear. Here now stop that crying. What will people think if they see the Judge making his wife cry? Any fool can see these are tears of joy.

Well in that case raise your glass and join me in a toast. Here's to us, may the future be just as good to us as the past. Don't you worry about that Mr. Kenton; it will be good, I promise, "starting tonight as soon as we get home." I'm sorry Roxanne; I have to go back to the courthouse tonight. Oh, you can go back, "just as soon as I'm finished with you at home."

"Do you mean?"

Yes, "that's exactly what I mean." Well let's drink to that also.

Get that waitress over here. Is everything ok with your meal? Yes young lady everything is great but we have to rush so can you bring us two doggie bags. Sure, "I'll be right back."

Leon, yes Roxanne. I love you man...

CHAPTER 19

Your Honor before we began I would like to inform the court of a new witness who has just been put on the docket, said Mr. Vonhart. Objection, we were not made aware of any new witnesses.

Mr. Vonhart, "who is this new witness?" Her name is Katherine Levens Your Honor. From what I've been told, she will be able to help us all make sense of this whole mess. We strongly object!

Gentlemen, please approach the bench. Go ahead Mr. Jackson; I want to hear your concern.

We haven't had time to investigate this witness Your Honor. Mr. Vonhart, "when were you made aware of this new witness?" About ten minutes ago Your Honor, "she is just as much a mystery to me as she is to Mr. Jackson." I haven't even had time to interview her. Then why would you put her on the stand as your witness? I have it on very good authority that she has vital information.

"Who is this authority?" I can't say. I see...and you expect me to allow it any way. "I sincerely hope so." This is not one of your Hunches is it Mr. Vonhart. "No it isn't Your Honor."

What could it hurt if she truly does have vital information? Besides, she seems to be scared to death. I'm dying to hear what she has to say. Very well. "I will allow it," however I must allow Mr. Jackson the privilege of the same ten minutes that you have had Mr. Vonhart.

"No thanks Your Honor," I don't wish to waste the court's precious ten minutes. Are you sure about that Mr. Jackson? Your Honor, I've been doing this for a very long time, "I know what I'm doing." Have it your way Jackson but personally I think you're making a mistake. Don't give me that look Mr. Jackson, now have a seat.

Mr. Vonhart, "call your next witness."

Thank you Your Honor. If it pleases the court I would like to call Miss Katherine Levens to the stand.

Miss Levens, "please raise your right hand."

Do you swear that the testimony that you are about to give is the truth the whole truth and nothing but the truth so help you god.

"I swear."

Good morning Miss Levens. Good morning Mr. Vonhart. Would you please tell the court what your profession is? I'm a chemist. Who do you work for? I am currently unemployed but I used to work for Warrenton Pharmaceutical Products. Why don't you work for them any more? It's hard to work for a company on Long Island when you've been hiding in Canada for the past year.

"Can you explain Miss Levens?"

I'll try but I must warn you that I get very emotional just thinking about it. I was at the lab when my co-workers, my (sob) friends were killed.

Objection! Objection Your Honor.

Overruled!

Continue Miss Levens. Thank you. Like I said I was there. I saw everything and I can prove it.

Objection Your Honor. "Who is this person?"

Mr. Legitt you had an opportunity to find out but you turned it down.

I demand a recess right now!

No Mr. Legit, now sit down and shut up or I'll find you in contempt. Please continue Miss Levens.

Thank you Your Honor. This is what happened......

Objection!!!

***

Hello this is Veronica. We just received word that the Jury has reached a verdict in the Advernox case. We are now live inside the court room.

Foreman has the jury reached a verdict? Yes we have Your Honor. Bailiff would you please bring me the verdict. Here you go Judge. Ok, please return it to the Foreman.

Foreman how does the jury find BMX Pharmaceutical in the thief Advernox? The jury finds BMX guilty Your Honor.

How does the jury find BMX Pharmaceutical in the wrongful death of the four Warrenton Pharmaceutical Product chemists? The jury finds BMX guilty Your Honor. Thank you Bailiff.

Mr. Jackson, the court wants you and your client to rise. On this the 28th day of October, 2004 this court orders BMX Pharmaceutical to pay a total of fifteen billion dollars to Warrenton Pharmaceutical Products effective immediately.

Also each family that was directly affected by this terrible tragedy is to be paid a lump sum of one hundred and fifty thousand dollars, effective immediately.

I want Advernox removed from the shelves immediately! I want this to go out over all networks, newspapers, radios and all international media. I will assign a task force to make sure this is done immediately. I do not want even the slightest remains of this drug left anywhere on the face of this earth!

"The decision of this court is final." There will be no appeals. Do I make myself clear Mr. Jackson? I said do I make myself clear!

Yes, Your Honor.

Good, now get out of my court room!

"This court is adjourned!"

***

Well everyone you just heard the ruling for yourself. Here comes the attorney for the defense now. Let's see if we can get a statement from him. Mr. Legit would you care to comment on today's ruling? No I would not except to say that I will be filing an appeal first thing tomorrow morning. Mr. Legit the judge said there can be no appeal. When did he say that? Just now in court, you were there. I'm sure you must be mistaken; now excuse me I have other clients.

Well everyone it's obvious that Mr. Legit is still in shock over the ruling. Here comes the attorney for the Plaintiff. Let's see if we can get a statement from him.

Mr. Vonhart, "how do you feel right now?" We are extremely happy Miss Taylor. We felt that justice would prevail if given a chance. Thank God for people like Judge Kenton. It's a shame that he's retiring.

"The judge is retiring?"

Yes he just announced it.

Are you aware that the defense is appealing this ruling tomorrow morning? No I wasn't. A case like this cannot be appealed. Didn't you hear the Judge say that? Yes I did, however, Mr. Legit claims too have heard differently.

Don't worry about him, once the shock of what just happens wears off he'll come to his senses.... maybe? Well congratulations again Mr. Vonhart. Thank you Miss Taylor.

Well, there you have it. It's been three long months of reporting this story and we are all glad to see a happy ending.

Reporting for channel 12 news, I'm Veronica Taylor, "have a great day."

***

Veronica is your camera off? Yes, "it is Mr. Vonhart." I just want to congratulate you. Why do you say that? You have done a terrific job covering this story. I wouldn't be surprised if the more popular networks aren't beating down your door very soon offering you a better job, with more money and all the fringe benefits.

You're very kind but I doubt that will ever happen. I've been trying to get away from here for years but now I think I want to stay. Well you have definitely bought viewers back to channel 12 and for that alone they should reward you nicely.

***

Excuse me Mr. Vonhart. My name is Suzanne Edwards. My husband was the CEO for Warrenton Pharmaceutical. He was killed by someone at BMX Pharmaceutical. Although I can't prove it, I was hoping I could meet with you and discuss this matter.

Sure Mrs. Edwards. Here's the address to my office. When would you like to meet. How about tomorrow at noon? Ok, that will be fine. I'll see you then.

By the way that's a beautiful baby. How old is he? He will be one month old tomorrow. His name is Marvin Jr.

***

Congratulations Rick, this nightmare is finally over. Thanks to you Kathy the bad guys are about to be punished. We could not have done any of this without you Kathy. Thank you Rick.

After BMX pays Warrenton Pharmaceutical do you think they'll have enough left to pay everyone else? Maybe but I can smell a bankruptcy cooking at BMX right now. Well in that case we better hope that WPP does the right thing. Who knows stranger things have happened.

Well Rick what will you do with yourself now? I'm not sure Kathy. I hate to ask you this Rick but I have to know. Will it be Stacey or Candis? I can't believe you're asking me that. I'm sorry but you deserve to have someone special in your life. Thank you for saying that but the truth of the matter is I don't think I'll ever be able to trust Candis again and Stacey has completely shut me out.

She feels her disability is too much to ask me to deal with.

Is it permanent?

The doctors don't know.

I've tried to reach out to her but after she found out about Candis and me, she stopped speaking to me. But weren't you and her on the outs any way. I mean she did give you back the engagement ring right.

That's right but apparently she still feels betrayed. I'm sorry Rick but I don't blame her. Any woman in her position would feel the same way. So what's you next move?

Well Kathy these past three months have been horrendous. It's been one surprise after another. I think a trip to a tropical island would be nice but I should probably try to find a job first. I don't think Bartell Pharmaceutical is the right place for me.

Finding a job is high on my priority list also Rick but I like the idea that you have about the tropical island better. I need a vacation too; maybe we can catch the same flight. Maybe we can Kathy.

Why don't we talk about it over dinner, said Kathy and if things work out we can be on a plane headed to that tropical Island by this time tomorrow? Sounds good, I know this great little Italian restaurant down town. You like Italian don't you Kathy?

"Yes Rick"...I do.

***

Mr. Winters there are two police officers in the lobby. They are asking to see you. Should I send them in sir? Hello, Mr. Winters are you there?

I'm sorry officer but he's not answering his phone. Is he in there? I'm sure he is. He was having a meeting with the company's CFO and I haven't seen him come out. Try him again.

Mr. Winters the police are here sir. What should I do? I don't understand why he's not answering. That's ok miss we'll just let our self in. But no one is allowed to see him with out an appointment. We don't need an appointment.

Let's go in Eric. The door's locked Kevin. Miss please unlock the door. I don't have a key. That means we'll just have to kick it in. Kevin do you want to do the honors? Sure Eric, I've never kicked a door in before.

Oh my.... Miss you had better call an ambulance.

What's wrong?

Please just call an ambulance. Do it now!

Kevin, let's check for a pulse. I'm afraid we are too late for this one. What about the other one? No pulse here either. Forget the ambulance we better call the coroner these guys have been dead for at least an hour. Why do you think they would do this? They knew we were coming for their sorry asses. It looks like they over dosed on whatever was in these pill bottles. Better bag those bottles.

Do you think we should call the news also? Of course not the captain would have our ass. Maybe you're right but I'm going to give that cute little reporter from channel 12 a call. What cute reporter? Veronica Taylor...from channel 12. Who's Veronica Taylor? Where have you been for the last several months Kevin, living under a rock or something?

Channel 12 has been all over this story; it's only fitting that they be the first one here for this. Come to think of it I think I did hear something about her. Well suit yourself man, just don't mention my name. Operator please get me channel 12 news. It's an emergency.

***

Hello, I'm Veronica Taylor reporting with late breaking new from the BMX headquarters in Burlington, New Jersey. The police came here today to serve a warrant to the company's CEO, Mr. William Winters. However, when they arrived they were surprised to find him on the floor of his office dead of an apparent suicide. Lying next to him was the company's CFO, Mr. J.T. Barrows. They apparently over dosed on some of their company's product.

Both men had been with the company over twenty-five years. The police believe that these two men were the masterminds behind that terrible fire at the WPP lab last year. If you remember five people died in that fire.

The only question remaining is how could the fear of losing the company's pension have driven two well-respected men to do this? Could there be more to this story than meets the eye. You be the judge on this one. Join us tomorrow when we discuss how to invest your company's pension wisely.

I'm Veronica, reporting for channel 12 news. See you later.

***

Hello Miss Taylor? My name is Lloyd Banks from channel 7 Cable Network. How would you like to work for us? Thanks but I'm not.....before you say no, please listen to what I have to say. We'll make it worth your while. Ok, "I'm listening."

***

Who is it? It's me Candis. Hey come on in. Give me a hug, Miss big time reporter. Please tell me that you took the job offer from channel seven.

"Yes I did." That's wonderful, I'm so proud of you. This calls for a celebration. Candis, I'm sorry, I can't stay long. I just wanted to say thanks for everything. Veronica there's no need to thank me. I simply pointed you in the right direction and you did the rest.

Have you told Rick about me yet? No I'm ashamed to admit that I haven't. I've been trying to reach him for the past two days but he hasn't returned my calls. I love him so much but I haven't been completely honest with him about everything. I'm sure he's not ready to hear about you. But you didn't really lie about me, said Veronica. Sure I did.…. by omission. Don't worry sweetheart no man can stay away from you too long. I'm sure he just needs a little space. I hope you're right, we both know how long it's been since I've had a man in my life.

Just wait you'll see, he'll be running back to you in no time. I hope you're right about that little sister because I love that man.

I have to go now. I have to be in Thailand by tomorrow afternoon. What's happening over there? I'm not sure yet but I'll let you know as soon as I find out or you can tune in to the number one cable station in the country and find out when I tell the rest of the world. You are on your way. Thanks to my big sister, said Veronica. I love you Candis. I love you to Veronica. Call me when you land. I will.

***

According to a report from a hospital here in Thailand five women were admitted into the hospital last night. These women share two things in common. They are all four months pregnant and they are all taking a prescription drug called Advernox. We'll have more on this story tonight.

I'm Veronica reporting for…wait just one minute, we have just got the news that the deaths of William Winters and J.T. Barrows have been ruled a double homicide. Apparently these two gentlemen did not commit suicide as was first reported. The coroner is certain that they were poisoned; apparently there are traces of a fatal drug in Mr. Winters bottle of aspirin. We will keep you informed as this mystery become clearer to us.

I'm Veronica reporting for channel 7 news good night.

CHAPTER 20

Rick we better hurry or we'll miss our flight. I only need a few more seconds. I'm trying to get this silly fax machine to work.

Can't we fax it once we get where we are going? I guess but you can never be sure about those island resorts. I'll be finished in a few minutes. Ok, but if we miss this flight we'll have to wait until tonight to leave. Stop worrying I think the fax just went through. Thank God, now let's get out of here.

Rick before we fly half way around the world I have to know something. I thought you were in a hurry. What is it? Are you still in love with Stacey?

I can't believe you are asking me that but if you must know, a part of me will always love her but she is my past, you are my future. Do you mean that? Yes I mean it, now can we please go. Wait just one more question...what about Candis Lockhart.

What about her?

Do you still love her Rick?

I'm not sure I can ever love someone that I can't trust. Are there any more questions woman? No I think I have my answer. Good, now can we just go please?

Where are you headed today Miss? To Maui, oh you are so lucky and will this gentleman be accompanying you? Yes he will. Why do you ask? No reason, it's just some girls have all the fun but you'd better hurry; I think your flight is boarding. See Rick I told you.

Oh stop your crying; what's the worst that can happen? If we miss this flight I'll just get us a room and make love to you all night and then we'll catch another flight tomorrow. Oh you're going to make love to me all night but we'll be doing it in our room or on the beach tonight in Maui. Calm down there's the terminal now. I'm not going too calm down until we are on the plane, sitting comfortably in our seats.

May I have your boarding pass sir? Here it is. Thank you. By the way you two make a nice couple. Thank you.

Oh Rick...I'm so excited. I never get to do anything like this. This past year has been such a drag. I bet it has but things are different now. Here are our seats.

Stewardess may I have a drink of water please? Sure sir, I'll be right back. Here you go. What's the movie for this flight, said Rick?

It's a long flight so I think it's a fist full of dollars. Great, "I love that movie." Yeah me too, there's nothing better than a good western to fall asleep on.

Well as soon as we are airborne and the captain turns off the seat belt light I'll bring you both a headset, but for now I'm going to have to ask both of you to have a seat and fasten your seat belts.

***

Good afternoon everyone, we'd like to welcome you to Southwest flight 1487, nonstop to Maui. This is a five-hour nonstop flight. I am your host Tracey, I'm a little nervous because this is my first day. Please direct your attention toward the front as we go over our pre flight instructions.

In case of a drop in cabin pressure a mask will drop down from the overhead compartment. We do not anticipate this, however, it is important that you understand how to operate this equipment. If you have a small child please secure your mask first and then that of your small child. Also note that the bottom of your seat cushion can be used as a floatation device.

If you are sitting in a row with a sign marked exit you will be responsible for opening that door in the event of an emergency, if you feel that you are unable to perform this task please inform us and we will reseat you now.

We have been cleared for take off. Everyone please make sure that your seat is in the upright position and that your tray tables have been placed in the locked position.

"Thanks for flying Southwest."

***

Excuse me sir, do you still wish to see the in flight movie? Yes I do. That will be six dollars. What about you miss? No thanks, I've got a book to read. Very well enjoy your flight. Thank you.

That was a good movie. I could watch it again. Good because I think it's the only one they are showing. I'm sure they are not showing the same movie again. Let me check for you. Excuse me Stewardess, when will the next movie start? There will be a fifteen minute intermission before the next movie. If you want to watch it, it will be an additional six dollars.

What's the name of the movie? It called For Your Eyes Only. Great, that's an old James Bond classic. Oh it's a classic alright Rick, isn't that the one with the lady that they found out years later was really a man? Do you have to take the fun out of everything woman.

I'm going to the bathroom. Here's my six bucks. What about you miss? No thanks, I'm not really a James Bond fan. I understand. With a man like yours who would be? Excuse me?

I'm sorry miss, "I didn't mean any disrespect."

Well he's taken, so keep your little comments to yourself.

***

Stewardess, please help us. It's my wife, something is terribly wrong. What seems to be the problem? I'm not sure, she seems to be going into labor but it's too soon. Is there a doctor on the plane? Attention everyone this is Tracey your flight attendant.

"Is there a doctor on the plane?" If so, please come to row six?

Are you a doctor, said Tracey?

Yes, "I'm a doctor," my name is Derrick.

What seems to be the problem Stewardess? We have a pregnant lady back in coach. What's wrong with her? I'm not sure but she appears to be in a lot of pain. Please come quick. I'll be right there let me get my bag.

***

Calm down, I'm a doctor. Now young lady what seems to be the problem? Doctor, I think I'm about to give birth. I'm sorry miss but you don't look pregnant. My name is Carla and I'm three months, I have two kids and this is exactly how I felt when I gave birth to them.

Was either of them premature? No doctor they weren't. Please help me doctor I'm in so much pain. Ok, I'll do everything I can but first I have to ask you a couple of questions.

Doctor, "I'm in too much pain to be answering questions?"

The first thing I need to know is what type of prescription you are taking. The only medication I'm taking is for fatigue, dizziness and stomach pain, which I'm having a lot of right now. What is the name of your medication?

Doctor my name is Barry; my wife's medication is called Advernox. Did you say Advernox? Yes, I said Advernox. How long has she been taking that? Our family doctor prescribed it two months ago. Yes...my stupid husband forgot and left it on the bedroom dresser.

"Do you have any doctor?"

"No I don't have any!"

"It's the only thing that's works for her pain," said Barry.

"Doctor what's wrong?" "Why are you looking at my wife like that?"

Son...for Christ sake don't you people read the newspaper or listen to the news, said Derrick? I don't understand your question doctor. Here Barry, hold this on your wife's stomach until I get back.

Stewardess is there somewhere that we can talk in private?

"Yes follow me."

Listen carefully; she said she's taking Advernox.

Advernox.... Isn't that the drug that's causing woman to.....? Shhh, "yes it is." What did you say your name was?

It's Tracey. Well Tracey; you had better tell the pilot to land this plane right away.

"I'm afraid he can't do that." We are over the ocean right now.

How long before we can get to land?

"It will be at least two hours."

I'm afraid that's not quick enough, said Derrick. That woman needs to be in a hospital emergency room as soon as possible. Now Tracey you go tell the pilot to land this damn plane in the next hour.

I'll go tell the captain, doctor but I'm sure we can't land. Well...Tracey I know this is your first day but if we can't get her to an emergency room in less than two hours I suggest you prepare to inform your passengers that they will be sharing their flight with a dead woman and her unborn baby.

***

Captain we have a crisis back in coach.

What's the emergency?

We have a lady who is three months pregnant. She claims that she is about to give birth.

Is she having a miscarriage?

Captain I'm not sure what she's having but she is on that medication called Advernox.

Advernox! That's the same medication my sister was taking. She was four months pregnant with twins and lost them. She's lucky to be alive but she can't ever have any kids because of it. She was devastated.

I'm so sorry to hear that Captain Matthews. I thought they told everyone to stop taking that shit and took it off the market. Apparently not everyone got the word sir. What in God's name are we suppose to do?

There is a doctor with her right now but he said that if she isn't in a hospital in one hour, she's not going to make it.

Doesn't he know that we are over the got damn ocean right now?

Yes he's aware of that but he said that there is nothing that he can do. She needs the attention of a hospital emergency room. He says if we can't get her to an emergency room, we should prepare the passengers for her death.

What are we going to do? I have an idea. Get on the intercom and tell everyone to sit down and fasten their seat belts. Ok but why? You don't want to know but I advise you to have a seat also.

Isaiah...yes Captain. Let's see what this bird can do.

What are you saying sir? Do you mean...?

Yes, "that's exactly what I mean."

But Captain no one has attempted that in modern times, there are just too many aircrafts in the air these days, not to mention that it will take us completely off course and we'll basically be flying blind for the next three to five minutes.

Listen Isaiah; we are almost two hours away from any kind of land but if we do this, it will cut that time in half.

Do you realize how fast we would have to go to do that? For God's sake, it's too risky Captain!

I know it's risky but we have to give that woman and her baby a fighting chance. But sir what about the other passengers? We have two hundred other people that we have to consider!

I'm going to get her to a hospital or die trying.

Well you're going to have to do it with out a co-pilot.

So be it!

Please sir, you're not thinking clearly. Remember you only have one more year until you retire. If you do this they will fire you, take your license and your pension.

"Think about your wife and kids."

I am thinking about them Isaiah. If I know my family and I think I do. My kids will say dad you should have done something. My wife will say, what if that was us?

"Sir you're not thinking clearly right now." I know you want to help those poor people and so do I but not like this. If you do this and we survive your career as a pilot is over, whether that women and her child lives or dies. You will not be known as a hero, all they are going to think about is all the people lives you risked to save those two.

Please Captain, you heard what Tracey said; the poor woman has been taking Advernox. It's probably too late for her. Am I'm right?

"Sir am I right!"

"Yes Isaiah you are right," oh how I hate the got damn Pharmaceutical Companies!

***

Rick I have to talk to you. Rick take off that damn headset! I was in the bathroom and I overheard something.

What did you hear? The stewardess was talking to a doctor. Apparently there is a young pregnant woman back in coach. She's only three months pregnant and she's in a lot of pain. The poor woman thinks she's in labor. Guess what medication she's been taking for the past two months?

No way.... said Rick. Yes Mr. Naylor, she's been taking Advernox. How can that be? It's been over two months since it was all taken off the shelves. Where would she get it from?

I have no idea but we have to do something. What can we do? I'm not sure but we have to think of something fast. If she's taking Advernox the only thing might save her life right now is to get rid of the baby. Oh, no, we can't do that.

Come on you know the side effects of Advernox as well as I do, so what would you suggest, said Rick? I'm afraid that I'd suggest the same thing that you just did. Unless...unless what woman? I think I have an Idea. There is one thing that we can try. I can't believe I didn't think of this sooner.

Well for Christ's sake Miss Lockhart spit it out!

"Everyone this is Isaiah your co-pilot."

Please make sure your seatbelts are fastened. Tracey please make sure the passengers are all seated. Then secure your own seatbelt, I think we are in for a bumpy ride.

"Everyone, "this would be a good time to pray."

What the hell is he talking about Candis?

I don't know...but it seems like we are going faster...

CHAPTER 21

Mr. Naylor are you in there? Mr. Naylor are you in there?

Is someone at the door?

Yes it's me Ralph the doorman.

Good morning Ralph.

How are you feeling today Mr. Naylor? For some strange reason, I have a terrible headache. Other than that, I'm just fine Ralph.

You must have really tied one on last night. What are you talking about Ralph? Well sir you were so wasted that your friends practically carried you to your room.

"What friends?"

It's obvious that you are still a little hung over sir. I just wanted you to know that you have an urgent message and you also have a visitor down stairs.

What's the message?

Someone named Stacey has been calling the front desk all morning. She says that she is your fiancée and that she's been trying to reach all night but you're not answering your phone.

That's right; I turned my phone off so I could get a quick nap after work. I didn't realize I would sleep all night long, I'll call her now.

But sir you didn't sleep all night. You left late last night with a friend and when you returned, your friend and another gentleman had to carry you to your room.

They said that you really had a good time at the party. Ralph, I don't remember any of that. That's obvious Mr. Naylor. That must have been some party.

What about your visitor sir?

What visitor are you talking about Ralph?

The man waiting for you down stairs. He says he's an old friend of yours. Should I send him up? He says that he really needs to speak to you.

Who is he again?

He says his name is William Winters.

"That's impossible Ralph."

"William Winters is dead!"

He was poisoned by Cliff Miller.

Well this man looks very alive. What does he look like Ralph? He's a large man, he appears to be in his late fifties and he's wearing a very expensive Italian suit. He arrived in a limo. Did he say who he worked for? As a matter of fact he did, I think he said BMX Pharmaceutical.

Ralph this has to be someone idea of a bad joke.

I don't think so Mr. Naylor. I think that bump on your head has you talking crazy.

Are you telling me that I dreamed this entire thing?

I don't know what dream you are talking about but I really must get back to the front desk. I suggest that you have a doctor look at that bruise on your forehead. It looks rather bad.

I couldn't have dreamed this but I must have. Are you sure this isn't some kind of stupid joke Ralph?

"I take my job very serious Mr. Naylor."

I even checked his I.D.; the man down stairs is definitely William Winters.

"He can't be Ralph!"

"I tell you he can't be!"

I refuse to believe that I have been dreaming all this time. My God Candis..."this would mean that you don't even exist."

Oh my, "I think I'd better sit down." My head is really starting to pound fast and it hurts so bad.

Can I get you anything Mr. Naylor?

Listen too me Ralph, I see you reading the newspaper every morning. Do you remember reading anything about a case involving a terrible drug called Advernox?

No Mr. Naylor, that name doesn't ring a bell.

"Come on Ralph think!"

This drug was responsible for the deaths of pregnant women and their unborn babies. It made world news.

No I haven't heard of anything like that. I think you better get to a doctor as soon as possible Mr. Naylor

Ralph just one more question. What about a woman named Candis Lockhart? She stayed here with me for a couple of weeks, tall, brown hair, hazel eyes and the best butt that you could ever hope to see on a woman. She would have had to pass your desk everyday to come up here.

Mr. Naylor, if a woman like that came within twenty yards of my desk even once, I'd remember her.

Now what about Mr. Winters? He is really starting to get impatient down stairs. Is he a friend of yours or not?

William Winters is not my friend Ralph. He has no friends. I see....so should I send him up or not? He says it's urgent....

***

Is someone's knocking at your door Mr. Naylor?

I didn't hear a knock Ralph.

Did you hear it that time? Would you like me to get the door for you?

No Ralph, I can answer my own door.

"*Who is it?*"

Please open the door Rick.

I really must speak to you, it's urgent. How's your head?

What...who are you and how do you know about my head?

I was there when Cliff hit you with the butt of his gun.

Who are you?

"It's me Rick."

"*Didn't Peaches tell you that I was coming?*"

"The End"

Or is it just

"The Beginning"

"ABOUT THE AUTHOR"

Rick Naylor currently resides on the East Coast. He was born in Meridian Mississippi on April 3rd 1964. At the age of 4 his family moved to Enterprise Mississippi where he remained until he joined the U.S. Army in July of 1982 at the age of 18. His first assignment was the 101st Screaming Eagles Air Assault Division located at Fort Campbell Kentucky. He also served two years with the 1st Armored Division in Bamberg Germany. Sergeant Ricky Naylor received an Honorable discharge in July 1986.

Rick currently works in the Pharmaceutical Industry as a Manufacturing/Packaging Supervisor. His twelve year career in this field has allowed him to work for three great Pharmaceutical companies in three states, including assignments over seas. No part of this book is a reflection on any employer that he has worked for. "Any similarities are simply that."

"The Advernox Project" is book one of "The BMX Conspiracy" trilogy that includes "The Chester Project" and "The Norwegian Project " You can expect to see the complete collection in time for Christmas 2006.

Other completed books are: "The Gas Attendant" and "Defining Moments" which is a collection of seven terrific short stories.

235692